LOVE & OTHER GREAT EXPECTATIONS

Becky Dean

DELACORTE PRESS

Text copyright © 2022 by Becky Dean
Jacket art copyright © 2022 by Libby VanderPloeg

All rights reserved. Published in the United States by Delacorte Press, an imprint of Random House Children's Books, a division of Penguin Random House LLC, New York.

Delacorte Press is a registered trademark and the colophon is a trademark of Penguin Random House LLC.

GetUnderlined.com

Educators and librarians, for a variety of teaching tools, visit us at RHTeachersLibrarians.com

Library of Congress Cataloging-in-Publication Data is available upon request.
ISBN 978-0-593-42942-6 (hc) — ISBN 978-0-593-42943-3 (lib. bdg.) —
ISBN 978-0-42944-0 (ebook) — ISBN 978-0-593-57255-9 (int'l edition)

The text of this book is set in 11.2-point Adobe Caslon Pro.
Interior design by Cathy Bobak

Printed in the United States of America
10 9 8 7 6 5 4 3 2 1
First Edition

To Mom and Dad, who taught me to love stories and adventures,
and to Russ, my favorite person to adventure with

CHAPTER ONE

Dreams are like knees—you don't realize how fragile they are until something rips them to shreds.

I sank onto the first row of bleachers overlooking Fairview High's athletic field. One hand rubbed the massive brace gripping my leg, which was tight after my cross-campus trek. The other clutched the strange envelope I'd found in my locker but hadn't opened in my rush to arrive.

Arrive, so I could leave before the game started.

Girls in royal blue jerseys and blue-and-white striped socks sat on the grass, stretching. I'd made it in time. Warm-ups, I could handle. Games, however, were more torture than physical therapy, a tactic that could've cracked terror suspects.

If I'd happened to schedule PT during the three playoff games the past two weeks . . . well, it was purely coincidental.

Several teammates waved from the field. One shouted, "We miss you, Britt. Can't wait to have you back."

My heart stutter-stepped as I returned the wave. They'd be

waiting a long, long time. But they only knew about the knee, not the rest of it.

When the soccer ball made its appearance, a shot of pain kicked through my chest.

I yanked my attention to the cream-colored envelope. Handwritten letters across the front spelled out my name: *Brittany J. Hanson.* A round, raised seal on the flap displayed the monogram *PCM,* the C larger in the center. The card inside read:

*The honor of your presence is requested
Today, May 20, at fifteen minutes past three
in the afternoon in classroom A-6.
A Unique Opportunity Awaits.*

It resembled the announcements we'd received when my sister and brother graduated college, but unlike those, this card didn't say who sent it or the meeting's purpose.

Three-fifteen was . . . I checked the scoreboard clock. Four minutes ago.

Was it worth the trip? I couldn't run, so I'd definitely be late. But it intrigued me.

I shouted "Bye" and hurried across campus as fast as the knee brace allowed.

Unique opportunity. The phrase set my pulse racing. I could use one of those. Didn't even have to be unique—I'd settle for any old opportunity. It had come knocking once this year, but after I let it in, it bolted without the courtesy of a goodbye.

Granted, unique opportunities were rare. I shouldn't get my hopes up. But it was better than the ninety minutes of fingernail-extracting, tooth-yanking misery of a soccer match I couldn't play in.

Plus, someone who used calligraphy might serve snacks like tiny sandwiches or something wrapped in bacon. I never passed up bacon.

A-6 was my English classroom, but why would our teacher, Ms. Carmichael, invite me to anything? Her comments on my essays frequently included the words *uninspired, lack of thought,* and *disappointing.* Was she the mysterious *PCM* who had access to my locker?

When I reached the room, Amberlyn Hartsfield was sitting in the front row. Spence Lopez, a guy from the football team, lounged a few seats away, and another boy slouched in the last row with a book, long hair hiding his face. No one else was present. Also, negative on the bacon snacks.

Fancy invitations for four people? Weird.

Amberlyn grunted, showing my lack of punctuality had not gone unnoticed. "Some things never change."

Her muttered words reached me, which I'm sure she intended.

"Like your constant uptightness?" I dropped into the seat next to Spence, smothering a sigh of relief to be off my feet. "Whatever this is, it hasn't started yet. What's the big deal?"

She straightened a colored notebook and the invitation in the exact center of her desk. The stationery looked natural in her manicured hands. Her mail probably always arrived this way—party invites, credit card offers, and political flyers delivered on heavy cardstock in engraved envelopes.

Her gaze flicked to my leg, and I saw the condescension drain from her face. For a second, she resembled the girl who used to share secrets and red Skittles with me.

Pity-politeness based on failed friendship. Fantastic.

I swallowed a growl. "No spring practice today?" I asked Spence. "Don't you have freshmen to train?"

He shook his head, making the longer hair above his undercut flop. "Girls took over our field for a strange sport called soccer."

I punched his shoulder.

He grinned. "The other guys are watching the game. They were talking about how much the team misses you. Will you be able to play summer league?"

Every time I received a similar question, it felt like a ball to the gut at short range, the air physically forced from my lungs. "Not sure. I might be on my yacht, cruising the Riviera."

He snorted. Our small town south of Santa Barbara, California, contained two types of people—those who owned yachts and those who cleaned them. Spence and I did not own yachts.

Actually, I did know the answer to his question. I just hadn't told anyone. The doctor's diagnosis constantly echoed in my head. Phrases bounced around like out-of-control soccer balls: *blood clotting disorder, blood thinner, no contact sports, change your diet, watch out for sharp objects. Be careful, be careful, be careful.*

But as long as I was the only one who knew, as long as I never spoke the words, I imagined I could contain it. Undo it.

"Any idea what this is about?" He lifted his chin to point to the front of the classroom.

"Nope. I was hoping for snacks." I glanced around, but no bacon had magically appeared.

The guy in the back sprawled in his seat, wearing a Captain America shirt and reading a beat-up paperback with a spaceship on the cover. I recognized him now—Peter Finch, a sullen guy I'd had classes with for years. He looked up and caught me staring. His blank gaze didn't change, but his lip curled.

I thought that expression was reserved for supervillains but apparently not. He aimed his sneer alternately at me and Amberlyn. What was his problem? Captain America was supposed to be nicer than that.

Groaning, I faced front. Whatever this opportunity was, it'd better be good.

"Do you think this is a psychological experiment?" I tapped my non-braced leg against the desk. "To see how long we sit here?"

"No, Ms. Hanson," a proper British voice said from the doorway. "It is not."

My posture straightened at the familiar accent.

Our English teacher, Ms. Carmichael, glided across the room and settled at her desk.

As was usual in her class, she presided. There was no other word for it. In her first year teaching here, she already ruled the school. Her styled, short hair was a pale blond probably called Champagne Bubbles or Old Money. Glasses dangled from a beaded chain around her neck, always accompanied by pearl earrings and flawless makeup that made her appear younger.

"Thank you for coming." She regarded each of us. "As your invitations stated, I have a unique opportunity for you."

Her expression didn't reveal anything. Her cultured voice filled the room, each word enunciated in a crisp British accent.

"I've decided to try something rather exciting. I called you here because I am offering each of you a chance to compete for a prize of one hundred thousand dollars."

A wild laugh escaped my throat.

Spence made a strangled noise.

Amberlyn gasped and sat up straighter.

Our questions tumbled over each other—"Is this for real?" "How is that possible?" "You're joking, right?"

She waited until we fell silent. "Yes, this is real. It's not a joke."

A hundred grand was . . . a lot of money. So much I couldn't comprehend it. And hardly information you dropped so casually. My brain conjured images of stacks of bills, of Scrooge McDuck swimming in a pile of gold coins.

Another image replaced those: the letter from UCLA, saying if I still planned to enroll in the fall, I owed ten thousand dollars by September 1 for registration, housing, and a hundred various fees, many I suspected they had made up.

And that was for this year, to say nothing of the following three, when I wouldn't have partial help. Even if they let me keep this year's money, no more would come. People don't pay for work you can't do.

Since my original Life Plan had been forced into an early retirement, I needed a new one. As my mom and siblings enjoyed pointing out so frequently, most Life Plans required a college education. One I no longer had a way to pay for.

Until now.

This prize would cover those made-up fees and more.

Next to me, Spence leaned forward, his hands gripping the sides of the desk.

Amberlyn capped and uncapped her pen repeatedly.

Were the others dreaming of what they'd do with the money? College, a new car, traveling the world. It seemed too good to be true.

"Where's the money coming from?" I asked. "Is this school-sponsored?"

"The school has approved this trip," Ms. C said. "But it is something of a personal endeavor. I've been blessed with resources and wish to help others."

"I didn't realize teaching paid so well," I muttered to Spence.

"Who said the money came from teaching?" Ms. Carmichael met my gaze.

"Who cares where it comes from," Spence said. "What do we have to do to win?"

Good question.

"Is there an application?" Amberlyn asked. "Do we have to write something?"

"Like a book report or an essay?" I added.

Or something equally likely to eliminate me? I'd had my chance at earning money, and it certainly hadn't involved academics. My odds of winning anything from an English teacher? Whose class discussions I avoided and whose books I found tedious? I might as well leave now.

Ms. Carmichael folded her hands and rested them on the desk. "Ah yes. Now we come to the fun part."

My hopeful heart pounded in my ears. My brain kept repeating that this couldn't be real. The rest of my body ignored the logic. *Don't get excited. You can't win anyway.*

"The contest will be a scavenger hunt," she said.

That sounded promising. Action-oriented, physical, concrete. I might stand a chance.

"Inspired by classic British literature," she continued.

Not so promising. I held my breath.

"To take place in England." She smirked like she knew she'd saved the best for last.

Sweet. I finally breathed. The laugh bubbled out again.

Amberlyn squeaked. Spence met my gaze, his eyes wide and bright. Even Peter grunted behind me.

But . . .

"That's not exactly cheap," I said. "Assuming we need the cash prize, how are we supposed to pay for a trip across the pond?" I tried to mimic her accent on the last three words.

"That will be taken care of."

"You're paying for us to go to England *and* giving one of us cash?" I drummed my fingers on the desk. "What's the catch? Do we have to use this for college or books or something?"

Amberlyn raised her hand even though there were only four of us. "Is this like when the French club went to Paris or the student council to DC?"

"They didn't get cash prizes for those," I said.

"That you know of," Amberlyn replied.

"There is no catch." Ms. C's face remained calm. "You may use the money however you see fit. Consider it an investment in your future."

I tapped the desk. "So how does it work exactly?"

"I'll handle the arrangements, speak with your parents, and ensure you have adequate supervision while overseas. All you have to do is decide if you're willing to be challenged and possibly learn about yourself in the process. Travel tends to have that effect."

Learning about myself didn't sound fun, but I never said no to a challenge. A scavenger hunt in England was a better way to spend my summer than watching from the sidelines as my team played soccer without me. Or wearing a chicken costume on the main drag, holding a sign for the Lord of the Wings restaurant like my siblings had.

"Why us?" Spence asked.

Peter still hadn't spoken, but his posture had straightened and he'd been listening to Ms. C with wide eyes.

"I selected each of you for a specific reason that will be made clear in time." A glint in her eyes, the slightest quirk of her mouth, said Ms. C was enjoying this.

What possible reason could she have for me? English was far from my best subject.

But I could win this, with less contemplation and more action. The familiar pregame energy built inside me—a feeling I'd missed the last few weeks—making my muscles tense, my senses sharper.

Deep breath through the nose, count to ten, release slowly. Better not to imagine how winning could change my life. Wanting things rarely ended well, especially things I didn't have control over. Even things I thought I had control over were ending badly recently.

Indifference was a proven armor.

"When do we leave?" Amberlyn uncapped her pen again and poised it over her notepad. "How long will it take? What can we do to prepare?"

"If you agree, you and your parents will sign a nondisclosure agreement, and I will provide your plane ticket. You'll leave at the end of June and be gone for ten days. Though you'll begin in London, where I will meet you for the start of your journey, the trip will take you throughout the UK. Other details—including the specifics of your tasks—will wait until you arrive."

Amberlyn's grip tightened on her pen, and I could practically hear her teeth grinding. Personally, I figured not being able to prepare favored me.

Plus—London. I'd never been farther from Southern California than the Grand Canyon. If I didn't win, at least I'd be getting a free trip to England. Images of men in red uniforms and tall, black hats paraded through my mind. I couldn't contain a giant grin.

"Why the mystery?" I asked.

"When it is your money involved, you may be as mysterious as you wish." This time she fully smiled, telling me she didn't mind my interrogation.

My mind whipped through questions. Would Mom let me

go? Would I be better off getting a job that guaranteed money? Would I stand a chance against Amberlyn, Peter, and Spence?

Overthinking never accomplished anything. Action was better. Despite my efforts not to get excited, desire ignited inside me. I needed to believe something good could still happen to me.

I nodded once. "Where do I sign?"

CHAPTER TWO

A month later, I crossed the tiny gap between the airplane and the gangway—my first step onto a new land. My heart skipped, and my feet wanted to join it, my enthusiasm overcoming the fact that I felt like I'd been run over by a bus.

Amberlyn, with her sleeping pills, doughnut-shaped pillow, and travel-size makeup bag, looked ready for a photo shoot. She frowned as I waved goodbye to my businessman seatmate. "I bet he's never had a worse flight. You're so rude."

The doctor had told me to walk once an hour to keep my messed-up blood moving, plus do exercises for my knee, so I'd barely slept, and I'd made the guy next to me move so many times he eventually offered me the aisle seat.

"When you have your knee cut open and metal screws attached to the bones," I said to Amberlyn, "then you can comment."

She turned away.

Forget her. I was in England! Accents were different. The overhead announcements sounded fancy. And besides LAX to fly here, this was my first airport experience, so even signs directing us to customs put a spring in my step.

I couldn't believe I'd convinced Mom to let me come. For being a latecomer to the overprotective-parent thing—and by latecomer, I meant two months ago when she decided an opponent's incompetent slide tackle was somehow her fault—Mom seemed determined to make up for lost time. But sad faces, lots of chores, and a call from Ms. Carmichael won her over. Playing on her desire for me to "make something of myself" like my siblings hadn't hurt, either. Although, I doubted a week in England would lead me to Cal Poly grad school like Drew or law school at Stanford like Maya.

After clearing passport control, we trooped toward baggage claim. The carousel was awfully colorful. Strewn among the suitcases were the contents of a bag—T-shirts, underwear, toiletries. Several people chuckled or clucked as they freed bags from the flood of laundry.

The blood drained from my head.

No.

Those colorful panties were mine.

I wasn't into fashion, but I always imagined if I were in one of those bank robberies where the criminals forced everyone to strip to make sure they didn't have weapons or phones, I would give them creative underwear to laugh at.

There went my Snoopy briefs. The bikini-style with cartoon frogs. Rainbow polka dots, Harry Potter, and Superman.

Ugh. Was that my toothbrush on the metal belt? So much for getting rid of airplane breath.

I spotted my duffel bag, royal blue with our school name in white. Gaping open and mostly empty. Also, preventing me from pretending I had no idea who owned that stuff until everyone was gone, embroidered letters spelled *Hanson* across the side.

"Hey, Britt, isn't that yours?" Spence wasn't even attempting not to laugh. Or to keep his voice down.

Amberlyn retrieved her enormous, perfectly zipped pink plaid suitcase, pushing aside one of my sports bras.

My clothes were joyriding on other people's luggage. I had no other option but to suck it up. Head high, fighting a blush, I elbowed my way forward, shoulder-checking Spence as I passed, and snatched the empty duffel bag, then started scooping clothes into it. The bag smelled like grass and sweaty shin guards, but I hadn't had another.

Spence kept laughing and made no effort to help, not that I wanted a guy touching my underwear.

Amberlyn crouched beside me, silent. She handed me T-shirts and a hoodie, attention locked on the luggage rather than me. I snagged my deodorant, running shorts, jeans, and socks, cramming everything into my bag in a jumble.

Then Amberlyn cleared her throat. My Ninja Turtle panties dangled from one finger. "Really, Britt?"

Her tone held more humor than mockery, and I was briefly caught in a time warp, transported back six years to when we used to be friends. She dropped them into my bag and straightened, and the time warp collapsed so fast I doubted its existence, leaving rubble in its wake.

I thought I'd found everything, but I waited through another cycle of the conveyor belt to be sure. When I zipped the bag and stepped away, I sensed eyes on me.

I looked around, but most people's gazes flickered away before I made eye contact.

"I'm missing the TARDIS ones," I announced in a loud voice. "I know someone has them. Come forward now, and I won't press charges."

Quiet chuckles greeted my words.

I learned a long time ago if you make a joke and laugh first, they can't laugh at you.

"C'mon, Britt." Amberlyn's voice rolled its eyes.

I slung the duffel over my shoulder and headed for my class-mates with my head high. This would not dampen my spirits.

Peter and Spence carried fancy backpacker-style backpacks. Amberlyn towed a set of matching pink suitcases.

As if the flight hadn't been bad enough. Amberlyn had spent hours poring over notes from the last year of English, covering every book and poem we'd read. Peter scribbled in a journal, implying he wrote for fun, which Ms. Carmichael probably loved. And Spence pulled out a guidebook on England, forcing me to distract him by reading through the seats and pointing out funny place-names like Catbrain, Felldownhead, and Great Snoring.

Since Ms. C had been vague about the contest details, I'd figured there wasn't much to do to prepare, besides getting my passport. England had too much literature to read every book, even if I wanted to. Which I did not.

My competitors had a head start before we landed. Now,

before leaving the airport, I came across like a rookie who couldn't close a zipper.

Attention, airport travelers: Britt Hanson is in over her head.

Whatever. Luggage didn't matter. People seeing my underwear didn't matter. Winning mattered.

Focus on that.

Peter smirked as I passed. "Cool socks." He nodded at my leg. "Making a fashion statement?"

Kneeling had undone two snaps on my workout pants, revealing the compression socks I'd tried to hide. The tight, white sock came to right below my knee, swallowing the bottom few inches of my scar.

My heart skipped a beat. I quickly redid the snaps. "They help circulation. I do have screws in my knee, after all."

I speed-walked toward customs before anyone had a chance to mention the socks again. The last thing I needed was my classmates asking questions.

Outside, a man in a dark suit holding a sign that said CARMICHAEL greeted us. A town car limo, like the president rode in, waited at the curb. Was that for us? No way. Although, if Ms. C had the money to award a hundred grand, a limo was vending machine change.

"Can we maybe stop at a drugstore?" I asked. "I need a new toothbrush."

Peter snorted, and Spence broke into fits of laughter.

"Of course, miss," said the driver as he loaded our bags into the trunk and opened the back door.

Leather seats faced each other, and glass separated us from

16

the driver. Spence stretched out, and Amberlyn sat properly, glaring at his tennis shoes on the leather seat. Peter hunched in the corner as if the car were too small for him and the three of us, his eyes saying he hated me, the world, and puppies and rainbows.

On the new app we'd downloaded, I sent my mom the required text to let her know my plane hadn't gone down over the Atlantic, then drank it all in.

The city streets were packed. Old-fashioned-looking black taxis contrasted with giant red buses that looked like they'd driven out of a children's cartoon. Pedestrians crowded the sidewalks, and several incredibly brave bicyclists shared the road with tiny cars dwarfed by our beast of a vehicle.

I wanted to press my face to the glass like the world outside would suck me in, swallow me into its excitement. To burst out of the car bubble, plunge into the crowd, be part of the thrill.

The driver took a scenic route past Buckingham Palace, Big Ben, a giant church, and an ornate drawbridge. My eyes leaped from one sight to the next, a fascinating blend of new and old, grand and sleek, quaint and modern. My heart pulsed with the city beat.

This couldn't possibly be real. I blinked hard, and London was still there. Laughter bubbled in my chest.

Amberlyn provided a running commentary on the sights like a tour guide until Peter's glare made her falter and fall silent. I almost—*almost*—felt bad for her, except her knowledge put her one more step ahead of me.

We ended in a posh neighborhood of tree-lined streets

and white buildings with columns. Flower boxes and sculpted houseplants decorated every balcony. The driver parked in front of a row of apartments.

While he opened the car door for us, another man exited the building. He directed us up the sidewalk and into a lobby with polished marble floors. My tennis shoes squeaked, and I felt the crystal chandeliers and gleaming wood panels turning up their noses at my American-ness.

A fancy brass elevator operated by a man in a dark suit carried us to the top floor. The penthouse apartment had creamy walls with gold molding, floor-to-ceiling windows, and dark hardwood floors with plush rugs.

Ms. Carmichael waited, perched on an armchair, as we tromped in. Her coral-colored skirt suit and pearls could've come straight from the Queen's closet.

Amberlyn was the only one fancy enough for this place, in her leggings, cute sweater, and ankle boots. Not only was I underdressed, but I smelled after a day of travel, and I definitely needed mouthwash.

Ms. Carmichael rose. "I trust you had a pleasant flight. I'm sure you're tired, but the best way to overcome jet lag is to keep busy."

After a meal served on real china in a formal dining room, we settled on leather couches while our teacher took the chair. The setup reminded me of class. I couldn't stop my foot from jiggling. The city had temporarily distracted me from the challenge ahead.

Four unfamiliar people now stood against the wall. Two women, one wearing a black-and-white dress and one with a blouse and skirt. And two men, both in suits. All appeared to be in their mid-twenties to mid-thirties.

The men were too young for Ms. Carmichael and too old for me. Still, that didn't mean I couldn't appreciate the view.

I caught Amberlyn's eye and wagged my eyebrows. Her lips pressed together as she fought to hide a smile, but she did nod as if to say, *I know.*

"Do try to stop drooling, Ms. Hanson." Ms. Carmichael raised a hand, and one of the pieces of eye candy brought her a stack of envelopes.

A thrill zipped through me. Time to find out what I had to do to win.

"Now, for the details. You will receive a series of clues telling you where to go and what task you must complete to obtain the next clue. There will be eight in all. The tasks and locations will correspond to various works of classic literature."

Amberlyn's notes might've come in handy right about now.

"You will also find a journal. This competition is inspired by *The Canterbury Tales,* and as such, I'd like you to record your experiences as a series of tales. You will give these to me at the end of the adventure."

Writing tales. Journal. Books I barely remembered or hadn't read. I was in serious trouble.

She handed the envelopes around. I shook the contents into my lap. Along with the papers, notebook, and pen, I found a flip phone that I wouldn't bother using since it didn't have data, and a smaller envelope full of colorful bills that felt like Monopoly money.

"The phones are prepaid, for emergencies," Ms. Carmichael

said. "They're programmed with my number and the number of your chaperone."

"Chaperone?" I scanned the people standing along the wall, and my gaze lingered on one of the handsome men, with deep brown skin and full lips. "Can we pick?"

"You have been assigned someone to accompany you." Her lips twitched. "They are not to provide assistance. You'll essentially be on your own. They will observe, make sure you remain safe, and oversee the challenges."

"Like a babysitter," I said.

The youngest lady on the end, in the skirt and flats, sniffed.

I smiled at her, and she raised an eyebrow at me.

Ms. Carmichael drew one deep, slow breath. "Should you encounter trouble, they will be there to help as a last resort. Now, you also have two hundred pounds for transportation, meals, and lodging. When you require more, your *babysitter* will provide it. Within reason. I've assigned you each a room in this flat, should you need it, or if you'd like to leave anything you packed."

She eyed Amberlyn's massive pink suitcases, which possibly contained her entire library, her little brother, and enough clothes to stock a thrift store. Or, in her case, a fashion boutique.

"You have nine days. I expect you to hand in your journals on the morning of July seventh."

A set date? I tapped my foot and squinted at her. "It's not a race?"

"Not in the sense that the first to finish is the automatic winner," she said.

"What's the fun in that?" Time was measurable. A tangible thing that would let me win.

"I know, right?" Spence said.

"This is about the experience," Ms. Carmichael said. "You should not be so focused on rushing to the next place that you fail to appreciate where you are."

I leaned toward her, resting my elbows on my knees. "So, how do we win?"

"I will review your tales and hold a private interview with each of you. That's all I'll say now. I want you to have open minds to experience and write what you will, without preconceived ideas from me."

The odds of me writing anything remotely inspiring were low. I wished I knew what she wanted.

Ms. C shifted slightly. "Any questions?"

Too many to know where to start. The main one being, why was I here?

The assistants came forward, and the young woman who'd acknowledged my joke approached. "I'm Alexis. I will be accompanying you."

"It's okay," I whispered loudly as I stood. "You can say *baby-sit*. I can tell you totally used the same word yourself."

"I believe I used the term *nanny*." She didn't smile, but her eyes held a twinkle.

"Fair enough. Call me Britt."

My nanny was in her mid-twenties, shorter than me, with a shoulder-length, brown, wavy bob and big brown eyes. Her blue blouse was tucked into a narrow black skirt, accompanied by sensible but stylish flats. Even though she looked and sounded like an elegant pixie, I didn't sense judgment of my casual clothes and loud voice.

"Call me Al," she said.

Unexpected. "That's fun. When we were little, my brother, Drew, was obsessed with Batman. He pretended we had a butler named Alfred and always asked Alfred to do things for him." I paused. "I don't suppose you're driving me around England in a Batmobile? That would be awesome."

"I believe Ms. Carmichael expects you to use public transportation," she said. "Besides, I've heard the Batmobile has terrible fuel efficiency."

"Like those crazy red buses? Cool." I studied the other chaperones, who were talking with my classmates in other parts of the room. "What exactly do you do for Ms. Carmichael?"

"I babysit Americans."

"Does that pay well?"

She raised an eyebrow. "I've a dreadful suspicion there isn't enough money in England to pay me to keep up with you."

"I like you, Al."

"Then all my dreams have come true."

I grinned. We'd get along fine. "I need a plan. Oh yeah. You're not supposed to help. Can you show me to my room? Or am I supposed to guess which one's mine?"

"I believe that falls within acceptable assistance parameters."

"Acceptable assistance parameters," I repeated in a horrible British accent. "Thanks."

She grabbed my duffel bag, and I followed her down a hall to a room with dark, modern furniture—a twin bed, small dresser, and nightstand. Out the window, the sky was light despite the late hour. Treetops and buildings spread below us.

"I'll be outside if you need me." Al closed the door and, I assumed, positioned herself in the hall like a security guard. Weird.

I plopped onto the bed and immediately rolled up my pant legs. The tight, itchy socks had to go. The doctor recommended I wear them for three days after arriving, but *recommend* did not mean the same thing as *require*. Take that, vocabulary tests. I rolled the socks down and yanked, wiggling my toes when they were free.

With my legs stretched out, I noted that my tan lines were fading. My knees and thighs had always been a nice golden brown, while my lower legs, usually covered by shin guards, were pale. The tan lines had made me proud. They were an identifying mark, clearly stating I was a soccer player.

But I wasn't. Not anymore.

Yet another reason to wear pants. Hide the scar. Hide the tan line. Hide the problem.

I tugged my pant legs down.

Better to look forward than back. I pulled out the first clue.

The envelope also contained a page titled "Guidelines," but that sounded boring. I focused on the good stuff.

All I needed to do was figure out clues, write a few stories, and win some money.

No problem.

CHAPTER THREE

I chewed my pen as I reread the first clue, presented on a thick card similar to our invitations, also written in calligraphy. Our principal needed to know that grading papers wasn't keeping Ms. C busy enough.

At Lane's End lies a place with a new Twist on an old social ill;
Pip, David, and Oliver's ghosts echo still.

Perform an act of kindness to brighten a day
Before receiving a clue and going on your way.

I could do this. Twist. Oliver Twist? We hadn't read the book in class, but based on the movies, Oliver was an orphan. Maybe Pip and David were, too? Orphans could count as a "social ill." Did that mean I should visit a place with orphans?

I dug out the cheap smartphone Mom had bought before I left, with a bare-minimum international plan, primarily for mandatory check-ins. Knee surgery, her new venture into concerned parenting, and a ticket to England had finally made her upgrade my prepaid flip phone.

"Hey, Al!" I called toward the door, assuming she was standing in the hall awaiting my commands.

The door cracked open, and her face appeared.

"Is there Wi-Fi here?"

"England isn't the Dark Ages, Ms. Hanson."

I wiggled my phone. "Are you allowed to tell me the password, or do I have to solve a clue to get it?"

One corner of her mouth lifted. "It *is* a literary quote. Think *existential crisis.*"

I chucked a pillow at her.

She caught it and set it on the dresser. "The password is *to be or not to be.* No spaces."

Seriously? "Thanks. I guess I'll see you in the morning."

"The anticipation will keep me awake all night." She exited and closed the door before I could send my other pillow flying.

A basic search confirmed all three names in the clue were Dickens's characters who were orphans. Gold star for me. Also, depressing much, Charles? Another search revealed many orphanages, plus charities helping kids, throughout the city. Helpful. But one, at the far eastern edge of the city, was called Lane's End Children's Home. An act of kindness sounded simple enough. Once I arrived, I'd come up with something.

Now that I had a plan, I wanted to begin. But it was too late to crash an orphanage where the kids were probably sleeping.

Had the others solved the clue? Hopefully, none of them

could begin tonight. We had to sleep. And this wasn't a straight-up race. Which was too bad, because I stood a better chance at winning a race than writing a hundred-thousand-dollar journal.

I sighed. Community college was looking increasingly likely. There was nothing wrong with that. It made sense. But images of UCLA refused to leave my head, with its green lawns and grand quad, new people to meet and things to see, the promise of attending football and basketball games, even if soccer was out. And I had two siblings working on advanced degrees, which tended to set lofty familial expectations. No one expected me to meet those expectations, but that didn't stop them from existing.

I needed to win—that was all there was to it. I might be in over my head, but I wasn't going down without a fight.

My alarm blared early the next morning. My head felt stuffed with cotton, and my eyes full of sand. But I had money to win. I shoved the items from Ms. Carmichael into my messenger bag and left the duffel since I didn't know where I'd be going. Best not to risk a repeat of the underwear incident.

In the dining room, dishes of fried eggs, toast, bacon, beans, and tomatoes filled the table. Al sat alone, sipping tea and reading an Agatha Christie novel. There was no sign of my classmates.

I gulped strong, hot tea, swallowed the daily pill that was a new lifelong companion and ensured yesterday's flight wouldn't kill me, and grabbed two pieces of toast. "Ready?"

She tucked the book into her purse. Today she wore a business skirt and a blazer.

"Does the clue involve attending a board meeting?"

She raised an eyebrow. "How would I know? I'm not allowed to help, remember?"

I gestured to her outfit. "You look . . . formal."

"This is what I wear."

I glanced at my jeans, T-shirt, and blue tennis shoes. "Whatever makes you happy. The guy I sat next to on the plane said London has a great tube system. Does telling me where the nearest stop is fall within acceptable parameters?"

"I believe that would be permissible."

I headed for the door, hoping she couldn't tell I had no idea how to navigate the train station once I arrived. But I learned better by doing, so I'd figure it out when I got there.

Al directed me to the station, marked by a sign with a red circle and blue line across it that said UNDERGROUND. Thank you, London, for making public transportation easy.

Once I stood in front of the tube system map, I was less impressed. The image reminded me of the summer my sister attempted to learn knitting and the yarn got tangled into a rainbow mess. A dozen curvy lines, each a different color, with hundreds of tiny names. Who thought this was a good idea? I tried to remember everything my plane neighbor had said about lines and stops.

People bustled past. Everyone knew where they were going,

so certain and determined. I elbowed my way through them, clearly traveling the wrong direction, toward the sign that said TICKETS.

In a voice that made giving directions sound classy, the man behind the window answered my questions about traveling east and getting around the city. He gave me a day pass for as many rides as I needed throughout London and told me how to reach the platform.

He ended with, "Welcome to London, mum."

It took a second to realize *mum* meant *ma'am* and another to decide I liked his manners.

I handed over money, unsure of the true cost because of the exchange rate.

"Get a receipt," Al said from behind me.

We joined the line going downstairs to the platforms, and I craned my head to look at everything. Al tugged me to the right side of the escalator, and I understood why as someone charged past us on the left.

"This is so cool."

"You enjoy crowds, queues, and dark tunnels?" Al asked from two steps behind me, which seemed to be the official unspoken spacing rule.

"A magical world could be waiting down there."

"Your optimism is truly boundless."

"I sense I'm going to need enough for both of us. This will be a great week. You'll see."

I'd thought Al's outfit formal, but once we boarded the tube car, I realized many people were dressed up. Black dress shoes that must've been the unofficial footwear of British males over the age of eighteen. Perfectly tailored suits on trim men who totally pulled them off. Others wore leather jackets, trench coats, dresses, jeans. Most read papers or stared at phones or listened to earbuds.

A cross-section of life, riding the same train. Since Southern California wasn't big on public transportation, the experience added to the British feel. All these people, and they were so English. Hundreds of strangers with stories and accents. I wanted to talk to them all.

The train was packed. I wedged my way inside and reached for a rail, until a man stood, motioned to his seat, and let me take it.

British manners. I barely stopped myself from hugging him.

The girl next to me couldn't have been more than a few years older than I was. She wore a silk dress and shiny flats.

"Londoners are fashionable." I gestured to her and to my tennis shoes. "It's totally obvious I'm a tourist."

"S'all right. We get lots of tourists here. Nobody minds what you wear."

"Are you on your way to work? Do you always ride the tube?"

We chatted until the train approached its first stop.

"Please mind the gap between the train and the platform," a cool female voice announced from the speakers.

My loud laugh escaped, the one I couldn't control that woke bears from hibernation and forced old men to turn down their hearing aids. I blamed the accent, the odd phrasing—did people fall into the tiny gap?—and the jetlag.

People glanced at me without making eye contact. Apparently, when Brits put on their suits, they also put on indifference and a straight face.

The girl smiled, a soft one that didn't show teeth. "'Mind the gap' is a London thing. They have shirts and everything."

I had to get one.

As we headed away from the city center, the train slowly emptied. I tapped my foot and tugged on a chunk of hair. Al sat nearby, staring into space. Clearly not one for conversation. How was I going to spend nine days with no one to talk to?

I listened to the voice announce stops until I heard the one I wanted, one of the last, at the city's edge. But the station was several blocks from the children's home.

"Do you know where we're going?" I asked Al.

"Ms. Carmichael informed us of the clues. And I've been here before. This way."

"Acceptable assistance parameters. I like it."

We walked through neighborhoods with attached houses like condos and onto a street where brownish-red brick homes had private yards. The street seemed normal, except the shapes of the windows, the makes of the cars, the colors of the stone buildings, were just different enough to remind me this was another country. I spotted the correct number, and we passed through a waist-high gate and up a cobblestone driveway.

"So the kids here are orphans?"

"Some. Others might have parents who are unable to care for them."

"That sucks."

"Indeed."

Game plan: Do something nice. Write a tale.

Were they expecting me? I rapped the lion door-knocker several times. No one answered.

"They're likely too loud to hear the bell," Al said.

"If you disapprove of loudness, you're in for a long week with me."

"Indeed."

I grinned. "Do you come here often?"

"Part of my job for Ms. Carmichael is assisting with her charitable endeavors."

I slid her a glance. "She has lots of those?"

"Quite a few."

"Where does she get the money? Did she rob a bank?"

Al's expression didn't change. "If so, I was not asked to drive the getaway car."

Oh well. Worth a shot.

I knocked again, harder.

The door opened. A girl of maybe ten peeked out, all wide blue eyes and freckled nose.

I bent to her eye level. "Hi. I'm Britt."

"You talk funny."

"*You* talk funny," I said, even though a kid with a British accent was the cutest thing ever.

Her hands flew to her hips. "We talk the same. That means you're the odd one."

"Fair enough. What's your name? Can we come in?"

"I'm Nadia." She grabbed my arm and yanked me inside. "Come play."

She dragged me past a woman around my mom's age, with

short gray hair and a kind smile, who sat at a table with a boy younger than Nadia.

"Hullo. Alexis, good to see you. Welcome. I'm Harriet," she said to me. "The kids are in the garden."

"I want to play," the boy said.

Harriet returned her attention to him. "Once you finish your maths homework."

"Maths, plural?" I gave the boy a grimace. "I thought one was bad."

"I'll help." Al took Harriet's place at the maths table, looking happier than I'd seen her yet. Better her than me.

I followed Nadia to the back door. In the yard, ten kids ran around. Some were elementary-school age, like my new friend, but most were young teens. Spence was with them. His babysitter was leaning against the fence.

"Do you like football?" Nadia asked. "I love football. But they don't always let me play. But if you play, you're a girl, and they have to let me."

Her cute accent distracted me enough that I forgot *football* meant *soccer*.

The kids were passing a ball. A beautiful, perfect soccer ball.

A wave of longing crashed over me, tugging me toward dangerous depths. What would it hurt? I'd been cleared to jog, so my knee wasn't an issue as long as I didn't make any sharp turns. As for the blood condition . . . well, this wasn't a full-contact, competitive match. I'd be fine. Right? As long as I was careful?

The words Mom asked when I proposed this trip echoed in my head: *Since when have you learned to be careful?*

My feet carried me closer. The springy grass welcomed my steps. My gaze tracked the movement of the ball with laser focus. I almost felt it at my feet.

I drifted even closer.

A boy kicked the ball. It sailed over the heads of his companions.

Moved in slow motion.

Headed straight for me.

CHAPTER FOUR

Instinct took over. I trapped the ball with my thigh so it dropped at my feet and passed it to the boy who'd kicked it. The ball cleared the others and landed right in front of him.

He waved.

I froze. Trembled. Swallowed. That one simple act was like embracing a long-lost friend, taking a ball to the gut, and losing a family member rolled into one.

The kids kept playing, and slowly the world came back into focus. I'd done it. Kicked a ball for the first time in months. Nothing disastrous had happened, at least not physically. I should walk away now, though.

I tried to linger at the edge of the yard, but the boys kept passing me the ball. Returning it felt so good—so right—that I couldn't stop. My feet inched forward no matter how many times I told them not to.

Don't get attached. This can't last. This won't end well.

One ball came high, and I sent a perfectly aimed header to a boy in a Chelsea jersey.

Next time I got the ball, my girl shadow charged me. Years of practice controlled my body. I faked right, nudged the ball to the left, then dragged it backward and spun around her. Several kids hooted.

"Britt Hanson is back, folks," Spence said in an announcer voice.

Before I realized how it happened, we were playing a game with trees as a goal on one end and patio chairs on the other.

My knee only twinged a couple of times. I wanted to steal the ball, dribble all over the yard, send powerful kicks toward the goal. Feel the air rushing past as I raced down the field. Whoop and yell and cheer.

When I passed Spence, he nodded at my knee with a teasing glint in his eye. "Sure you should be playing?"

One small comment dumped a heaping pile of reality on my head. He didn't know the truth. He was messing with me, nothing more. But his words stopped me faster than an illegal takedown.

No, I wasn't sure at all. Uncertainty on the field was a new sensation. This was my domain. Once. No longer.

I made myself pass to the boys, run interference for Nadia, and set up others to take shots.

Surely this was safe enough, right? Because it was like I imagined an addict felt. I'd had a tiny taste after going cold turkey for weeks, and now I couldn't get enough. I craved more, more, more. But I'd be forced to give it up again soon, which made the one taste both precious and dangerous.

Spence, not content to let me play backup, dribbled toward me, a determined set to his jaw.

My mind calculated the exact angle for a slide tackle. I could take him. I shifted my weight. And remembered a slide tackle was what landed me here in the first place.

I scrabbled for an alternative that didn't leave me looking like a coward. "Nadia, quick, get him."

She charged.

"What's wrong?" Spence glanced up long enough to meet my gaze with narrowed eyes. "Afraid to lose?"

Yearning to show him up burned inside me, fueled by my blazing pride. But what if I fell? What if my knee gave out? What if he kicked me, which I was used to, but never when a simple bruise could prove deadly?

"Didn't want to embarrass you in front of the kids," I said.

I thought Spence would escape Nadia, but he slowed and let her steal the ball. I cheered as she darted in the other direction.

He shook his head at me, and I shrugged and grinned to hide the fact that I wanted to scream.

Soccer was the one thing I could always count on dominating. I loved trash-talking and shutting up people like Spence by playing well. I squeezed my hand into a fist and drew a deep breath, but air couldn't fill the massive chasm in my chest.

After half an hour, I was breathing hard, my thigh muscles burned, and my knee was sore. Being forbidden from running the last several weeks had messed me up. Despite the cool, cloudy weather, sweat beaded on my forehead.

Light rain had started to fall, which didn't faze the kids, but I bowed out to cheer from the edge of the yard.

Spence joined me. "Can't take the rain?"

Knowing he expected a joke, I forced a lighthearted tone. "Can't take your smell."

He laughed. "I thought you were tougher than that."

Why did he care? Was he hoping I'd hurt myself and have to go home?

"No one's tough enough for that, dude."

"Is your knee okay? Won't slow you down this week, will it?"

"You wish."

My knee was fine. The doctor had cleared me to go without the brace weeks ago. He knew I was coming here and would've told me if walking around England would be a problem. Why did Spence have to bring it up anyway? Jerk.

"Hey, Spence? Why do you need the money? With sports and your grades . . ."

He lifted a shoulder. "I received partial scholarship offers, but I want to go to USC for undergrad and law school, and they didn't give me anything. It's way too expensive for seven years of loans. My family thinks I should stay home the first two years, go to community college. But I'm ready to move on, you know? And this prize is way more than I ever made busing tables or mowing lawns."

I understood all of that. The desire to experience something new. The minimum-wage jobs. And numbers racked up in my mind of the loans for my sister's law school and my brother's master's degree, despite their academic scholarships.

"I didn't know you wanted to go to law school." I could see him as a lawyer, hounding criminals the way he did opposing receivers. "My sister's at Stanford. Even with a scholarship, the loans are ridiculous."

"Yeah, I don't want to do that if I don't have to. We can't all be stars like you. I wasn't good enough for a football scholarship, and my family can't help. So now it's up to me, and I'll do whatever it takes to win."

Being a star hadn't gotten me as far as he thought. "Why do you think Ms. C picked you for this?"

"Because I'm charming and brilliant?"

"Are those synonyms for *egotistical* and *full of crap*?"

His eyes widened in mock surprise. "You know the word *synonym*?"

"Ms. C picked *me* for my wide vocabulary." She *had* complimented my vocabulary in multiple essays. Her issue was with how I used the words I knew.

Spence's smile faded. "Why do you need this? You got an offer from UCLA ages ago."

Any lightheartedness melted away. "Partial. But . . ." I lifted my leg.

"They withdrew the scholarship when you got hurt?"

I refused to meet his eye. "Something like that. Doesn't hurt to have extra funds, right?"

"Right. Well, I'm out of here. Break a leg."

"If I do, it'll be yours." I tossed him a smile.

Spence smiled too, saluted, and strode away.

A guy I hadn't seen earlier now sat on the ground by the house, reading to three younger kids under the overhang. He was about my age, with thick-framed glasses. Hair fell across his forehead almost to his eyes, and red Converse sneakers peeked out from under his crossed legs. Cute, in a nerdy way.

I headed toward them, walking slowly to hide my limp.

"Heads up," someone shouted.

I spun. The ball was shooting toward the guy reading, flying straight at his face.

I launched myself. Once again, muscle memory ruled. I jumped parallel to the ground, lifted my left knee, and swung my right leg. I'd done enough bicycle kicks to execute it perfectly. My hands came down to brace my fall, followed by my butt. I landed on the ground in front of him. The ball sailed back toward the field.

The guy looked up and blinked. "Thanks."

I froze, lying in the dirt. Why had I done that? Had I re-injured my knee? Was I bleeding? Bruised? Was I going to die?

Nothing hurt. I knew how to land for one of those kicks. I wiggled my toes. Flexed my knee. Took a breath. I was okay. I hadn't done something incredibly foolish. Well, I had, but I'd gotten away with it. Hopefully. I'd have to watch for bruises.

"Are you all right?" A male voice drew my attention to the present.

"Oh. Yeah. Fine." Other than embarrassed that it looked like I'd lost a battle with a lawn mower. I stood and brushed off the dirt and wet grass.

"Why'd you do that? I'm grateful, of course. But . . ." The guy studied me like he couldn't figure out what exactly I was.

I examined him. He had a slight chin dimple and eyes somewhere between brown and gold. "Glasses."

"Glasses?"

I waved at his face.

"I'm going to need more than that."

I drew another breath to confirm I was still alive. Yep. I plopped next to him. "You want the whole story?"

"Absolutely. Dee, why don't you fetch another book?" He handed the one he'd been reading to the boy in his lap, and the young kids ran inside.

I focused my attention on the cute guy. "Okay, then. I started playing soccer at the age of four. By the time I was seven, I was basically convinced I was ready for the US national team. Because three years of kiddie soccer is an eternity."

Though he sat very still, his intense gaze focused on my face like his whole mind was present and listening. It was both intimidating and flattering. My stomach fluttered.

"My favorite player as a kid was Carli Lloyd, a forward for the US. Amazing accuracy, scores tons of goals." I found myself leaning forward, voice growing animated. "One day, I was practicing in the backyard. My dad was outside, too, gardening. I decided it was the perfect opportunity to show him I was a top goal-scorer, too. I planned to perfectly curve the ball around him and hit the goal on the other side, some old-school bending it like Beckham."

I made a curving motion with my hand.

The guy groaned in sympathy.

"Yeah," I said. "Not the first or the last of my brilliant plans that ended in complete failure. Not only did I break his glasses, but they shattered and cut his face. I was lucky I didn't blind him. Now I have radar. If a ball's headed for anyone with glasses, I can sense it from a hundred feet and I have to save them." I spread my hands. "I can't help it. It's my superpower."

"You throw yourself in front of loads of strangers, then?" One eyebrow lifted a fraction.

"Better than throwing myself *at* them, right? I could've tackled you." Ugh, really? Way to give him an inappropriate mental picture. "I mean, I chose the politer option of kicking the ball."

He didn't blink at my awkwardness. "You were too far away to tackle me."

"Good point."

"Half those boys"—he nodded to the kids—"will now demand you teach them to perform that kick."

"Um, yeah. Maybe later." Could I teach without having to do it again? Because even I wasn't impulsive enough to repeat that move anytime soon. Unless they aimed the ball at Glasses again. "You might want to go inside for that. Could get dangerous."

"What if I take my glasses off?" He slid them from his face, giving me a clear view of his golden-brown irises.

My throat went dry. What was wrong with me? Cute boys rarely fazed me. But I was used to athletes. Maybe my immunity didn't extend to attractive nerds.

I squinted, pretending to examine him. "I dunno, depends how badly you need them. Will you be able to see the ball heading for you? Because I only save people with glasses. Without them, you're on your own."

His lips quirked. I realized he didn't move much. Through my whole story he'd barely shifted, slight changes of expression without lifting his shoulders, hands, anything else. Stillness surrounded him. That wasn't something I had experience with.

"I'm Britt, by the way."

He put his glasses back on. "You don't sound like a Brit."

I let out my loud laugh. "I thought that was the most obvious joke possible, but you're the first person to say anything. Congratulations."

That earned a smile, which leaned slightly to the right side of his face. "Luke Jackson."

Before I could reply, the door opened and Al stepped out.

"Morning, Luke," she said.

He nodded at her. "Alexis. All right?"

"All right."

"You two know each other?" I glanced at one, then the other. Someone tugged my arm.

"Come on. Teach us how to do that." Nadia grabbed my hand and pulled.

"I warned you," Luke said.

I let the girl drag me to my feet.

Al made a noise in her throat. "Are you sure you should be doing this?"

My jaw clenched. "Who told you?"

"Told me what?" Her too-wide eyes screamed *guilt*.

"Does Ms. C know everything?" Of course she did. Because she was like a spy or a ninja, with *proper British schoolteacher* as a cover. "Did she get her money from hacking private databases and selling personal information?"

"I—"

"I'm fine, Alexis." I spun away. "I'm going to play with the kids."

If only I could take out my frustration on the field. Kick as hard as possible. Dribble far and fast until the last three months were too far behind me to have any sway over my future.

I shouldn't have come out here. After several weeks off, to know I could still make that bicycle kick. Dribble the same. Ignorance might've been better. But I couldn't disappoint the kids, so I gave them pointers and set them loose to practice, then trudged toward the house. Luke was no longer sitting there, and my heart sank. Silly. But I wouldn't have minded talking to him more.

Nadia followed, skipping beside me.

Did teaching soccer skills count as an act of kindness? Simply playing with the kids? Or should I do more?

"Do you like it here?" I asked her.

"It's all right. Better than the last place. Ms. Harriet is nice."

I stopped at the door but didn't enter. "How many places have you lived?"

Her face scrunched. "First there was Gran, but she got sick. Then a couple of foster carers. I thought a family might adopt me, but they moved to Liverpool and changed their mind."

"How long will you get to stay here?" I gestured toward the house.

"Until someone adopts me. But I'm nearly too old for that. I've a better chance than Jimmy, though. No one wants teenagers." She said it so matter-of-factly, a pang hummed through my chest.

"Well, I would want you if I lived here and I was, you know, a real adult. I bet a family will come along."

"You're nice." She threw her arms around me. "Even if you do talk funny."

At first, I was too surprised to react. Then I wrapped my arms around her small frame and hugged her, too.

It was nice they had places like this, like a home. Better than the workhouses in Dickens's time. Or picking pockets on the street. The kids didn't seem unhappy. But it had to be sad to think you'd never have parents. Would I have ended up somewhere like this if something had happened to Mom? Or would my dad have returned from wherever he ran off to?

Nadia released me and pulled me to the ground. I let her braid my hair, undo it, then redo it again.

This didn't seem like a hard task. It might scare antisocial Peter, who never talked, or annoy Amberlyn, who didn't like kids because they were loud and messy. I thought it was fun, if sad. Based on their reactions to Luke, Spence, and me, I didn't think people played with the kids often.

And yet, Nadia's voice hadn't held a note of self-pity. Could I say the same about myself the last few months?

Charles Dickens, already forcing me into self-contemplation.

When Nadia declared my hair done, she hugged me again and skipped off to rejoin the soccer game.

Someone cleared their throat. I jumped and whirled to find Ms. Harriet behind me.

"Sorry to give you a fright," she said. "Thanks for spending time with the kids. They always enjoy when people visit."

"It was my pleasure. Really. You're amazing."

She waved a hand. "This is for you. Cheers." She handed me a card and nodded before heading toward the kids.

I leaned against the wall and opened the envelope.

Tour streets familiar to the man known as Boz.
Despite being Fleet, remember to pause

At the public house where many great writers did eat.
You must be quick as a Dodger to get what you need.

I dug out my phone and learned that *Boz* was a nickname for Charles Dickens. Maps traced routes for self-guided tours of Dickens sights. Boring. Ooh. "Entertaining and historical" Charles Dickens walking tours. Bingo.

As for the rest, hopefully the tour would visit the correct public house. And I assumed the second part of the clue referred to the Artful Dodger, a character from *Oliver Twist*, not the baseball team. But he was a pickpocket who led a group of criminal children.

Seriously? Was that my next task? Pick a pocket to get my clue?

This was going to be interesting.

I found Al inside. Luke sat on the floor, surrounded by the younger kids again. An open book lay in front of him. A flutter went through my chest. I was glad he hadn't left.

I needed to move on. But Luke's smooth voice pulled me in. I edged closer, trying not to be seen.

The story had dragons and knights and princesses. His voice was deep and smooth, with a crisp accent, like a movie voiceover or a hero in the Jane Austen movies Ms. Carmichael made us watch. He didn't stumble once. The kids' round eyes fixed on his face. Mine surely matched.

Some mouthed the words along with him. Did they have so few books that they'd memorized the words?

I crossed to Al on the far side of the room. Keeping my voice low, I asked, "Would Ms. Carmichael mind if I used leftover money she gave us to buy them books and stuff?"

"She frequently donates to this facility. I'm sure she wouldn't mind." She kept her gaze on Luke. "That's nice of you."

"How do you know Luke?"

"He's my cousin."

Huh. "You greeted him like a business acquaintance."

"We don't know each other well. He needed something to do this summer, and I suggested he volunteer here."

My attention returned to him. While reading, he used no extra movement. A finger to turn the page. A smile that didn't use every facial muscle. His restraint made me feel loud and obvious.

"Luke, why does the knight always chase the dragon?" A boy bounced near Luke's shoulder. "I would leave it alone so I didn't get toasted like the other knights who tried to kill it."

Luke closed the book, focused his attention fully on the boy. "Because it's a fairy tale. Fairy tales are exciting stories that are fun to read, but they also teach us that good beats evil. Knights are brave, honorable, and noble, and they fight the monsters to show us we can fight monsters, too."

"Like Bill in my school? He smells like a troll. He might be a monster."

I covered my mouth to hide my laugh.

"He might be," Luke said, and I gave him credit for not laughing. "Or he might be lonely like the hermit in the forest. When the knight was kind to him, the hermit gave him stew and a map to the dragon's cave."

"So if I'm nice to Bill, he might help me find treasure?"

One corner of Luke's mouth dimpled, but his face remained serious. "You never know, Dee."

As Luke spoke, I recognized something in his face. He loved what he was doing, but it was pleasure tainted by sadness. Or regret.

It was like seeing my insides turned out and pasted on his face.

He looked up and met my gaze. Time froze.

A hint of a smile was stuck on my face, but twisted sideways with near panic so I resembled the beast in his story.

He adjusted his glasses and returned his focus to the kids, leaving me feeling like he'd read me as easily as the pages before him.

The air closed in, warm, stuffy. Tight in my lungs.

I bolted to the front porch.

The cloudy sky had darkened, and a fine mist hung in the air. I sucked a few breaths.

The door cracked behind me.

I jumped.

"Sorry." Luke stopped beside me, hands in his pockets, staring out at the street without moving. He was taller than I would've guessed, towering several inches above me, not thin but wiry. He smelled of soap and pine, a nice change from the body spray–drenched guys at my school.

The silence felt full of heavy things.

"You're a natural." My voice came out higher-pitched than I would've preferred. "You could, like, read audiobooks for a living. You love books, don't you?"

A wistful expression crossed his face, like he was thinking about something wonderful he could never have. "What about you? The older boys were practically drooling when they watched you play football."

I was pretty sure my face mirrored his expression. I knew I was now thinking of something wonderful I could never have. "I played."

The rest of the story got stuck between my brain and my mouth, same as it had for the last several weeks.

He pressed his lips together in a sad almost smile. "It's better not to love something, isn't it? It's harder to get hurt if you don't care."

I didn't answer. I couldn't. Not after he so perfectly captured what I'd tried not to think about for weeks. *Change the subject.* But for once I couldn't find anything to say.

"You're not supposed to play, are you?" His question was quiet. Gentle.

Heat pricked my throat and eyes. But I hadn't cried in years, not when my knee snapped with the worst pain I'd ever felt, or at the doctor's office when I got the news.

"Well, it was nice to meet you, but I have places to be." I stepped toward the edge of the porch.

Luke didn't move.

I glanced back. His eyes were sympathetic, despite my rudeness.

He withdrew an umbrella from his bag. A spoke caught on the opening, and several items tumbled onto the pavement. One was a small box, which popped open to reveal a gold watch. Luke snatched it up, snapped it closed, and shoved it into the bag in a hurry. The other items littering the porch were books.

"You carry a library with you?" I knelt to help him pick them up.

The first book my hand encountered was *The Canterbury Tales.*

I froze. Ms. Carmichael had said this book inspired the competition. Was it a sign? I paused in a squatting position despite my screaming knee. Cleared my throat. "Do you like impossible-to-understand literature as a general rule, or are you partial to Chaucer?"

He crouched next to me and gathered the other books, his arm brushing my knee as he reached around me. He grasped his glasses at the spot where the right earpiece met the frame and adjusted them. The gesture was sophisticated, not the typical nerd pushing up glasses by the nosepiece. "Chaucer's not hard to understand if you read it right."

"I must've been reading it wrong." I fanned the pages with my thumb. "Is this a setup? Did Al put you up to this?"

"I'm not sure what you mean." His eyebrows drew together.

I studied the book in my hands, a paperback with worn pages, nothing special. "Have you ever been on a pilgrimage? Like these guys?"

"Do people still do that?"

"Kind of." I eyed him again. Smart, educated, cute. Funny in a dry way. Plus, I wouldn't mind listening to him talk. Unless he planned to ask more questions I didn't plan to answer. "Interested in helping with one?"

"What type of pilgrimage are we talking about?"

I handed him the book and eyed Al, who stood on the edge of the porch pretending not to listen. "What are you doing this afternoon? And how do you feel about Dickens?"

CHAPTER FIVE

"I never suspected the literature of Dickens made for a popular pilgrimage destination," Luke said as we sat on the tube. "Social inequity, child labor, and homelessness hardly say *Come visit me.*"

"I guess I need a better term than pilgrimage." I tapped my fingers against my thigh. "Quest? That sounds epic."

"Fool's errand?" he suggested.

"No one said you had to come."

"I was otherwise unengaged."

"You talk like Al."

My words were lighthearted, but I recognized the shadow in his eyes. It said he had something he should be doing but wanted to forget about. The look matched the one I'd seen in the mirror the past few weeks.

Only three other passengers sat in the train, which was silent other than the clacking of wheels on the tracks. As the city flew past, I kept my voice low and explained the reason for my trip to England, leaving out the things I thought the confidentiality agreement covered—mainly, the fact that my teacher was loaded. But if Luke's cousin worked for Ms. C, he might know.

Al sat several seats away reading, making no move to stop me. Did her instructions include enforcing the guidelines or reporting to Ms. Carmichael if I violated them?

"So, you have to visit places?" Luke asked, his head tilting.

"And do tasks and write tales. Hopefully not in Old English, since I can't read it."

"The Old English writers are easier read aloud. Their spelling differed, but many of the words are remarkably similar."

"Maybe you'll have to read it to me." To help me understand, not because of his hot reading voice. "Sounds like you know a lot about literature."

His brow furrowed but cleared after a single blink. The half smile returned. "Sounds like you don't."

"I'd be offended if you weren't so right."

"Is this sort of competition"—he worked his lower lip— "common in America?"

I couldn't contain a loud laugh, which bounced through the car. The other passengers glanced our way. I shifted and lowered my voice. "It is so uncommon I still can't believe I'm here."

"That's a relief. I was worried more mad American students might be set loose in our country. I don't think we could handle that."

"Just me. And three classmates, but don't worry. I'm by far the craziest."

"That's also a relief."

I laughed again. His even voice with the fancy accent, and the slight curl of his lip, made everything funnier.

"For you," muttered Al. "I'm the one who has to keep an eye on her."

"Admit it," I said. "You're having fun."

She didn't reply, but her mouth twitched.

The train whooshed as we pulled into a station, the opening doors sending a rush of cool air through the car.

We exited to change lines. I stared at the signs, and Luke placed his hands lightly on my shoulders and angled me to the left. Then winked as we continued, heating my cheeks.

When our new train was moving, I asked, "Have you ever taken a Dickens tour?"

"I've not actually been in London long."

"Where'd you come from?"

He adjusted his glasses and peered at me. "Don't parents have that talk with you in America?"

I rolled my eyes and elbowed him.

His smile faded. Did my casual touch bother him, or was he thinking about something else?

"I grew up in Oxford. I've seen the historical sites in London but not the tourist attractions." His flat tone said it was something personal. I hoped. "Is this what your clue said? Take a Dickens tour?"

"Sort of. Here." I dug in my bag and laid the first two clue cards on his knees. "I'm not cheating, Al."

Luke scanned the lines, and I didn't mention that I hadn't fully interpreted the new one.

"I get eight clues total. Then I have to write about my experiences. It's inspired by *The Canterbury Tales*."

"Canterbury. You really are a pilgrim." He flipped to the next page. "Did you read the sheet called 'Guidelines'?"

"Nope. Easier to get out of trouble if you can claim ignorance."

"It says no help, Pilgrim."

"You're not helping. I figured out the clues. I'll write my own stories. You just happen to be along for the ride. Lots of people will be on this tour, I bet. Besides, Al would stop me if I broke the rules." I waved at her.

"Would I, though?" she asked without looking up from her book, ankles crossed, posture straight, like she was sitting at a table for tea rather than in a musty train car reading a murder mystery.

"Are you even reading, or are you pretending so you can spy on me?"

"It's called multitasking." Her lips quirked a fraction. "And I would never spy. I am the epitome of politeness."

I snorted.

Luke straightened the cards on his lap and shifted, revealing a flash of his red shoes. "So, if you solve these clues and write about them, then what?"

"One of us wins a cash prize."

"What would you do with it?"

Another question I'd been trying not to consider. One step at a time—win. And avoid the chicken outfit. "Go to college. What about you? Are you in school?"

"Just finished." He handed the papers to me. "This is mad. You do know that?"

He was as skilled at avoiding uncomfortable subjects as I was. "Yes, but it's also different, and I've never traveled before, so I couldn't say no. Plus, I really need that money."

That feeling returned, pressing to get out, like I might burst with longing and desperation and *need*.

"At least it's fun, right? You had a good time with those kids." He slanted a glance at me. "Even if you were trying not to."

Curse his determination to analyze me. And his accuracy. But two could play that game. "Like you? You clearly enjoy books since you're carrying half a library. And you were having fun, too, but you wished you weren't."

A light dimmed in his eyes, but he blinked, and they returned to normal almost before I noticed. Almost.

"Books are like adventures," he said. "They take you to new places and let you be new people. The best ones teach you about life or inspire you."

"Maybe I'm reading them wrong. I like books okay, if the story is exciting. But I'd rather have my own adventures and meet real people."

"Then this contest is perfect for you, Pilgrim." His eyes sparked, and one corner of his mouth tucked in, making a tiny dimple.

That stupid flutter returned to my chest. "Pilgrim, huh? Is that how it's going to be, Professor?"

Even though I smiled and my voice teased, something dark flitted across his face.

The train slowed and Luke stood. "This is our stop."

Okay. No calling him Professor. It sounded like a way better nickname than Pilgrim, but I obviously hit a nerve.

We exited the tube, Al trailing us, and climbed to street level.

A man sat against a building outside the tube stop. He wore a black jacket with a hood over his head, and a blanket covered his legs. An empty paper Starbucks cup rested beside him.

Luke dug through his pocket and dropped coins into the man's cup. "All right?"

"Ta." The man bobbed his head.

Luke returned the gesture and kept walking.

He read to orphans and gave change to homeless people. Definitely a step above the guys at home.

I nudged his arm with mine. "Are you trying to be one of those knights you read about?"

He brushed hair out of his eyes. "It was just a couple of pounds."

"To you," I said. "To him, it was a meal."

He ducked his head, his cheeks pink.

The website said this tour started at the corner, so we joined five people waiting. One of them, I recognized.

Peter greeted me with his usual hostile expression, hands stuffed into the pockets of faded jeans. He wore a Starfleet Academy shirt, and shaggy hair hung in his eyes in a manner much sloppier than Luke's.

Al greeted the hot guy, who must have been Peter's babysitter. He'd lost the jacket and rolled up the sleeves of his shirt. Ms. C either had a strict dress code or only hired fancy dressers.

I marched to Peter, and Luke followed. "Do you scowl at everyone, or is that particular expression reserved for me?"

Peter's lip curled. "You really don't know?"

"Know what? That your face is stuck like that?"

He snorted, but not in an *I think you're funny* way. "Typical. You don't honestly think you have a chance of winning, do you?"

"I don't lose."

"There's a first time for everything. I plan to win, so you're about to learn how." His gaze darted to Luke. "Already getting other people to do your work?"

"It's called making friends. You should try it." I grasped Luke's arm and dragged him to the other edge of the group.

"You're quite popular," he said, a teasing glint in his eyes.

"We've been in class together since we were kids, but I've never really talked to him. He's not the most outgoing person. And he seems to hate me, but I have no idea why."

Despite our years together, I didn't know much about him. Why had Ms. C picked him? Why the rest of us? She must've had a reason, but I couldn't ask Peter like I had Spence.

I released Luke's arm so he didn't think I was looking for reasons to touch him. "So, tell me about you."

He lifted one shoulder. "Not much to tell. I'm rather dull."

"Family?"

"What about them?"

I rolled my eyes.

He unsuccessfully tried to hide a smile. "Just my dad and me."

"It's just my mom and me, too. I have siblings, but they're

57

older. Maya is in law school, and Drew's studying architecture. They got the brains in the family."

"You don't seem dumb." His mouth quirked. "Perhaps a bit excitable. Maybe loud. But not dumb."

To avoid telling him I wasn't as smart as he thought—and I'd needed Google to solve the clues—I pointed to a store with maps in the window. "I'm gonna stop in there before the tour guide arrives."

Using the map on my phone took too much data.

Luke trailed me into the shop, which contained other London-y gifts like mugs and snow globes and the Mind the Gap shirts my tube friend mentioned.

I selected a map of the United Kingdom and, once we were outside again, pointed to the title. "Can you explain? I keep hearing 'UK.' I thought I was in England."

"England, Wales, Scotland, and Northern Ireland are separate countries that make up the United Kingdom. Anyone from anywhere in the UK is British, but they're only English if they're from England. If they're from Wales or Scotland, it's better if you call them Welsh or Scottish."

I flipped the map over. "Regular Ireland?"

"Not part of the UK, and if you suggest it, you might get escorted out of the country."

"Got it."

"Did you get a receipt for that?" Al asked.

"It cost, like, two pounds." I dug the paper from my pocket and handed it over. "Do you paper your wall with these?"

"Good record keeping is nothing to mock." She smoothed out the wrinkles.

Before I could reply, the tour guide approached. His maroon jacket with long coattails, puffy tie, and flat cap made him look like a Dickens character, which I guessed was the point. He carried a polished walking stick topped with a brass knob.

I grinned. "Can I adopt him? Or shrink him to pocket size and take him home?"

"Greetings," he said. "I am Rupert, and I will be your guide today through the world of Charles Dickens."

I might have had little interest in Dickens, but this guy was adorable.

Like a cluster of five-year-olds chasing a soccer ball, we huddled behind him as he led us to a small, slightly run-down park, chattering about Dickens.

I tried to focus, to make sure I didn't miss the public house I was supposed to find, but there was so much history, and I kept getting distracted by the fact that I was actually walking around London. This was a new country, and I was here, and home was far away, and an adorable man in costume was speaking with a delightful accent as we walked along a street filled with red buses under cloudy English skies. I didn't mind the gray sky—it perfectly matched my mental image of London.

When we stopped near a wall, I forced myself to concentrate.

"This was the site of the infamous Marshalsea Prison." Rupert swept an arm toward it. "Home to criminals, yes, but home mainly to debtors. Dickens's father was sent there for failure to pay his bills when Dickens was twelve. Eventually Dickens's mother and siblings chose to live in the cell with Mr. Dickens to avoid the workhouse."

A brownish-red brick wall with two gates and one small

sign was the only thing left. Good thing people didn't get sent to prison for debt anymore. My family would've gone when Maya's first college bill came due—and if not then, certainly a few weeks ago when the doctors' bills arrived. I swore they were breeding on our kitchen counter, like rabbits run wild.

It seemed appropriate somehow. One wall remained of a horrible place that ruined lives. A single line down the center of my knee was the only visible sign of something larger that had ruined my life. Although, technically, the thing that destroyed my life was completely invisible.

We trooped behind Rupert down the crowded street. Standard square buildings lined the road, but not too far away a pointy skyscraper stabbed the sky like a shard of glass, more modern-looking than anything we had even in LA. Our next stops were an impressive cathedral and a huge market under a curved glass ceiling with stalls of food I longed to sample, as we made our way toward "the River Tems."

I didn't tell anyone I'd been pronouncing *Thames* wrong.

Also, I fully loved this city. The fact it had existed so long, alongside the signs it continued to thrive, the sheer feeling of aliveness that made me feel more alive, too.

We paused at the base of a plain concrete bridge, where Rupert detailed the history of London Bridge and its role in a Dickens book I hadn't read.

"I thought it was supposed to be falling down," I muttered to Luke.

He shook his head, but his lips twitched.

"If I were naming a structure after my town, I'd pick that one." I pointed to the fancier bridge downriver to our right with gray stone towers, bright blue railings, and a drawbridge that I'd seen our first day.

"I'll forward your suggestion to Parliament," Luke said.

Parliament. Because they had a parliament, not a congress, because this was England!

We crossed the boring bridge and headed into the city's heart, past a domed church I'd seen from miles away. My knee was growing stiff, but I forced myself to walk normally, grinding my teeth against the discomfort. Instead, I focused on the people, the blend of buildings, the city that felt so alive, and despite the pain, I gave in to the desire to skip.

Rupert stopped us on Fleet Street to tell us its history and how a young Dickens worked there in a law office.

Fleet, like the clue. We must've been close.

"Hey, Britt," Peter called from the far side of the group, so everyone looked at him. "Remember when Ms. Carmichael told us Dickens worked as a barrister, and you thought it meant he made coffee at Starbucks?"

I glared at him. "I was joking."

I hadn't been joking. But I hadn't said Starbucks, only the coffee part.

The rest of the group chuckled. One old lady shook her head like I'd insulted the Queen.

My brain searched for a defense, another joke, but Luke's presence made my thoughts sluggish. I'd just met him, so I didn't know why I cared so much, but I couldn't bear the thought of him thinking I was an idiot. Thanks to Peter, I was losing my edge and Luke was reevaluating his opinion of my intelligence.

"Actually," Luke spoke over the laughter, "Dickens worked

as a clerk but never an actual lawyer. He hated lawyers. And politicians."

"Right indeed," said Rupert, and as he continued his talk, the others shifted their attention away from me.

Comfortable warmth seeped through my chest. I shot Luke a grateful half smile.

He brushed his hair out of his eyes, straightened his glasses, and nodded as if to say *Case closed.*

Take that, Peter. You aren't the smartest guy here.

The tour led to a series of charming garden-like courtyards and a pub in a narrow alley. Rupert stopped us outside. The building consisted of dark wood on the first floor and brown brick on the second, and a round, hanging sign read, "Ye Olde Cheshire Cheese, Rebuilt 1667."

England had a bar older than my country. Crazy.

"Dickens loved to wander these streets." Rupert spun, making his coattails flutter. "He walked several miles a day to observe the people of London. He wrote many of his early works here in this public house and published them anonymously before he was confident enough to sign his name to his writings."

Public house. My ears perked up.

Peter elbowed his way closer to me. "You should've written your essays anonymously so Ms. Carmichael wouldn't have known who to give all those Cs to."

"They were B-minuses, thank you very much, and I'd rather get a B in English than an A in jerk-hood."

Hopefully, Luke didn't know how the American grading system worked.

"Many other writers frequented this pub as well, such as Tennyson, Twain, and Doyle," said Rupert, confirming this was the place I wanted. He twirled his cane. "This area inspired part of *Oliver Twist*, which was the first novel-length example of Dickens's concern for poor children and desire to awaken the upper class to the plight of the poor through fiction. His stories exposed injustices and made people sympathetic enough that many reforms were implemented in the years following publication of his books. His stories changed society."

"Okay." I edged away from Peter and leaned into Luke. "That's pretty cool."

"Dickens is one of my favorite writers." His eyes shone. "Not only was he a skilled storyteller, but he was passionate about a cause and used his talents to make a difference in a unique way."

I wished I had skills to make a difference, to be remembered centuries later. Now that I didn't have soccer, I didn't have anything.

The tour ended at an inn, and Rupert directed us to the nearest tube stop. Luke and I stood while the others filtered away, Peter throwing me a glare as he vanished around a corner, like a demon returning to Hades.

"You're like a hero in a Dickens book. Standing up for the oppressed and downtrodden." I shook my head. "Not that I'm comparing Peter making fun of me to orphans in workhouses. Man. Sorry. I'm not that self-absorbed, I promise."

"I do understand jokes."

I shoved my hands into my pockets. What now? I'd had fun with Luke, and I wouldn't mind getting to know him better, but

I had to get on with the competition, and he probably had places to be. After only half a day, he saw beneath my intentionally carefree exterior more easily than anyone at home. Maybe it was smarter to part ways.

Then again, who said I was smart?

Luke and I drifted down the street, both of us dragging our feet. The rain had become more than a drizzle. I shouldn't have left my waterproof warm-up jacket at Ms. C's. Luke pulled out his umbrella again and held it over us. His right arm pressed into my left, warm and solid. Our dry bubble felt safe, protecting me from Peter's attempts to humiliate me, the squashed hope today's soccer game brought on, the looming threat of my mother's disappointment if I couldn't win this competition.

By unspoken agreement, we hesitated at the corner.

I scuffed my tennis shoe on the pavement. "Thanks for coming with me."

"I had fun. Better than—" He pressed his lips together.

What would he have been doing if he hadn't come? I sensed he didn't plan to finish that thought.

"I need to visit that pub, the cheese one."

He nodded. He'd seen the clue.

"I'm eighteen. I guess that's allowed?"

"That's the legal drinking age here. Besides, pubs are like restaurants. Families go there."

"Oh. Cool." My stomach let out an embarrassingly loud growl, reminding me I hadn't eaten since toast several hours ago. "I don't suppose they serve fish and chips?"

Luke smirked. "It's London. Everywhere serves fish and chips."

I fiddled with the strap of my bag. Pictured myself eating alone or with Al, who would read and refuse to talk to me.

"Wanna come? Al's treat." I raised my voice so Al could hear. Her expression didn't change.

Luke took his phone from his pocket and frowned. The screen showed several missed calls from "Dad." His mouth tightened. Then he blinked, emotion gone.

"Sure." He shoved the phone into his pocket. "Why not?"

CHAPTER SIX

We retraced our path to the public house, which I now knew meant a pub. Inside, the dim lighting, dark ceiling, and white-washed walls made me feel like we'd entered a cave, one that smelled of beer and cooking oil. The feeling strengthened as we descended stairs to underground rooms. It contained a mixture of regular tables, bar tables, and booths, plus lots of little nooks, but few customers in the late-afternoon hour. Over the bar, a stuffed dead parrot in a glass box stared down at us. The whole thing felt properly historic.

I didn't see Peter. Was he hiding, waiting to jump out at me? Or had he finished the task already and slunk out a back exit?

And the others. Had they been here yet? I didn't want to fall behind on day one.

Since I needed to finish my task, I tried to stop thinking about them.

Luke and I selected a table. Al pulled a book from her purse and took another, alone.

"I'm supposed to commit a crime here," I muttered to her. "Shouldn't you be keeping an eye on me?"

"I am. From afar. Someone needs to remain unconnected to this fiasco to bail you out, in case you get caught."

"Don't scare off Luke. Besides, I'm the Artful Dodger. This will go great." I hoped.

"Again with the optimism." Her eyebrow quirked up. "It truly is boundless." She stuck in earbuds and bent over her novel.

Did she plan to do this all week? I saw many lonely meals in my future.

"Well"—I turned to Luke—"good thing you're here. I don't want to be alone for my first fish and chips experience."

Luke pulled out my chair, and I glanced up as I brushed past him to sit, our eyes meeting briefly. A spark zipped through me.

Once we settled at the table, I ordered fish and chips, and Luke requested a burger. The waiter brought us the tiniest water glasses I'd ever seen.

"So . . . I'm going to think out loud, and you shouldn't answer because it's about my clue."

He pressed his lips together and nodded once, eyes crinkling.

"It said I had to be like the Artful Dodger. Which is crazy, right? He was a pickpocket. I can't see my prim, proper teacher deliberately leading me into a life of crime."

Only one other table had customers, and they were ignoring us. They looked like regular people, so why would they have my clue?

Luke lifted his shoulders extra high.

"It is completely insane that I'm currently contemplating who I'm supposed to rob."

Luke made a *Yes it is* face and nodded again.

Who knew winning a book-inspired contest would involve committing petty theft?

The waiter arrived and dropped plates on our table. As he left, I spotted an envelope sticking out of his back pocket.

I waved at Luke and pointed forcefully. The envelope's cream color and square shape matched my first clue.

A short laugh erupted from Luke.

"Am I seriously supposed to pick our waiter's pocket?" I hissed.

Luke spread his hands. Silent, no help.

"Ugh. Let's eat first."

My fish resembled chicken fingers, glistening with oil. Next to it and thick fries was a dish of squishy green stuff.

"Guacamole?" Not my usual French fry condiment, but I was from California, so it worked for me.

Luke smirked. "Mushy peas."

"Excuse me?"

"Think guacamole made from peas instead of avocados."

I lifted a piece of fish to my mouth instead. The batter was crispy and greasy, perfectly tasty in the way fried things are. The fish inside flaked apart instantly. Heat seared my tongue. I started to spit out the bite before my mouth suffered third-degree burns but didn't want Luke to think I had the manners of a barn animal. I forced myself to swallow and chugged the tiny glass of iceless water in one go.

Luke's shoulders shook, and I suspected I hadn't hidden my suffering.

When my tongue recovered, I savored the next bite more slowly. Real fish in a real pub with a real British boy. Even if I lost the competition, this moment was worth it. Not that I intended to lose.

I eyed my empty glass. Perfect. I waved to the waiter and lifted the cup. Not the best manners, but neither was stealing from him, so there we were.

"To eat it like a Brit, you need vinegar on top." Luke indicated the bottle.

I splashed dark liquid on a couple of fries and tried a bite. The vinegar soaked into the potato, which dissolved in my mouth, soggy, leaving a sour taste. "Yeah, sorry, no. Give me good, old-fashioned ketchup."

The waiter approached, his face blank, no indication he knew I was planning to Artful-Dodger him. My heart did quick-feet drills in my chest. My hands twitched. I could do this.

But the man set my new glass down and moved away so quickly I suspected he was intentionally making my life difficult.

I grunted and Luke laughed again.

"Oliver Twist must've had a super-stressful life," I said. "I wouldn't want to do this every day to survive."

"Perhaps that's the point of this task? To deter you from a life of delinquency?"

"It's working." I returned my attention to the fries for now. I needed another plan.

A tiny dish with minuscule ketchup packets rested in the center of our table, but a glass bottle sat on the next one. I leaned over and snagged it.

"This is more like it." I shook the bottle.

A strangled noise escaped Luke's throat.

The white lid rolled across the floor next to a trail of red sauce.

"Whoops." I stretched out to grab the lid. When I straightened, I froze.

The ketchup hadn't just gone across the floor. It had coated Luke as well.

Large globs smeared the front of his shirt, his collar, his shoulder. *Inside* his collar. How did that happen? He angled his head to see his shirt. A spot in the middle of the left lens of his glasses. Another trail across his face and into his hair.

My breath caught in my lungs. What had I done?

The laugh bubbled up. I couldn't stop it. I shouldn't laugh. Luke was a new friend. A nice, cute boy I hadn't scared off yet.

And I'd covered his white shirt and his face in ketchup.

But the abundance of bright red substance and the look on his face—the same calm, expressionless one he'd had all day—was hilarious. I pressed my lips together and busied myself collecting napkins. When I glanced up to hand them to him and caught sight again, the laughs erupted once more.

"Sorry, I'm so sorry." I shoved the napkins at him, tried to dab at his shirt from across the table.

He calmly wiped at the ketchup.

I'd made a scene—again—this time at his expense.

Stop laughing. Stop laughing. No matter how many times I commanded myself, I couldn't. He was going to think I was awful. Mean. Heartless. Too embarrassing to be with in public. I choked back another giggle.

The waiter approached. "Is everything all right, sir?"

"I'm fine. It's only ketchup." Luke kept dabbing.

"*Only* ketchup." I snorted again. "Did you think he thought it was blood? Like I stabbed you with my fork?" Laughter garbled my words. "How would you stab someone to get blood all over like that?"

He grabbed another napkin and wiped his face.

Was he mad? Had I ended our new friendship with an unlucky condiment catastrophe?

The waiter returned with a wet rag. "Here, sir."

Luke stood. "I'll be back."

The waiter scooped up the pile of used napkins that looked like evidence a ketchup murder had been committed and crouched to wipe the floor.

My heart jumped. This was my moment.

I joined him, kneeling nearby, and when his attention focused on the ground, I eased my hand toward the envelope. Which also happened to be near his rear end.

I really hoped the other customers weren't watching.

A little farther . . . I closed my index and middle finger around the envelope. When he stood, I stood with him, pulling it free and instantly whipping it behind me.

"Thanks, sir. Sorry about the mess."

He gave no indication if he realized I'd taken the envelope or if he suspected the ketchup mess was an evil distraction ploy. Curse the British and their straight faces.

I settled into my seat, tucked the envelope under my leg, and stared at my plate.

Now what? Opening the envelope in the place I'd stolen it

71

felt like flaunting my crime. I'd wait until we left. But was I supposed to wait for Luke, or could I keep eating? What made me appear most contrite?

I put the lid on the ketchup bottle, but it wouldn't twist.

See! I wanted to say. Totally not my fault. Defective equipment. The restaurant was to blame.

Of course, I hadn't had to shake the bottle. And I could've kept a finger on the lid. But how was I supposed to know this place didn't conduct sauce safety inspections?

I decided to be polite and drank another glass of water instead of eating. A collection of empty cups now decorated the table, but I wouldn't be summoning the waiter again. Flaunting the crime and all.

When Luke returned, the globs were gone, but orangey-red stains spotted his shirt. The left side of his head dripped water onto his shoulder.

He dropped into his seat.

I held my breath.

And he grinned. "Next time, please use the vinegar."

I laughed again, this time relieved. "I'm so sorry. I'll buy you a new shirt. Least I can do for laughing. I couldn't stop. I'm sorry."

"You said that." He stole one of my vinegar-soiled fries. "Don't worry about it. I figured out the moment we met that you were dangerous, but I stayed anyway. This is all on me, really." The twinkle in his eyes and the small dimple beside his mouth from a suppressed smile finally relaxed me. "You can put this in your tale, if you like."

"Absolutely. But . . . I will get you a new shirt."

"It's fine. Are you planning to eat those fries? Least you can do now." He leaned over and stole another.

I grabbed my fork and pretended to stab his hand. "I really am sorry."

"Stop saying that, or I'll put vinegar on the rest."

I carefully poured ketchup onto my plate from the faulty bottle. "Now you smell like ketchup. It kind of makes me want to lick you."

Did I say that?

Luke's face turned pink.

"Um. I mean. Dip my fries in you? Ugh, that's worse. I'm shutting up now."

We both laughed and the awkwardness evaporated.

"Something good came of your ketchup bath." I leaned closer. "I got my clue."

"I missed your first step toward delinquency? Now I can honestly claim innocence since I wasn't here to stop it."

"Not my first step. I stole a bag of gummy bears when I was seven. Drew, my brother, made me take it back."

"I am shocked. Appalled. I knew America was a land of rampant lawlessness."

As our gazes met, his crooked smile made my insides dance.

He blinked first. "You know, this is quite brave."

"What? You staying to eat with someone who weaponized ketchup?"

"Exactly." His eyes crinkled. "But also, visiting a new country and mucking about on your own."

Warmth swept through me. "I've upgraded from crazy to brave? Thanks."

"The two aren't mutually exclusive." His grin emerged, and I wrinkled my nose at him, which made his smile bigger.

When we finished our meal, I paid from my stash of weird currency and gave Al the receipt.

"See? No one got arrested," I told her.

She raised her eyebrows. "The trip is young."

I shook my head and wandered until I found a bench where the city surged around us.

I tapped the edge of the envelope on my thigh. I didn't want to open it in front of Luke. I'd made extensive use of Google for the last clues, which Luke figured out in a single glance. What if this one was more difficult, I couldn't solve it, and he regretted spending the day with an idiot? But I didn't want him to leave. . . .

"Are you planning to open that or stare at it all evening?" Luke asked with a smile.

Great. *Thanks, Luke, it was fun while it lasted.* I withdrew the card.

> Legends abound on Pendragon's isle;
> Locate the Tor and face a great trial.
>
> Strange knights you must gather to aid in your quest
> To recover the grail and pass the next test.

Someone had had too much fun with the rhyming dictionary. I'd solved the first clues. I could figure out this one, too.

74

Pendragon meant King Arthur. We'd read Arthurian poems, and I'd seen movies that definitely lacked historical accuracy. Problem: King Arthur was a legend. One of the few things I recalled from class was Ms. Carmichael saying everyone and their dog had a different theory regarding the identity and location of King Arthur and his court. Okay, those weren't her exact words, but the end result was the same—other than checking every wardrobe in the country for a secret door, how did I visit a mythical place?

At least knights and a grail sounded like a quest I could get behind, once I figured out where to go.

No avoiding this. I needed internet again. I opened my new map and spread it across my knees. Too bad a city called Camelot didn't appear out of nowhere.

Hoping I didn't use all my data on the first day, I dug out my phone. A site in Wales might have been Camelot. Wales sat across the channel, though, requiring a lengthy trip. Wait. The clue mentioned an isle. Avalon. I searched for that instead. Italy seemed unlikely. Sweet—another site was a place with a tor, like in the clue.

"Glastonbury." I sounded it out. Glanced at Luke. "Do you think nodding if I solved it right counts as helping?"

His lips tilted at the corner. He reached over to pick up the map, adjusting it on my lap and letting his hand linger with his thumb resting over southwest England. I squinted until I located the tiny city name.

"It's Glastonbury," he said, pronouncing it "*glass*-ton-bree" instead of "glass-ton-*berry*" like I had.

"Say it again."

He did.

"Once more."

He raised an eyebrow.

"What? I like the way you say it."

His face flushed.

I tried to contain a grin and focus. Would asking for travel advice be considered help? This would be faster if I could hire a private car. I was too young to rent, and besides, I wasn't about to subject these people to my trying to drive on the other side of the road.

I fiddled with the map. "I don't suppose you could give me an overview of public transportation to other cities? Like, to somewhere in western England? Theoretically speaking."

"The major stations have a variety of trains and coaches. Paddington is a safe bet. Certain towns with possible ties to King Arthur likely require three or four hours of travel."

By the time I retrieved my things from Ms. C's, found the train station, a three-hour trip . . . I wouldn't arrive until late. I sighed.

"Not a fan of trains?" Luke asked.

My shoulders must have slumped. "Trains are great. But I have to finish eight clues in nine days. I don't want to run out of time."

"That's wise."

Not a word people generally used to describe me.

"Best to give yourself leeway and time to write," Luke continued. "Things always go wrong when you're traveling."

"Like attacks by evil knights?"

He raised one eyebrow and, in that gesture, I saw his resemblance to Al. "Or missing a train or getting your passport stolen."

"Your imagination needs practice. It's far too practical."

"That's me. Always practical." An undertone of bitterness flavored his words.

"I didn't mean it like . . . practical is good. If I'd been practical, I wouldn't need to win this competition so badly."

Ugh. Why had I said that?

He did his head tilt, which I recognized as an invitation to continue.

"I mean, thanks. That's all."

I bent over to shove my phone into my bag and hide my face. I'd avoided discussing the recent past long enough; I wasn't diving into it with a stranger. With Luke, I had someone who didn't know what happened, didn't feel sorry for me. He might suspect something was going on, but he didn't know for sure. I wanted to keep it that way.

An image flashed through my head of Luke accompanying me, us getting cozy on a train, sharing an epic quest, while he teased me with that delicious accent. Stupid idea. I forced it away. "Thanks. You realize if I hadn't met you, I would've walked to the nearest station and winged it?"

"If you win, you can give me a cut."

I crossed my arms. "*When* I win, you mean."

He met my gaze. "*When* you win."

"Thank you." I folded the map in sharp moves.

"Glastonbury," he said, emphasizing the word, "is supposed to be an interesting place. Lots of myths and legends."

"Have you been?"

He shook his head.

"Have you traveled much in general?"

"Not really. School trips, an occasional holiday. My dad worked a lot. You?"

"Hardly at all. This was my first airplane trip, my first tube ride. When I was younger, we did a few family trips in California, but we never had the money to go anywhere big." I fiddled with the clue card. "There are so many places in the world. I have a huge wish list."

"Hopefully, England was on it, so you've checked the first one off."

His eyes were warm, and his intense focus sent a pleasant hum through me.

"You know, this trip sounds fun." His smile was one of the biggest, most genuine I'd seen yet. His eyes lit up, and his face appeared younger, carefree. "I don't suppose you want company? Not that my cousin isn't a delight to be with."

His tone was joking, but the glint in his eyes revealed he was half-serious.

"Depends. Are you offering?" I nearly matched his light-hearted tone, but tried to sound a touch more serious in case he meant it. Leave him an opening.

"You might require supervision to ensure you're pronouncing words correctly. You'd hate to offend someone."

My heart thump-thump-thumped, and I hoped he couldn't hear. "It would be tragic if you missed the fruit of your lessons. And you were carrying Chaucer. It's like a sign."

Our eyes met and darted away. I resisted the urge to play with the map. The idea sent a thrill through me, but I didn't want to seem too eager.

His gaze met mine again. "Is that allowed? No help, remember? I wouldn't want to disqualify you."

"It's a free country, right? If you showed up at the station tomorrow and happened to be going that way, it's not like I could stop you."

"Are you certain?"

Luke didn't talk much, but he was funny and he got my humor. He knew way more about literature than I did. I dreaded the thought of seeing England and having no one to share it with. And he seemed like he was searching for something. Wasn't that the point of quests?

On the other hand, did I want him to witness my ignorance when I inevitably reached a clue that stumped me? Plus, I already liked him more than I should. It was easier not to get close, the way Al traveled with me physically but wasn't really *with* me. I should say goodbye now before I got attached.

"I'm sure." The words escaped before I could stop them. "If you're willing to risk it." I gestured to the ketchup stains on his shirt. "I'm clearly hazardous."

"I'm willing to risk it." The heat of his gaze seared me. "Alexis," he called without breaking eye contact with me. "Would your boss mind if I accompanied you?"

"Shouldn't you ask if *I* mind?" She removed one earbud. "I'm the one who has to put up with you for the next week."

"I mean"—I spoke to her but also kept my eyes locked with

his—"is it allowed? He wouldn't help. I'll figure out the clues and write my tales."

Al shrugged. "I don't imagine it would be a problem. But your dad—"

"No longer gets a say in what I do." Luke's tone clearly said *Discussion over.*

"Are you sure you want to?" I lowered my voice, my words for him alone. "Don't you have things to do? Kids to read to. People to save."

We still hadn't broken eye contact.

"It's volunteer with the kids. Ms. Harriet will understand if I take a few days off."

"No job or anything?"

His jaw twitched. "Not at the moment."

"So . . . we're doing this?"

Unsure what answer I hoped for, I held my breath.

He chewed his lip, eyes watching something far away. He was probably imagining things he did need to do, other than traipsing around the country with a stranger. But his expression hardened.

His attention focused on me again, and one corner of his mouth lifted. "Meet you at Paddington Station at eight tomorrow, Pilgrim."

CHAPTER SEVEN

When I returned to Ms. Carmichael's flat, Peter was in the living room, reading a companion book on the mythology of the popular Elven Realms series. Because regular history wasn't bad enough. There was no sign of Amberlyn or Spence. Were they already in Glastonbury? Maybe I should have picked a pocket and run rather than staying to eat.

A dull ache spread through my knee after a full day of walking. I threw myself onto the couch, dangling my sore feet off the side so I didn't soil the furniture. Ms. Carmichael surely had a maid, but since she held my future in her checkbook, I didn't want to make her mad.

Now that I had Wi-Fi again, I sent my daily message to my mom, telling her I hadn't been mugged or carried away by pigeons in London. Not exactly what she wanted to know, but the competition had barely started, so I didn't have much to report.

"Where's your friend?" Peter sneered. "Off preparing to do your work for you?"

"I'm perfectly capable of doing my own work." It didn't seem wrong to ask an organized friend—one who happened to know his way around the country—for advice on transportation. I wasn't cheating. I was utilizing available resources.

Ms. Carmichael entered the room.

I checked to make sure my feet weren't touching the couch. "Oh." I jumped up. "Can I ask you something in private?"

"Of course."

"Gonna tell her about the friend who's helping you cheat?" Peter called after us.

Ms. C led me to her office, which held an enormous desk and wall-to-wall bookshelves. "You wanted to ask me something?"

"Can I use leftover money to buy new stuff for the kids at the orphange? Like if I stay in cheap places and don't eat much?"

"I'm certain I can arrange that."

"Cool." I gripped the back of the wooden chair that faced her desk. "What Peter said, about the friend I met. He's Al's cousin. He volunteers at the orphanage. I figured out the first clue before I met him, but he's new to London, so we brought him on the Dickens tour."

She opened her laptop. "The guidelines said no help. They did not say no making friends."

"If it's not specifically forbidden, it's allowed. I like the way you think." I squinted. "So, the rest of the trip . . ."

"I have no control over who boards trains in this country." Her lips pressed together like she was fighting a smile. "Have a good journey, Ms. Hanson." She started typing, dismissing me.

Paddington Station was a cavernous building of trains, tracks, and people that could've fit multiple football fields. It had tube platforms—for the Underground within London—and train platforms—for longer-distance trains to other parts of England.

I exited the tube with my duffel bag slung over my shoulder and followed signs to the train area. Al walked behind, offering no help whatsoever, wearing a trench coat over dress pants. She rolled a tiny suitcase.

"Today you look like a spy," I said.

She straightened her coat. "Wearing it saves space in my bag."

Amberlyn needed to take packing lessons from her.

At last, I spotted a ticket counter. Luke leaned against the wall nearby, a large backpack at his feet. My heart leaped and my shoulders relaxed. I'd feared common sense would take over once he got home.

"You look surprised." He pushed off the wall and hefted his backpack, shaking hair out of his eyes. He nodded at Al. His jeans, red Converse, and gray jacket over a faded T-shirt matched yesterday's outfit. How did he make something so simple so adorable?

"You didn't change your mind, did you?" One corner of his mouth lifted. "I went to loads of trouble packing. It took nearly ten minutes."

Seeing him convinced me I very much had not changed my mind. I shrugged and grinned. "I thought you might chicken out. I am dangerous, after all."

"Some things are worth the risk."

He met my gaze, and the temperature jumped ten degrees.

We bought tickets and navigated to the right platform. The

train had comfy, individual seats with tall seat backs and screens on the back of each one. No cheap benches or cracked plastic. I sat by a window.

Al lingered at our seats. "You do know where we switch trains? I don't fancy ending up in Wales."

"Ooh, that's an option?"

Her lips twitched. "Did you find a hotel?"

"No point. I don't know how long we'll be there. What if I go somewhere else today? We'll wing it."

She sighed. "I miss my office."

"You're weird."

"You are," Luke agreed.

She ignored us and moved farther down the car.

We passed through the city, and then buildings gave way to green fields that screamed at me to run across them with a ball. I imagined the smell of grass, freshly mowed and covered in dew. Cool air on my face, wind in my hair.

Desire and sadness twisted together in my chest. I shoved the feeling down and enjoyed the view of what I pictured as classic England.

"How's your journal coming?" Luke asked.

"I was too tired to work on it last night. Jet lag. And writer's block. Severe writer's block."

"You can do it now. I won't peek."

Of course he wouldn't. He was too nice for that.

Determined to smash that block, I took out the journal and jotted notes about the kids, the tour, the pub. Nowhere near a story, which the ketchup-slash-thieving incident should have been.

I could use these notes to write thrilling tales later, after everything had time to soak in. My brain needed time to process the experiences.

I wanted to win, but this was not my thing. I crammed the journal into my bag with more force than necessary.

Luke eyed me.

"What?"

"Nothing. That was fast, is all."

I sighed. "English isn't my best subject. My teacher complimented my grammar and wide vocabulary, but that was the only thing I did well. And those are thanks to my sister, who forced me to learn her Words of the Day."

"So, what's the problem?" He focused on me with the same direct gaze as at the orphanage.

"Ms. Carmichael's most frequent complaint was that I summarized books instead of analyzing them. Apparently, it demonstrated a 'lack of critical thinking.'" I tried to imitate Ms. Carmichael's proper voice for the last part. "My journal has to be really good. She'll want more than 'I went here and I did this.'"

"You'll figure it out." He studied me. "Do you want advice? Not help. Just advice."

"Maybe . . ."

"The competition is inspired by literature, right? The point of most literature classes is critical analysis. You can find plot synopses on the internet. What matters is the message and how it speaks to you personally."

"Why does it have to speak to me?"

"Think of it this way." Luke grasped his glasses. "What makes a book a classic?"

You tell me, Professor. "Leather binding and fancy words?"

"A classic says something about life. Makes the reader think. Tells one particular person's story but makes you feel like it could be about anyone, anywhere." As he spoke, his eyes lit up and passion flooded his voice. The enthusiasm made him even cuter.

"But how many of these writers thought, hey, I'm going to sit down and write something to torment students for centuries to come? What's wrong with just reading a good story?"

He lifted a shoulder. "Nothing, except you said you needed more to win."

He had me there. If I had any hope, I needed to figure something out.

To change the subject, I recalled Luke's words from the day before, saying I was reading things wrong.

"This is your chance to prove you were right about Chaucer." I lifted my chin and stared him down. "Did you bring it?"

"You're on." He dug through his mobile library and produced a book. Then he cleared his throat and started to read.

With his smooth voice and sexy accent, I forgot to listen to the story and just enjoyed the way his lips moved and the fancy sound of his vowels. I caught myself leaning in. After a few minutes, though, I realized they almost sounded like actual words telling the story of two knights fighting over a woman.

When he stopped, I said, "You can read to me every night."

His eyebrows lifted.

I coughed. Seriously, why did I keep saying inappropriate-sounding things around him? "I mean, I could've used you in English class last year. I might not have needed Google for my essay on *The Canterbury Tales*."

His mouth twitched and, though I'd only known him a day, I knew it meant he was preparing a sarcastic reply. "I hear Google is an expert on everything."

"If it's on the internet, it must be true."

"Yes, I believe that's part of the appeal. Truth and accuracy on every page." He closed the book and set it on his leg. "The words sound odd to us, but Chaucer was revolutionary because he wrote in the vernacular."

"Yeah, Ms. C mentioned that. The language of the common people." I paused. Smirked. "I bet they just wanted a good story, too."

CHAPTER EIGHT

Glastonbury was much different than London. Colorful shops lined the downtown streets, decorated with hanging baskets of flowers. Windows displayed items like crystals, polished rock spheres, stone carvings, and necklaces with stars. Other stores sold bath oils and candles.

We'd missed the town's famous music festival, but street musicians were playing guitar or sax. One guy had a recorder, sounding like he'd wandered out of a Renaissance fair.

"I played one of those in first grade," I muttered to Luke.

He patted my shoulder. "I'm sure you were brilliant."

"Oh, I was."

Everywhere the scent of incense hung thick in the air, like someone had dumped a truck full of herbs onto a flower garden and set the whole mess on fire.

I rubbed my nose. "This place is weird."

Luke's face screwed up like he needed to sneeze. The expression didn't change until we left the main street he called High Street and were on our way to the Tor.

I'd assumed *tor* meant *tower* since the words sounded similar, but apparently, it meant *hill*, and the hill just happened to have a tower on top. The climb was steep. Within minutes, sweat dampened my face and arms, but my knee seemed okay.

"This is a strange place for King Arthur." As we trudged up the steps, we passed a group of women in white gowns, sitting in a circle meditating. "I pictured mysterious woods and ancient castles, not hippies and New Agers."

"How do you know King Arthur wasn't a hippie?" Luke's face had gone an adorable shade of red, and his words puffed out as he tried to breathe.

"Now I'm picturing a guy with a beard and a sword wearing bell-bottoms and driving a VW van instead of a horse, so thanks for that."

He huffed out a laugh.

By the time we reached the top, the crazy-strong wind tore at my ponytail. The view was worth it, though. I could see all the way to water glinting in the distance.

I aimed for the square stone tower, but a group of people moved to block my way.

They wore black knight-like tunics and brandished plastic swords.

Excellent.

One stepped toward me. "What is your quest?" His voice boomed.

Was there a correct answer? "I seek the grail."

"Nice," Luke said.

A few of the knights chuckled. They looked about my age, and there were ten of them. Local college theater group?

"To obtain the grail, you must assemble your knights and prove your worth."

He motioned to items I hadn't noticed—four piles of prop shields and swords, the shields in four different colors.

I glanced at Luke, who shrugged, and Al, who raised an eyebrow. My eyes narrowed in response and I grinned. A challenge.

"Want to be a knight, Al?"

"My salary does not include dismemberment."

"If you get dismembered by a plastic sword, you're doing something wrong."

"I'm not supposed to help. I'd hate to get you in trouble."

I shook my head at her smirk.

Others nearby were staring at the knights with curiosity. Gather strange knights. Strangers? I could do that.

The red pile contained fewer shields, and I noticed Amberlyn clutching an armful, wandering along the hillside, so far without any recruits. It was a miracle she hadn't rolled her ankle in those booties. With the amount of luggage she'd brought, surely she had other shoe options. I was happy in tennis shoes. She saw me watching, angled her head briefly to acknowledge me, and moved on.

I selected blue, our school color, which I'd worn to win two state championships, picked up shields, and lasered in on a nearby young couple.

"Greetings, good sir and fair lady. Would you be interested in joining me on a noble quest?"

They looked at each other.

"Why not?" the guy said.

"What do we need to do?" asked the woman.

"Once I have assembled my knights, we will take the castle!" I swept a hand toward the tower.

They laughed. "Sure."

I tapped the man on each shoulder with my sword. "I dub thee Sir . . ."

"Jason."

"Sir Jason." I handed him a shield and sword and did the same to the woman. "And I dub thee Lady . . ."

"Tina."

"Lady Tina. I thank you both for your bravery."

They waited while I approached a family with two kids, who accepted the challenge. The kids immediately started swinging the swords at each other.

"Save your courage for the enemies, brave knights." I winked at them.

A group of teens turned me down, but an older couple agreed to help. As I roamed the hillside searching for recruits, my path led near Amberlyn. I eavesdropped as she approached a couple.

"I need volunteers," she announced. "Will you help? It's easy. You just need to swing a sword. It won't take long."

They eyed her, frowning, and shook their heads. Her tense shoulders screamed of frustration and made me certain she'd received many rejections.

No wonder she only had two people so far. This task was about the legendary King Arthur. She needed to inspire, to cast vision, to make it sound like a fun adventure they'd be missing out on if they refused. Not like a trip to the dentist.

Did she still want to be an event planner, like when she was younger? She'd nailed the ordering-people-around part but might want to work on the inspiring-people angle.

I led my new knights toward the tower. One shield and sword remained. I gave Luke an evil smile.

"Are you ready, Sir Luke?"

He sighed. "If I must."

He took the sword, his fake-put-upon look shifting to twinkling eyes. When I turned, he jabbed my arm with the weapon. I spun. His eyes widened in innocence.

I swished my sword in front of him. "Hey. You're on my side. Save it for the enemies."

His crooked grin emerged.

I knighted him and stood in front of my knights. They clutched plastic swords and shuffled their feet, hardly appearing like fearless soldiers. I needed to motivate them. Deliver a rousing speech worthy of Aragorn or King Arthur.

"Thank you for answering the call to complete this noble quest. The grail lies within." I pointed to the tower with my sword, where the other knights had formed a line. "Our enemy is strong, but you are the bravest and best knights in all the land, and your courage shall win the day." I spun and raised my sword. "For glory and Britain!"

I raced toward the waiting knights with my recruits behind me. The lead knight moved to meet me, and I swung my sword. He blocked, and I had a moment to hope these guys weren't trained stage fighters before the thunking of plastic swords and shields surrounded me.

Surely plastic swords couldn't bruise me, right? Ms. C wouldn't do anything to injure us. But if she only knew about my knee, she might not know that something simple could be dangerous.

After exchanging blows with my opponent, I blocked his swing with my shield and smacked his side with my sword.

He stumbled and fell to his knees. "Alas, I am slain." He slumped to the ground dramatically.

Definitely a theater student.

I spun to find one of the kids hacking at a female knight. Both were laughing.

"Courage, Sir Jeremy," I said.

The kid charged and I grinned, spinning to fight another.

Soon, all the knights lay in the grass, unmoving.

I raised my sword. "Huzzah."

"Huzzah," cheered my knights, even Luke.

The path now clear, I entered the tower. A fake metal chalice sat on the ground inside, with an envelope taped to the bottom. I grabbed the cup and returned to the group, holding it high.

"Thanks to your service and bravery, the grail has been found. We could not have prevailed without you. Victory is ours."

They cheered.

As the knights rose, my new friends tossed their props into a pile, waving and grinning as they wandered away.

"That was fun. Thanks," said Jason.

"I want to be a knight now." Jeremy slashed with his sword before his mom made him drop it.

"We'll see," she said as she smiled at me.

The lead knight raised his sword in salute. "An excellent battle."

"Indeed. I'm Britt."

"Steve."

"You guys students?"

"Yes, from the University of Bristol Drama Department."

Knew it. "You were worthy opponents. Thanks."

"Good luck on your quest."

One knight ducked into the tower holding a second grail. The others resumed their positions. Amberlyn approached hesitantly with four people who appeared less than enthusiastic.

"Okay, everyone, let's do this," she said.

I might suck at writing, but I had conquered this task way better than Amberlyn.

We moved away to give her tiny army some room to fight.

"That was epic," I said to Luke.

"I can't believe I did that."

"Admit it, you had fun."

"I wouldn't have done it for anyone else. You made an impressive King Arthur."

"I know," I said to hide the way his words warmed my insides. Louder, I called, "Al missed out."

"Some people are happy as clerics," she said.

I gasped. "Was that a D&D reference? Is Al a gamer?"

"I have siblings. I know things."

Tucking the grail under one arm, I circled Amberlyn's knights to return to the inside of the tower. Two doorways without doors, on opposite sides, provided a glimpse through the structure and impressive views.

A tour group of old people shuffled up. I edged closer to eavesdrop.

"Thousands of years ago, this hill was an island and that"—the guide swept an arm toward the view—"was underwater. Legend tells us this was the site of Avalon, the magical island of enchantment where the dead passed to the other world, where King Arthur found healing, and where he waits to return to the land when we need it most."

Awed expressions crept onto the people's faces, like this was a religious experience. They'd obviously missed our awesome battle.

I focused on breathing deeply, staring at the horizon, trying to calm my heart rate and feel something in the wind. Whatever magic they felt, I didn't. I shoved my free hand into my pocket to protect it from the wind and held tightly to the grail and envelope.

The group wandered off, and Luke appeared beside me.

"Are you surveying your kingdom?"

"Nah. I'd make a terrible queen. I was thinking about people being desperate to believe in magic or the supernatural."

He shoved his hands into his pockets. "People want something to believe in. Everyone desires something greater. Like we realize this world alone can't satisfy and there's more to life than what we see."

"That sounds familiar."

"I paraphrased a C. S. Lewis quote."

I had lots of unsatisfied desires. Did that mean I'd been looking for solutions in the wrong places? The thought prickled my brain like a burr lodged under a shin guard.

"Something tells me he didn't mean people selling magic rocks in Camelot." I watched cloud shadows flicker across the hills. "Ms. Carmichael said many King Arthur stories are about identity and destiny. Who you think you are, what you're destined to do."

He tugged his jacket tighter. "Do you believe in destiny?"

"Not anymore." My answer came too quickly.

"You thought me having Chaucer was a sign I should come with you."

Feeling a burst of knight-inspired bravery, I nudged his foot with mine. "Maybe I just thought you were cute."

One corner of his mouth dimpled.

Ignoring the unsettling but not unpleasant effect his expression had on my insides, I tried to grasp that feeling, like we were destined to be here at this moment, but came up with nothing.

"I used to think there were things we were meant to do. Or that if you wanted something, you fought for it and it could be yours. But now I think you take each day as it comes and see what happens. Sometimes you can't control it, so why try?"

A line formed between his eyes. "It's good to feel you have a purpose."

"*Does* everyone have a purpose? I don't think I do." Not anymore. "I'm done here. Let's see what's next."

I strode away. The knights were reassembling, so Amberlyn's uninspiring squad had apparently succeeded. Spence now stood nearby, clutching an armful of green shields.

"Want to join me?" he called.

"I fought my battle. I'm retiring to enjoy the fruits of victory."

His gaze latched onto my grail. "Don't suppose you want to share?"

I hugged my grail. "Do your own work, Lopez."

He grinned. "I'll fight you for it."

"Focus on those knights," I said. "And watch out for the pointy ends."

I debated lingering to watch and see how he did. I expected him to fare better than Amberlyn. But if he nailed the task, it might be better for my confidence if I didn't know. Instead, we left him and headed for town.

CHAPTER NINE

As we strolled along High Street, we passed an old lady exiting a shop, struggling with overflowing packages of bundled herbs, fabric, books, and what I hoped was leather but suspiciously resembled skin. One bag slipped, and crystals tumbled across the sidewalk.

Luke ran to assist her, tucking items into bags.

"You like to help people," I said when he returned.

"In a way, you help them, too." He resumed our trek.

I trotted to keep up. "What do you mean?"

"You like to talk to people. Ask them questions. Let them feel heard."

"Everyone has a story."

One corner of his lips lifted. "I thought you didn't like stories."

"No, I don't like reading." I poked his arm. "There's a difference."

"Books are like that. They let you get to know fictional people, and if the author is good, the characters seem real and it helps you understand real people better." Luke rubbed his nose as we passed a particularly vile incense shop. "What do you like about people?"

"I don't know. Learning why they chose their job or their spouse. What it's like to live their life, especially if it's different from mine. What makes them special, because everyone is unique and has something that makes them, *them*."

"We like the same things, I just prefer to do it through books. Less chance I'll say the wrong thing." He adjusted his glasses. "I admire your ability to talk to people. I never know how to start a conversation, so I carry their bags or give them my change."

"You're still acknowledging they're important when you do that." I did a double take as I dodged a sign with a live owl perched on top.

"Like you."

"I guess so."

"I know so. Don't argue with me." He gave me a lopsided smile.

No one had ever seen my talkative, inquisitive nature as a good thing. Luke managed to find things about me that annoyed everyone else and turn them into things he liked.

What I couldn't decide was, did I appreciate his insight? Did he understand me better than I knew myself? If so, could he help me figure myself out?

As we strolled past colorful storefronts, I watched for a place to eat. Being a knight had made me hungry.

"Okay, I've seen restaurants named after geckos, turtles, and monkeys," I said. "What's up with the inedible animals? Unless you eat those here . . ."

"No, but you should try a pasty," Luke said. "Those are British."

"Pass tea?"

"A pasty. A meat pie." He steered me to a café with a sign for PASTIES.

"I would not have guessed that was a word for food. More like a club for pale guys."

Luke shook his head and smiled. "Do not mock the pasties."

Inside, a display case held rows of half-circle pastries with handwritten signs for things like beef, pork, chicken, sausage, even lamb.

I picked beef and potatoes, and we took a small table.

It felt good to sit. My feet and knee ached from walking. I planted the grail in the middle of the table.

Al sat at our table, and I squinted at her.

"Would you sit with me if Luke weren't here? I thought you planned to keep your distance. Observe."

"I'm not supposed to influence your journey in any way. I'm merely supposed to act as a backup should anything go wrong." She paused to stir a packet of sugar into her tea. "I get the sense that's more likely to happen with you than the others."

"So, is Ms. C punishing you, or does that mean she trusts you more than the other chaperones?"

She quirked an eyebrow. "Are you certain you want me to answer that question?"

I grinned. "Are the other babysitters sitting with my class-mates or ignoring them? Isn't it lonely to travel with someone but not actually *with* them, you know?"

Luke opened a bottle of a strange purple drink. "Lots of people go through life that way."

When he phrased it like that, I realized my words could apply to me. All the people I met, the stories I listened to, and I couldn't tell anyone mine. I needed a new topic now, before they noticed the gaping wound inside me. "Are you allowed to give me advice?"

Al added a splash of milk to her cup. "If you're boarding a ferry to France, I can advise you to stop."

"There's a ferry to France?" I pretended to stand. "Do we have time for that?"

Her eyes narrowed. "My employment contract only covers the UK. Beyond the borders, you're on your own."

I might have considered it, if I didn't have a deadline and a contest to win. "Have you done this before?"

"This is the first time Ms. Carmichael has attempted this particular competition."

"I'm a guinea pig. Great. Has she done others? Where'd she get the money? Counterfeiting? Printing press in the basement?"

Al sipped her tea. "You should focus on the contest. Doesn't winning the money matter more than where it came from?"

"She's right." Luke's cheek dimpled. "You may have walked where King Arthur once lived and died. Fought in his footsteps. Doesn't that inspire you?"

I chewed my lip. "I did have fun. I liked convincing strangers to do something crazy. People probably thought King Arthur's round table idea was crazy, too, but he got people to join him."

"He convinced people to see potential, share in the vision," Luke said. "Like you did."

Huh. Too bad it was easier to believe in other people's potential than my own.

To escape my thoughts, I stole Luke's purple drink and took a long swig. I licked the excess off my lips, drawing his gaze, which he quickly averted. My heart fluttered. I set the drink down and grabbed the pasty.

Flaky pastry surrounded chunks of meat and potatoes. Not as good as the fish and chips, but I wanted to sample as much local cuisine as I could. "Okay, I'm feeling properly British. Let's do this."

I opened the new envelope.

These moors once played host to a mysterious dog.
At Harford you'll camp amid the hills and the fog.

Begin by locating a boot from of old,
Then follow the trail as you decipher the codes.

I focused on the paper, hoping Luke couldn't read calligraphy sideways. Dog. We'd read a Sherlock Holmes book in class called *The Hound of the Baskervilles*. A detective would fit with deciphering codes. Camping sounded fun. But how many moors did England have, and how was I supposed to remember the exact one?

In the book, moors were like foggy hills, which meant lots of nature. I unfolded my map and spread it across the table. Luke watched, head tilted.

I scanned the green patches, hoping they indicated parks like in America, and spotted potential names: North York Moors, Exmoor, Dartmoor. I didn't see Harford anywhere.

Without looking at Luke, so I wouldn't know if condescension filled his face, I dug out my phone. Apparently, Harford was in Dartmoor. Another search confirmed *The Hound of the Baskervilles* took place in Dartmoor, too.

"Looks like we're going camping," I said. "Am I supposed to buy tents? It says Harford has a bunkhouse and a campground."

Al sighed dramatically. "Tents are taken care of. I was dreading this part."

"It's a tent, not a coffin. I think you'll survive one night." I shifted to Luke. "How do you feel about camping?"

Had we decided he was coming for the whole trip, or had he just tagged along for the day? I didn't want to assume he'd stick around, but I hoped he'd come.

His gaze was warm. "I've never been, but I wouldn't mind."

I returned his smile, tension in my chest unclenching.

"Great," Al said. "You can do my job for the night."

I gasped dramatically with a hand to my chest. "You're supposed to keep an eye on me, Al. What if wolves attack while I'm in the wilderness, and you're safe and snug in a five-star, miles away?"

"We don't have wolves in England."

I checked travel to Dartmoor and discovered it would take hours to reach the city nearby, not to mention getting into the park, setting up tents . . .

"We should stay the night here and start in the morning." I hoped that was the right decision and my classmates weren't already on their way.

"And you mocked when I asked about a hotel," Al said.

"What else is there to see here? Let's drop off our bags and explore."

I asked other customers and the café staff for suggestions until one woman recommended the 8 Owls Bed and Breakfast, which fit the town's random-animals theme.

We followed her directions down a narrow alley next to a New Age shop, through a small garden, to a metal owl sign guarding the door. The rooms were small but clean, with owl-shaped pillows, owls on the walls, and a blanket made of fake feathers.

I hoped they were fake and no actual birds had died in the decorating of this room.

I sent a short text to my mom telling her I was okay. Her reply came almost instantly.

It said, *Hope the competition is going well!* followed by emojis of a trophy and several bags of money.

No pressure or anything.

The B&B was a block from our first stop, Glastonbury Abbey, an old church mostly in ruins. Towering remnants of stone formed graceful arches and crumbling walls, some covered in ivy. It must have been incredibly impressive in its prime, because even ruined, it stirred something inside me. Awe. Reverence. A sense of timelessness.

On the grounds, a small plot of grass had a sign proclaiming it to be the site of King Arthur's tomb.

I stared at the insignificant display, the weight of sadness pressing my chest. "Seems too small for such an epic hero."

"Are you a King Arthur fan?" The nearby man who spoke could be nothing but an American tourist, with his fanny pack, giant camera, and floppy hat. "You should visit the nearby castle ruins. Legends say it was the location of Camelot."

"Sweet. Thanks."

After I let one final glance linger on the small sign, we caught a taxi for the half-hour drive to South Cadbury, through more patchwork fields and rolling hills that filled me with both thrill and inexplicable longing.

In the town—if you could call it that—everything was named after Camelot. Hotels, guesthouses, pubs.

"They take the legends seriously." I jerked my chin at a bar creatively named the Camelot.

"Or they like the tourism money," Al replied.

"That's not working out so well for them."

Hardly anyone else occupied the road. The taxi parked in a small lot after nearly running over a half-dozen chickens that roamed free. Ours was the sole car.

We dodged the pecking birds and started up the hill. Even though it was afternoon, the weather had stayed cool with nice stacks of gray and white clouds.

The beginning of the path led through ancient, gnarled trees, and I almost believed Arthur's knights rode through here hundreds of years before. Past the trees came a grassy hill. My out-of-shape thighs complained, but my knee didn't threaten to collapse.

When we got to the top, it was flat, like someone had sliced off the peak. Walls of earth, or stone long since covered by earth, gave a rough idea of where a castle had been. A stone marker pointed out sights on the horizon, including Glastonbury Tor. The 360-degree views included hills of green fields and little groves of trees, houses like Monopoly toys, and tiny ant-cars.

It was not the ruined castle I'd expected. I'd thought it would be like the abbey, with part of an actual structure remaining.

"Supposedly this was Camelot?" I made a slow circle. "Where's the round table?"

"Is that all you know about King Arthur?" Luke wore his dimpled half smile.

"I also know he pulled a sword out of a stone. I saw the Disney movie."

He nodded solemnly. "A literary classic if there ever was one."

"Don't forget the holy grail." I jumped up to sit on the waist-high stone. "Monty Python taught me that."

Luke stopped.

"Why is your mouth hanging open?" I asked.

He adjusted his glasses as if he needed to see me more clearly. "You've seen Monty Python?"

"Sure. Hasn't everyone?" When his gaping mouth didn't close, I added, "My brother liked it."

We swapped movie quotes until we could no longer form words through our laughter.

"You both," Al said, "need help."

She planted herself in one spot, hands behind her back, and refused to move.

"How can you not like that movie?"

"I prefer historical epics or documentaries."

"That's not normal, old woman."

"And killer rabbits, shrubbery, and coconuts *are*?"

"Well," I said, "at least she's seen it."

A gleam lit Luke's eyes as we shared a grin, and the light of it pierced my chest like a shot of sunshine. I needed to move before it blinded me to the impossibility of our future.

I wandered and then sat, enjoying the smell of grass and fresh air, trying to imagine knights and horses, sword battles and epic-ness, occurring here centuries ago.

Then I caught a whiff of cow.

They appeared in front of me, ambling up a terrace, coming straight at me. A pack of them, like wolves, and way too friendly.

Did I have a sign that said FREE SUGAR CUBES? Was I putting out a cow scent indicating I was ready to mate? I barely had time to scramble to my feet before they surrounded me.

Wet noses pressed my side, my shoulder, my cheek. One snorted on me with an alarming amount of mucus. Another head-butted me in the ribs. I stumbled into another that stared at me with eyes that were either adoring or calculating my destruction.

"Um, Luke?" I called. "Al? A little help?"

I scanned the herd for an opening, but they crowded tighter than a football huddle. Was I the playbook or the opposing quarterback?

Another nosed me, smearing goo down my arm.

Laughter carried over the sounds of snorting and stomping.

"Guys?" I yelled again.

Apparently, they found laughing more enjoyable than rescuing me.

I spotted it. A small gap. As if this were a game, I treated it like a break between defenders and aimed for it. My arm brushed rough fur, and I passed too close to a rear end, but I was free.

So I thought.

I jogged toward Al and Luke, but grunts came behind me. The cows were following. Seriously, following me like I was their leader. Or their prey. I ran faster, and they kept pace.

Luke and Al were no longer laughing. When I reached them, the cows nipped at my heels.

"Run away," I said in my best Monty Python impression.

We scattered. Three cows kept after me. I tripped on one of the half-buried stones, but Al's hand closed around my arm and held me up. Her foot slipped, and she dropped to her knees.

I heard snorts. Our pursuers slowed, turned, and rejoined their partners in crime. The whole herd started grazing like nothing had happened, once more resembling innocent farm animals instead of smelly demons.

I turned to Al. "Thanks."

Al grunted. In rescuing me, she'd planted her nice, shiny flat in the middle of a cow patty and slipped. Dung coated her whole leg.

I laughed. I couldn't stop it. The noise rang out across the hilltop. A few cows jerked their heads up. I swallowed and quieted before I frenzied them again.

"I'll tell Ms. C you need a raise." I stuck out my hand to help her up.

"I'm not sure there is adequate compensation for this particular job hazard."

"Are you all right?" Luke asked when he rejoined us.

When I nodded, he let a laugh escape, so I pretended to wipe cow slobber on his shirt. Al scraped her shoe in the grass and plucked grass, attempting to rub poop off her leg.

"They should have called it Cow-a-lot," I said.

"Knights of the cow table," Luke added.

"Sir Gawain and the green cow?"

"Ex-cow-ibur?"

We both laughed uncontrollably again.

"The pair of you are positively hilarious." Al wasn't laughing, but I suspected I saw a twinkle in her eye.

I shot the cows a mock glare. "I think we're done. Let's get out of here."

Al lifted her chin. "I've never heard a better idea in my life."

The cab driver had waited like we'd asked. When we got into the car, he sniffed loudly.

Luke and I covered our mouths to stop the laughter. He sat between us, pressed against my arm, hip, and leg, to keep away from Al's dirty pants. His nearness was much more welcome than the cows'. But possibly more dangerous. With cow slobber clinging to me, I must've smelled great. How on earth was Luke managing to keep his hands off me?

When I caught my breath, I said to the driver, "Sorry about the smell. Have you been here before? Did you know they have a feral herd of deadly cows? King Arthur needs to return to fight off this horrible invasion."

I described our close encounter. His hearty chuckle boomed through the car.

"Why couldn't I have gotten that other girl?" Al crossed her arms. "I bet she doesn't get assaulted by cows."

I would've paid good money to see Amberlyn get chased by

cows. "You'd be so bored with her. You like me. I add excitement to your life."

"My life was perfectly fine, thank you." But I could tell she was fighting a smile.

One positive thing came of this side trip. Whenever I went back to my journal, I would definitely be writing about the cows.

CHAPTER TEN

Early the next morning, we were on another train. My journal sat in my lap. But after staring out the window trying to reflect on stories, I gave up. Silence and inaction were terrible ways to spend a beautiful day riding through the English countryside.

I turned to Luke. "Not a music person?"

"Hmm?" He looked up from his book.

I pointed. "No earbuds. I was starting to think it was a rule of public transportation here. Everyone wears them."

"Oh. Right." He shook his head. "My mates think I'm odd. I'm not a big fan of music. I know, it's weird."

"Nope, me either. I mean, I like music, but I'm not that into it. And I hate earbuds. I always want to talk to people, but I don't know if they can hear me, or if they're wearing the things to keep people from talking to them. So rude."

He smiled.

I glanced at the cover of his book. *The Screwtape Letters.* "We read that one in class. I didn't hate it."

Luke's lips pressed together, and a dimple formed. "That's a ringing endorsement."

I dug through my bag for a box of cards. "Want to play a game?"

He tried to peek through my hands covering the title. "What is it?"

"Would You Rather." I held it up.

"What?"

"Each card has a question." I pulled the stack out of the box. "Would You Rather. You get two choices, usually both bad, and you have to pick."

He squinted at me, unconvinced.

"Watch." I selected a card. "Would you rather eat poison ivy or a handful of bumblebees? See, now you pick one."

"What kind of question is that?" He angled to face me head-on, drawing one leg up onto the seat, and plucked the card from my hand. "Why on earth would I have to eat either one, ever? Exactly what type of camping are we doing?"

I matched his position, making our knees brush. He didn't move, so I left mine grazing his. "That's the point. It's silly."

He didn't blink.

"Fine. Try this one. Would you rather have the power of flight or invisibility?"

"Um. All right." A crease formed between his eyes. "Invisibility would be more practical. Although most of its applications would be criminal, so perhaps not. But—"

"Ohmygosh, you cannot analyze Would You Rather." I clapped a hand to my face. "New rule—you have to answer immediately. No thinking."

One cheek dimpled even though he narrowed his eyes. "You can't make up new rules as you go along."

"I can if you're going to pick your answer to a silly game based on logic. That defeats the purpose. Say the first thing that comes to mind. Flight or invisibility?"

"Flight."

"Excellent. Me too." I held the cards out to him. "Your turn."

His forehead wrinkled, but he picked a card, his fingers grazing mine.

"Would you rather be a giant hamster or a tiny rhinoceros?" His accent made the word *rhinoceros* sound sexy. "What does that even mean?"

"It's not supposed to mean anything. Giant hamster, I think. I'd get a huge ball and run around, rolling over people. You?"

"This is ridiculous."

I fake-glared at him.

"Fine. The rhino, I suppose."

I drew another card. "Would you rather be stranded on an island for ten years alone or with someone you hate?"

"Alone." His lips quirked. "I don't have to ask you."

"Why not?"

"Because you have a stranger accompanying you on a personal quest. You'd rather be with anyone than by yourself."

"If that's true, and I have low standards, it doesn't say much for you." I poked his knee.

"It tells me I was a sucker to talk to the pretty girl who saved my glasses."

A tingle darted through my chest. "That'll teach you to

show gratitude." I grinned. "You're right, though. I'd prefer to be with someone. I could get them to like me in days, tops. Except maybe Peter."

Luke made a show of shaking his head.

We played a while longer, and I learned Luke would walk barefoot in a gas station bathroom before wearing bowling shoes without socks, live at the bottom of the ocean instead of outer space, and visit the past rather than the future.

His answers were the opposite of mine on silly questions, but he surprised me on the serious ones. We agreed we'd spend time with friends over our families, skip Halloween but not Christmas, and do what we love and be poor rather than be rich and unhappy.

We'd rather rely on ourselves than others.

Despite our different backgrounds and varying interests, he understood me. My family loved me but didn't get me. I kept my friends at a distance, not letting them close enough to know the real me, and few tried to go deeper. But after two days, this boy from across the world saw me, identified with me, and—I thought—liked me. It was unsettling but comforting, like eating homemade cookies while getting an X-ray.

When the train stopped in Plymouth, Luke checked his phone. "There's a Poundland nearby. Before we enter the park, we need snacks."

He led the way down a busy street that resembled home except the cars were on the wrong side of the road and the sky was too gray. We came to a path alongside a park, ending at a stone courtyard across the street from a church with a tall tower and a giant high-rise. Luke aimed for a tan building, its pale stone streaked with black.

So far, Plymouth was a letdown in the "charming country town" department.

I studied the name of the store—POUNDLAND. "I get it. A pound is a dollar, so it's like a dollar store. That's fun."

The store sold exactly what I'd expect—tons of random items. In the food aisles, I selected things with funny names— Jammie Dodgers, wine gums, Monster Munch, and Wotsits— and the strangest flavors of normal foods, like steak-and-onion potato chips and beef-burger snack mix.

I held them up for Luke to see, laughing loud enough to draw disapproving glances from other customers. Luke mopped up behind me with glances that said *She's American, what are you going to do,* but he smiled, too.

Luke stocked up on that purple black-currant-flavored drink called Ribena and packages of Digestives.

"What in the world are those?" I inspected the package. "Do they aid in digestion? Like, make you regular? You're such an old man."

"They're biscuits," he said patiently. "With chocolate."

"Chocolate biscuits?"

"Biscuits." He angled his head. "Cookies."

"Oh. Chocolate cookies. Cool. Why give them such a terrible name?"

He shook the container in my face. "Wait until you eat one, and you won't care what they're called."

Next to the register, a display contained small boxes labeled

INTIMATE SITUATIONS CHEWABLE TOOTHBRUSH. The image showed a close-up of a smiling mouth with freakishly white teeth.

I snorted. "Please tell me you've never used one of these."

He held up a hand as if swearing in court. "I have never used one of those."

"What do you do, carry it in your pocket? Then if you think, hey, I see an intimate situation coming up. Better eat my toothbrush? I love it here."

Even though I'd replaced the toothbrush defiled by baggage claim, I added one of those to the pile. Then hoped Luke didn't think I was anticipating an intimate situation.

Once I handed Al the receipt and texted my mom to alert her I'd be venturing into the wild and might not be able to contact her that evening, we returned to the train station.

Our next stop was a small town called Ivybridge, which, appropriately enough, had an ivy-covered stone bridge across the river. Definitely a step up on the charming scale.

"I'm going to change." Al vanished into the train station bathroom and emerged wearing spotless hiking boots, black hiking pants, a thermal shirt, and a rain jacket.

I pretended to search the terminal. "Who are you, and what have you done with Al?"

She raised an eyebrow.

I gestured to Luke's jeans and bright red Converse. "Do you want to change?"

He looked at his shoes. "Why? Are we planning an expedition?"

"You never know."

"I'll take my chances."

We stood in the station, clutching our bags, resembling vagabonds. Now, how did we get into the actual park?

I approached the gray man behind the counter—gray hair, gray cardigan, grayish skin. "Can you tell us how to get to Harford?"

He aimed a finger over my shoulder. "There's a trail, Two Moors Way. Only a couple of miles."

We followed the gray man's directions to a footpath through the trees that led to a narrow road. A broad hill to our right curved up and out of sight, stretching, I guessed, into the moors. A low stone wall covered in vines ran alongside the road.

"There." I pointed to a small stone with a sign that said DARTMOOR NATIONAL PARK and had an outline of a horse.

Voices behind us drew my attention.

A family approached, parents, two girls, and a boy. I blinked. All five sported blue plaid button-down shirts, knee-length khaki shorts, thick socks, and hiking boots.

"Wow," I said.

The dad fumbled to set up a tripod as the others assembled by the sign.

I strolled over. "Want me to take your picture?"

"Would you? That'd be great." I couldn't place his accent. Something British-ish but not the same as Luke's and Al's. Maybe one of those others—Scottish or Welsh. He handed me the camera.

The family gathered next to the sign, a huddle of identical shirts and pasted-on grins. I raised the camera, and, as if on cue, they lifted their hands as one and gave a thumbs-up.

"Wow," I muttered again as I snapped two pictures. Were they for real?

The dad collected his camera.

"Are you guys doing the trail?" I gestured to their hard-core outdoor attire.

"Camping." He jerked his finger toward an RV, smaller than an American vehicle but still enormous on the narrow road. "And you?"

"We planned to hike to Harford."

The oldest girl, maybe twelve years old, frowned at Luke. "Those shoes aren't approved hiking gear."

He scuffed his Converse on the pavement. "We're not going far."

The dad shook his head. "Nonsense. You can't hike in those. It's quite mucky out there. Come with us." He clapped his hands. "Kids! Make room for new friends. To the camper van!"

Surely serial killers didn't travel with kids, wear matching clothes, and take pictures at park signs. I shot my own thumbs-up and intentionally cheesy grin at Luke and Al.

Al lifted one eyebrow. Luke adjusted his glasses. Both regarded me with blank expressions that said they were plotting my painful death.

The family sang as they filed toward the RV. A marching chant. In perfect harmony.

Luke's eyebrow imitated Al's. He was either impressed with their vocal abilities or considering abandoning me on the moors.

The RV must've been made for a family of hobbits. I had to edge between furniture and still earned a table corner to the hip, a chair to the shin. A couch, TV, and tiny kitchen had clearly been arranged by a Tetris expert. A half-drawn curtain revealed a bed and bathroom barely wide enough for one person.

How did five people travel in this without killing each other?

Snacks filled a wire rack on the small kitchen counter, in alphabetical order, because why wouldn't you eat your food from *A* to *Z*? One shelf contained books ranging from Elven Realms to Anne of Green Gables to Nancy Drew. A table in the middle of the space held a stack of board and card games, arranged by size to form a pyramid.

"We're the Humphreys, by the way. I'm James, that's Jennifer"—he pointed to his wife—"and Jessica, Jocelyn, and Jamie."

Wow. I could *not* use that word enough. "I'm Britt. They're Luke and Alexis. Thanks for the ride."

"Our pleasure. Make yourself comfortable." He disappeared up front, leaving the rest of us to sit on top of each other in the living space.

The mom opened a small video camera. "Day One of Dartmoor National Park. The weather is lovely, cloud cover but no precipitation. We've made new friends. Spirits are high." She aimed the camera at the youngest, the lone boy. "Jamie, anything to add?"

The boy was probably seven or eight. "I'm hungry."

I snorted, and she sicced the camera on me. "Tell me about yourself. What brings you to the UK?"

"Oh, uh. Traveling."

"What do you think so far?"

"It's nice. I'd never left the country before."

"Did your family take vacations like this?" Her disembodied voice pursued me relentlessly from behind the camera.

Way to get personal, fast, lady. "Not exactly. We visited the Grand Canyon once, but I got sick and barely saw it."

"Ooh, the Grand Canyon? Kids, did you hear? We'd love to go one day. Was it grand?"

I shrugged. "I mostly remember the puking."

"Gross," said Jamie in a voice that sounded like he meant *Cool*. "Do you play backgammon?"

"Can't say that I do," I said. "Would you like to teach me?"

Anything to escape the interrogation.

We tucked into the table, where our knees knocked beneath it.

He opened a black-and-white board with triangles and round, black-and-white pieces. "Do you play games in America while you travel?"

His quick fingers laid out the pieces.

"Uh, I Spy." I glanced out the window. "But there isn't much to spy out here other than rocks and grass. Or the license plate game. But that's not helpful, either."

The RV filled the entire road, brushing eight-foot-high shrubs on both sides. If we met another car, things would be interesting. At least ours was guaranteed to be the larger vehicle. I'd take that in a game of chicken.

"Luke, I don't suppose you're handy about the house?" Mom J. peered out from behind the camera. "The sink leaks, and James is rubbish at fixing things."

120

"Oh." He blinked. "All right."

He opened the cabinet and poked his head in.

The oldest girl sat next to Al on the tiny couch and inspected her outfit. "These are approved hiking clothes. Where did you get them? What's your favorite place to hike?"

Luke snorted from under the sink.

"Who wants a snack?" The middle girl opened a container of homemade scones and distributed them.

Mom continued filming everyone.

Luke peeked out from under the sink long enough to give me a look that said *Are you kidding me*. Mine replied *I know, right.*

This family was too perfect. The kids behaved. Mom and Dad got along.

A memory surfaced, one I hadn't thought of in years—Dad and me camping in the nearby Los Padres National Forest.

Not long after, Dad decided raising three kids was too much work and split. Which meant no vacations and definitely no camping.

I wasn't sure if today made me miss him. I rarely thought of him—it was easier not to.

Instead, I lost semigraciously at backgammon to an eight-year-old.

Less than an hour later, we parked in a campground nestled in green hills and piled out of the RV. The campground held an assortment of vans, RVs, cars, and tents, as well as a bunkhouse.

"Great camping here." The dad swept out an arm. "And you couldn't ask for better scenery."

I hefted my bag onto my shoulder. "Thanks for the ride."

"Our pleasure," he said. "Enjoy your trip."

We said goodbye and watched them close the RV and march off into the hills.

Once the family left, everything was twenty times quieter.

"Well," I said, "that was . . ."

"Torture?" Al suggested.

"Fun." I narrowed my eyes at her. "My family vacations were never that pleasant. When we took them. What about you?" I asked Luke.

"Our trips usually involved museums."

"Fun," I said in a completely different tone of voice.

Al nodded. "That sounds like your dad."

His eye twitched. He nudged her shoulder. "That didn't remind you of your childhood?"

I gasped. "Al was a child? Not possible."

Al shuddered. "Thank heavens we never wore matching shirts. But the games, the camper, the . . . bonding. I was hoping I wouldn't have to experience that again."

"You had a family that got along and took trips together, and you didn't like it?" I couldn't imagine that. Either the happy family or her reaction.

She shrugged.

I imagined her like my sister on trips, reading, ignoring everyone. Something inside me simmered. Not everyone had the money for family vacations. Or family members who could stand to be in the same room with each other for five minutes.

"Did it occur to you that some of us might hope to experience that someday?"

She raised an eyebrow, as if she knew their shared gesture was starting to drive me crazy. "Not all of us."

I scowled and marched away.

"I hope for that, too." Luke's quiet voice came from right behind me.

I stopped.

He braced his hands on my shoulders to keep from bumping into me.

I spun, and he stood so close I noticed faint freckles across his nose. His hands fell, but he didn't move away.

"Sorry about Al." He brushed hair out of his eyes. "She doesn't like people, so she doesn't appreciate growing up with a big family."

I drew a breath to calm myself. "I had a big family, but even before my dad left, we didn't have trips like that. Maya ignored us. My mom and Drew wanted to go to museums. My dad and I wanted to do outdoor stuff. And we fought over everything."

"Does it count as family when it's you and your dad, and he barely acknowledges you?" His mouth twisted into a wry smile. "The best trip I ever went on was with my friend Nick's family. Sad, huh?"

I stared over his shoulder at the moors. "I always imagined when I had kids, we'd load into a car and drive to parks where we'd camp and hike and do things I never tried, like fishing or whitewater rafting or horseback riding. We'd play car games and eat candy and sing along with classic rock songs." I risked a glance at his face. "Does that sound dumb?"

His gaze was soft. "No, it sounds like fun." A twinkle entered his eyes. "As long as you throw in one or two museums."

"I guess I could live with that."

We shared a smile.

Wait. Why was I planning future family vacations with a guy I just met? I hadn't realized I hoped for those things until today. I couldn't believe I'd let that family make me . . . nostalgic? Hopeful?

Whatever. Not like I'd ever find anyone I trusted enough to have a family with anyway.

"Come on." I dropped the smile. "Let's find those tents."

I left him behind, brushed past Al, and avoided glancing at the Humphreys' Camper Van of Family Fun.

CHAPTER ELEVEN

Al directed us to a guy guarding a pile of camping gear. Several sleeping bags and unassembled tents remained, but matching tents were set up nearby in two groups.

Who had beaten me? And would my third classmate arrive soon? I imagined us as pieces moving around the game board of England, one jumping ahead, the others catching up, trying to stay even.

I selected three tents and aimed for an unoccupied patch of land, where I dumped out the poles. I hadn't used a tent in years, but surely they weren't hard to assemble.

Al and Luke stood next to each other, heads bent over the instruction booklet.

"Really, guys?" I plucked the book out of Luke's hand. "You don't need that."

"This is going to end well," said Al.

"What are you, my grandmother? Do you also read the small print at the bottom of commercials and listen to airplane safety briefings?"

"Airplane safety is a serious matter."

Luke watched the guide longingly as I tossed it aside.

"You too?" I asked.

"Have you done this before?" He grabbed one end of a tent pole and helped me unfold it.

"Yep. Well, not exactly. I watched. Last time we camped, my dad set up the tent, but we haven't been since he left."

Luke's head tilted. "When was that?"

"Eight years ago. No big deal."

"I think it's a big deal." He held the tent pole, so I had to either let go or meet his gaze. "My mum left, too, but when I was quite young. It's hard to miss what you never had. I don't remember her."

That deserved acknowledgment, but I had no idea what to say. Was it worse to have no memories, or did that make life easier? Instead of replying, I tugged on the pole. "Did your dad teach you how to pitch a tent?"

"No."

One clipped word conveyed more emotion than he probably intended.

"I'll do it," I said.

Another tug, and our pole reached full length. A memory returned, of my dad and me jousting with them. I'd forgotten about that, too.

This trip was dangerous.

"Having fun yet, Al?" I asked to escape the past as I moved on to the second pole.

She didn't answer, glaring at her tent bag.

126

"She thinks gardens have too much nature." Luke unrolled the tent and shook it out.

"I don't see why these clues couldn't have taken us to libraries," she muttered. "This *is* literary themed."

After we fiddled with poles and sorted through tent fabric, Al scowling all the while, three small tents stood in the clearing.

I tossed my duffel bag into one. "And you thought we needed instructions."

Luke laid a hand on his chest and bowed, grinning at me. "I'm sorry for doubting you."

"We still might die," Al said.

Now that our lodging was set, time for the clue—find a boot from of old. I planted my hands on my hips.

A large green field stretched in front of me, dotted with a variety of tents, plus an area for campers like the Humphreys'. Trees lined one side, and a bunkhouse with a porch, a second wooden building, and a selection of picnic tables sat scattered throughout. A few people were throwing a Frisbee or relaxing in camp chairs, but the campsite was fairly quiet.

Al sat at a picnic table and opened her book. Luke glanced from her to me as if debating how involved he wanted to be.

"You can stay with Al if you want," I told him, mainly so if I missed something super obvious, he wouldn't be at my side to see it.

Once he joined her, I took a deep breath of fresh air. I was Sherlock Holmes. I would observe the tiniest details invisible to mere mortals, spot anything remotely out of place, catch the monstrous killer, and restore justice to the world.

Okay, not that last one.

Our tents sat near a stone wall separating the campground from the moors, so I started there. Nothing but rocks and moss. The shrubs that came next held nothing, either, nor the trees.

What happened if I didn't find the clue and spent the entire week in Dartmoor, failing miserably? Al might kill me. Or leave me here alone.

I moved to the fire pit in the middle of the field, surrounded by logs serving as benches. There. Something black, resembling leather, poked out from under a log. I tugged on it. *Please don't be covered in spiders.*

It was a man's boot, with laces and a buckle. Thankfully, I didn't have to stick my hand far inside to test the spider theory before I found a familiar card, except instead of a clue, it had a series of numbers. They were separated into groups, like words. Decipher the codes. Could it be as simple as one for A and two for B?

Tucking the boot under my arm, I retrieved a pen from my tent. Luke and Al watched as I scribbled the alphabet and numbers and translated the card to: *seek a light in the window.*

Only two permanent structures had windows. Inside the wooden building, I found bathrooms, metal sinks, and showers without doors, which I would definitely not be using. Nothing in the windows, though.

This reminded me of a team scavenger hunt last year, defense versus midfielders versus offense, as my teammates and I raced around town. Except far more was on the line this time than bragging rights and free pizza.

I needed to channel Sherlock. I was nowhere near as brilliant, but I related to his single-mindedness, his determination to finish a case. Good thing no one's life depended on this one. Except mine.

The other building was the bunkhouse. Nothing on the porch except mud-caked hiking boots, two umbrellas, and a towel hanging over a chair.

Sherlock would've made deductions about the lodgers based on the items. A woman with feet my size had an unfortunate encounter with a bog. Someone had prepared for storms. And if the owners needed those umbrellas anytime soon, someone else was going to have a very wet and useless towel.

But that didn't help me.

I'd circle it before I attempted entering. Around back, a row of windows overlooked a sprawling vista of rock-strewn fields.

What was that, in the windowsill? Without a porch, the windows were nearly above my head. But sitting in one was a bronze candleholder and a candle. Like a character in *The Hound of the Baskervilles* had used to signal someone in the moors.

I jumped, brushed it with my fingers to knock it off, and caught it. Wrapped around the white candle, so both stayed in the holder, was another card.

I was a regular detective. Sherlock would be proud.

This card showed random letters in chunks like words, but they weren't actual words: *F UNUJ ZSIJW YMJ XYFNWX.*

If it resembled the last card, letters could stand for other letters. A single-letter word could be *a* or *I.* I returned to the page where I'd scribbled the last code and studied the alphabet. Maybe shifting the letters over would work. Starting with *a* under the *f*, I wrote out the letters again and translated the code.

That gave me "a pipe under the stairs." The bunkhouse had stairs. Perfect.

I crawled under the steps and found a pipe with a paper rolled inside it. This one had a string of letters all in a row: *MDEHFINTPA.*

Word jumble? Fat Mend Hip, Hemp And Fit, Tip Fem Hand . . .

"Find the map," I said.

I flipped the cards over. No map. Where hadn't I searched? I ran to a kiosk near the RVs and discovered a display of maps of area hiking trails, under glass. Beneath the display was a box with paper copies. I flipped through them, finding one with a dog sticker on top, showing the path to Western Beacon.

Excellent. An adventure on the moors. Like Sherlock.

Waving the map, I skipped to the table where Luke and Al sat. "Who's up for a trek through the moors?"

"Because nothing could possibly go wrong with that idea," Al muttered.

"What was that, Al?" I cupped my hand around my ear. "I couldn't hear you."

"I can barely contain my excitement at the prospect of hiking through bogs with you, Ms. Hanson," she said with a blank face.

"That's what I thought you said."

We found the trailhead and set off. Patches of bright blue peeked through brilliant white clouds. My steps were light.

"Sure you want to wear that?" I pointed to Luke's Converse and jeans.

"I've never done the hiking thing."

"Obviously."

Luke rolled his eyes good-naturedly. "You seem to like hiking."

"I haven't been often, but I like exploring, seeing new things, and physical activity, so I guess so, yeah."

"Activity like football?" Slyness filled his sideways glance.

That was my intro. A perfect chance to tell him something real about me, other than that I'd rather eat a bar of soap than drink a bottle of dishwasher liquid. But I wasn't ready to share my whole story, and now we knew each other well enough that telling part of it felt like lying.

"Activity like walking across moors." I increased my pace, not waiting to see if he and Al followed.

"Be careful of the bogs," Al said.

"That's a good one. Would you rather be licked to death by a hellhound or swallowed by a bog?"

Luke snorted. "Bog, I guess. It's quick, but the lack of oxygen preserves you. At the British Museum, there's a man they found in a bog who's hundreds of years old, but you can tell he's human."

"Awesome."

Two figures appeared ahead, hiking toward us. I recognized Spence, in a rain jacket with the hood up and worn hiking boots. He must've already visited the trail's end.

I waved and he saluted.

"Seen any dogs yet?" he called. "I heard it might be dangerous out here."

"I think the bogs are worse than the dogs," I replied as we neared.

"Better watch out, then. I'd hate for anything to slow you down." He smirked, and we continued past each other.

The air smelled of tangy dirt, wet grass, and something sweet. I'd missed the outdoors. Exercise. Fresh air. I threw my arms out and laughed.

The moors just kept going, muted greens and browns stretching toward the distant sky. We followed a rough trail, paralleled a row of stones like an ancient giant had dropped toy blocks, and climbed a hill to find a chest-high freestanding stone pillar and panoramic views of rocky hills, green patchwork fields, and even a town in the distance.

Secured to the stone was another envelope. I shoved it into my pocket, since there was no cell service here and I didn't plan to read it without my friend Google.

After admiring the scenery, Luke and I sat on a rock. Al adopted her bodyguard stance several feet away, as if protecting us from invisible foes. The wind howled, whipping my hair and the grass.

Okay. I had nailed the tasks so far. But if I planned to win, I needed to figure out the journal part of this competition. Maybe I could learn something from Sherlock—or his author, considering how many books he wrote.

"Have you read Sherlock Holmes?" I plucked at the grass

growing from a crevice in the rock. "What would you say the hound story is about?"

"A giant demon dog," Luke said.

"Helpful." I tossed the grass at him.

He ducked and grinned. "I'm not doing your work for you."

"Think of it as helping me learn."

"What do you remember?"

I sighed. "A dog terrorized people. I think someone died of fright. Is that possible? So Sherlock made Watson come out here." I stared at the horizon and the endless, rolling hills. "Can you imagine that? It's so . . . bleak. And there are no people."

Luke's relaxed expression told me the lack of people was part of the appeal.

"I think there was a crazy guy living in the moors. And the dog had, like, glowing eyes. Or was that the modern version?"

Luke shook his head. "You're hopeless."

"I do better with movies." *Think, Britt.* "I know at the end there was an explanation for everything. Watson believed in the supernatural stuff, but Sherlock didn't, and that made him keep searching for a human answer."

"Preconceived ideas. Good. Think about that."

My only preconceived idea was what I'd do with my life, but that belief lay in wreckage now. "You sound like a teacher again."

"Sorry." He chewed his lip. Recognizing the habit by now, I assumed he planned to change the subject. Instead, he blinked and stared at the horizon. "I wanted to be one."

Trying to protect the moment, I kept my voice low. "You don't anymore?"

"It's complicated." He didn't elaborate.

"I understand complicated."

After two shaggy ponies ambled past, he asked, "What do you want to be?"

"A superhero." The answer came out before I could stop it, inappropriately flippant after he'd been so open.

He grunted and I glanced at him.

Fine. He'd been honest. I could be, too. "I don't know anymore."

He held my gaze, and I felt like he was reading my mind. Like he saw the truth written across my face—that I'd had a dream, but it had died, and now I was lost. Like he was saying he also felt that way.

A charge surged through me. I dragged my eyes away from the understanding in his.

Windswept grasses and scrawny trees leaned in the same direction, and piles of rocks crouching like beasts waiting to come to life filled my view. Now I remembered the bogs in the story—thick, hidden areas of mud capable of swallowing someone whole. The permanence of this place was both comforting and disturbing.

"Do you believe in the supernatural?" Luke asked.

"Like dogs from hell? No."

"Other stuff? God? Miracles?"

I needed many miracles—my future, college, this competition— so I wanted to believe in them. Maybe just being here was one.

"Yeah, I guess. Look at this." I waved my hand at the hardy trees and the beautiful clouds and the tiny flowers growing in the rocks. "It would be hard not to."

The weight of emptiness pressed in, heavy and full of too many thoughts.

"I'm tired of sitting. Race you to that rock." I jumped to my feet and took off running for a distant rock pile.

Though I carefully selected my steps on the uneven ground, I savored the wind and the way my breaths came faster. The doctor had said I could run, but it felt weird after several weeks with nothing but kiddie soccer. My lungs burned, but I kept going, sucking wind and forcing my tired legs to keep moving.

As I ran, the cloud shadows shifted and the sun disappeared.

Al's voice floated to me on the wind, warning me to be cautious. I ran faster. She had a point, though. What if I fell? I could bruise or cut myself on a rock. Who knew how long it would take to find medical care out here?

Fine.

I slowed to a walk, panting.

Luke stopped beside me seconds later.

I drew in a deep breath to make sure my voice came out steady. Couldn't have him thinking I tired so easily. "Not bad for those shoes."

Must've been his long legs.

"I'm not completely unathletic." His face was red, and his chest heaved more than mine. The wind had brushed his hair off his forehead, where it usually fell straight. He removed his glasses to rub them on the hem of his shirt.

How had I ever thought he looked nerdy? With mussed hair and no glasses, I saw the clear golden brown of his eyes and the arch of his brows. He slid his glasses on and turned those eyes on me. The breath I had just caught whooshed out again.

"Both of us are about to regret our footwear choices." If he'd noticed me ogling him, he gave no indication, thank heaven.

"Why?"

He pointed up. Gray clouds filled the sky. As I leaned back, drops splattered my face.

I brushed a raindrop out of my eyelashes. "There's that English weather I heard about."

Al approached, extending two blue ponchos.

"Aw, Al, you take such good care of me."

"I couldn't live with myself if anything happened to you," she said, deadpan.

I yanked on the poncho, which swallowed me, reaching my ankles. I would have worried about its complete unattractiveness except Luke and Al donned theirs, too. "Way to be prepared, Girl Scout."

"Worst two years of my life."

I whipped toward her. "Wait, for real?"

"Girl Guides. My older sister loved it, so my parents made me join."

"Ah yes, I'm well acquainted with the joys of older sisters who like different things. Sorry you were forced into that. But also, I will never let you live it down."

"I would be shocked to hear otherwise."

Luke and I shared a smile before we moved on.

An ache thrummed deep inside me. The space seemed too big, too empty. Where was a nice city when you needed one? Full of noise and people and distractions? The only sound was the soft plunking of raindrops on the plastic ponchos.

I'd always liked the outdoors—early mornings on the dew-covered soccer field, swimming in the icy Pacific, hikes up the hills with view of the ocean and the islands on clear days. But the outdoors I was used to was filled with people. Out here, I felt alone in the world.

And I wasn't sure I liked it.

CHAPTER TWELVE

Near the campsite, we passed two more people—Peter and his chaperone, heading toward the beacon. Peter's head hung low. Unlike Spence, he had no hat or hood, and his wet hair clung to his face and neck. His shoulders slumped. Bad timing for him. At least we'd made it partway back before the rain. He glanced up long enough to see me and glare, as if I were responsible for the weather.

The expression wiped away any sympathy I might have felt for his drowned-rat situation.

By the time we reached our tents, mud caked my shoes, Luke had ditched his glasses after wiping them dry multiple times, and frigid silence flowed off Al in waves that threatened to knock me over.

A fourth set of matching tents sat in the clearing, which meant my classmates and I were tied once more.

I glanced at the Humphreys' RV, but it was closed and dark. A breath escaped me. I was relieved for Al's sake. Not because I couldn't handle another happy family meal. My stomach rumbled. Actually, one of those scones sounded good.

The rain had died off, of course, now that we had the option of shelter. Luke and I sat at a table and broke into the snacks we'd bought.

"That does not count as a meal." Al crossed her arms. "I'm surprised at you, Luke. You're usually so prepared."

"I am prepared." He shook the bag he was holding. "I have food, don't I?"

"Biscuits and crisps are not a meal."

"I'm a bloke. This is a perfectly acceptable meal." He shook the crumbs from the bag of steak-and-onion chips into his mouth without breaking eye contact with her.

She retreated to another table to eat an energy bar alone.

Luke shrugged and opened a new package of Digestives.

"You don't strike me as the kind to eat junk food for a meal." I plucked a cookie from the package. "I mean, I'm perfectly fine with it. But you seem too . . . cultured."

"I'm not sure if that's a compliment or an insult. When you live with a father who doesn't cook, you learn to live with whatever's around." He glanced at me sideways. "I *can* cook, though."

"Really?" That surprised me less than him eating cookies for dinner.

"Sure. But like I said, I don't mind the occasional bag of crisps."

I broke open the Wotsits, which were like puffy Cheetos. "My mom cooks some, but she works long hours. When it's my

139

night, we usually have macaroni and cheese from a box or grilled cheese sandwiches."

"There's nothing wrong with a meal that consists primarily of cheese." To prove his point, he grabbed a handful of Wotsits from my bag.

Despite the late hour, the sky was bright, so when Luke retrieved a book and sat under a tree, I remained at the table and tried to write in my journal.

The day offered plenty of material. I attempted to describe the family and how it made me feel to spend time with one so different from mine, yet so similar to what I hoped for. But I couldn't capture the eerily matching outfits, the enthusiastic filming mom, the friendship among the kids. I jotted sentence fragments about the clues I'd found and the hike through the moors. My talk with Luke about miracles and beliefs rattled in my head. Those were the kinds of things Ms. C probably wanted to know, how Sherlock was making me introspective, challenging me to learn about myself and life.

But I didn't know where to start in putting down my feelings. Writing them on paper seemed awkward, like whatever I wrote would never capture my actual thoughts. I'd only record something weak and inaccurate that, once put in ink, could never be changed.

I closed the book and sat, shivering slightly and watching the sky go dark. Too bad the fog was blocking the stars. Another thing my dad used to do—take me to a secluded beach to see the stars come out over the ocean.

I didn't know how long I'd been sitting there when something warm wrapped around my shoulders. Luke dropped to sit beside me, tugging the other half of his sleeping bag around him. He sat close enough that his body heat, combined with the sleeping bag, helped me stop shivering, but not so close that I thought he was putting moves on me.

My foolish heart sank.

"This is nice, this camping thing." He drew the sleeping bag tighter, pressing us close, and my heart thrummed faster. "Peaceful."

The sleeping bag burned my nose with mingled scents of mothballs and something resembling the dorm I'd stayed in during my UCLA visit. "I forgot how much I like it."

Possibly I'd forgotten on purpose since those memories were tied up with my dad.

"What do you like about it?" he asked. "I'd have thought you preferred cities, where there are people and things to do."

"True, but I guess I like the challenge. Building your roof for the night. Making fire. Easy stuff becomes a problem to solve."

"That makes sense, I suppose." I could make out his profile from the light of a lantern somewhere in the campsite. "I like that it's quiet. It's a nice change, lets you escape."

I longed to ask what he was escaping from but held back. "I don't know how you do it," I said instead.

"Do what?"

"I don't know, stay so calm all the time. Sit silently. Be so . . . self-contained. I get bored too easily. I always have to be doing something."

"I admire how much energy you have. You're so enthusiastic

about everything. It would be exhausting to watch if I weren't so fascinated."

I'd never been called fascinating before. That sounded like an adjective you'd use for a rare flower or a museum specimen. My heart expanded, too big for my rib cage. He saw me, the real me, and liked what he saw.

"No one ever put it that way. In school, I was too excitable. At home, I was too loud. 'Why can't you sit quietly and read like your sister? Why can't you be like your brother and do your homework?'"

A soft huff came from Luke's throat. "I'm sorry."

"What? Why?"

Nearby, a man doused a fire, while another couple extinguished lanterns and climbed into their tent.

"Because it sounds like your family made you feel you weren't good enough, and that's terrible."

"Why, because family is supposed to love you for who you are and support you no matter what?" The words held more sarcasm than I intended.

"That's how it *should* be." His tone implied he knew better but wished for it anyway.

"That's not how you and your dad are?"

He waited so long to answer I thought he might not. "It's complicated. I'd rather not go into it."

He'd used the same excuse when he spoke of wanting to be a teacher. Were the two issues related?

I leaned back to study the sky again. "Okay."

"Okay? That's it?"

"Why wouldn't it be? You don't have to talk about it."

He shook his head. "I'm not used to someone . . ."

"Respecting your wishes?"

"Letting things go so easily."

"I'm great at letting things go. Now be quiet so I can listen for the hellhound sneaking up on us." The beast would have to be awfully stealthy, because no other sounds filled the camp-ground beyond the wind in the grass.

Luke chuckled, and his shoulder brushed mine, warm and solid. He left it there in a way that might or might not have been purposeful.

I hoped it was.

Don't get attached.

But I didn't move away.

"Why did you want to come with me?" I asked softly. "Some-thing to do with your dad?"

He twitched. "How did you know?"

"All the missed calls you ignored and the look on your face when you mention him."

He didn't answer right away. "You could read that? Most people say I have the best poker face. No one can ever tell what I'm thinking."

I shrugged, which shifted the sleeping bag. We both grabbed it, his fingers covering mine. The contact sent my heart into overdrive. Luke adjusted the fabric and removed his hand. How could he stay so casual? Did he have any idea what this was doing to my insides? Did it affect him at all?

"It's a long story. For another time." He didn't sound hostile, just tired, so I thought he might tell me eventually. "Why did you agree to let me come? I could've been a serial killer. Didn't you learn not to get in cars with strangers?"

"Instinct told me you weren't a psycho. And logic said if you were, I was strong enough to beat you up. Especially if Al helped."

He laughed. "You're probably right." He was quiet a moment. "Seriously, though, Pilgrim. It had to be more than not wanting to be alone."

"That was part of it. Experiences are better when you share them with someone. I guess . . . I saw something in you I recognized. Like you needed this, too. A break. An adventure."

The dark made it easier to tell him the truth. I wasn't talking to Luke, but to myself and the night.

Sheesh, this place was making me poetic. I needed to get away from nature.

"Darn," Luke said. "I thought it was my stunning good looks."

I recalled the way he had bent over his book, flipping pages without moving more than a finger, adjusting his glasses. His face, flushed and glasses-free, after running across the moor. The calm expression after I coated him in ketchup. Funny how many images I already had of him in two days. "That was definitely a point in your favor. Your turn."

"For what?"

"You never answered my question."

"You're right. I needed to get away."

I sensed that was all I was getting. For now, it was enough.

Something dragged me from sleep. I'd taken forever to fall asleep in the first place, so what had woken me? I rolled over and opened my eyes.

It was really freaking dark. No streetlights, no headlights, lanterns and fires extinguished, so the tent walls were pitch-black.

A long, low moan split the silence.

I jumped. Shivered.

"Psst. Luke. You awake?" I hoped his tent was close enough for him to hear me.

He groaned. "Why aren't you sleeping?"

"I heard something."

"A hound from Hades coming to get you?"

A flicker of light passed across the side of the tent, briefly making the fabric glow orange.

"There. Did you see that?" I sat up.

"I'm trying not to see anything except the back of my eyelids, but for some reason I thought it was a good idea to camp with a mad American who doesn't believe in sleeping."

Another moan filled the air, rising to a high-pitched wail.

"Sure you don't believe in ghosts?" Luke asked.

"No," I said firmly. "There's a human explanation."

"If you say so, Sherlock."

"It's probably Al. I bet Ms. Carmichael told her to play tricks on us to make it like the book."

"Yes, Al's the practical-joke type."

I crawled out of my sleeping bag toward the tent flap.

The moaning came again.

I jumped, then laughed. "I'm going to check it out." I shoved bare feet into my tennis shoes, drew back the tent zipper, and crawled out.

"Don't fall in a bog," he said.

Outside, there was no hint of the light I'd seen. The moaning had stopped, too.

Using my phone screen for light, hoping the battery didn't die, I took a few steps. A light appeared in the distance, illuminating a ridge away from the campsite on the open moor. The steady glow implied flashlight, not fire.

The wail returned, a low howl that built slowly and trailed off. The light went out.

More of the story came back to me. Sherlock stayed in an old stone hut. A guy took food to his escaped-convict brother. And when Watson and Sherlock had their final standoff with the hound, sheets of fog blanketed the moors, like tonight.

I'd meant what I'd told Luke—I didn't believe in ghost dogs. But out here, with the fog and the dark and the smell of earth, I understood how someone might.

My phone made little headway against the mist, but I aimed for where I'd seen the light. There was no dog out here. Probably night hikers. Possibly Al.

I picked my way across the uneven ground.

"Pilgrim, wait," Luke whispered from behind me.

He stumbled toward me, pulling on a hoodie.

I stopped. "Protecting me from the hound?"

"I can't let you walk around at night alone. It wouldn't be right."

"No, it wouldn't," said a second, resigned voice, and Al appeared.

Okay, not her out there with the sound effects.

"Did you set this up?" I squinted to see her in the meager light. "Ms. Carmichael's orders? Trying to scare us?"

"I had nothing to do with it." Her voice sounded like the thought offended her. "But I figured if you heard it, too, you'd be out here."

"You know me so well."

"Here, take a torch."

"You don't have flashlights in England?"

She handed me a flashlight, using another to illuminate her face.

"Oh. That's what you call them here. Thank you for the torch, Girl Scout," I said in a British accent.

"Please stop," Luke said.

We continued across the moor. The thick mist blew in gray gusts and coated my skin in moisture. After several minutes, the light came again, farther to the right. We adjusted our course.

I blew on my chilled hands. "Think it's an escaped convict?"

"You *did* read the book," Al said.

Luke snorted.

I huffed. "I do not appreciate your tone of surprise."

Another howl pierced the air.

"Sounds more like a dog being tortured than one out for a midnight snack." But goose bumps broke out across my arms.

"Quiet," Al said.

When we reached the ridge, Al shined her light, illuminating muddy ground that contained a footprint. Well, paw print. A large one, twice the size of my shoe. Al continued her sweep. Nearby, there was another. I spotted one more before they disappeared into the bushes. With prints that big, the dog would've been the size of a small dinosaur.

I laughed. "Seriously?"

Had Ms. Carmichael put someone up to this? Part of the challenge to see how I'd react? Or one of my classmates could've been behind it. Spence would find this amusing.

Had the others heard the noise? I wished Amberlyn were here. When we had sleepovers as kids, strange noises made her imagine all kinds of things—serial killer, UFO, government spy drone. She was so easy to fool, it had been fun. The fake spider in her ice cream. Waking her up while wearing the *Scream* mask the night we watched the movie. Pretending I was transforming into a werewolf after her dog bit me. I thought she'd never believe that one, but she had.

But I didn't scare so easily. "This is disappointing. If someone wanted to mess with me, I wish they'd at least brought an actual dog."

"Who do you think it was?" Luke asked.

"One of my classmates, probably."

"Or that family," Al said. "Never trust people who sing."

"We didn't tell them why we were here," Luke pointed out.

I turned toward camp. "Let's go. I'm tired."

As we walked, I aimed the flashlight alternately at the

ground and the moors around us, hoping to catch a glimpse of someone or something. I craned my head left. Right. My toe clipped a rock.

My ankle rolled. Not hard, but my leg bent at a strange angle. Something twinged in my knee. It gave out, and I fell to the ground with a grunt.

"Britt?" Luke immediately knelt by my side and rested a hand on my arm. "Are you all right?"

Al aimed the flashlight, blinding me.

"Fine. Help me up." I grasped Luke's hand and stood, testing my weight. My knee seemed okay. It hadn't hurt, just felt like something shifted. I took a couple of steps, still holding Luke's hand. "I'm okay. I had knee surgery recently. But it's good now. I stepped wrong, that's all."

"You had surgery, and you're out here hiking in the dark?" His hand tightened on mine.

"No big deal. My doctor said it was fine."

"To hike in the dark?"

"That exact activity didn't come up." I dropped his hand and started walking again. Traitorous knee, making simple walking hard. And traitorous hand, missing the warmth of Luke's.

Part of me wished he'd insist on helping, put an arm around me. The other, logical part argued I was perfectly fine on my own and certainly didn't need to rely on someone who'd only be with me for a week.

I stopped. We'd almost reached our campsite, but something looked wrong.

"Um, guys?" I pointed. "Isn't that where our tents should be?"

CHAPTER THIRTEEN

I dug through the limp fabric that puddled where my tent had stood minutes ago. "Someone stole our tent poles."

I spun in a circle, pointing my flashlight, but saw no one. Who would go to the trouble . . . ?

"Peter."

Spence might've done the howling and fake paw prints, but he wouldn't go this far. Peter, though . . .

"He must've planned that dog thing to draw us away." I stomped to the edge of the campground and rustled through the bushes. Circled the perimeter of our area. Nothing.

Luke put a hand on my shoulder before I could march to every tent in the campground.

I clenched a fist and forced myself to breathe. Had he watched Luke and me all evening? Had he seen us talking before bed? Creep.

Calmer now, I continued my search—bushes, rocks—but there was no sign of the poles. Surely Ms. C wouldn't approve of theft. This was *so* going in my story. Even if the fake dog was part of the challenge, sabotage wouldn't be.

Luke crouched next to his used-to-be-a-tent. "Does he hate you that much?"

"You saw him on the tour." I toed the tent. "I guess we could sleep under the stars."

Except the stars weren't visible through thick sheets of fog, which gave off nearly as much moisture as rain clouds.

Actually, real drops were falling now.

A growl came from the direction of Al's tent. I spun. Had the fake dog returned? Oh. It was Al.

Luke tilted his head toward the sky. "Or not."

"As if my back weren't already going to hurt," Al muttered.

"Stop being an old woman. We can figure this out." I lifted my tent so I could unzip the door. At least Peter had left my sleeping bag. We needed a way to keep the roofs up. "Remember those tiny tents we saw out on the moors? The personal-sized ones?"

"They're called bivvies," Al said. "And I was thankful we weren't using them."

"We are now. We can prop up the roofs with the backpacks and Al's umbrella."

I grabbed her big golf umbrella and wedged it into my duffel bag. Luke held the tent up. I tucked the bag into the corner of the tent, and he draped the fabric over the tip of the umbrella. The result was a three-foot-high peak that sharply dropped off.

"If I use my bag as a pillow, it might work." I climbed in and lay down. The ceiling drooped inches from my face, and the rest sagged onto my body like a blanket. "Good enough."

Luke and I did the same to his tent, using his backpack frame. Al glared at the tents like she blamed them for dismantling themselves, so we fixed hers, too.

"Sweet dreams, I guess." I crawled into the tent but couldn't find the door zipper, so I left it open. The roof kept the rain off my face, at least.

I might not have fallen for the dog trick, but it sure provided an effective distraction. On the bright side, my story would be entertaining. If I didn't die of hypothermia.

"Thanks, Peter," I mumbled as I fell asleep.

I woke with wet fabric plastered to my face. Sometime during the night, the umbrella had slipped. My face, hair, and shoulders were damp, and the tent clung to me like a soggy cocoon.

My nose and ears ached with cold, and my eyes and throat felt full of sand. The damp had made my hair a tangle of frizzy waves. I yanked the rubber band out and tried to smooth it before pulling it up again, hampered by numb fingers.

I didn't immediately rise. As my brain woke, I remembered the night before. In the chaos of fixing our tents, I'd forgotten what I'd admitted to Luke—the surgery. What if he asked about it? I didn't want to lie, but I wasn't ready to talk about the terrible health stuff that followed my knee injury. Plus, Al already monitored me constantly. I didn't need Luke babysitting, too.

I gritted my teeth and peeled off the tent. Couldn't hide all day, so I might as well face him.

Despite last night's grumbling, Al looked fashionable and put together as always in dark jeans and her trench coat in place of the hiking clothes—curse her British style—but Luke also had damp hair and tired eyes. Too bad *his* hair didn't look like an electrocuted poodle when it got wet. I would've preferred he not see me with damp bedhead first thing in the morning, but he smiled at me like nothing was wrong as he and Al folded their tents, a task made easier without poles.

We packed up, left what remained of the tents near the bunkhouse where we'd found them, and walked down the road. No RV waited to give us a ride, but buses ran from the campground into town.

"You mean"—Al drew a deep breath that flared her nostrils—"we could have ridden a perfectly lovely bus yesterday instead of suffering through the camper van debacle? I need a coffee."

"Wow, you must be extra grouchy if you want coffee instead of tea."

Chips and cookies didn't make as good a breakfast as they did a dinner, so we rode the bus to town and stopped for egg, bacon, and tomato sandwiches on the way to the train stop. I slipped my blood thinner medicine into my mouth, trying to hide the act. Al's gaze flickered to me, but she focused on her coffee without drawing attention.

Now that I had cell reception, I took out my new clue.

It should've stirred excitement over where I might be headed next, but solving them in front of Luke and trying to hide my ignorance was exhausting. I squared my shoulders and tried to maintain the blank expression he always wore, but couldn't stop my foot from jiggling.

If I could handle knights and ghost dogs, I could handle Ms. Carmichael.

As soon as I read the words, I groaned.

Sample waters of healing when your health starts to fade
In this place where Jane's heroines used to take a parade.

At high noon Assemble in great Rooms, one and all,
As you enjoy the trappings of a true Georgian ball.

My King Arthur–Sherlock confidence died a swift and brutal death.

Jane Austen. Of course Ms. Carmichael would torment me with her. Most girls in our class loved *Pride and Prejudice*. We'd also read *Northanger Abbey,* and Ms. Carmichael had made us watch film versions of *Emma* and *Persuasion,* for a grand total of more than half of Austen's works.

I didn't get the obsession, though. Which meant I'd skimmed the books, done squats and lunges during the movies, and used Google to help write my essays. Looked like my good pal Google would be making another appearance. No matter how long I spent thinking, I wasn't going to come up with anything.

I searched for "Austen healing waters" and learned that people in Austen's day thought the waters in Bath had healing powers. Sea bathing was also popular for health in Brighton, Weymouth, and Lyme. What about taking a parade? I recalled a room in *Northanger Abbey* that the characters visited simply to sign their names in a book and walk in circles. I couldn't think of a more pointless way to spend a day, but that also happened in Bath. And apparently, Bath had Assembly Rooms where balls and concerts took place. But Brighton did, too . . .

I knew Jane Austen was my kryptonite.

"May I?" Luke reached for the clue.

I shoved it toward him.

He glanced at Al before asking, "Have you discovered anything?"

That I was the only girl in America who didn't know anything about Jane Austen. "I'm gonna go to the bathroom."

So I could make a plan without them staring at me.

On my way back, I'd decided to take a chance on Bath when raised voices drew my attention. Amberlyn stood at the ticket counter, arguing with an official.

I paused. Did she need help? Her tense shoulders, red face, and the dangerous swing of her blond ponytail screamed frustration. She spun to point at something, and her gaze latched onto me. Her desperate expression seemed to plead for assistance, but with a single blink, indifference took over.

I stepped toward her. Hesitated. Would she want me to get involved? Probably not.

She whirled back to the man at the counter, so I moved on. And bumped into someone.

"Whoa." Spence's voice greeted me. "Where's the fire?"

"Apparently, Amberlyn's trying to light it under that guy's feet."

Spence glanced toward the counter and chuckled. "It would be a shame if she had a problem that slowed her down."

His half smile indicated he wouldn't mind one bit.

"How's everything going for you?" he asked. "Did you enjoy the moors?"

I narrowed my eyes. "Nice try."

He lifted a shoulder. "Just curious. What about your tales? I'm writing mine in the styles of the original authors."

He knew how to do that? Was he lying? Trying to intimidate me? I couldn't ask, not without admitting my journal progress. Or lack of. I tried to keep my face neutral and hide the tidal wave of panic. "Good for you. To be truly authentic, you should use a quill and inkpot. I bet Ms. C would love that."

"Great idea. Thanks."

Like the type of pen we used would matter. The words themselves concerned me more. I could barely manage complete sentences, and he was attempting nineteenth-century grammar?

"Well, I have places to go." I edged away. "See ya."

Bath might have waters of healing, but I needed greater magic than that to win this competition.

Al took the first free seat. "Wake me when it's time to switch trains."

Spence boarded the same train, raising his eyebrows as he passed Luke and me. I twisted and watched to make sure he didn't sit too close.

Luke and I sat beside each other, near enough that I noticed a trace of stubble that made him look older and deliciously dangerous. What would he look like if he didn't shave all week? If his stubble were combined with the scent of pine, now tinted with hints of rain and dirt, I'd be in so much trouble. I tried not to breathe too deeply.

I felt his eyes on me. Here it came. Funny how I could tell now, by the expression on someone's face and the breath they drew, when they planned to ask.

"What happened to your knee?" Luke nodded at it like I might have forgotten where it was.

"Surgery." I bit out the word, hoping to imply he should stop there.

"You mentioned that. Do you want to tell me what happened?"

Rather than returning his gaze, I stared at the dark screen on the seat back in front of me and ran my finger over the smooth surface. "An opposing player who never learned to slide tackle correctly."

He winced. "Sorry."

"Not your fault. I should try to update my journal."

He held up his hands. "Sore subject, huh?"

"I had surgery. It's healing." I shrugged. "No big deal."

"You like to say things are no big deal when, in fact, they sound like big deals to me." His direct stare burned a path straight to my soul.

I bent over my bag and rummaged for my journal. "I can't change it, so what is there to get upset about?"

"Getting upset and acknowledging that knee surgery sucks are two different things."

"Fine." I straightened and returned his gaze. "Surgery sucks. Physical therapy sucks. And people who don't know how to slide tackle suck. I need to write." I waved the journal.

"If you say so."

He refused to talk about his father, yet expected me to discuss the injury that led to the death of my future? Nice try.

I scribbled in the journal, attempting to describe the tent incident and the dog sounds. Those were the only new topics since my pathetic attempts the night before, but as long as I kept the pen moving, Luke wouldn't interrupt.

I scanned over what I'd written so far. Ugh. Awful. My words didn't capture the desolate beauty of the moors. Trying to explain how it felt to run again sounded dumb. So did my attempt to explain why I liked camping. And getting lured from our sleeping bags by a fake dog to return to dismantled tents should've been hilarious but came across as stupid.

Was Spence emulating Doyle in his journal, describing his sleuthing skills to make himself sound like Sherlock? In this scenario, I was poor Watson, always five steps behind.

A brief wave of heaviness weighted my shoulders.

I slammed the journal closed.

Endless green hills flashed by. My eyelids drooped.

Next thing I knew, Luke was nudging my shoulder. "Time to switch trains."

My head jerked up.

"You drooled, Pilgrim." He pointed, grinning.

Crusted spit had dried on my chin. I rubbed at it. "I didn't drool on you, did I?"

"Thankfully, no."

"Ah, well, maybe next time." I forced a smile to hide my embarrassment.

"I can hardly wait." His eyes twinkled.

Of course, for me, sleeping on a cute guy's shoulder would end with slobber.

After we switched to a new train, I pulled out the cards. Anything to keep him from attempting a real conversation.

Luke groaned. "Not again."

I tapped my fingers evilly. "Would you rather go without television for the rest of your life or without junk food?"

"Hmm, I could live without either." He'd be more believable if he weren't snacking on Digestives. He offered me a cookie. "I guess television would be easier to give up."

"Not me. I'm addicted to reality competitions. *Amazing Race, American Ninja Warrior, Survivor.*"

A quiet chuckle escaped Luke's nose.

"What?"

He waved a card. "This one's good. Would you rather be the star player on a losing team or sit on the bench for a winning one?"

I froze. My brain, my heart, my body. It was a stupid question. A game. Not a commentary on the rest of my life.

"I don't lose. The premise of that question is flawed. Next." Feeling strangely out of breath, I plucked the cards from him before he could object. "Would you rather be able to lie without getting caught or always be able to tell when others are lying?"

Now he went still. "Tell when others are lying. I hate when people lie."

159

Did he mean me, avoiding his questions? No, he was scowling at the seat in front of him, upset about something larger. His dad?

Who knew this game could turn dangerous so quickly?

"Me too," I said. "That's why I tell the truth, even if it gets me in trouble. Like this one time, my mom made cookies and left them to cool. Then our neighbor got sick, and my mom waited with her for an ambulance. So, I bet my brother I could fit more cookies in my mouth than he could. He usually never gave in to my crazy ideas, but peanut butter cookies are his favorite. By the time Mom came home, we'd eaten the entire batch. Drew wanted me to lie and say I'd been playing soccer in the house and knocked over the cooling tray. But I was so proud I'd fit six cookies in my mouth, I had to tell her. My brother was so mad, especially when he got a stomachache and I didn't."

By the time I finished my story, laughter had replaced Luke's scowl.

Mission accomplished.

I shoved the cards under my leg. Enough personal questions for the day.

We spent the rest of the ride discussing the trouble we'd caused as kids—mine mostly involved breaking things and accepting dares I shouldn't have, while he tended to correct adults and mess things up because he insisted on doing them himself.

Our route wound through more small towns and rolling hills, then past an old stone bridge and a Roman aqueduct.

Get your mind in the game. I was visiting Bath because Jane

Austen heroines went there. In her time, I would've made this trip in a carriage or coach, getting ready to socialize and find a rich husband at a ball.

I preferred balls I could kick.

Thanks for nothing, Jane Austen.

At the train station, Spence quickly marched off. It was after noon, so hopefully since I'd seen Spence on my train and Amberlyn at the station, it meant the ball was at noon tomorrow and I hadn't missed it.

Luke grabbed a map listing the town's main attractions. I'd decided the clue intended me to visit the Pump Room, where Austen's characters went to be seen—aka take a parade. It was connected to the Roman Baths, where a person could sample the waters that Austen's characters drank for their health.

We wandered into town, down a pretty pedestrian area with flowers and benches.

"We should find a place to stay," I said, shifting my duffel bag. "Drop off our stuff."

"I found a list of hostels." Luke held up his phone.

"You didn't like the way I found a place in Glastonbury?"

"Just trying to be useful," he said. "And those owls were disturbing."

"You win the award for best travel agent." I smiled at him. "Lead on."

He guided us to a tan stone house with a lawn and picnic tables out front. After we checked in, the hostess showed us to a room with several sets of metal bunks. Three beds had bare mattresses with blankets folded at the foot.

"Pick anything that isn't taken." She vanished out the door before she finished her sentence.

"I'm too old to stay in places like this." Al grumbled the words and darted to the bed in the far corner, leaving a bunk for Luke and me near the door.

"I think you don't really mind," I said. "You just like to pretend you do."

She knelt next to her suitcase, ignoring me.

I stared at the bare mattress. "Um . . . where do we get sheets?"

Luke laughed. "You don't."

"I'm supposed to sleep on a mattress?" It didn't sound overly hygienic, but I could live with it for a night.

"You're supposed to bring your own."

"Your own sheets? Who carries those?" I scanned the other beds. Apparently, everyone but me.

Al withdrew folded sheets from her small suitcase and stood. "They were on the packing list Ms. Carmichael provided."

"Oh." I coughed. "That."

"This is why we read instructions, Ms. Hanson."

"I read the packing list. I just . . . didn't remember everything."

She sighed. "I knew I should have checked your bag before we left London."

"Too bad we didn't keep those sleeping bags."

Luke took my duffel from me and set it on the floor. He stepped close and leaned in.

I froze. What was he doing? Did he plan to kiss me? In the middle of a hostel with his cousin in the room? I started to lean away, then closer, then settled for not moving.

He put his hands on my shoulders. His gaze darted to my mouth, and his face went pink. He dragged his eyes back to mine and cleared his throat, a teasing smile lifting a corner of his lips. "You owe me so big for this. I cannot wait to collect."

I swallowed hard. Forced my mind to shift from thoughts of kissing to his words.

"Owe you?" My voice squeaked.

He released me, leaving me swaying from the loss of his hands and the unexpected proximity. He pulled two sets of sheets from his backpack, dropping one set on the bottom bunk and tossing the other on the top. I glimpsed the same small box with the watch I'd seen on the porch the day we met.

I pointed to his bag. "What's that?"

"Nothing." He closed the backpack so fast I thought he might catch his finger in the zipper.

Hmm. Another sore subject.

Would Al report me for letting Luke find a place to stay and for not reading the packing list? And why had my mind jumped straight to kissing?

Luke stopped making the bottom bed and stared at me. "Please tell me you know how to put sheets on a bed."

"Oh. Yeah." I jumped to action, and we tugged sheets onto the bottom mattress together. The act was awkward, intimate, even though there were twenty other beds and the room smelled like my gym locker. "Why'd you bring extras?"

"I suspected you wouldn't know to pack them."

"Wow." After one day together, he'd known me well enough to pack for me.

His mouth quirked. "I believe the word you're searching for is *thanks*."

"Right. Thank you." We moved on to the top bed.

"I get the top bunk," he said as we smoothed out the last sheet.

"I'm perfectly capable of climbing up there. You don't need to baby me." Knee surgery shouldn't stop me from climbing a tiny ladder.

"I wouldn't dare. I promise." He tossed his backpack onto the bunk. "But I never got to sleep in a bunk bed before."

My eyes narrowed. "For real?"

"Honestly." His clear, brown eyes held nothing but sincerity.

"Okay, then."

I wasn't entirely convinced he was telling the truth, but his gaze hadn't once strayed to my knee and I couldn't read pity or lies on his face, so I'd go along with it.

I rubbed my hands together. "Time to see the baths."

CHAPTER FOURTEEN

The Pump Room was located off a large circle with cobblestone streets, columns, and hanging flower baskets. The stone columns and triangular top reminded me of pictures of Athens. Etched in stone were the words KING'S AND QUEEN'S BATHS, and a smaller hanging sign said THE PUMP ROOM.

"It looks like Greece," I said.

"Or perhaps Rome," Al said. "As in, the Roman Baths."

"What would I do without you, Al?"

"I shudder to think of the possibilities."

Luke snorted and elbowed me, and I shoved him. The friendly teasing offered less uncertainty than that charged possibility of more-than-friends, which was scary—and pointless. I didn't intend to start something with someone in another country, no matter how much I liked his smile, his eyes, his intelligence, his humor. . . . Besides, I could be reading him entirely wrong. I had no frame of reference for this type of relationship. He probably wasn't interested anyway. I thought we'd been flirting, but maybe he saw it as friendship? I was bad at this.

Better to focus on the competition.

Inside, dark, polished wood lined the lobby walls, stretching to cavernous ceilings. We paid and Luke took the map. The first stop was a small room with pale green wallpaper and a crystal chandelier. The space wasn't much bigger than my English classroom, and no one else was lingering in it.

A small balcony offered views to the bath below. The water was green. Not in a mountain-lake, ocean-on-a-sunny-day way. In a revolting-things-grow-and-die-in-there way.

I turned back to the room. A sign on the wall said PUMP ROOM.

"Did people in Jane Austen's time really think this was a big deal? It's tiny. They couldn't fit twenty people in here if they were walking in circles."

Luke choked a laugh. "I think the sign means the actual Pump Room is through that door."

Now that he mentioned it, the sign did sit above a doorway. I peeked through. The opening led to an enormous dining room with monstrously high ceilings.

"Oh. That makes more sense."

Tables draped with white linen filled the dining room, along with a grand piano. A curved second-floor balcony looked down on the room, and above that, a high ceiling with white columns and domes let in natural light.

"Okay, I guess this room could hold lots of people. If you took the tables out."

Luke shook his head and smiled.

I tried to picture it crowded with people in gowns and those tight breeches and boots the actors wore in Austen movies.

My mind formed an image of Luke in tight breeches and boots. In the movie in my head, he bowed, I curtsied, and he extended a hand as if asking me to dance.

"What?" He blinked. "You're staring at me."

I hid a cough. "Nothing."

"Are we stopping for tea?"

"I'm going to take a parade around the room, like a proper Austen lady. This room. Not that one." I jerked my thumb toward the tiny space behind us. "Want to come?"

He shifted and scanned the room. People in nice clothes occupied several tables, sipping tea from china cups.

"Come on." I slid my arm through his, and we strolled around the edge of the room.

"Would this have been allowed in Austen's time?" I asked. "Weren't people, like, not supposed to be alone?"

"Not without a chaperone. As an unmarried couple, we'd be causing quite a scandal."

Was Luke hinting we were a couple sneaking alone time, with Al the chaperone we'd ditched? I considered ending this stroll right now before I gave him ideas, but the feel of his arm under my fingers and his warmth seeping into my side urged me to enjoy the moment.

This wasn't Austen's time. Today, a walk was just a walk.

Keep telling yourself that.

Luke stood straight, his elbow crooked. My hand rested on

his arm. The pose struck me as very proper. Jane Austen would not approve of my improper desires to feel that arm around me or run my hands through his hair. *I* did not approve of those desires. *Don't get attached.*

When we reached the door again, Luke bowed. "Do you feel yourself connecting with Catherine Morland and Anne Elliot?"

"I do." Although I hadn't remembered their names.

Past the dining room, a walkway extended above the baths a level below. From this angle, the water appeared no better. Definitely not something I'd bathe in. Statues of men in Roman clothes—skirts, robes, plumed helmets, and laurel crowns— lined the walkway. In the background loomed a giant church.

People at the water's edge snapped pictures, read guides, and studied the water. Before following the path inside another building, I spotted a familiar face.

Peter. His head tilted up as if he'd sensed me. I scowled. He glared.

"Great," I muttered.

"What?"

"Peter's here."

Luke leaned against the wall to view the area below. "Good thing we left our bags at the hostel so he can't steal them."

The next part of the building contained a museum dedicated to ancient Rome. People packed the space, lingering over models of Roman cities, old coins, and stone carvings. Boring. I wanted to see the water up close, so I elbowed my way through the crowds.

When I reached the final door, I remembered what Luke said about liking museums. Did he want to stop? I shouldn't have rushed.

Too late now. We stood beside the water, uneven stones underfoot, gray sky above the open-air space. No rail guarded the water, which was a lawsuit waiting to happen. Columns led to the upper level, where the stone Romans lorded over us. The green water was fairly smooth, but a few places bubbled.

"Do things live in there?" I edged closer and wrinkled my nose. "Radioactive monsters with scuba gear?"

"It's from the natural springs," Luke said.

"People bathed in that? It's revolting. Wait. I'm supposed to drink the waters . . ." It looked like something my drain would spit up.

Luke laughed. "Not that muck. The pure mineral water straight from the springs. It's inside at the end."

I grimaced. "Can't wait."

Despite the disgusting water, the baths were cool. Seagulls soared overhead. Off the main pool, several dark nooks held remains of actual bathing rooms from Roman times. Hard to believe these buildings had existed so long. One pool sparkled with coins. Apparently, that was a tradition everywhere.

As Luke and Al roamed on, I sat on a stone by the water to think, rubbing my finger over the worn rock. Jane Austen wrote lots of stories. If I connected with her, it might inspire me to write mine.

Her books featured manners, polite society, and marrying for love versus money. But Ms. C had also talked about how the heroines grew to see themselves more clearly. They were willing to grow as people and learn from their mistakes.

This trip was showing me that was the crossroads I faced, no matter how hard I tried to avoid it. I had a choice. Would I grow,

169

or would I be an annoying side character like the younger sister who ended the book as obnoxious and clueless as she started?

I'd certainly rather end up with Darcy than Wickham, so there was that.

I stood carefully. The last thing I needed was my knee going out on uneven ground.

A guy in an official vest stood nearby, hands clasped in front of him. Was he a tour guide, a bodyguard, or a lifeguard?

"How often do people fall in?" I asked him.

"We get more jumpers than accidents, a few per year. Mostly middle-aged men having a midlife crisis. They have a row with their wife and get the urge to come jump. Personally, I don't know why you'd want to." The guy shuddered. "It's quite slimy, and ducks do hideous things in there. We had one bloke do it naked. Left his clothes inside. He was escorted off the premises without his trousers."

My loud laugh escaped. "There were way too many unpleasant mental images in that sentence."

He nodded as if the images haunted him, too.

I thanked him and spotted Al and Luke on the other side of the water. I made my way toward them, watching where I stepped.

I sensed someone behind me. Started to turn.

Someone bumped me from the side, hard. I staggered. My toe caught on an uneven stone.

And I was air-bound, flying straight for the green, slimy, duck-infested water.

CHAPTER FIFTEEN

I hit the slime pit face-first, my eyes and mouth wide open.

I choked on a mouthful of water, swallowed. The taste defined *green and slimy*. The temperature reminded me more of a lukewarm bath than the chill I'd expected.

Wet clothes dragged at me. I kicked to the surface and came up spitting. My hands scrabbled for the edge but slid off mossy stone. Hair clung to my face.

A warm hand grasped mine, and Luke appeared above me. He hauled me out and bent close, wiped a trail of water from my temple. His finger lingered on my cheekbone.

"Are you okay? You're not hurt, are you?"

"Just mad." I stepped away from the edge.

My tennis shoes squished; my hair dripped. I spit again, not caring that everyone was staring.

I gagged once more and squeezed my hair. Green rivers snaked down my arms. I rubbed at them, leaving a sticky coating on my palms.

"Where did he go? I'm going to kill him." I would wrap my slime-covered hands around Peter's skinny neck, shove him under the water, and make him swallow duck-contaminated sludge.

"Who?" Luke asked.

"Peter. Someone pushed me, and he was here. You didn't see him?"

Luke and Al shook their heads.

"You're sure you didn't jump?" Al asked. "That sounds like something you might do."

"Please. If I'd jumped, I would've made sure you were watching first. It had to be him."

Then the scent hit me.

I smelled like duck poop.

My laugh erupted, the inappropriate kind I could never control.

The friendly vest-wearer had ditched his friendly expression. He strode toward us clutching a giant towel.

I kept laughing. Bent-over, hands-on-my-knees, shaking laughter.

A weight settled over my shoulders as I was bundled up and marched away. Past huddles of staring tourists, past whispers and snickers and snorts of disgust.

Like he had to force me to leave. All I wanted was a shower.

The man led me straight to the exit and out into the street, where I stood, oozing and smelly, like something that washed up after a storm.

He yanked the towel away and left me in sopping clothes.

I should've pressed charges. "This wasn't my fault. I have rights," I called after him. "I didn't realize England tolerated such rampant lawlessness. Is this the way you treat victims?"

People walking down the sidewalk altered their paths, veering away from me.

Luke grasped my arm and drew me against the building so we didn't block the way. "Al, why don't you go find Pilgrim a dry shirt?"

"Aw, that's sweet. Thank you." I opened my arms and stepped toward him like I planned to hug him.

He grimaced, shrugged off his jacket, and started to drape it over my shoulders.

I shook my head. "No point in both of us being defiled by ducks."

Instead, I wrapped my arms around myself, shivering. The weather hadn't been too bad this trip, but the air felt colder when I was soaking wet.

On this pretty, flower-decorated boulevard in a quaint town, I looked and smelled like a sewage monster. My anger seeped out along with my body heat, replaced by a desire to crawl into a drain and hide. Possibly forever.

"I didn't get to drink the water," I said.

"It's disgusting anyway. Warm and full of minerals."

"Can't be more disgusting than what I did swallow. Hopefully, it counts that I drank something, even if it's not the water I was supposed to." I gagged again, then stared at the exit, watching for Peter. "Maybe it's good that he's hiding. I want to punch him when I see him."

"Have you ever punched someone?"

I shook my head. "Elbows and knees during corner kicks."

"I bet you were a hair puller."

I glared at him.

He grinned. "I'd be happy to punch him for you."

"Have *you* punched anyone?"

"Once. I was eight. I swore I'd never do it again, but I'm willing to make an exception."

"Thanks." I stepped closer, pretending to hug him again, and laughed at his grimace.

Al returned with an oversized University of Bath T-shirt. I tugged the shirt over my wet clothes, and we trudged to the hostel—my jeans chafing, hair dripping down my back and into my face, and shoes leaking green liquid.

In the community bathroom, I took the hottest shower ever, washed my hair three times, and rinsed my clothes, then draped them over the towel rack.

"If I die mysteriously," I said as I rejoined the others in the bedroom and pulled my wet hair into a ponytail, "tell them to test that water for killer germs."

"Here, take these." Al handed me her hiking boots—she'd returned to flats once we left Dartmoor—and I left my soaking tennis shoes to dry.

Luke sniffed me, because my day hadn't been embarrassing enough. "You smell better."

"That never happens to heroines in books. They get invited to balls by handsome gentlemen and attend symphonies. I think I'm cursed."

"Do you *want* to get invited to balls and attend symphonies?" Al asked.

"Good point. I'm trying not to think about tomorrow's task."

"Being with you is certainly an adventure," Luke said with a crooked half smile.

But did he like adventure?

I had an unfortunate tendency to end up in situations like this, so I'd grown used to the craziness, but having Luke around made me more aware of how I appeared to others. I wished I knew what he was thinking. Nothing to be done now except move on.

I took the map. "Let's eat dinner before the parasites get me. I hope I didn't have any open wounds."

My heart lurched. Open wounds. I didn't have cuts, did I? An elbow scraped on the stone? A hand sliced on the rock? The germs might not have time to kill me if I was bleeding. I was under strict orders to see a doctor immediately for any injury that drew blood.

No, I would've noticed the sting in the shower. I was okay. For now. I carefully released my breath so the others couldn't tell I'd been holding it.

The first location in the guide was a restaurant called Sally Lunn's, which served buns.

"I'm starving," I said. "Let's try that. It rhymes, which means it must be awesome."

"Your logic is, as always, impeccable," Al said.

Inside the restaurant, a hostess led us down an extremely narrow hallway and up a creaky flight of stairs into a room packed with tables. The sign on the door said JANE AUSTEN ROOM. That should win me points.

Luke pulled out my chair and steered me into it with a hand on my lower back, the contact jolting through my midsection, making my stomach heavy and jittery all at once.

"This is possibly the girliest place I've ever been," he said.

He didn't complain about the pots of tea, though. Those were British, not girly.

The restaurant was in an old house, and it sagged. I could see the ceiling and floor curving from where we sat. Totally not straight lines, like buildings should have.

Bath had far too many life-threatening situations for my taste.

"This place must've been here in Jane Austen's time." I added four sugar cubes to my tea.

"Earlier." Luke stole the sugar dish before I could reach for number five. "It's the oldest building in town, built in 1482."

"How do you know these things?"

He raised an eyebrow. "There was a sign over the door."

"Oh. Well, stop being so smart." I poked him, and his cheek dimpled.

A family at the next table distracted me with their glances.

"Do I have slime on my face?" I whispered.

Luke inspected me. "No, why?"

"Those people are staring. Can I help you?" I asked in a louder voice.

A girl a few years younger than me asked, "Are you the girl who jumped in the baths?"

"No, I am not."

Her face fell.

"I'm the girl who got *pushed* into the baths, thank you very much." I didn't mind owning it, but I at least wanted them to get the story right.

Her eyes widened. "Why would someone do that?"

Before I could stop myself, I straightened and faced her. "I'm Britt. I know, I know. I'm American, and the name is funny. You can laugh now." I paused for chuckles. "I'm visiting England with classmates, here to learn about classic books. One of those classmates is my nemesis, who waited until I was unsuspecting, and then . . . he struck."

After another short pause to let the statement sink in, I continued.

"It was a peaceful day at the Roman Baths. Green water bubbling under gray skies. Tourists enjoying the history and the architecture and the view. I, myself, was contemplating Jane Austen, who I'm sure you know spent time here and wrote about this place."

As I spoke, my spine straightened. I made eye contact with each person at the table, and my muscles relaxed. Their gazes fed me, added fuel to my words, which flowed without thought.

"As I strolled along the ancient stones, I sensed a presence. Lurking. Approaching. I tried to turn." I half looked over my shoulder. "But I was too slow. Someone bumped me. Hard. And I was soaring through the air." I motioned with my hands.

My listeners' eyes widened.

"There was no thought. No worry. Just a moment of weight-lessness, before I plunged into the foul water. The smell of sulfur. Of ducks. Of slime, green slime, which went down my throat, coated my hair, choked me." I shuddered.

"Tragically, my attacker escaped." I spread my hands and shrugged. "And I was blamed for his evil deeds, but don't worry. I don't hold your fine country responsible. However, if you visit the baths . . . only drink the approved water. The green stuff? One hundred percent do not recommend."

When I stopped, the room was silent. Apparently, my voice carried and everyone had been listening.

Laughter and applause erupted.

My philosophy of having others laugh with you instead of at you made the retelling far less embarrassing than living it had been. I grinned and waved, the attention washing away some of the morning's humiliation.

As the other tables returned to their meals, Al tried to hide a smile and an eye roll at the same time, but Luke chewed his lip and a line formed between his eyes.

"What?" I asked. "Was that totally ridiculous?"

"Of course not."

But he remained quiet and thoughtful as we ate open-faced sandwiches on soft rolls with soup and lots of tea. The tea was growing on me, as long as I had plenty of sugar.

What wasn't growing on me? The idea of tomorrow's challenge, which I could say with a good deal of certainty would not be nearly as fun as sword fighting.

After a cold breakfast at the hostel, we headed for my destination—the Assembly Rooms. The square stone building with columns faced a wide cobblestone street that would have offered a perfect driveway for carriages in Austen's time.

When I approached the doors, squaring my shoulders, they opened for me, revealing a man of around thirty in long black tails with tight breeches.

He bowed. "Greetings, Ms. Hanson. We have been most eager for your arrival."

I wished I could say the same. "Let's do this."

"It's a ball, not an execution," Luke murmured.

"Same difference."

Orchestra music played ahead as the man ushered me down a hall with polished wood floors. We turned left into a ballroom. High ceilings, pale blue walls, and a giant chandelier that probably cost enough to finance college registered in a heartbeat. My attention quickly shifted to the couples dancing. At least forty or fifty people twirled around the room in old-fashioned coats and gowns.

"You've got to be kidding me." I wasn't sure if I felt out of place in jeans or was extremely relieved no one had made me wear a dress.

Wait. I wasn't the only one not in costume—my classmates were here, too. As if I hadn't dreaded this enough. And I'd been the last one to arrive.

Amberlyn wore a cute, short sundress and a braid crown across the top of her head, leading to perfect waves. She looked ready for a party. Spence wore chinos and a short-sleeved collared shirt. Peter was the only one, like me, in a T-shirt, which made me wish I'd thought to put in some effort beyond choosing the least wrinkled top I could find.

The sight of Peter made yesterday's anger at the unplanned bath well inside me.

The gentleman bowed again. "May I have this dance?"

I eyed Luke. I'd rather dance with him.

His lips were pressed like he was trying not to laugh. "I cannot wait to see this."

"Oh, shut up. Why do you hate me, Jane Austen?" I accepted the guy's hand.

I had to do it. Might as well dive in. Was I supposed to act like an Austen lady, all demure and polite? Or be myself? How many ladies in her time pretended to be sweet and well-mannered to snag a guy when they'd rather be elsewhere?

As a new song started, the man led me to the dance floor. He bowed, so I pretended to curtsy, and we formed a circle with three other couples, including Spence. We joined hands and marched in a circle. That was easy enough. But then everyone split up, linking arms with their partner and twirling. Just when I realized what was happening, we changed partners, and a new man took my arm. Another swap, the next man wearing a red military coat.

If this was supposed to mimic a ball, these guys were far too old to be suitable husband material. Although, in Austen's time, eighteen was old enough to marry, and plenty of women married older men. I shuddered. I'd take the chicken costume and community college, please.

After I twirled with Spence, avoiding his eyes so we didn't

both start laughing, we separated again into individual couples, and I tried to follow along as my partner led. I was agile, light on my feet, fast—on the field. Here, I was a linebacker, barreling into people and stomping around.

Eventually, I realized if I pretended I had a soccer ball between my feet and let my partner keep hold of my hands and twirl my arms whenever I was supposed to, I could manage not to step on his shiny boots.

I shifted my attention to him. "Aren't we supposed to talk during dances? That's one reason Elizabeth didn't like Mr. Darcy. He was too quiet."

My partner smiled. His eyes were kind. "What would you like to talk about?"

"Shouldn't you have introduced yourself before asking me to dance?"

He spun me again. "Technically, I shouldn't have spoken to you at all until someone introduced us."

"Right. Because ladies couldn't be trusted to meet people on their own. Are you supposed to be in character, or can you tell me who you really are and who these people are and how you all learned to dance like this?"

"My name is Ben. I work in a shop nearby. We're students at a local Regency dance group. My girlfriend talked me into taking lessons. We were invited to help today."

"Trying to teach Americans how to dance?"

He twirled me again. "Precisely."

Now we were prancing. Skipping. Whatever. I was so not looking at Luke, or I might laugh. Or die of embarrassment.

Next came more group spinning. My knee was holding up, but I was getting dizzy. Oh, great. An individual couple entered the center, and the woman had a solo dance. A second couple copied them.

My heart pounded, and not from the exercise. I was definitely about to look like a giant idiot.

Spence and his partner took their turn. It was supremely unfair that women had to do all the work while he stood there, smirking.

When my time came, I tried to imitate the last lady as she wove in and out of the others. *Pretend you're dribbling around defenders. Pretend this is a field and you're going to score a goal.*

This was ridiculous. How long did these songs last anyway? This was the dance that never ended. No wonder getting trapped with Mr. Collins was such torture.

I rejoined Ben, and he was smiling. "Well done."

"No need to lie. I know Jane Austen is turning over in her grave."

He chuckled.

Oh, thank heaven. The music wound down. We paraded down the center, one couple at a time. Ben bowed, and I curtsied and fought the urge to wipe sweat off my face with my shirt.

"Thanks for not letting me fall on my face."

He smiled, and another, older man approached.

"May I have the next dance?" At least, I assumed that was what he asked. His thick accent made it hard to tell.

How many of these did I have to do? One had been more than enough.

I accepted his hand, and we began a dance with different steps, which seemed quite rude since I had finally caught on to the first one. Since I could barely understand him, I settled for asking my new partner questions and smiling and nodding at his answers.

Voices and scuffling from the group next to us made my steps falter. I glanced over in time to see Amberlyn and Spence collide. She glared at him and flipped her hair. The rest of the dancers stood in disarray. Spence smirked.

After one more new partner and new dance, the latest, a primary school teacher named Andrew, bowed and offered me an arm. "Would you care to sit and enjoy a game of cards?"

"The correct answer is yes, isn't it?"

His lips twitched. "I believe so."

Had to be better than dancing.

"Lead on."

He deposited me in a smaller room, its walls painted yellow, with tables scattered throughout. We stopped at one with two older people and Peter.

I barely stopped myself from asking Andrew if we could dance again.

"Good luck," he said.

I plopped into the empty seat and faced my companions. "This isn't Uno, is it? Go Fish, maybe? Spoons?"

Peter snorted, and not with humor.

"The game of the day is called *whist,* young lady," said an older man who reminded me of my grandfather.

I partnered with the older lady as they instructed us in suits and tricks. The game involved little strategy, no action, no bluffing.

I almost missed dancing.

Based on his furrowed brow, Peter to my right either really disliked his hand or wanted me to drown in the murky depths of the Roman Baths.

What did people talk about during cards? Probably not the Dodgers or the latest superhero movie. Peter shooting me glares made it hard to think, especially when the topic I most wanted to discuss was his stunt the day before. I had just enough restraint not to yell at him in front of strangers.

Time passed quickly as I asked the older people about their families, how often they played ancient card games, and how someone talked them into spending a day in the Assembly Rooms with American students.

"What about you?" the woman asked. "Off to uni?"

"I'm planning to start in the fall." Assuming I won this week . . .

Peter grunted.

"Very good. And you, young man?"

He didn't answer.

"No shame in not knowing," said the man.

Peter glanced at me, scowling. "Creative writing program," he mumbled. Then glared at me as if he expected a challenge.

Why would I judge that? He knew what he wanted to do, which was more than I could say.

"What's that like?" I asked.

He ignored me and played a card.

"Yes, I'd love to hear," said my partner. "That sounds fascinating."

Peter's shoulders tensed. He wouldn't answer me, but did he have enough manners not to ignore a sweet old lady?

"It's a six-month program, with time to write and classes and workshops and stuff."

I'd seen him with his journal but didn't realize he studied storytelling. Was he writing a novel? I had Spence emulating Charles Dickens. Now I was competing against a budding novelist, too. I definitely needed to step up my game.

"Fascinating," said the lady. "And your parents are supportive?"

He stared at his cards. "I get to try it. Then I might go to college after."

His subdued tone implied his parents weren't necessarily supportive and he'd rather not go to college afterward. But since he rarely showed enthusiasm for anything except tormenting me, I might've read him wrong.

"That's why you want to win . . . things?" I asked.

Peter rolled his eyes. "You should look up the word *subtlety* in a dictionary."

He fell silent, and the lady must have sensed his discomfort, so we continued playing without talking.

Since thinking about Peter's writing skills threatened to discourage me, I shifted my thoughts to Jane Austen. Did she like cards or dancing? Ms. Carmichael had said that Jane never married. So she came to these events, danced, played games, mingled, all the while crafting novels in her head full of sometimes-scathing social commentary. She never settled and never conformed.

Maybe she wasn't so bad after all.

After winning one game and losing one, the lady rose. "Ready for the next part, dear?" she asked me.

Surely it couldn't get worse than dancing.

When I stood, she linked her arm through mine as the man gestured to Peter. They escorted us to yet another room, this one bright and cheerful with columns on the ground and second floors. A large table contained a spread of tea and tiny sandwiches—unfortunately without bacon. Many of the dancers milled around, holding cups.

I would've preferred Gatorade after all the sweating. Hot tea hardly sounded refreshing, and by now I'd drunk enough to fill the Roman Baths. But Peter and I each accepted a cup—along with an envelope—from a server behind the table.

Peter started to move away.

"What's wrong with you?" I hissed.

He spun. "Excuse me?"

"Pushing me into the baths? Not cool, Finch. I could've been hurt."

"What are you talking about?"

I snorted. "Nice try. Yesterday. You. Me. Duck-defiled water."

He blinked. "I didn't push you."

"I saw you there."

"Of course I was there. It was part of the clue." He smirked. "You fell in?"

I started to cross my arms before remembering I was holding a cup of tea. "I didn't fall. I was pushed. Which you know, because you did it."

"It's not my fault you have terrible balance."

I was a competitive athlete. Or I had been. But still. My balance was great. "Whatever. Just stay away from me."

"Gladly."

He slunk straight for the door. I glared after him before lifting the tea to my lips, then made my way around the room, chatting with several people, thanking them for coming. They were more like the theater-student knights than the random strangers I'd recruited, but I appreciated them spending a day on such an unusual endeavor. I spotted Spence bolt as soon as he received an envelope. Amberlyn leaned against a wall, scribbling in her journal.

After talking to as many people as I could, I wandered toward the front doors and found Luke and Al waiting.

Luke's eyes twinkled.

I pointed at him, then Al. "If either of you says one word about the dancing, I will shove you into the next disgusting body of water I can find."

They gave me eerily similar fake-innocent faces that said I'd totally been a topic of conversation.

"I'm a proper Austen lady now. Let's see what's next."

We went outside, and I opened the new envelope.

Wizards and kings fill magical tales
Crafted by friends who dreamt here over flagons of ale.

Host a discussion of which they'd approve
To imagine new lands and receive your next clue.

A half second before I finished reading, Luke stiffened. The same tension overtook him when he mentioned his father—or the place he grew up.

In class, Ms. C had mentioned that C. S. Lewis and J. R. R. Tolkien used to meet at a pub to discuss books and help each other write stories. I didn't know they'd lived in Oxford, but Luke's reaction made Google unnecessary. I'd worry about the exact place later, though.

"Oxford it is," I said.

The slightest grunt came from his throat.

Doubt churned in my stomach. Maybe our time together was over.

"You don't . . . I mean, if you don't want to come . . . I know you have a life. You've been away for several days. I'm sure you have stuff to do in London. The kids need someone to read to them." I was rambling, but I didn't want him to feel forced into going somewhere he'd rather avoid.

He blinked, wiping any real emotion from his face, and fixed me with a stern look. "You can't abandon a quest before it's over, Pilgrim. I'm coming. If you still want me."

The tension drained from me, even though he was only prolonging the inevitable. "Yes, I want you. I mean, I want you to come. As long as you want to." *Stop talking, Britt.*

His face softened, and his eyes were bright. "Good. That's settled, then."

CHAPTER SIXTEEN

Since Luke seemed in no hurry to return to his hometown, I said, "Let's take the scenic route to the train station."

"This way, I think." He steered us down the street. "There's a park you'll like."

"I never understood the obsession with Jane Austen," I said as we walked. "Especially Mr. Darcy. Sure, the actors are hot and the accents are nice. But it's dumb how women had to find a rich husband, behave all the time, and not do anything interesting."

"Austen has many things to appreciate. Social commentary. Keen insight into human behavior. Humor."

"Wow, you like Jane Austen more than I do." I shoved his shoulder. "You're such a girl."

He stuck his nose up. "One does not have to be female to appreciate good writing."

"Uh-huh. I bet you wish you were a hero in one of her stories. Which girl would you pick? Lizzie? Emma? Jane?"

"I shall decline to answer that question."

Probably better that way. I didn't need to know if he preferred sweet, well-behaved girls with perfect manners. "I always sympathized with Lydia. Sure, she made terrible choices, but everyone admired her sisters, and she was the loud, annoying little sister. Like me. Maybe if they'd been nicer to her, she wouldn't have run away."

He spun and walked backward so he faced me. "Please don't tell me you like Wickham, though. You seem like too good a judge of character for that."

I scoffed. "Please."

I might not have paid a lot of attention to the story, but I was smart enough to spot a player.

We came to the edge of a park, with huge trees and expanses of grass. Luke led the way down a path.

"What do you look for in a hero?" he asked.

"I don't know, kindness. Compassion. Someone who listens."

Wait, what? Before this trip, I would've said someone adventurous and bold, spontaneous, funny. Had my injury changed me, or had Luke single-handedly altered my view of a suitable boyfriend? Because I'd described him perfectly.

"Well." I cleared my throat. "Whatever it is, I obviously haven't found it yet."

"No boyfriend?"

"Never had one."

He stopped next to a huge tree with leaves the size of my head. "Really?" When I nodded, unconcerned, he started walking again. "Your choice?"

"Pretty much. I went to school dances, a couple of dinners. I let one guy take me to a Lakers game, but he knew I was using him for free tickets. There's never been anyone I liked enough to get serious with."

I had lots of guy friends. We played pickup ball, watched sports, and ate pizza. But none had looked at me as a potential girlfriend, the way Luke seemed to. And the one or two who might've, who I could've truly cared about, well, I avoided them before it progressed that far. A thought struck me—surely Luke didn't have a girlfriend, right? Or he wouldn't be spending a week with me?

"What about you?" I tried not to reveal how much his answer mattered.

His lips twisted. "Believe it or not, literary knowledge isn't a big draw for girls."

"There's more to you than that, though. You're funny and smart and you read to kids."

"And the elderly." His eyes widened and his face turned pink, like he hadn't meant to let that slip.

"What?"

He cleared his throat and ducked his head. "I also volunteer at a center for old people. I read to them and help them write letters."

Could he be any more perfect? "There you go. You're patient, and clearly brave, because you've been with me for three whole days and haven't run away. You could be a Jane Austen hero."

He remained silent as the path leveled out and curved past stone monuments and a pavilion. Hopefully, my light tone didn't reveal my actual thoughts. The last thing I needed was for him to get ideas about us, considering we lived on different continents.

"You're more like Austen's heroines than you think," he finally said, and it wasn't at all what I expected. "They care about people. They speak their mind. They do what's right."

Uh-oh. Ms. Carmichael had said that love in Jane Austen's books started with appreciating someone's character. I liked Luke. Enjoyed spending time with him. Admired him. And he felt the same.

Those feelings were a long way from love. But still, this couldn't end well. We'd reached the point when I usually backed off, but Luke and I were stuck with each other for several days unless I told him to go home.

I should've told him to go home.

But I didn't want to.

"I think you have a higher opinion of me than you should." I sped up, hoping to leave the topic—and my complicated feelings—behind.

As the train approached Oxford late that afternoon, Luke grew quiet. He stared at his book without turning pages.

He'd lived here until recently. What happened to make returning so hard? Did it relate to the father stuff he kept avoiding? And what did it mean that he was willingly going because of me?

"So . . . should we have dinner at the pub?" I'd found the

name of the exact place while we traveled, before once more unsuccessfully trying to write in my journal. "Find a place to stay first? Walk around town?"

Luke spent a great deal of effort dragging his attention to me. "I can get us a place to stay."

His gaze wandered to his book again like he forgot we were having a conversation.

I cleared my throat. "Um, theoretically, or for, like, tonight?"

"Huh? Oh, right." He dashed off a text and returned to staring at the same page he'd been on for half an hour. His phone chimed. He glanced at it. "We're good. My friend Nick can put us up."

I nudged his shoulder gently. "Would you rather ignore me for the rest of the day or give me an idea of what's up?"

His shoulders lifted in an epic sigh. "I used to live here."

"Yeah, I kinda picked up on that."

"My dad lost his job five months ago. We moved to London. That's it."

His flat tone said that was most assuredly not it, but I wanted to support him like he had me, and in the past he'd appreciated when I hadn't pushed. I left my shoulder brushing his.

When we got off the train, Luke took the lead. I followed, raising my eyebrows at Al. Concern filled her eyes, and she shrugged. Neither of us knew if he'd be okay.

Oxford wasn't as pretty as Bath—it didn't have the quaint feel, the flower baskets. But it felt grand. Old. Distinguished. Like simply walking its streets was making me smarter.

Soot darkened buildings with many colors of brick. Square

courtyards hid green lawns. Elegant spires speared the sky. And, in a universal symbol of a college town, bikes were chained to every available space. I easily pictured Luke here.

Keeping his head down, shoulders hunched, Luke led us to a quiet side street lined with stone buildings. Near a door in the long wall, a guy our age was waiting, shorter than Luke, stocky but not fat.

He and Luke strode straight for each other and did one of those man hugs accompanied by slaps on the back.

"I'm glad you called." The guy ran a hand through his dark red hair so it stuck up at odd angles. "What are you doing here? I thought—"

"Nick, this is Britt, and you've met Alexis." Luke stepped toward us.

Apparently, Luke didn't want us to know what Nick thought.

"Hi." I waved.

Nick studied me with an intense gaze, like a judge deciding on a sentence. I returned the stare, my chin lifted.

He grinned. "Nice to meet you."

I must've passed inspection.

He nodded to Al. "Alexis."

"Nicholas."

"Would it kill you to act like you're happy to see anyone, ever?" I asked her.

Nick snorted. "Probably."

I liked him already.

Al raised an eyebrow. "Would you prefer I act American and run to greet him while screaming and hugging?"

"Yes, actually, I'd like to see that," I said.

"Get used to disappointment."

"Now she's quoting *The Princess Bride*. What is happening? Were you body-snatched?"

Laughing, Nick opened the tiny door. "This way."

When I stepped through, I entered another world. A brilliant green lawn, mowed in neat stripes, filled a large courtyard decorated with flowers and benches. A sidewalk ran around the outside of the lawn, next to the building. All four walls contained rows and rows of windows peering down on the grass.

Nick took us to a door in one corner and up three flights of stairs. Luke's gaze remained on his shoes. We didn't see anyone else. The hallway we ended at had doors along each side.

Nick swept his arm out. "Pick a room."

"They're empty?" I peeked in the nearest one, which contained a narrow bed, desk, dresser, and shelves on the walls. Basic dorm room. A pang shot through my chest. I'd stayed in one like this when I visited UCLA. And I'd planned on living in one soon. No matter how simple it was, I wanted this.

"No one stays here during summer term," Nick said. "But my dad works here, so he let me borrow a key."

"Cool. Thanks."

The room I'd opened overlooked the courtyard, which was nice enough, so I dropped my bag on the bed.

Luke set his backpack on the floor, dug through it, and handed me the sheets.

"I know, I know." I held them up. "I owe you."

"You do." He tried to smile as he zipped his backpack, but it wasn't convincing. He entered the room across the hall.

I dropped the sheets on the bed and checked my hair, which

was wild with frizzy curls, thanks to the impromptu bath and shower. I tried—unsuccessfully—to smooth it. Oh well. At this point, Luke had seen worse, and he hadn't run away screaming.

After several one-sentence texts to my mom, I probably owed her a real update. In my last check-in, I'd told her I was following Jane Austen, which she loved. I left out the bath, which she would not have loved, for the possible health implications.

Phrasing the message presented a challenge. I didn't want to straight-up lie about how the competition part of the trip was going.

I settled for: *Hey Mom, I'm in Oxford. Over halfway done. My knee is fine. England is great.*

Her reply came: *I hope you're having fun! Going to win that money so you can go to UCLA?*

I was definitely having fun. Winning the money, though . . . Glad she couldn't see my face, I replied, *Everything's good.*

She responded with a string of confetti emojis.

Yeah, that celebration might be premature.

I won't let you down, I typed.

You never could, sweetie.

She had to say that. She was my mother. But I wanted to make her proud, live up to Maya and Drew. Not be the family failure.

I'm off to my next task. Talk soon.

I clicked off the phone.

CHAPTER SEVENTEEN

I perched on the bare mattress in my room and stared, unseeing, out the window. *Win so I could go.* Did Mom think this competition was the only way I'd be able to attend UCLA? If I lost, too bad?

This was, to quote one of Drew's and my favorite movies, my only hope.

That meant figuring out the journal, but I'd focus on my immediate goal—host a literary discussion. I could do that.

I hoped.

Recalling my less-than-Austen-worthy ball outfit, I dug through my bag for a cute striped tank top. An evening at a pub seemed to call for more effort than I usually applied to clothes. Not that I wanted Luke to think I thought this was a date.

When I stepped into the hall, I spotted Nick and Luke in his room with the door cracked. They stood close and argued in hushed but intense voices. Nick waved his arms. Luke, as usual, was stone-still.

Luke shook his head and aimed for the door.

Pretending I hadn't seen them, I asked, "Ready to hit the pub?"

Nick exited behind Luke. "You don't seem like that sort of girl."

I opened my mouth, but Luke's laugh cut off my indignant reply. "She has to go to the Bird and Baby for a school project."

"I've not been there since . . ." Nick's gaze darted to Luke. "Never mind. I'm in. If you don't mind."

"Not at all." Friends often proved great sources of information about people. This could be fun. I knocked on Al's door, and we headed out.

"What did you call it?" I asked Luke as we walked. "I thought it was the Eagle and Child."

"Locals call it 'the Bird and Baby.'"

"So you can laugh at tourists who don't know?"

"Something like that."

Our route passed a huge, round building, sitting apart by itself surrounded by grass.

Luke paused. "That's Radcliffe Camera. It's a library with some of Tolkien's original manuscripts, and he said it resembled Sauron's tower."

The golden stone, columns, and dome on top hardly fit my idea of a dark lord's fortress, but it was a cool building.

We turned down a narrow street, and this time he stopped in front of a wooden door.

"Some people think this passage inspired Lewis to create Narnia. See the lion? And the fauns?"

In the center of the door, a carved lion's head regarded us, and on either side, two golden fauns flanked the doorway.

"And there"—Luke pointed ahead—"the lamppost indicating the wardrobe passage was near."

The lamppost did appear decades old. I didn't know enough about Narnia to confirm. Luke's voice sounded strained. Though it was costing him, he wanted to help me appreciate his city. When Nick continued on, I grabbed Luke's hand, squeezed, and smiled. His fingers tightened around mine as a tiny smile appeared on his lips. He kept hold for a few steps, like I offered a lifeline, before releasing my hand when we turned a corner. My fingers trailed after his like they weren't ready to let go.

The pub was unassuming, on a busy street in the British version of a strip mall. Old English letters spelled out the name across off-white stucco. A stand-up board on the sidewalk advertised fine brews. How long ago had Lewis and Tolkien lived here? Sixty years? Seventy? I bet everything had stayed exactly the same since.

The interior was dark and tight, but in a cozy way. A hallway led all the way to the rear, with little rooms off the sides, humming with voices. Pictures and quotes from Lewis and Tolkien decorated the wood walls. Scents of cooked meat and fried things elicited a rumble of hunger from my stomach.

It reminded me of the Dickens place in London. Apparently, to be a brilliant British writer, you needed a pub lair. I easily pictured two genius writers coming up with ideas in this place. I could write a masterpiece myself while sitting in here.

Okay, that was too optimistic.

We ordered at the counter and sat in the main room, which was brighter thanks to a ceiling of windows offering natural light. Luke sank into the corner seat, eyeing the door, shoulders tense. Al settled at her own table with a pint.

"I'm driving her to drinking," I whispered loudly.

Her lips curved slightly as she took a sip and pulled out her book.

A college-aged guy in distressed jeans and a T-shirt with a deep V-neck slid into the seat across from her, clutching his own glass.

She looked up slowly, raised an eyebrow.

"I hate to see a pretty girl drinking alone."

I blinked. Was he . . . hitting on Al?

Tonight, she wore a subtly patterned flowered skirt and short-sleeved blouse, more casual than her usual outfits. She easily passed for a college student. Looked at home here.

But. It was Al.

"Then don't look at me while I continue reading my book." Her half smile made the words politer than they could have sounded.

Luke chuckled quietly.

The guy shrugged and stood, returned to the bar, and joined a friend. Al went back to reading.

Picturing Al with a dating life was like glimpsing a parallel universe.

Okay. Focus. I was supposed to host a discussion worthy of the Inklings, the literary group Lewis and Tolkien were part of. Did it count with only two other people? I eyed the tables nearby. Recruiting strangers had worked well in Glastonbury.

But how to start? I looked at Luke.

He shrugged. "No help, remember?"

A drawing from *The Hobbit* hung on the wall, showing mountains, a lake, and trees, with a dragon in the sky. I had an idea.

I stood, cleared my throat, and ignored Luke's sigh that said he knew I was preparing to do something embarrassing, and Al burying her head in a book, pretending she didn't know me.

"I need opinions, people," I said loud enough for everyone in the room to hear. "I'm taking a poll. Would you rather visit Narnia or Middle Earth?"

Luke smiled. "Good one."

"Interesting question." Nick folded his hands and leaned forward as if we were in class. "Does this have to be during the time the books are set or anytime?"

"Books," I said, even though I hadn't read the Narnia books.

One old man in the corner turned away, muttering. Probably something about American tourists disturbing his pint. He should join Al, and they could be hermits together.

But a group of young people nearby shifted toward us.

"Is this for school?" one asked.

"Who cares?" said another. "Narnia, for sure."

"It depends on which book," Luke said, seeming to relax the longer we were here. "And where or who you were. Middle Earth wouldn't be so bad if you lived in Hobbiton or Rivendell during the events of *The Hobbit*. But if you were a human during the trilogy, not so fun."

"But you'd have a chance to do grand things and be a hero." Nick puffed out his chest like he was prepared to fight goblins on the spot.

Luke shook his head. "That's overrated."

I shoved his arm. "You're such a hobbit."

Nick hooted. "He totally is."

"I would live in Hobbiton," said one of the young people nearby. "They have the best ale and pipe weed."

"Nah," said the friend who'd spoken first. "I'd sail on the *Dawn Treader.*"

"Better than *The Lion, the Witch, and the Wardrobe,*" Luke said.

"Talking animals!" Nick threw his hands up.

"Turned to stone in perpetual winter." Luke grimaced. "No thanks. During later books when there's peace, Narnia would be brilliant."

"Exactly," said the *Dawn Treader* guy.

Their table continued the discussion, and I tried to listen to them while also eavesdropping on Nick and Luke's quiet talk.

"Speaking of boats, have you been on the water since you left?" Nick asked.

Luke shook his head.

"You sail?" I asked him as our neighbors discussed mythical beasts and magic portals.

"Punting," Nick said as the waiter brought our food, complete with a bottle of ketchup.

I glanced between the two of them. "What does kicking a ball have to do with water?"

"Punting is boating." Luke stole the ketchup and placed it out of my reach. "Small, flat boats on the river."

"How long are you staying?" Nick asked. "We could go tomorrow morning."

Luke didn't reply, but I read the longing on his face.

"We could make time," I said. "Get up early."

His eyes smiled at me. "Britt's turn," he said. "It's your discussion, so you have to participate. Middle Earth or Narnia?"

I reached for the bottle, and Luke blocked my arm, his grin emerging more easily. I made a face at him. Next to us, the people were mentioning names that sounded familiar from the *Lord of the Rings* movies, but half of what they were saying was like a foreign language.

"Can I vote for Hogwarts?" I asked.

Nick laughed.

Luke carefully poured ketchup on my plate for me. "That's blasphemy in this pub."

"But ghosts and moving armor and magic lessons! In a castle!"

Luke fake-scowled at me. "No."

I sighed dramatically. "Fine. Middle Earth."

"Good choice," Nick said. "Why?"

"Hot elves," I said. "And 'cause I've never read the Narnia books."

Nick laughed again and shoveled fries into his mouth like the earth might run out of potatoes tonight.

Luke clapped a hand to his forehead. "I am sadly disappointed in the American education system."

"It's my fault. I never liked to read." I felt the need to explain myself to Nick so he didn't wonder why his intelligent friend hung out with someone who'd choose Orlando Bloom over literary classics. "I preferred to be outside playing. But I do recognize how smart Lewis and Tolkien were, to create whole worlds in their imaginations. I couldn't do that. Let alone write as many books as they did. I can't even finish a simple journal."

"You could make up a language and write in that," Luke suggested. "Say it's Elvish."

"It might be the angle I need to set myself apart. Too bad it would never convince Ms. Carmichael."

Nick squinted at me. "What's this about?"

I explained the basics of my trip, the assignment, and the quest, leaving out the cash prize.

"You're going with her?" Nick turned a serious face toward Luke, who nodded. Nick frowned like he wanted to ask more but didn't.

I recounted our adventures.

Nick was grinning by the time I finished. "That's brilliant. Are you going to write about me? Will you make me taller?"

He ran a hand through his hair again, adding an inch in hair height.

"Considering my writing is pretty terrible, you might prefer if I left you out."

"Big surprise," a familiar voice said.

Amberlyn. Fantastic. My ears found her American accent loud and grating after days with British companions. Of course, that might've been the owner's fault.

Could this day get any better?

She swept toward us. "Who are your friends?"

"Nicholas Davies, at your service." Nick stood and pulled out an empty chair. He waited until she sat before taking his seat again.

Her white jeans, ruffled shirt, ankle boots, and gold jewelry were perfectly suited for a night out in a college town. Despite my cute shirt, my jeans were faded, and I was still wearing Al's hiking boots.

Amberlyn's white pants were asking for another ketchup "mishap," but Luke would never believe it was an accident if it happened again.

"Amberlyn Hartsfield." She let Nick take her hand, and I thought he might kiss it.

Luke studied her but without the awe Nick did. His gaze met mine. I must've been scowling, because he raised his eyebrows as if to ask if I was okay.

I made a face before asking Amberlyn, "Having a good time?"

"That hardly matters." She opened a menu. She didn't plan to join us, did she? "We're here to win."

"Winning is fun. And you're allowed to enjoy the trip. Ms. C won't pick a winner based on who's most miserable."

"She won't pick you anyway, so I don't know why you care."

Gritting my teeth, I tried to keep my voice light. "Why do you want to win? Still intend to start that event planning business?"

She blinked. "You remember that?"

"Hard to forget the way you planned weddings for your Barbies and critiqued every class party and took over that engagement party for your aunt and she got so mad." I chuckled.

"Hmm. Well." I couldn't read the expression on her face. "Yes, that is exactly why I plan to win. Congratulations on knowing me so well."

I blinked at the sharp tone.

She flipped her shiny blond hair and turned to the boys. "Are you guys fans of Tolkien? Personally, I'm so impressed with the world he created. Languages, history, everything."

It seemed unfair to steal my friends for her quest. Not that my literary discussion had been impressively deep. I hoped I'd done enough for it to count.

Nick scooted his chair closer. His face glowed like he thought he was in the presence of an elf queen. Too bad he didn't know she was a queen of darkness. "Several dialects of Elvish alone. Did you read Elven Realms? They have nearly the same level of detail."

"I prefer true classics," Amberlyn said.

From her table nearby, Al snorted.

"I read *The Lord of the Rings* when I was eleven," Amberlyn continued. "The Dark Riders scared me so badly. I tried to get Britt to read them, but she isn't into that kind of thing."

That's right. Dumb Britt who hated to read. "Insulting my IQ doesn't make yours any higher."

"How are you enjoying our country? I hope you feel at home." Nick's expression said he'd be willing to make that happen if she answered no.

"It's marvelous," she said, because *marvelous* was a word American teenagers used.

I rolled my eyes.

"I've visited so many fascinating places." She closed the menu and pushed it away. "The Dickens Museum was so interesting. It was like stepping back in time."

"Museum?" The word slipped out before I could tell it to stay in my head.

"And we visited Jane's house in Bath."

"I didn't realize you two were on a first-name basis."

Had she added those because she was a textbook over-achiever? Would that impress Ms. Carmichael? Should I start cramming in more side trips?

Oblivious to my thoughts, Amberlyn plunged on. "I hurried here from Bath so we could take a walking tour and visit the Bod."

I snorted. "Is that a wrestler?"

"It's a library," Nick said.

"The most amazing library ever," Amberlyn said.

I choked on my drink.

Luke patted my back gently, like he was reassuring me, not clearing my airways.

Nick glanced at me. "Your trip sounds much different than Britt's."

Uh-oh. Did he plan to repeat my embarrassing stories?

"What did you like most?" Luke cut in, shooting me a sympathetic grimace.

She rambled on, but I tuned her out until I heard the word *themes*.

She and Nick were discussing themes of Tolkien, but she finished with, "I'm tying all my stories to the themes of the books. I need additional opinions."

She rose and confidently marched to the next table. "Have you read *The Lord of the Rings*? What do you think the primary themes are?"

It sounded less like discussion and more like interrogation.

My mind fixed on her comment about her stories. That was a good angle. Luke and I had discussed some of the themes. Ms. C would love to know I was contemplating them and trying to learn at each stop. But now I couldn't use that without seeming like I was copying Amberlyn.

Amberlyn questioned multiple tables and even the guy at the bar. Luke watched her with narrowed eyes. He'd retreated into silence again. When she rejoined us, she said something that made Nick laugh.

Why wouldn't Nick like her, though? She was attractive, stylish, and obviously into the whole college-scene-sit-around-and-talk-about-smart-people stuff. I was the girl who guys called when they needed another player for a basketball game, or they planned to do something crazy and wanted me to participate and bring female friends to witness their coolness. Amberlyn was the one they flirted with, the one they tried to impress, the one they dated.

Even worse, she was the type who won literary competitions.

"Aren't pubs supposed to be big on darts?" I jumped to my feet. "Let's play."

"Sure," Luke said. "There's a board in back. Come on, Nick."

I understood the best-friend tone that meant *You better do what I say or else,* even though it had been years since Amberlyn would've listened to me the way Nick did to Luke.

"Ugh," Amberlyn said. But since Nick and Luke stood, she followed, too.

The faded dartboard hung on a wooden wall. I yanked out the darts, rolled the metal grip between my fingers, tested the weight.

This was more like it. A game with a clear winner. Simple and straightforward. Where I could throw sharp objects with great force.

Amberlyn crossed her arms and leaned against the wall.

"C'mon, Am." I shook the darts in my hand. "You're at a pub in England. I bet Lewis and Tolkien played darts when they needed a break from being smart."

I winked at Luke.

"They loved darts," Luke said with a straight face. "They said it helped inspire their imaginations."

I hid a smile. "See? It's completing your experience."

I held the darts out.

"Fine." She flipped her hair and grabbed them like she didn't care, but the gleam in her eyes said she wanted to do well. She adjusted her feet, watched Nick's stance, and copied his movement.

Instead of the second ring, where his dart hit, hers bounced off the wall.

"Oi," a guy called from behind the bar. "Don't be putting holes in my wall."

I snorted. Loudly.

She glared at me and tried again. The second one pinged off the metal surrounding the board and clattered to the ground.

"Getting closer," I said.

She grunted. "This game is stupid."

"You say that about anything you're not good at."

"So do you."

Fair point. "Don't swing your arm so much. This isn't baseball."

Her last one stuck in the edge. She marched up, yanked it

out, and picked the others off the floor. She shoved them at me. "This is pointless. It's how simple people fill their time when they have nothing intelligent to talk about."

She'd meant to insult me, but I grinned like I did the rare times I found something I was better at than she was. "Go talk to intelligent people, then. If you're afraid to lose."

We kept score, and it came down to Nick and me. My efforts were aided by imagining the dartboard was Amberlyn's face.

"You're going down, Red." I rolled the darts between my palms.

"Ginger," Luke said.

"What?"

"Ginger is what we call people with red hair." Luke had his hands in his pockets, leaning casually against the wall, but a devious glint lit his eyes. "And he hates it."

I waited until Nick lifted his arm.

"C'mon, Ginger, show me what you've got," I called.

His next shot barely hit the board. He scowled at Luke, who grinned and winked at me. My stomach fluttered. I shook my head to regain focus.

My final dart landed in one of the double rings to put me ahead by four points. I threw my arms up. "Woo-hoo."

Luke raised a hand for a high five, but instead of slapping mine, pressed his palm to mine and left it for two heartbeats. I hid a shiver.

Nick bowed to me. "Well played." To Luke, he muttered, "Thanks for nothing."

Amberlyn remained the only one not smiling. "Well, it's been lovely, but I need to go."

"We'll walk you out," Nick said.

"Hey, you. The girl with good aim." The bartender waved me over.

"You guys go on."

Nick, Amberlyn, and Al left as I approached the bar, but Luke remained with me.

"Got something for you." The bartender handed me an envelope. Amberlyn must've received hers already when she interrogated the guy about his opinions on elves.

"Is this because I led a rousing literary talk?" I asked. "Or because I didn't add to the holes in the wall?"

He rolled his eyes and smiled.

"Thanks."

Luke watched as I opened it.

An ambitious Scot called this castle his home.
You'll have double the trouble if there you don't roam.

Find your way through the twists and the turns;
In the center arrive, and a clue you will earn.

Ooh, a castle. In Scotland. Excellent. Too bad it didn't mean Hogwarts.

I should have recognized what sounded like a quote. My first few searches of "classic literature set in Scotland" gave me novels I'd never heard of. Finally, I stumbled on *Macbeth*, which wasn't a novel but a play, and that was an extremely unfair trick. Especially since Luke was probably lamenting my ignorance of the greatest playwright of all time.

The map search results loaded. Not only was Macbeth's

castle in Scotland, but it was all the way at the top of the entire island.

"Where are we off to next?" Luke asked.

"Cawdor Castle."

He nodded. "Macbeth."

I shoved him gently. "Show-off."

He opened his mouth like he planned to speak but shook his head and remained silent.

I scanned the map. "How long will that take? I guess there's a train."

"Might have to change in Edinburgh."

"Ooh, let's stop there."

His eyes crinkled. "Whatever you want, Pilgrim."

We turned to leave as someone new entered the pub.

Peter.

He paused right inside the door. No scowl marred his face. His eyes were wide. He looked . . . awed. Impressed. Like he was having a moment. He lifted a hand toward a plaque on the wall but didn't touch it.

If he liked to write, and I knew he read science fiction and fantasy, it made sense that this was his type of place. I would've been curious to stay and watch him try to talk to strangers.

When he moved from the door, his gaze found mine. His eyes narrowed, his face wiped clean of any emotion that might have made me sympathetic.

I grabbed Luke's hand and pulled him with me, and we passed Peter and joined the others on the street.

Once we were out the door, I wanted to keep Luke's hand,

but I didn't want the others to see, so I released it and shoved my hands into my pockets.

"So," Nick said. "Punting tomorrow?"

"You bet," I said. If we were splitting up the trip anyway, we could delay long enough for that, especially since I sensed how badly Luke wanted to go.

"Would you care to join us?" Nick asked Amberlyn. "You can't visit Oxford without going punting."

"I shouldn't waste time. I have a competition to win, and boating is not on the agenda."

Of course she knew what punting was.

"I bet Lewis and Tolkien loved to punt." I gave Luke a pointed look.

"Absolutely," he deadpanned. "Every morning before pints."

"Really?" Amberlyn asked.

Luke nodded solemnly. When Amberlyn faced Nick, Luke grimaced and shook his head.

I coughed to cover my laugh.

"I suppose I could go," she said. "If it doesn't take long."

"We'll start early," Luke said.

"Fine."

After Nick gave them the details for the morning, Amberlyn and her chaperone, Priya, left. Nick stared after them before turning to us.

"I'm glad you came, mate." He and Luke hug-slapped again, he hugged me, and he headed off, too.

We strolled to the dorms, passing a field where people were playing pickup soccer.

My feet slowed.

Luke stopped a couple of steps later and turned to face me. I sensed his gaze on me while I watched the game. These guys had skills. I could hang with them. It would be more serious than with kids, though. They might've been playing pickup, but they were playing to win. Like I did. And that kind of game spelled danger.

Still, I edged closer, drawn by a magnetic pull.

Al cleared her throat.

That small noise worked like a bucket of ice water over my head. I made myself move away, striding past them, not looking back.

When would I be able to watch a game without this miserable, twisting, yearning, bubbling pain inside me? Pain that, in a way, I welcomed because it meant I was close to what I'd had before, even if I could never hold it again.

CHAPTER EIGHTEEN

"Wait here," Luke said once we stood alone in the quiet dorm hall, after Al told us good night.

"Um, okay."

He vanished into his room and returned holding something behind him. "Come on."

He took my hand and led me downstairs without letting go.

Like the rest of him, his grip was steady, reassuring, and slightly terrifying all at once. I'd never considered how fast I walked, or that I tended to gallop down stairs like an avalanche picking up speed, until I tried to pace myself to someone else. But we fell into a rhythm and exited into the quad, our linked hands swinging between us.

Silence blanketed the courtyard, an occasional car or bike bell sounding distant and muffled. Luke guided us to the grass, and we sat near a golden light casting a glow over the stones.

"What are we doing?"

"You said you've never read *The Lion, the Witch, and the Wardrobe*." He produced a small book and slid his hand free of mine, fingers trailing along my palm as he let go. "I'm supplementing your education."

Tingles darted up my hand and into my arm, leaving my fingers cold in the absence of Luke's.

He started to read in that smooth voice, keeping his volume low and intimate. I lay on my back, the grass cool through my shirt, my attention locked on his face. Though his body remained still, his expressions fluctuated with the ups and downs of the story. He swept me away to an old manor house in the English countryside and the wintry landscape of Narnia, made talking animals come alive. His skill in reading and his obvious enjoyment reminded me of the day we'd met, offering me a peek inside his heart.

I didn't know how long he read until he cleared his throat, sounding hoarse, after a chapter ended.

I sat up. "It's *pretty* good, I guess." I smiled so he'd know I was joking. "Thank you. You can take a break now and finish tomorrow on the train."

He closed the book and set it aside before returning the gaze with a faint dimple in his cheek. "Yes, mum."

We studied each other. Luke chewed his lip and lay the way I had been. I lay next to him, not quite touching, both of us on our backs looking at the sky.

Luke cleared his throat softly. "Those people playing football . . . There's more to the story than surgery, isn't there?"

I didn't want to tell him. And yet I did. Constantly avoiding the issue because I feared it had grown exhausting. I rolled my head sideways to study Luke. He stared back without moving, his open expression welcoming me to share.

"Yeah. There's more." I turned my head to the sky again. My foot jiggled. I forced it to stop. Plucked a few pieces of grass. I closed my eyes. I could say it. Needed to say it.

"You don't have to tell me." His voice was kind, gentle. "But not telling me won't make it go away."

He was right. I'd been ignoring the issue like my siblings used to ignore me—hoping if they did it long enough, I'd stop bothering them. I never did. And my problem wouldn't either.

I was suddenly breathless, like I'd sprinted up and down stadium stairs, my muscles shaky. Icy fingers clawed at my throat. *Say it.* Just blurt out the words.

"I can't play soccer again." I opened my eyes and met his look directly. "I can never play again. There. I said it."

All breath left me, leaving my chest emptied out, a chasm inside. But as I made myself suck in air, a giant weight lifted. Pressure I hadn't realized was squeezing my insides for the last few months eased.

Luke's eyes went wide. "What . . . wow. Why? What happened? Your knee?"

My gaze shifted to trace the outline of the building. Old stones that had stood for centuries, protecting this secret courtyard, standing firm. They could handle my words, protect them, too, and remain upright.

"I tore my ACL during a game. It was no big deal. I mean, I had surgery, but it was standard. Plenty of athletes come back from that, so I was nervous, but . . . determined, I guess. Afterward, though . . ."

Now came the part I'd been avoiding. The secret. Those fingers returned to grip my chest with ice.

Luke waited, silent, patient as always.

"After surgery, I got two blood clots. They ran tests. Turns out I have this genetic condition that makes you prone to clotting."

The emotions of that day flooded back. Confusion over how I'd lived eighteen years without knowing, with no signs. Anger mixed with fear, because unlike the ACL, this wasn't something I could fight head-on. No amount of PT and hard work would fix it.

I cleared my throat. "Now I have to take medicine that thins my blood. For the rest of my life. It means I can't play competitive sports. I can't risk scrapes or bruises or anything to make me bleed. Casual stuff is fine if I'm careful—jogging, hiking. But nothing high-contact."

When I'd received the news, it had taken several minutes for my brain to comprehend it. Soccer didn't involve contact like football or hockey. But there was lots of bumping, cleats that could cut. Over the years, I'd had countless grass burns, bruises, scrapes.

As the truth sank in, I'd watched the doctor realize I was understanding him. The sympathy on his face, him searching for a Kleenex, except I'd refused to cry. Clenched my jaw tight and stared at the wall and then walked out in silence beside my mom and shoved the truth so deep, I'd hoped it would vanish into the depths.

It had taken on life down there, like a trapped beast, ugly, full of sharp angles and vicious claws. And yet, opening the door hadn't released the terror I'd expected. Instead, it felt like freeing something dark from my soul. Avoiding it for so long had made it feel bigger and scarier than it was, but the only power the truth had was what I'd given it. Putting it into words confined it, made it smaller.

"The worst part . . ."

Luke waited.

I destroyed more grass. "I had a scholarship. To play for UCLA." I let the grass pieces flutter to the ground. "That was my dream growing up. It's nearby, and one of the best soccer schools in America. Several US national team players went there. I led my high school team to a state championship two years in a row, and I got invited to try out for the US Under-19 team, and I earned the scholarship. Everything was perfect. But now . . ."

I dug my fingernails into my palms. Sharing the truth of the past might have helped, but the future was an entirely different beast, waiting ahead. Still to be dealt with.

"That's why this contest means so much?" Luke spoke carefully, gently.

"I'll get to keep my partial scholarship this year, but I won't get more money once they find out I can't play. I don't even know what I planned to study. Soccer was all that mattered. My grades are okay, but not good enough for a scholarship. My siblings are in grad school, got great grades. Mom constantly reminded us we had to go to college, make something of ourselves. Now if I fail this . . ."

Luke grasped my hand. "Thank you for telling me. For trusting me. And I'm so sorry."

I dreaded how he might look at me now. But nothing had changed in his face, in those open, caring eyes.

I studied his strong, solid fingers wrapped around mine. The simple contact sent waves of assurance through me, along with something lighter, shivers of happiness.

"It sucks, but I can't change it. So, I'm here to move on."

"I believe you will move on, but it's okay not to be okay." He squeezed my hand. "To be disappointed or angry or to grieve. Same as if you'd lost a person. Because you lost something important, too."

I'm afraid. But I couldn't admit that. "That's the first time I've said it. My team, my friends, they don't know. I found out a few weeks before Ms. Carmichael invited me here, and my knee gave me an excuse not to play. I guess I hoped if I didn't tell anyone, it wouldn't be real. Or if I won this, at least everyone wouldn't feel sorry for me."

His thumb made circles on the back of my hand, slow, like he didn't realize it was moving. "Do you still want to go to UCLA? If you can't . . . you know."

I shifted my gaze to the building again, its strength and endurance. "I did love it. It's the only place I ever wanted to go, but not because of school. Would it help to have part of my dream? Or would it make it harder that I'm on campus and I can't play? I don't know."

His fingers further tightened on mine. "Oh man. I didn't help, did I? Those Would You Rather questions. Asking if you believed in destiny. I'm sorry."

"It's not your fault. I have to face it eventually. I was just hoping to put it off longer. This stupid competition, though . . ." My laugh sounded strangled. I pulled my hand from his. "She did warn us that travel forces you to learn about yourself. I knew that sounded terrible."

We sat in silence. I'd trusted him, said the words. The world hadn't ended. Luke wasn't treating me any differently. The silence felt softer.

"What's the story of you and that girl?" His voice sounded deeper than usual.

His pretending to forget her name sent a warm surge through my heart. "We used to be best friends. In junior high, she decided I wasn't smart enough for her, and she ditched me. Sometimes she forgets she's a brat and is accidentally nice. But usually it's more like tonight."

"Her loss," he said.

Hers, but mine too. Not that I wanted to hang out with the Amberlyn of today. But I missed the old one, who baked cookies and painted stripes on her nails and laughed at my jokes instead of at me.

Luke gathered my hair that had spread across the grass and tucked it behind my shoulder. I went still.

His fingers brushed my neck before he put his hands behind his head. "Did you know Lewis and Tolkien had a falling-out? Despite having such similar opinions on writing and stories and life?"

"Did one of them decide the other was dumb and use inside knowledge to ridicule the other?"

"Not exactly. There wasn't one particular issue, but they had

221

theological disagreements, differences in opinion on the direction of their writings. They drifted apart."

"That's sad."

If there wasn't hope for brilliant men with an epic friendship, no wonder Amberlyn and I didn't last. I appreciated the shift to a normal subject. I'd dropped a giant truth bomb and he'd listened, respected my pain, accepted it, and continued to treat me the same as before. My chest threatened to burst with gratitude.

"Sometimes people aren't who you thought they were." Luke's expression darkened, and I didn't think he meant Lewis and Tolkien.

So many questions lurked at the surface of my mind. I settled for one I didn't think would scare him. "Nick's cool. You guys been friends long?"

"Since we were kids."

It was a sad contrast after telling him about Amberlyn. I hadn't been close to anyone since her. Hadn't had my own Nick. Hadn't shared as much with anyone until meeting Luke.

"You know." Luke's voice caught, and he cleared his throat. "You know how Nick's dad works here?"

"Yeah. What does he do?"

"He's a professor. That's how I met Nick. My dad used to work here, too. Until last semester."

That explained Luke's intelligence, love for learning, and skill at teaching. "What did he teach?"

"Literature. Right up there." He lifted his hand to point, and I followed the line of his arm to a top corner where two sides of the square met.

And that explained his extensive book knowledge. "You said he lost his job, though?"

"He was fired." His words came out tight.

I had a million questions, but it felt like Luke planned to keep talking, so I didn't ask them. I wanted to take his hand but held my breath as if the sound of breathing or any movement might make him stop. He'd listened to me, been patient. I wanted to do the same for him.

"He was fixing grades for money. He'd been doing it for two years, and they finally caught on."

Wow. Not what I'd expected. In college situations, especially somewhere as old and distinguished as this, that had to be a huge scandal.

"I'm sorry." I turned my head sideways to watch him more closely. "What's he doing now?"

He faced the sky, expression blank. "Private tutoring. He's trying to get hired at a secondary school in London. Like a public high school. So far, the only places that will talk to him are academy schools, in the estates. Inner city, rough economic areas."

I tried and failed to picture Luke leaving the grand streets of Oxford to live in a tiny London flat. "So you had to leave your school and everything?"

"I attended a sixth form school here. It was my final year. But Dad didn't have the money for me to stay. So now I'm a Londoner."

I stretched my fingers out to link my pinkie finger around his. "I'm sorry."

The words themselves felt weak, and I put as much feeling into them as I could. From him, they'd been enough, since I knew he cared. I hoped mine would be, too.

He crooked his pinkie more tightly, then released it and twined the rest of his fingers through mine. My heart thrummed to an unheard rhythm.

"That's not the worst part." Luke wouldn't look at me. "I was set to come here in the fall. Study literature. Eventually teach, like him. But now . . ."

"They won't let you?" I started to sit up. "That's totally unfair."

He tugged on my hand. "They'd let me. But would you want to attend university where everyone knew your dad and what he'd done?"

I relaxed onto the grass again. "No, I guess not."

Our thumbs slowly circled each other as the cool silence wrapped us up.

"What are you going to do?" I asked quietly.

He turned toward me. I shifted, too, so we lay on our sides, faces inches apart, hands clasped between us. Light glinted off his glasses. I wiggled until I could see his eyes.

"Nick's worried for me. You asked why I came with you, and I said I needed to get away. I just finished A-Levels, which are important exams we take to officially get into university. My dad had been riding me about them. But all I could think was, what right does he have to tell me that when he cheated? When I finished, I planned to get a job this summer, and my dad hounded me about that, too. I needed a break from him. So I ran away."

I knew that feeling, the weight of decisions and stress and life pressing in. "It's like you're on a quest, too."

"I guess it is, Pilgrim."

He fell silent and tugged my hand so I inched closer. He lifted his other hand and ran the side of his finger down my cheek. His breath tickled my face.

Mine caught in my throat. "Are you finding what you're looking for?"

"Better," he said. "I found something I wasn't looking for."

He closed the distance between us, bringing his face closer and closer to mine. Our eyes locked. Mine fluttered closed. He hesitated inches away. Time suspended.

And reality flooded in.

I jerked to a sitting position.

What was I thinking? I had less than a week in England. Anything beyond basic friendship was pointless. Kissing him would definitely cross that line—and make it harder to say goodbye.

I withdrew my hand from his and stood. "We should get to bed. Separately, I mean. Not, like, together." *Way to make it worse, Britt.* "I'm tired. That's all."

Luke was a silent ghost by my side, up the stairs, to our rooms. I couldn't read his face—uncomfortable, disappointed, mad? I hesitated at my door long enough to give him a chance to speak but still almost missed his quiet "Sleep well."

CHAPTER NINETEEN

Last night replayed in my mind as Luke, Al, and I walked to the river to meet Nick in predawn light. Luke and I had shared our deepest secrets. Something like that created a bond, but ours was one formed in darkness. How would it affect us in the light? Especially given the awkward way it ended after I ran away.

Luke's expression remained calm, and I tried not to let him catch me watching him. What was he thinking? I hoped he didn't feel I'd rejected him. Although, really, I had. I'd wanted nothing more than to let his lips meet mine, but if I did, I'd get more attached than I already was. Had I made things weird between us?

The back of my brain couldn't help but wonder what it would've been like if I'd let him.

Maybe if I pretended nothing had happened, he would, too.

I certainly didn't plan to bring up the health stuff again. That would stay in the dark. Though the free feeling from last night lingered.

When we arrived, Luke wandered to the water's edge and Nick drew me aside. "I'm glad you're making him do this. He's had a rough year."

I nailed him with a look. "But yesterday you thought he shouldn't be doing it?"

Nick flinched. "Did he say something?"

"No, you seemed upset with him." I heaved a sigh. "Last night he told me about his dad. I didn't know."

"I told him he should be working, figuring things out, talking to his dad, but I was wrong. He needs a break." Nick studied me. "You're good for him. I've not seen him this happy in months."

My gaze sought Luke, who stood on the bank, hands in his pockets, staring at the river. His face was always calm, but I realized that before, it had lacked something, rather than contained something. Now I could tell the difference—now it contained peace.

Sharing must have helped him, too. I hoped that meant the rest of the night hadn't hurt him.

"Okay, let's do this." Amberlyn strode toward us, wearing running leggings, a fleece jacket, a high ponytail, and a headband that covered her ears.

"Are we rowing to the Arctic?" I asked. Sure, clouds were blocking the sun, but it was no colder than spring mornings in Southern California.

"I like to be prepared."

"For running a marathon in subzero temperatures?"

She ignored me.

Luke, Nick, and I would have to suffer in street clothes.

Al stared at Amberlyn before settling on a bench nearby. "I'll watch the bags."

"You don't want to come?" I asked.

"I'm a landlubber." She pulled out her earbuds.

"You got enough boating as a Girl Scout?"

"You're never going to let that go, are you?"

"Absolutely not. Aren't you supposed to keep me out of trouble?"

She stuck one earbud in. "It doesn't seem to be working. I thought I'd try a different strategy."

"Complete indifference?"

"*Partial* indifference." In went earbud number two.

I laughed.

"I'll stay, too." Priya, Amberlyn's chaperone, sat near Al.

A row of low, flat boats tied together stretched from the bank to the middle of the river. They were squarish with flat bottoms and had four low seats that faced each other. We had to climb over half a dozen boats to reach ours.

Amberlyn made it to the third one before she stumbled, sending the boats rocking and the rest of us clutching for handholds.

"We all have different gifts, Am," I said as I hopped from boat to boat, praying my knee wouldn't give out. "Yours isn't anything requiring grace or hand-eye coordination, but don't worry. You have many other redeeming qualities."

Nick slid a hand around her waist to steady her.

"I think he fancies her," Luke muttered.

Oh good. He was still talking to me. *Act normal.*

"Already?" Nick seemed too smart for that.

Now Nick was offering his hand to help Amberlyn into the farthest boat.

"He falls in love with every pretty girl he meets."

He hadn't fallen in love with me. But I'd shown up with his best friend.

Luke and I sat together, Amberlyn facing us, and Nick stood on a small platform behind her with a pole he used to push us along. Mist curled over the surface of the water. The sun prepared to breach the horizon. Though many other punts lined the banks, few floated on the river. Apparently, smart people waited for daylight and warmth for this particular activity.

At first, I couldn't turn off my brain. Was Luke sitting closer than usual or farther away? Was he afraid to touch me now? And why did that thought make me sad?

Trees lined the banks, and we floated under two stone bridges. The slow pace finally helped me relax. Even Amberlyn remained quiet.

Nick sneaked glances at her as he steered. I wanted to warn him there was no possible way that crush would end well.

After several minutes, he and Luke switched places. I watched Luke for a while before asking, "Can I try?"

Nick eyed me.

"I bet she's strong enough," Luke said. "She's an athlete."

"All right."

"We're all going to die," Amberlyn said.

Luke ignored her. "See how I'm standing."

I studied his stance, legs wide, knees bent.

"And how I hold the pole."

He held it over the right side of the boat, plunged the pole into the water near his feet, let it slide down a little. He walked his hands to the top so the pole was behind him as the boat moved on. Then he yanked it out of the water, moving hand over hand back to the middle. "It helps if you twist as you pull."

I'd never thought of him as particularly buff, but his shirt stretched across his shoulders and biceps as he moved. He'd pushed his sleeves up, and muscles tensed in his forearms. His hands were sure and steady, reminding me of how they'd felt clasped with mine.

"It's a bit like paddleboarding," I said.

"Except don't let the mud steal the pole."

We traded places, his hands brushing mine as he gave me the pole. Did he do it on purpose? Was he testing me? Ugh. *Focus.*

The balance part wasn't hard. I held the pole, feeling it out, the wood worn smooth beneath my hands.

I stuck it in and mimicked the movement of his hands. We moved faster than I expected, and my hands reached the top before I was ready. I twisted and pulled. The mud pulled back. I would not lose the pole. Or fall in the water again. After a solid yank, the mud released the pole and I walked my hands down it.

"Good." Luke nodded. "When it's in the mud, you can steer. Just push to one side or the other."

This time I was ready. Before it got all the way behind me, I tried pushing sideways. The boat turned. Nose-first toward the brushy bank. I pushed the other way. As soon as we straightened, it was time to yank it out again.

Once I fell into a rhythm, it was a good workout but relaxing. My arms strained in a pleasant way with each push. I saw why this was popular. I wouldn't want to try when other boats were out, but on a quiet morning, with the current carrying us, I almost forgot how my future depended on the next few days.

"She's good," Nick said.

"Yeah." Luke met my gaze with a crooked smile that showed no hint of resentment. "There isn't much she's *not* good at. But don't tell her that. She'll say you're lying."

His tone remained light and teasing, lacking the intimacy of the last time he'd complimented me. But last time, we'd been alone.

Amberlyn rolled her eyes. "Please."

I pretended not to hear them, but Luke's words stayed with me. They disturbed my peace. I was good at soccer. Most sports. I was good with people. But school wasn't great. I got bored too easily. I'd never enjoyed music or art or student council like my siblings.

I could always move here and be a punter.

Nick took us upstream and tied up the boat. More people were out now, and the sun was burning up the mist. I was glad I'd done this for Luke.

"Thanks. That was fun. Wasn't that fun, Am?"

"If you like that kind of thing."

Pretending she hadn't spoken, I turned to Luke. "Did you used to do that often?"

"Almost every weekend."

I wanted to say sorry. I wanted to say I understood that it

sucked not to be able to do something you loved. I wanted to ask him if it got easier. But too many people were around.

"I see why you like it. I'd go all the time, too."

My answer took too long. No one but Luke noticed, but his lips slid into a sad smile like he'd read my unspoken thoughts. He squeezed my hand briefly as we climbed across the row of boats. I returned the gesture, hoping we were back to normal. If he didn't fear casual touches, maybe he was willing to ignore last night, too.

When we reached the bank, the others rejoined Al and Priya, who were laughing together. Good to know Al talked to someone.

Luke stopped me with a hand on my arm. "Why don't you think you're good at anything?" he asked quietly. "I saw your face when I said that."

I dug my toe into the wet grass. "Something my dad said before he left, how it was a good thing I had soccer, since I had nothing else. Doesn't matter."

"You're doing it again, saying things don't matter."

Nick's voice interrupted. "So, uh, I was thinking . . ."

Saved.

We joined the others, but I sensed Luke's frown.

Nick retrieved a large backpack and ran a hand through his hair. "I have a free day. Where are you going next?"

He turned hopeful eyes toward Amberlyn, but she stared at him like he'd spoken Elvish.

"North." I eyed Amberlyn. I didn't plan to say the name aloud. "Way north."

She whirled and opened her mouth, then closed it with a huff. "Of course you are."

"We have the same clues, genius." I faced Nick. "I thought I'd stop in Edinburgh for the night. Seems like a city I should see."

Amberlyn stared again.

"What?" I asked.

"I was thinking the same thing."

Of course she was. She'd probably arranged stops at famous literary places in the city, even though it wasn't on our official schedule.

"Edinburgh sounds brilliant." Nick clapped his hands. "We can go together."

Brilliant, indeed. We were competing. The last thing I wanted was Amberlyn along to witness my ignorance in all things literary.

But I liked Nick, and hanging out with him cheered up Luke.

I expected Amberlyn to argue, but she didn't. Did her silence mean she didn't mind? That she wanted to keep an eye on me? Or that she anticipated a chance to mock me?

When Nick led the way to the train station, Luke hung back, so I did, too.

"Sorry," he said. "I had no idea he'd invite himself."

"He's not the one I mind. I like him."

"Yes, but if he weren't coming, we could avoid Amberlyn."

"Having her along reminds me how smart she is." I sighed. "How she deserves to win a contest like this. How she has her life planned."

"You deserve it." His voice was fierce. "Besides, it's fine not to have your life planned. You're eighteen."

"I did, though. That's the problem."

"She obviously needs help, too, so maybe her plans aren't as perfect as you think."

I hadn't considered that. Why *was* she here? Her grades were excellent. She joined every council and community event. But . . . she had missed school one semester. I assumed she'd been on an elite study abroad program. But I'd never heard about it, and that's the kind of thing she would've bragged about.

Huh. Maybe Amberlyn had secrets, too.

CHAPTER TWENTY

The four of us boarded a train to the transfer hub of Birmingham and took seats forming a square. Amberlyn burrowed into the window and immediately started scribbling in her journal.

Nick attempted to ask questions about her family, hobbies, and career plans. She gave noncommittal answers, but they didn't deter him.

I wanted to talk to Luke, but I didn't want Amberlyn to overhear. She'd mock Would You Rather. Revisiting last night would be too personal. Although, I did welcome the excuse not to discuss the almost kiss. Instead, I got out my journal, too.

Luke raised an eyebrow.

"What?"

He shook his head.

I tried to write about Lewis and Tolkien before shifting to jotting words like *Amberlyn sucks at darts* and *Career option #6—Punter.*

Luke leaned into my shoulder and peeked at the page. He

choked on a laugh. Then he took the journal and pen from me, wrote, and passed it back.

In small, neat writing, it said, *Career option #7—Swim instructor.*

"Very funny." I bumped his shoulder with mine and added, *#8—Darts champion.*

He wrote, *#9—Cowgirl.*

I pretended to shudder but couldn't hide a smile. *#10—Tent builder.*

He added, *#11—Street musician.*

My loud laugh refused to be contained. Luke's shoulder pressed into mine as we shook with laughter.

Amberlyn shot us a glare and stood, shoving her journal into the outer pocket of her backpack before she navigated down the aisle toward the bathroom.

I swallowed a final giggle and eyed her bag. Had she written about me? Was she really examining deep literary themes and tying them to her personal journey while I barely managed to summarize events?

"Don't even think about it." Luke's low voice tickled my ear. His arm rested against mine.

"I wouldn't."

He ducked his head and peered at me over the top of his glasses.

"Fine. I *would* think about it. But I wouldn't *do* it."

He leaned back.

"*You* could, though," I said. "Look. If you stood and tripped, it would fall out."

"Why are you so curious? It's not like you can copy it."

"I wouldn't copy." But I would like to know if her tales sounded brilliant and thoughtful.

Spence had his literary styles, Peter the creative writing skills, Amberlyn the themes. Based on my essays from the last year, Ms. Carmichael would assume I'd provide a straightforward summary of what happened. But we'd established that was what she didn't want. And the only thing I knew how to do.

I needed to find an angle. Go deeper somehow. But . . . what if I didn't have anything deeper inside me to find?

We disembarked in Birmingham to change trains. As we trudged through the giant, fancy station resembling a shopping mall, I nudged Amberlyn.

"Doesn't that remind you of Mr. Brucklehorst? In the red sweater."

She huffed a breath, like I'd interrupted something other than her walking in self-righteous silence. "What?"

"That guy." I nodded at the man walking toward us. "Mr. B, right?"

A small smile formed on her lips. "Yeah."

"He even has the comb-over."

"And the mustache. Remember how he used to comb wax through it every morning before class?"

I laughed. "And Seth Carson switched it with shoe polish."

She laughed, too.

"Man, I wish we'd taken pictures that day."

We watched the man pass, and I remembered the days when this was normal. When I told her my thoughts and she understood rather than judging.

Amberlyn's laugh died out first, slowly replaced by her mask of indifference. For a moment, I'd forgotten she despised me.

I kicked a stray food wrapper.

While Nick and Luke studied the board listing the train platforms, and Amberlyn moved on, Al stopped beside me.

"I take it you and Amberlyn have a . . . history."

"You could say that. We used to be friends." I dropped my duffel with a thump. "She decided she was too smart for me. Found new friends. Whatever."

"Whatever?"

"It ended years ago. I'm over it." I craned my head and pretended to read the board. "Besides, we're too different. Being friends when you're ten doesn't mean it's destined to last a lifetime. People change."

"May I . . . offer advice?" The words sounded forced, like she didn't want to say them.

"I thought you weren't supposed to help."

"Not with the competition. This is about life." She shifted.

"Sure, why not? But I'm not good at taking advice."

"I'm astonished." Her tone didn't change. "It sounds like you need to talk to her. To clear the air. She hurt you, and now you dismiss her and the situation. You need closure."

"Our friendship is over. That's closure."

"Did you ever tell her she hurt you?"

"She didn't hurt me. We moved on. That's life."

Al's silence spoke her disbelief. Then she said, "Perhaps both of you being here is no accident. This could be your opportunity to make things right."

I nudged my bag with my toe. Despite the bright, cavernous space, the concourse was way too claustrophobic. "Why are you saying this? Babysitting is now counseling?"

"A good nanny cares for her charges," she said in her flat, sarcastic tone.

I rolled my eyes. "How did you get into this anyway? Working for Ms. Carmichael?"

She remained silent so long I thought she wouldn't answer. "Much like she's doing with you, she offered me an opportunity at a time I needed one most."

For private Al, that was pretty personal. "What else do you do?"

"All of us helping this week work for her charitable foundation. I do accounting."

Wheels turned in my mind. "Finances, huh?" Explained her obsession with receipts. "Does that mean you know where her money comes from? Does she launder it?"

"I assume she made you sign a confidentiality agreement? Which somehow didn't prevent you from telling my cousin nearly everything?"

How did she sound? Judgmental? Amused? Like she might get me in trouble or like she didn't care? "The agreement was kind of vague."

"I'm sure it was," she said. "Mine was not."

"Aw, just when I thought you were getting fun, Al."

"My goal in life has always been to be considered 'fun.'"

Luke and Nick headed toward us, cutting off further conversation. Nick immediately veered off to join Amberlyn, who stood several yards away, texting. When we rode the escalator down to our next platform, Nick trailed behind her, chattering. Couldn't he see she wasn't interested? Even if she was, what would he do?

Luke watched his friend with an expression that said he was used to this but didn't like it.

We stopped near the tracks. A crowd was forming, people packing the platform. Amberlyn tried to inch away and pulled her bag in front of her to rummage through it.

Voices muttered, and people shifted. A man burst through, elbowing people aside as he ran. He bumped Amberlyn, sent her stumbling toward the tracks.

"Am!" I wrapped an arm around her and yanked her away from the edge.

Her stuff went flying, spreading across the ground, items tumbling toward the train tracks.

I released Amberlyn and lunged for her bag. I fell sideways, bounced off a person. Tripped on another. Plummeted to the ground.

Pain exploded through my chin. Lights flashed in my head.

Somewhere above me, Luke shouted and Amberlyn shrieked. Her voice pierced my skull. My chin throbbed with pain, in time with every beat of my heart. I rested my cheek on the cement briefly before pushing myself up.

An arm came around me. Which was good, because the

world was tilting wildly. Or was that my head? Drops of rain spattered my face. Wait. Rain. Weren't we indoors? I wiped them off, and my hand came away red.

Red. That was bad. Why was that bad?

"Careful." Luke's voice, low, in my ear.

He helped me sit and whipped off his jacket and T-shirt. I barely registered his naked chest. He pressed the shirt to my chin, which no longer throbbed. I no longer felt anything at all.

Luke gently guided my hand to the shirt. "Hold this."

When I obeyed, he zipped his jacket on.

Amberlyn screeched nearby, but her voice sounded muffled. Distant.

"Sorry, Am. I tried." My words came out slurred.

She turned to me. Her face paled. "Oh my . . . blood."

Her hand flailed until it connected with Nick. She clutched his arm.

Blood. My breath escaped in a massive whoosh. I wasn't supposed to bleed. Bleeding was bad.

"I'm the one bleeding," I mumbled. "Why do you look sick?"

But she'd never been able to stand the sight of blood.

She shouldn't be seeing it now. I shouldn't be bleeding. Couldn't be.

What happened if I bled? I was supposed to do . . . something. Ugh. My brain felt sluggish, thoughts bogged down somewhere inside my head. *Think, Britt.*

Amberlyn whirled away, peering over the edge of the tracks. "I can see my notebook. Should I get it? There's no train, but I obviously shouldn't go on the tracks . . ."

I watched her, my brain trying to figure out why I should worry.

Luke made sure I held the shirt before whirling toward Al. "We need to get to a hospital. Call a taxi?"

She took out her phone.

Luke knelt by my side again. His fingers closed around mine and drew them away from my chin. His other hand grasped my cheek and angled my head. "It's deep. You'll need more than a plaster, possibly stitches. Did your . . . is there anything you're supposed to do?"

No idea what he meant by "plaster," but I tried to nod. Couldn't tell if my head moved.

"It's all right." Luke returned the shirt to my chin. "Keep pressure on it. Everything will be fine."

Other than the blood dripping down me, I didn't feel anything. Was that a problem? When I opened my mouth to ask, Luke put a finger on my lips.

"Don't talk. Keep it still."

Nearby, Amberlyn hovered as someone used a trash grabber to pick up her belongings from the tracks.

She flipped through a rumpled journal. "I should be able to copy everything into a new book."

Luke turned a blank gaze on her, but something in it must have conveyed that she needed to shut up, now. He kept an arm around my waist as he helped me upstairs and through the massive concourse, where the bright lights and swooping white ceiling only worsened my disorientation.

Concentrate on stepping. Don't trip.

We exited onto the street, where gray skies were spitting light rain. A taxi waited.

Luke didn't remove his arm until he inserted me into the backseat. Which was good, because the world was still spinning too fast.

"Your arm is nice," I tried to say to Luke. Fortunately, I didn't think the words were understandable.

We couldn't all fit in the cab, so Nick, Amberlyn, and Priya said they'd meet us at the hospital and bring our bags.

I jostled between Luke and Al as the taxi sped through town. The car bumped and lurched, and my stomach lurched with it. I swallowed hard to keep my fried eggs from reappearing.

Luke guided me into a beige waiting room. *Beige* was a funny word. Beige. My tongue tried to say it, and Luke hushed me again while steering me to a chair.

"Al, stay here." He marched to the counter. He kept his voice low, but the room was small, and the two other people were silent, so I heard every word.

"My friend has a fairly serious cut on her chin that may need stitches. She's taking blood thinner for a medical condition, so she needs attention immediately." His voice was calm but firm, soothing me even though he'd spoken my secret.

Al shifted in the seat beside me. "I'm sorry. I failed at looking out for you."

"I'm sure Ms. C won't blame you."

"I'm not worried about getting in trouble with my boss." Her sharp voice focused my attention. "I'm worried about *you.*"

I blinked. "Oh."

"Do you want to call your mum? Or for me to call?"

Good question. This seemed like something a mother should know. But if she found out I'd gotten hurt, would she insist I come home? Given the time difference, she'd be sleeping now, so I had time to decide how to spin this.

"I'll check in later."

Al held my gaze before nodding.

Luke returned to my side and took over holding the shirt.

"It smells funny in here," I mumbled. Even in England, hospitals smelled like a chem lab, disinfectant, and sick people. *Beige* sick people.

The others piled into the emergency room. The burst of light and noise from the open doors sent a flurry of darts through my head.

Nick made a beeline toward me. "Are you going to be all right?"

"She'll be fine," Luke said.

"I can talk." But my words slurred.

"I'm aware of that. But you shouldn't move your chin, so please refrain from speaking for now." His eyes held a gentle smile.

A man in a white coat came through the double doors. His gaze circled the room, landed on me. He approached.

Luke jumped up and met him halfway, drew him aside, and spoke in a low voice.

I tried to beam a thank-you from my brain to his.

The doctor strode toward me. "I'm Dr. Smith. Let's get you back and have a look."

My Doctor Who joke got stuck between my brain and my mouth. I stood, and Luke's arm came around me again. I wanted to tell him I was fine, but I didn't want to fall over in front of Amberlyn.

"Al, you take care of payment. I'll go with Britt."

Luke's phone buzzed in his pocket. He pulled it out, glanced at the screen, and silenced it. He took my hand, and we followed the doctor through double doors. "Have you had stitches before?"

"Not that I was awake for. During the surgery . . ."

Images flooded my mind. The hospital. My knee.

The news.

I stumbled. Put a hand on the wall as it hit me.

CHAPTER TWENTY-ONE

Last time I'd gone to the hospital, I thought I'd only hurt my knee. The actual news had been so much worse. News that changed everything.

What if today ended with more than stitches? What if it happened again?

Shaking consumed my body, and blood roared in my ears.

Luke squeezed my hand and bent his head close, forcing me to look at him.

"Everything will be fine. It's just a cut. Breathe." He brushed hair out of my face and tucked a strand behind my ear, his gentle touch tickling the sensitive skin behind my earlobe. "They'll stitch you up, and we'll be on our way."

I nodded, sucked in a deep breath. How did he know what worried me? No one had taken the time to understand me so well, let alone know exactly what to say. Having him sense my fear, my insecurity, when I hadn't said a word was scarier than the scrape on my face.

Luke's phone buzzed again. He ignored it and led me down the hall after the doctor. "Nick had stitches once. On his chin, like yours. He was trying to show off for a girl while punting but fell overboard. Hit his chin on the boat."

The doctor gestured to a small exam room. I sat on the table, crinkling the paper beneath me. I winced. Exactly like home.

"He made a giant splash," Luke continued as he drew the extra chair to my side. "It was a rare sunny day, so the river was full."

The doctor made me follow his finger with my eyes, tell him my name and the day, and count backward from one hundred by sevens. Satisfied with my answers despite the pauses I needed to do the math, he prepared a syringe and a small bottle of clear liquid. "Are you allergic to any medications?"

I shook my head. Air vents hissed. Footsteps squeaked in the hall. Loud breathing filled the room. That was me. I forced myself to do a breathing routine to slow my heart rate.

Luke tugged my hand until I focused on his face, brushed another strand of hair off my cheek and away from my chin. "Everyone nearby hollered and cheered. But Nick drenched the girl, too, and she was furious about her new jumper. She demanded he take her straight to shore and ignored his messages. He didn't ask out another girl for a month, which for him is an eternity."

I tried to return his smile and squeezed his hand. He was right—stories did help take your mind off things.

Until the doctor plunged the needle into the bottle, filled it, and did that evil squirt-a-bit-out thing like villains preparing to torture people. Still, I'd been put under for knee surgery, and I preferred this, even though the giant needle heading for my face was disturbing. At least there would be no surprises waiting when I woke. Better to be alert for everything.

A sting pricked my chin, and feeling faded from the lower half of my face.

I clutched Luke's hand, an anchor in the sea of numbness. It creeped me out knowing the doctor was touching my face but I couldn't feel it. Touching Luke, knowing he was real, grounded me. His gaze didn't leave my face, and the gold flecks in his eyes glowed brighter under the harsh hospital lights.

The doctor swabbed my chin with something that made my nose burn and picked up a needle. He bent his head close, glasses over his eyes, blocking my view of Luke. I focused on the gray streaks in the doctor's hair, waiting for him to announce something was wrong.

But he only produced a pair of scissors, I assumed to snip the thread.

"All finished." He set the scissors down and removed his gloves. "The stitches will dissolve within a week or two. Don't get them wet for forty-eight hours."

My hand drifted toward my face.

"And try not to touch them." He offered me a kind smile. "In fact . . ." He rummaged in a drawer and produced a piece of gauze, which he taped over the stitches. "There. That will protect them."

"All right?" Luke asked.

I nodded.

"Good. I'm going to find you a clean shirt." Luke stood and

waited until I let go of his hand, rather than releasing mine. I tried to thank him with my eyes. "I'll be right back. I promise."

I glanced down. Blood drenched my T-shirt. Hard to believe, when I couldn't feel anything. How much had I lost? Too much? How much was too much? Surely I'd pass out if it was too bad. Luke had told the doctor about my medication, and the doc hadn't been concerned.

Luke reappeared, carrying the top from a set of teal scrubs. He helped me pull it over my shirt, careful not to touch my face.

He'd used his shirt for first aid. That made two I'd ruined. At this rate, I'd owe him a new wardrobe.

After the doctor exited, Luke gathered me into a gentle hug, angling to keep his shoulder from pressing into my chin. He smoothed a hand over my hair. "You did great. You're going to be fine."

I closed my eyes, nestled my head into his neck, and breathed deep, the nasty hospital smell drowned by the now-familiar scent of Luke.

I held on longer than I should have. The hospital felt removed from the real world, like what happened here was outside of time, so I clung to him, enjoying the last few moments before I had to let go.

When we rejoined the others in the lobby, Amberlyn was the first to stand. "Are you okay?"

"She's fine," Luke said, which was good because everything below my nose was numb and I didn't know if I could talk.

"Good. Priya and I are heading out, then." Whatever expression formed on my unfeeling face made her shift and look away. "This is a competition, after all."

And I was falling behind. I didn't want to be the last one to finish, racing to Ms. C's with seconds to spare, scribbling in my journal as I ran, while my competitors lounged around eating scones, laughing at me.

Amberlyn shifted toward the door. I was surprised she'd stayed this long. Still, that was the thanks I got for trying to help?

Her gaze avoided my face, but her eyes softened a fraction. "Good luck, Britt."

Al aimed a pointed look at me. I knew she wanted me to mend bridges or build fences or whatever. My mind couldn't come up with the right words. Since I couldn't talk, I didn't know what she expected.

I waved a hand, less saying goodbye than shooing Amberlyn out the door.

"She was trying to help you." Luke gave Amberlyn a teacher glare. "I've not heard a thank-you."

"Thanks for trying, Britt." Her quiet voice sounded surprisingly sincere.

And she was gone.

"I can't believe she left like that." Luke frowned after her. "Even if you two aren't close now, you used to be friends."

I didn't bother replying. People left. It was just what they did.

Luke didn't leave, said a small voice in my head.

Nick watched her go with more longing than Luke had, then focused on us. "I should head home. Let you rest rather than take a wild group tour of Scotland."

This time, my wave was friendly. I shot him a thumbs-up.

"Glad you're all right. Be safe. And take care of Luke." He squeezed my shoulder, said something quiet to Luke. They shook hands, and he left, too.

I rummaged in my bag for clean clothes and changed in the bathroom. After I ignored Al's attempts to convince me to stay in Birmingham for the night, we returned to the station to catch the next train to Edinburgh. We'd arrive by evening, just without Nick and Amberlyn or time to sightsee.

I remained silent—mostly because I couldn't feel my face. Thoughts were trapped in my head with nowhere to escape.

I'd tried to help Amberlyn without thinking. I was so used to jumping into things, but now I had to retrain my mind. Knowing I shouldn't join a soccer game was one thing, but it was entirely different when an opportunity appeared with no time for me to think it through. How did you change eighteen years of habit?

After settling on the train, Luke resumed reading *The Lion, the Witch, and the Wardrobe* where he'd left off in Oxford.

I couldn't concentrate, though. Memories filled my thoughts, of how he took charge, stayed calm, knew how to keep *me* calm. Of his arms around me. I wasn't used to having someone take care of me. After my siblings left for college, Mom worked a lot and I was basically on my own. I hadn't thought I minded. I liked independence, not relying on others. Other people let you down.

Except Luke hadn't today. And I'd appreciated having him there. I might not have made it without him—or, at least, I wouldn't have wanted to.

I was in so much trouble.

With a quiet sigh, I rested my head against the window, watched the scenery, and listened to Luke.

After an hour, he took a break from reading.

I scribbled in my journal and held it up: *You have to talk since I can't.*

His lips curved. "This must be killing you. You *do* like to talk."

I glared at him.

His face grew contemplative. "There is something I've been wanting to say. Now seems a good time since you can't argue . . ."

I raised my eyebrows.

"What you said about football being all you had . . ." His words were careful. Testing. "You don't really see yourself that way, do you?"

I stared at the stupid journal. What else was there?

His eyes clouded. "I get it. You built your identity around football, and now that you can't play, you feel like you don't know who you are."

Once again, he read me too well.

A frown creased his forehead. "Who you are isn't what you do, though. You're still *you* whether you play football or not."

The problem was, I didn't know who I was.

"I've been thinking . . ." He chewed his lip.

I waited.

He seemed to change what he planned to say. "Can I see your journal? If you didn't write anything about how brilliant you think I am, of course."

Don't flatter yourself, I wrote. I started to hold it out but snatched it away. *Promise you won't laugh?*

"I solemnly swear."

That sounds ominous. But I gave him the book and refused to watch as he flipped through it. He was going to think I was an idiot.

"Hmm. You *aren't* a writer, are you?"

Yet another reason for him to realize I wasn't smart enough for him. I shoved his shoulder with my fist.

He laughed. "Sorry, kidding. It's not the end of the world."

I grabbed the journal back and wrote, *I'm supposed to write. So yeah, it is. Ways the world might end: asteroids, zombies, robot uprising, terrible stories.*

"You're supposed to tell tales. Like Chaucer. You like stories. Listening to other people's. Even reading them."

If they're short and have explosions.

"How did Chaucer's pilgrims tell their stories?"

Around a campfire?

"Exactly. They wouldn't have known how to write, but they told stories." The thoughtful expression returned. "You know at lunch in Bath? When you described falling in the water? Everyone in the room was listening."

Yeah, because a dumb American falling into the Roman Baths was funny.

I must've looked doubtful, because he continued. "You're a storyteller. The cabbie in Glastonbury, when you told him about the cows? On the train when you distracted me with the cookie incident?"

I thought of those times. I liked entertaining people, knew how to read their faces and time jokes. But when I spoke, I tended to exaggerate. *How does that help? Tell my stories out loud and have someone write them down?*

He shrugged. "It was something I noticed you're good at, that's all."

Would it be cheating to have someone write the tales for me if they were my words? Could I teach myself to write the way I talked in the next week? Unlikely.

I'll think about it.

"Good." He squeezed my knee.

I smiled. Tried to. I'm not sure it resembled a smile.

Luke's phone buzzed.

I pointed to it and raised my eyebrows.

He ignored me, opened the book, and resumed reading aloud. I alternated listening and dozing on his shoulder, and before I knew it, we were in Scotland.

Despite the weariness, a small thrill shot through me. Another new country.

From the station, we walked down brick streets with solid lines of tan stone buildings full of shops, restaurants, and hotels. The air held more of a chill, and I shoved my hands into my pockets. I was ready for this day to be over, no matter how exciting this city might be.

We checked into a boring hotel, ate a late dinner at the hotel restaurant, where I settled for soup since the numbness had worn off and left my face sore, and went to our rooms.

Al stopped me. "Do you need anything? Are you sure you're all right?"

"I'm fine." The rare combination of a serious question and concerned gaze made me uncomfortable. "Really."

"Get some rest."

In my room, I lay down, but I couldn't sleep. The anesthesia had worn off, and my chin felt weird and tight. I did PT stretches. I texted my mom a nightly check-in, leaving out today's excitement to avoid the inevitable debate we'd have about my coming home. I tried to write in my journal, but no words came. I unpacked and repacked my bag, hoping to find magical aspirin I knew I hadn't brought.

Finally, I tiptoed next door to Luke's room. I knocked, lightly, so if he slept, I wouldn't wake him up, and so Al wouldn't hear from across the hall.

The door opened immediately. Luke was still dressed.

He leaned an arm against the doorframe above his head. "Can't sleep?"

I shook my head. "I napped too much on the train. And my chin is throbbing. Do you have aspirin? Tylenol. I can't take the other stuff."

He opened the door wider, and I followed him in. He handed me a bottle of water and a packet of approved painkillers.

"Are you sure you should be talking?" he asked.

"It's fine."

We sat side by side on his bed, farther apart than on the train, but knowing he'd be sleeping here made it more personal.

He leaned in to inspect my chin, but I'd left the gauze over it, figuring the bandage would look less disturbing than stitches in my face. He gently, gently pressed the edges of the gauze like they were coming undone and withdrew his hand.

"Do you want to go out?" I blurted out. I wasn't sure why I said it. The sun hadn't set until nine, and since it was totally dark outside now, it had to be late. But I wouldn't be sleeping anytime soon, and how often would I get a chance to see Edinburgh? "To see the town, I mean?"

Luke gave me his level gaze. "All right."

I blinked. "Really?"

"Why not?"

If he couldn't think of good reasons why not—which was way more his strength than mine—I sure wasn't going to try. I jumped up and headed for the door.

CHAPTER TWENTY-TWO

The hotel was a few blocks from what Luke called the Royal Mile, a broad boulevard packed with people. Performers juggled and breathed fire. We passed bar after bar and turned onto another popular street where music seeped out of hidden clubs, the bass vibrating in my bones. I imagined we'd gone back in time to the Prohibition. If they'd had that in Scotland, which seemed unlikely.

A chill made me wish I'd grabbed a jacket. The moisture in the air muffled sounds and blurred lights, softening the edges like a melting watercolor.

Too many people, though. The thick air clogged my lungs. I flinched when someone jostled me. Usually, I'd find this place fascinating, but tonight I wanted peace.

Luke was rubbing off on me.

He kept my hand grasped firmly in his. I told myself it was to keep the crowds from separating us, until the crowd thinned and he twined his fingers through mine. He hadn't tried to kiss me again, but I wasn't discouraging his attention.

Holding hands was no big deal. Lots of people held hands. It didn't mean anything.

We paused when we spotted a group circling someone. I edged forward. A guy not much older than us was juggling. A glint of light hit an object in midair. Correction—he was juggling *knives*.

"Awesome," I said.

"Someone has a death wish," Luke muttered.

The guy caught his knives, swept off his red plaid hat, and bowed. I clapped along with the crowd.

"I need a volunteer," the juggler said. "You." He pointed at Luke.

"Not a chance," Luke said.

I stepped forward. "I'll do it."

Luke grasped my arm. "Are you sure that's a good idea? You've already made one hospital trip today."

"Exactly. My bad luck is all used up." It sounded stupid even to me, but I didn't want to live always scared to act. I wouldn't let a medical condition define me, make me someone different. I had to still be *me*.

With a dramatic whip of a towel, the juggler spread it on the damp pavement and directed me to lie on the ground. I did. Luke's grunt carried from where he stood.

Vaguely aware of the crowd encircling me, I stared up. The sky was dark, but lights from nearby bars blocked any trace of stars.

The juggler said something to make the crowd gasp, then laugh.

I should pay attention, considering he held large, sharp objects. Maybe this hadn't been the best idea.

He stood over me.

"Are you ready?" he asked in a loud voice.

The crowd yelled, although he was asking me, not them. I nodded, my ponytail catching on the ground.

A devilish grin played across his mouth. He threw one knife in the air. And another. And a third. They spun above me, dark blurs flashing occasionally when light hit a blade.

I held my breath for the first few rotations, waiting, wondering. From this angle, they looked surreal. They weren't real knives, with real blades, flying mere feet above my head. This was a dream. A trick. I smiled.

Somehow, I felt freer. Like I was staring the future straight in the face and saying *Do your worst.* Because, honestly, life had already taken my father, my best friend, my future. What were a few pieces of—albeit large—flying cutlery in the face of that?

The juggler caught the knives one by one and swooped into a bow. The crowd cheered. His hand appeared above me, and he helped me to my feet, twirled me to display me. I bowed, too. The people clapped again.

I pretended to feel my limbs as if making sure they were intact. Laughter bubbled up around me.

Luke's face, pale and grim, stood out. Not smiling like the rest.

I slid my hand from the juggler's, waved at the crowd, and returned to his side. "You okay?"

"I wish you hadn't done that." He adjusted his glasses with a shaking hand.

"I'm fine. He's a pro."

"You can't be a professional at street performance."

"Well, he's as close as you can come. Nothing happened."

He ran a hand through his normally neat hair. "I know. But after earlier, seeing you covered in blood . . ."

An unusual burning sensation tightened my throat. I'd never considered my crazy choices affecting someone else, but he'd been worried.

"I'm sorry I scared you." I squeezed his hand. "It's over. Let's do something else. Any ideas?"

"Something that doesn't involve weapons."

Keeping my hand, he led us down the street. Stopped. "I have an idea. If I can find it. Wait here."

He darted to a group and spoke. One guy gestured. Another shook his head and argued, pointed in a different direction. They all nodded. Luke waved and jogged back.

"Come with me," he said.

I followed him. "Where are we going?"

"You'll see."

"Not even a hint?"

He smothered a smile. "Nope."

"You said no weapons . . ." I pretended to think. "Poetry reading?"

"I like literature, not torture."

"Beer pong? Folk music concert? Skinny-dipping in the river?" I purposely named things he'd hate. The crowds had energized me, and I was ready for a new adventure.

"Yes," he said. "It's skinny-dipping. How did you guess?"

His raised eyebrows sent a rush of heat to my face. Why had I said that?

He smirked. "We're here."

I stared at the dingy sign with a faded lion. "A seedy Scottish bar? You know how to show a girl a good time."

He bypassed the beer-scented patrons and headed for the rear, steering me gently with his hand on my lower back. The simple contact sent shock waves up my spine.

I didn't spot the door until he pushed it open. "You hardly need speakeasies when everyone out front is holding pints."

Then I stopped.

The room was larger than I expected, with a small stage containing a single microphone stand and a stool. Folding chairs filled the rest of the space. A guy in a kilt stood next to the stool and held the mic.

"A comedy club?" I asked.

"More like a bar that allows people to perform."

We sat and listened to the guy joke about football, the English, *Doctor Who,* and his toddler.

I had to concentrate. His Scottish accent was stronger than the juggler's. Several times, a word translated slowly in my head, and I laughed later than everyone else when I got the joke.

After it happened for the fourth or fifth time, the comedian noticed.

His eyes locked on mine. "Ach, it seems we have someone who's a wee bit daft."

"Maybe your accent is a bit daft." The words came out before I could stop them.

Luke snorted.

The audience laughed.

The comedian stepped to the edge of the stage and peered out. The room had no true stage lights, so he spotted me easily.

"American, eh? How did ye find your way to Edinburgh?"

I didn't know much about Scotland. Certainly not enough to make jokes. Clichés about whiskey, kilts, and *Braveheart* wouldn't get me far. But I remembered Luke's comment on the Scottish and Irish.

I looked around the room, pretending to be confused. "Edinburgh? I must've taken a wrong turn. I thought I was in Dublin."

That set him off on a lengthy Scots-versus-Irish monologue that might've been funnier if I'd been Scottish or Irish. But soon he strolled toward me again.

"Are you properly educated in the ways of Scotland, lassie? Go on, ask your questions."

I pursed my lips. Then nodded at him. "Is that real?"

"Me beard or me kilt?"

"I meant the beard. No one here wants you to prove your kilt is real." I gave a deliberate shudder. People chuckled.

He tugged his substantial beard. "As real as William Wallace's own." He squinted and pointed to my chin. "There's a story behind that, I'm betting."

"There is." I scanned the audience. "Are you ready for a harrowing tale of action, danger, and daring heroism?"

"Ach, here in Scotland we love tales of brave heroes."

"Okay, then." I stood and made my voice intentionally dramatic. "This story begins with a helpless girl, far from home and lost in a foreign land."

Reactions ranged from raised eyebrows to smiles to soft chuckles.

"This girl ventured into the great British institution known as a train station, a wild and terrifying place."

Shifting eye contact from person to person as I spoke, I spun a tale of poor Amberlyn, a tourist attacked by a dastardly criminal, and my brave efforts to save her from near death in front of a speeding train, endangering my own life in the process.

"This"—I motioned to my chin—"was a minor and acceptable wound in the face of ensuring the safety of a child in need. Many thanks to the fine hospital system of this great country."

I bowed and sat, and people laughed and smiled.

"Quite a tale, lassie. Ye could well be Scottish to spin a yarn like that." The comedian closed with a few more jokes and handed the mic to someone else. He stopped by our seats as he exited, bowed, and took my hand and kissed it.

The next guy wasn't as funny, so Luke and I slipped out.

"That was fun," I said when we reached the street. "How did you think of that?"

"I've seen the way you enjoy being in front of a crowd. I thought you might like it."

"Did you know it would be so . . . interactive?"

"They aren't always, but often amateur comedians interact with the audience. Plus, with you around, I suspected something like that was possible."

"I'm choosing to take that as a compliment."

"You're the kind of person things happen to, Britt Hanson, whether you like it or not. Though I suspect you do."

The warmth in Luke's gaze and voice made it sound like a good thing.

"Do *you* like it?" I suddenly needed to know.

"I know how to get home if I wanted to get away." Despite the light tone, his expression was serious.

But did he mean he liked the excitement I attracted, or me?

The two of us stood in a bubble, the rest of the street distant and muted. Luke leaned in, the space between us shrinking. I swayed toward him without making the conscious decision to move.

"Aye, awrite there?" a voice called.

I jumped and stumbled backward. The juggler from earlier approached.

"If it isn't my willing victim. I'm Max." He pulled off the plaid hat.

"Britt," I said. "This is Luke."

"Your boyfriend went quite pale when I suggested he help me, but when you were out there, he was positively white."

Luke didn't correct him, so I didn't, either.

Max smoothed his long hair. "I believe I should be flattered that you had enough faith in me to volunteer."

I shrugged. "I was feeling brave. How did you learn to do that? Did you wake up one morning and think, I want to chuck knives in the air over random strangers?"

He turned the hat over in his hands. "I learned to juggle when I was wee, but one night I saw a bloke here, he was juggling chain saws. People loved it. So, I moved from balls to clubs to wooden knives."

"Can I see your hands?"

"Eh?"

I took his hands, examined them. "You have all your fingers."

He laughed. "I didn't use real knives for a long time. Until I knew I could."

"What's the worst injury you've ever gotten? No, wait, what's the worst injury you've ever given an idiot volunteer like me?"

"For me, nicks and cuts. Never hurt a volunteer. Did drop a knife once. Gave the poor bloke a fright."

I could imagine. "How do you practice?"

"Hours every day, with dull knives the same weight and balance as the real ones."

"How does it pay?"

"Britt," Luke said.

"What? I'm curious if I could make a living as a street performer."

Max chuckled, not seeming to mind my rudeness. "I'm a student at the university. I do this for fun."

"Sorry she's so nosy," Luke said. "She's American."

I punched him lightly.

Max grinned and plunked the hat on his head. "No worries. It's nice to be appreciated. Wish me mum thought it was as cool as you do. Enjoy your time in Scotland." He waved and headed off.

CHAPTER TWENTY-THREE

We took a quieter street away from the Royal Mile, heading toward a castle on the hill. The building glowed like a giant lighthouse, but the streets had fewer lights, making the dark stretches last longer.

"Well," I said, "at least I learned street performer and stand-up comedian aren't terrible career options. Or maybe magician's assistant."

"How do you figure?"

"I don't mind having knives juggled over me. I could be sawed in half or vanished."

"They'd make you wear a sparkly outfit."

"Ugh. Never mind."

The shrill tone of Luke's phone pierced the air. I didn't know the exact time, but it was late for a call.

He turned it off.

"Still ignoring your dad?"

"I'm not ready to deal with him."

"That's why you came, right? To get away." We passed a pub with noise and light spilling out, then moved on, returning to the quiet. "Is it helping?"

He turned a serious gaze on me, his eyes full of flames searing my soul. "In so many ways."

Decoding that statement was definitely a bad idea. I cleared my throat. "What do you think he wants? He's called several times."

Luke kept staring at me, but when I refused to look at him, he said, "Probably to tell me to come home. To apologize again. To ask if I paid the water bill."

I kept forgetting his future was as undetermined as mine. He acted so calm, so assured, that it seemed impossible for him not to know something. "Do you have any idea what you'll do?"

"Got any suggestions?"

"I'm keeping a list for you, too." I ticked them off on my fingers. "Audiobook reader, travel agent—not tour guide but the guy who makes the arrangements, trivia show contestant, and RV plumber."

"Quite thorough. Thank you."

We passed a park that, during the day, would've been all green spaces and trees, but now held a collection of shadows. I stopped. Spun him to face me. Breathed like I was preparing to dive under deep water. "You need to be a teacher."

He grimaced.

I held up a hand before he could argue, hoping he wouldn't get mad. "Hear me out. I get why you don't want to go to Oxford. I do. But you don't have to go there to be a teacher. You're the most natural teacher I've seen. *I* want to learn when you say smart things."

His expression softened.

"You care about the subject and want the student to learn. You explain things in a way that makes sense. And even though you claim you're trying to get away, look how you chose to do it."

"What do you mean?"

"You're trying to escape studying literature, and yet you came with me on a road trip that is *based* on literature. You're helping me understand C. S. Lewis and Jane Austen and discussing themes and quoting authors." I waited for my words to sink in. "All I'm saying is, you must not have wanted to escape *all* of it."

He scuffed his feet on the pavement and started walking again, slowly. "Maybe I just wanted to spend time with a pretty, crazy American."

I smirked. "Did you call me *pretty*? Or was that a qualifier for the adjective crazy?"

"It was not a qualifier. It was two separate adjectives, both of which accurately describe you. Although after the knife incident, I believe *crazy* is coming through stronger."

"Way to ruin a compliment, genius." A wave of relief passed through me when he didn't explore the other way that answer could've gone. "You're changing the subject. We were talking about you and college."

"My favorite topic."

"You must have options. You're smart. What about here? Edinburgh University?" I assumed they had one. "Cambridge? Eton?"

"Eton is a boys' school."

The road veered uphill, past a church with arched windows, spires, and a tall steeple. The stone appeared black in the darkness.

"You know what I mean. England is a big country. There must be more than one place to go to college. Don't tell me you didn't apply anywhere else. You're too careful for that."

He shrugged. "I did list other universities on my application, but I already officially accepted the spot at Oxford, so it's too late now."

"I wouldn't have thought you'd give up so easily."

"Like some people, who give up before something has started?" A gleam flashed in his eyes. He shifted a fraction closer, moved his face in as if daring me, but deliberately stopped several inches away.

Did he mean us? My heart stuttered. Restarted too fast. I stared at his lips before focusing on a point over his shoulder, where town lights sparkled below us.

I swallowed. "I'm tired. Can we go?"

He didn't speak but, when I refused to meet his gaze, started downhill. Even though we walked without talking, he held my hand, our fingers laced together. I might not be giving us a chance, but he planned to take as much as I'd give him. I couldn't bring myself to pull away completely. Part of me wished he'd challenge me, call me out. Was he too much of a gentleman? Or did he care less than I thought?

He stopped outside my door.

"Thanks for going out. I had fun." I dug my key out of my pocket but made no move to use it. "Sorry if I made you mad."

"You didn't make me mad." His low voice hummed in the quiet hall. "I had fun, too."

"Do you do this often? Go out on the town?"

"It's not exactly my scene. I prefer to stay at home." Not surprising. "What about you?"

"I know you'd think so, but no. I live in a small town, and the only thing open late is the doughnut shop. Or the In-N-Out in the next town over. Plus, I was always focused on soccer. Eat right, get sleep, wake up early to run or train."

Not having close friends helped, too. My teammates invited me to things, but I usually only said yes if it involved a meal or a game.

We were silent. I needed to stop enjoying this so much, spending time with Luke. We had three more days, at the most. Besides, I didn't know how he felt. I knew he liked hanging out and had said he was glad he came. Gave me compliments. But with how badly he needed to get away, would he have felt that about anyone?

Oh, who was I kidding? He would've already kissed me if I'd let him.

The silence stretched to fill the hallway, warm and cozy, but laced with an undercurrent of uncertainty.

He cleared his throat. "We should get to bed. Early train in the morning."

I nodded.

"Remember to keep your stitches dry." His fingers trailed across my jaw, stopping short of the bandage on my chin, leaving goose bumps in their wake.

"Yes, doc." My voice cracked. My head leaned into his fingers like my skin wasn't ready to give up his touch.

"Good night, Pilgrim." He dropped his hand but waited a heartbeat.

When I didn't move, he shuffled to his door.

I fumbled with my key, and he waited, so our gazes remained locked as we stepped into our rooms, losing sight of each other at the same time.

As I changed into pajamas, I was oddly out of breath. It was getting harder and harder to resist him—and to remember why I had to.

I forced my thoughts in another direction. What exactly did I enjoy about tonight? Other than Luke's presence. Which I shouldn't have enjoyed as much as I did.

The rush of adrenaline from the knives. The crowd. Entertaining the audience. Learning about Max's knife-juggling career.

I felt like it meant something. But I didn't know what.

Pounding woke me the next morning. I rolled over and buried my head under the pillow. The pounding didn't stop.

"What?"

"Time to go." Al's voice was way too chipper for . . . I rolled over again. Six a.m. Ugh. Why was the sun up?

"Too early."

"It's a long way to Inverness," she said through the door. "You wanted an early start."

I did say that. Before I decided to stay out until two a.m.

"Fine. Coming."

I dragged myself out of bed, ignoring the ache in my chin, and dressed without showering. If I couldn't dunk my head under scalding hot water, forget it.

Al waited in the hallway with coffee, Luke with Tylenol. I gulped both as we headed to the train station.

I watched the hills roll by and drank the giant coffee. The farther north we traveled, the more rugged and wild the land became. I imagined a nice witch might bring a trolley full of wizard candies or a giant frog might hop past. Some of the worry faded, the tiredness slipping away. I was heading to an actual castle. My insides hummed.

"You must be tired," Luke said. "I've never seen you so quiet, except when you couldn't move your face." He poked at my chin without touching it. "You *can* move it today?"

I swatted his hand. I wanted to hold it but made myself ignore that impulse.

Time to get serious. I had one clue left after this, and I didn't need distractions from a cute boy I'd likely never see again. I needed to focus.

Later, though. When the coffee kicked in.

Inverness was bigger than I expected, considering it felt like we'd reached the edge of the world. We'd passed lonely castles and craggy mountains. The city had a wide river, a castle, and several church spires. Everything was the same bright green, like someone had dumped a bucket of paint—maybe Spring Leaves or Scottish Emerald—on it.

It was beautiful and wild and felt more foreign than London, the cool air laced with magic.

From Inverness, we took a taxi to Cawdor Castle, fictional home of the fictional Macbeth. I planned to tour the castle, the gardens, and the woods, saving the best part for last—the website said they had a maze, which matched my clue.

The exterior didn't look super castle-like. More like a big stone manor than a fortress.

The pathway to the entrance, lined with enormous bushes, led to stone walls decorated with a turret. One proper castle feature stood out—a drawbridge. Two beams extended over our heads from the entrance, with chains connecting them to a wooden bridge underfoot.

I leaned over, but no moat filled the space beneath the bridge, only a grassy ditch. "Do you think they had alligators? Or a troll?"

"Yes," Luke said, "I'm certain they had a troll."

"I'm just saying, I would totally want one guarding my castle."

"I'll make a note to buy you one as soon as you *have* a castle."

The idea sent sparks through my chest because it promised a future. Not that I'd ever have a castle. A hundred grand was hardly enough for that. But the idea of Luke in that future, in my life. I shouldn't let myself hope for that. I didn't like hope. It let you down.

An old bell was set into the wall above the gate, next to a sign that said BE MINDFUL and a carving of a deer skull.

"Cheery way to welcome people," I muttered. But it was a needed warning to watch my heart as well as my step.

There were no tour guides, leaving the three of us to explore the interior by ourselves. The first spaces resembled fancy sitting rooms, filled with knickknacks and family photos. Tapestries draped the walls of one room, while another contained portraits of men in plaid holding large guns or petting dogs.

"This doesn't seem very Shakespearean." Not that I knew anything about the furniture and art of Shakespeare's time.

"That's because the castle was built around a tower house in the fifteenth century," Luke said. "Macbeth takes place in the eleventh century. Plus, people live here."

I paused to examine a bed draped with thick, red curtains like I'd expect at a theater. I'd be afraid they'd smother me while I slept. "How do you know that?"

"I looked it up yesterday. I like to know things."

I stopped. The last few days played through my head. "All those random facts about authors and books and places we've been? You didn't just know them?" I put a dramatic hand to my chest. "I feel so deceived."

He shrugged, unembarrassed. "Some I knew. I *did* take a comprehensive literature exam last month. If we visited somewhere that I was unfamiliar with, I did research."

"For fun?"

He smiled as we went through an old kitchen decorated with antique cooking tools. "Yes, believe it or not. I find knowledge enjoyable. You seem to enjoy the 'random facts' as well."

Huh. "I guess I do. I would never think to look them up, though."

"Call it a hobby. Anytime I go somewhere I haven't been or hear of a new topic, I want to know about it."

"Well, thanks for sharing your knowledge."

Learning didn't seem boring when Luke dropped facts into normal conversation. He made me feel smarter. Like an equal. Not as if he needed to educate a dumb friend, but like he assumed I'd be interested and wanted to share the joy of knowing, to let me into his world. I couldn't keep a slight smile off my face.

We completed the house and moved on to a flower garden. Explosions of purple and pink erupted from bushes, and shrubs were pruned into intricate shapes so neat they probably kept an army of gardeners busy year-round. The gravel path led from the garden into a quiet forest.

Now I truly felt myself connecting to Macbeth. Trees covered in moss and vines lined the trail, with giant ferns hugging the trunks. An occasional break showed fields of pale blue wildflowers. A supersweet flowery scent filled the air, and creeks and tiny birds provided a classic forest soundtrack.

I paused in a clearing among ancient trees. "I can picture witches in a place like this, after dark, on a cold, foggy night."

"What would you want them to tell you?" Luke asked.

"Nothing. That didn't work out so well for Macbeth. Besides, it's not like the future is set in stone. Prophecies mess things up."

He leaned against a tree trunk. "They could act as a guide."

"But how many people can hear their future and not do something stupid? Even after reading the play, knowing how Macbeth took things into his own hands, if I learned what I was to become? I might still try to make it happen my way."

His cheek dimpled. "That's because you lack patience."

I nudged him, leaving my fist against his upper arm a second too long. "It's because I'm human. So what can you teach me about Macbeth, Professor?"

"One of the most common questions about the play is, would Macbeth have become king anyway if he hadn't killed the current one? Would the prophecy have come true eventually if he'd done nothing?"

"What do you think?"

"That it's your competition, and your opinion is the one that matters." He smirked.

"Helpful." I shoved him lightly.

He shoved back, like neither of us could bear more than a few minutes without touching somehow, so we reverted to the safety of teasing.

I swatted at a low-hanging branch. "I guess it goes back to that destiny thing. If he was meant to be king or if his ambition made it happen." I wasn't sure which option appealed to me more, that I couldn't change my future or that I might mess it up. "Did the witches know that telling him would set those events in motion? It seems like if they'd kept their mouths shut, the whole mess could've been avoided."

We exited the woods, and I spotted the best part.

"The maze." I skipped toward it. "I've always wanted to explore a hedge maze."

"I'll meet you at the exit," Al said. "If you can find it."

"Your doubt hurts me. If I don't come out in two hours, avenge my death."

"I'll send a search party," she said.

"That's not the same thing."

"Vengeance is above my pay grade."

"After all our time together, I am hurt that you wouldn't do it simply to honor our friendship, Al."

She left to find the café, and we aimed for the maze.

The well-trimmed hedges were at least eight feet tall, which was perfect. No cheating. Us versus the bushes. Bring it on, shrubbery.

To enter, we passed through a stone door wrapped in vines. It needed a warning overhead: *Beware, all ye who enter here.* We stepped into a cool, shadowed world. The castle peeked over the top in the distance.

"If we keep track of how many turns we make . . . ," Luke started.

"Do. Not. Finish that sentence. No logic in a giant maze. We're going to wander and get lost until we make it to the middle."

"That sounds like fun," he said in a voice that implied it wouldn't be fun at all.

"Thanks, *Al.*"

Soft dirt formed the path, muffling our steps. The hedges grew close together, blocking out most of the light, making the air cool and thick. The leaves smelled like pine and Christmas.

"This is so cool." I ran my fingers over small, shiny leaves. "Just like I imagined."

Two turns later, I rounded a corner and collided with something solid. My shoulder bag ripped, sending my journal, phone, and wallet into the dirt.

"Oh. Sorry." I stepped back, bumping into Luke.

My victim spun. My victim with a faded *Star Wars* shirt and too-long hair.

"Fancy meeting you here," said Peter as he bent to scoop up my journal.

CHAPTER TWENTY-FOUR

My hands formed fists. I stepped toward Peter. Luke's fingers on my arm stopped me. Based on his tight grip, I suspected he was fighting to hold himself back, too.

"Nice chin," Peter said.

"Give me that." I reached for the book, but he shifted it behind him.

I lunged, but again, Luke restrained me.

I crossed my arms so I didn't strangle Peter. "What's your problem? Not confident in your ability to win, so you have to mess with the rest of us?"

"I haven't done anything. Are you still on that?" His thumb fanned the pages. "First you trip, then you drop your things, and somehow it's my fault?"

Please don't read it. I scowled and shifted, bumping Luke, who lurked nearby like my personal Secret Service. "Where's your chaperone, anyway?"

"Ditched him."

Of course, at the time I most needed another witness. "Why do you hate me?"

"Figures that you wouldn't remember." His lip did the villain curl again. "Fifth grade? In the lunch yard?"

Seriously? "That was seven years ago! I barely remember what I ate for breakfast."

"'Journey to the Center of the Galaxy'?"

I hesitated. The phrase rang a bell, but a distant one I couldn't place.

His jaw clenched like he couldn't believe I remained clueless. "You found a notebook with a science fiction story in it, and you read it aloud. Everyone made fun of the writing and whoever wrote it."

"What's the—wait. You wrote it?" I knew he liked to write, but he'd started in fifth grade?

"I worked on that story for weeks. And your loud, annoying voice carries. You and Ms. Perfect laughed, and everyone else heard. They said the story was dumb and the author needed a life. Heather Long kept reading from it for weeks."

Why didn't I remember that? "I'm sorry. Really. I never knew who that notebook belonged to."

My apology didn't make a dent in his unpleasant expression.

"So . . . you've hated me since fifth grade?" Granted, that would be crushing. To keep writing after your classmates made fun of you showed courage. But that was a long time to hold a grudge, especially since I hadn't meant to hurt him.

He slapped his palm with my journal. "Should I read yours out loud and see how you like it?"

I shrugged, though my heart pounded. "Go ahead. Luke's read it."

Still, I didn't want Peter to know how bad it was.

He grunted like I'd taken away his fun, so I must've pulled off pretending not to care.

"I would've thought this of all places would remind you there's a difference between knowing what you want and going after it, and cheating to achieve it." I eyed my journal. "Obviously you have no problem with Macbeth's path, but you're lucky I'm not like that. I won't knock you out and leave you here, no matter how tempted I am."

"Huh. You *did* learn something." His mocking tone sliced the air. His gaze flicked to Luke, hovering by my side in tense silence. Letting me fight my own battles but standing close enough to provide backup if needed. "Is your British lackey teaching you things?"

I stepped toward Peter. "I think you'd better leave before I change my mind about the violence."

Peter smirked and turned to Luke. "Be careful. She only thinks about herself and doesn't care who she hurts."

With a final sneer in my direction, he chucked my journal over the nearest shrub wall, spun, and vanished around a corner.

"Hey! Stop, jerkface."

I raced after him. My shoulder brushed the shrub, and a twig stabbed me, but I kept going.

Peter disappeared around another corner, heading away. Chasing him mattered less than finding the journal. I skidded to a stop. How did I reach the next row over? I raced through narrow pathways, prickly branches snatching at me when I cut it too close.

I peeked around a corner. No journal, so I went the other way. Still nothing.

I kicked the bush.

My knee felt stiff. My lungs burned. And my chin throbbed.

Trying to slow my heart rate, I gulped deep breaths. Good thing my team couldn't see me now. I'd never live this down.

Who held a grudge for seven years? And who'd have thought a childhood event I didn't remember could haunt me this long? Our tents were one thing. Even the baths, which he denied. But my journal? What if I'd written award-winning tales? Did he think Ms. Carmichael would be okay with this?

The joke was on him, though. That journal wouldn't win. I needed another plan anyway. Peter's actions had only forced my hand sooner than expected.

That didn't mean I wanted it lying around a hedge maze for anyone to find.

I sucked breaths and stared at the dirt ground, the leafy walls.

In the process of trying to find my journal, I'd lost Luke.

I took off again, jogging more slowly. When I rounded a corner, I bumped into someone. My hands formed fists, ready for Peter.

But the person steadied my arms, and I looked up at Spence. "Whoa," he said. "Why the rush?"

I didn't want to confess any of it—Peter's grudge, my lost journal—so I shrugged. "Having some fun."

He released my arms and studied me, likely deciding I

didn't look like I was currently having much fun. "Find the center yet?"

"Wouldn't you like to know? Why, have *you*?"

He shrugged and grinned. "What about the others? Have you seen them?"

"I ran into Peter."

"Hmm. He's pretty awful to you. Too bad we can't trap him here, right?"

Tempting idea, but I cared more about finding that journal. And getting back to Luke. And reaching the center.

Trying to force a carefree smile, I edged backward. "I can win without messing with the rest of you. Don't get stuck in here forever."

"Likewise." He saluted, and we went opposite ways.

Once he was out of sight, I paused.

I stood alone in the middle of the hedge maze— well, not the middle, or I'd have my next clue. Small, infrequent drops sprinkled down. The scent of wet dirt filled the air.

The silence felt like a tangible presence, highlighting my aloneness. Mazes were creepier when you were by yourself.

Would Luke try to find me or stay in one place? The easiest way to find someone in a maze was probably if only one person moved. Luke would know I wouldn't be able to stay still, which meant he would. So I was good to explore.

The journal might've been a lost cause. Maybe Peter had stumbled across it and taken it with him. Maybe I'd get lucky and find it now that I wasn't looking. Or maybe it was gone, along with its pointless musings and half-written tales.

I turned and headed the way I'd come. "Luke? Where are you? Can you hear me?"

I kept calling as I rounded turn after turn, brushing against wet leaves, everything silent. And then a small, open space greeted me.

Along with three women in cloaks.

They held umbrellas and chatted, one staring at her phone. But when they spotted me, they quickly lowered the umbrellas, pocketed the phones, pulled up their hoods to hide their faces, and rose.

Macbeth's witches.

"Do you have a prophecy for me?" I asked. "Because I don't think I want to hear it."

Not that I believed they could see my future, but after my talk with Luke and remembering how badly that went for Macbeth, I wasn't about to let strange women in a hedge maze interfere with my future in any way whatsoever.

"We have an offer," said one as they moved into a line.

"Not about the future but about the past," said another.

"And the present," added the third.

They'd clearly memorized these lines.

"Would you like to know how your competitors are doing?"

"How their tasks went?"

"What they've been learning?"

"Who seems most likely to win?"

I paused. Not exactly prophecy, but information I'd wondered. I knew what my classmates had told me about their writing, and I knew we were fairly even in our progress, but I had no idea how most of the tasks had gone for them, whether they'd rocked them or barely squeaked by.

"Have you seen them yet? Did any of them accept your offer? No, wait, don't answer that."

The women waited. With their faces hidden, I saw no expressions to interpret, couldn't guess anything. I rubbed my arm where the bush had stabbed me.

This had to be a trap. Macbeth, ambition, prophecy. The correct move was to decline, request my clue, and move on. I'd know every outcome in two days.

But those days felt endless. My future, the UCLA letter, pressed against my mind.

I blinked hard and shook my head. "No. I'm good. The next clue, if you don't mind."

"If you're sure," said the one in the center as she stepped forward.

"It's only information."

"What can it hurt?"

"No, thank you." I held out my hand. This was how they taught us to say no to drugs. My elementary teachers would be proud.

The center witch produced a card from inside her cloak and handed me an envelope.

Again, I wished I could read on their faces if this was the decision I was supposed to make. I'd better get credit for resisting temptation. Before I could change my mind, I whirled, shoved the envelope in my pocket, and returned to the maze, leaving the witches behind.

"Luke?" I called his name through several turns.

"Britt. I hear you." Layers of leaves muffled his voice.

"Keep talking."

He did, and I tried different paths, some making his voice quieter, until it got louder and I saw him.

He stood casually, hands in his pockets, as if unconcerned he was in the middle of a maze in the rain.

"Were you here the whole time?" I asked.

"Once I realized I lost you, I stopped. Why?"

"Ha. I knew it. Take that, maze."

He plucked a leaf off my shoulder. "Did you find your journal? Or the center?"

"No to the first, yes to the second." I kicked the ground. "Good thing I didn't find Peter. I would've punched him, and then my hand would be injured, too."

His eyes widened, and he stepped toward me. "Your chin isn't supposed to get wet."

"It's not raining that hard." I ran a finger over the skin near my stitches, and it came away dry. "Ugh! Being useless sucks."

"Hey." Luke rested a hand on my shoulder. "You are not useless. You're good at many things. Kids love you. You'd make a great coach. You're funny. You're ridiculously good at all things resembling sports. You're good at reading people. Knowing what they need to hear. Knowing what *I* need to hear. So I want you to stop putting yourself down."

I stared at him, mouth hanging open. "That was . . . a very passionate speech. I'm not sure what to say."

He met my gaze, unapologetic.

Did he honestly see me like that? He made me sound like a superhero. Or like someone he . . .

I didn't know if I wanted to finish that sentence.

I settled on, "I've never been close to my siblings. They like being indoors, school, quiet stuff, which my dad never understood. So when I came along, I was just what he wanted. We played catch and one-on-one and soccer. But then . . ."

"He left."

"I thought if I'd been better, faster, he might've stayed. The one thing he cared about was me excelling at soccer. So that's what I did."

"And believed you weren't good at anything else?"

"Soccer was my constant, you know? The one thing I could control. Until . . . I couldn't. Until it abandoned me, too."

"It's terrible that you can't play anymore, but it's no one's fault." Quiet intensity burned in his eyes and voice. "Not everyone abandons you. Not everyone will. You can't live thinking that way."

I dug my toe into the dirt. "It's easier than getting hurt."

He put his hands on my shoulders as if to hold me in place. "It might seem that way, but what about the future? Are you never going to get close to anyone? Never make new plans or have new dreams?"

"Maybe." As I said it, though, I knew I didn't want to live that way. "I always fight for what I want. But now . . . I don't know, maybe I'm afraid."

"Because wanting something leads to fear of losing it."

"Yeah."

287

He chewed his lip, his mental-debate face. "You can't let fear stop you from the things you want most."

"I don't know what I want, though."

"I do." His gaze was intense.

What I wanted in life was a mystery, but seeing him in front of me, in the rain, eyes deep, hands warm and firm on my shoulders, I knew one thing I wanted.

Last time, fear had won.

I definitely shouldn't do this since I was leaving soon, but I stepped closer. Rose on my toes. And found his lips with mine.

He returned the kiss instantly. Determined. Insistent. One hand cupped my cheek, his fingers settling behind my ear. The other hand slid to my back, pressing me closer.

I ran a hand through his hair, traced one across his shoulders. Every cell in my body hummed with life.

When he angled his head, his glasses brushed my cheek. I slipped them off without removing my lips from his.

The rain fell harder.

My free hand explored the angles of his shoulder blades. His palms spread across my back, sending a thrill through my core.

I pulled away, gasping. I couldn't look at him. I chanced a peek. His face was serious, as always, but something gleamed in his eyes. Satisfaction, or fear.

A chilled breeze teased my hair and mingled the scent of rain with Luke's now-familiar soap and pine. We stood frozen, gazes locked.

"I wanted that, too," he said.

He brought his lips to mine again, gently this time, slow and deliberate. More what I would have expected from him than the passion.

I should've moved away. I didn't.

His fingers left a trail of goose bumps on my neck. My hand found the back of his head, brought him closer.

Time suspended. There was no air, no breathing, no maze or rain or competition. There was only Luke.

A cold raindrop slid down the back of my neck. I jumped, separating our lips.

Luke stared at me. I ran a hand over my wet neck as we both gasped for breath, eyes locked.

He ran a trembling hand through his hair, then looked at it. "It's raining." He sounded surprised.

I nodded, not sure I could form words. I already missed his closeness.

His eyes widened. "We need to go. Keep your chin safe." He reached to adjust his glasses, blinked when he found them missing.

I held them out, my cheeks burning, and focused on his shoulder instead of his face as he put them on.

Now what? Should I say something? Take his hand? Pretend nothing had happened?

He settled the issue by weaving his fingers through mine, a tiny, secret smile flitting across his face. We jogged through the maze, hands clasped, searching for the exit.

I relived the feel of his lips, his breath mixed with mine. My heart raced again, and not from running. I was surprised the rain didn't turn to steam as it hit my face. What had I been thinking? That was the problem—I hadn't been.

By the time we found our way out, I was damp. Not drenched, but definitely damp. And I still shook from the kiss. I'd wanted to do it. Was glad I had.

Even knowing I'd be gone soon.

Even knowing it would lead to disappointment.

CHAPTER TWENTY-FIVE

In the dry, warm café, we rejoined Al, who raised an eyebrow at our clasped hands.

After we'd secured hot cups of tea, Luke asked, "Where do you go next, Pilgrim?"

Oh. Right. The clue. That kiss had distracted me. My cheeks were warm, my insides fizzing. To distract myself from the desire to peek at Luke's lips, I pulled out the card.

Strange to think this was the last one. Well, plus the writing, which was the most important part.

> Pilgrims swapped tales and made new friends;
> Find their destination at your journey's end.
>
> Then join fellow travelers for one final test
> And share a tale before earning your rest.

Luke leaned into me so he could read. A small smile hadn't left his face since our kiss, and now it widened. "Told you you're a pilgrim."

Ms. Carmichael had said the competition was inspired by Chaucer. I should've guessed. Joining the others to share a story from the journal I no longer had sounded like a sure way to end this trip in disaster.

"Where's Canterbury?" I asked.

"Not far from London," Al said.

"That's a long trip."

"There's a sleeper train," Luke said. "Travels overnight, beds in small cabins."

I nudged him. "Thanks, tour guide. That sounds fun."

As we left in search of a taxi, a dark, England-worthy rain-cloud threatened to blot out the sunshine feeling still warming my insides. I couldn't stop glancing at Luke, our eyes meeting, smiles flickering, gazes skittering away.

The competition was almost over. Our time together nearing an end.

I shoved the cloud away. I'd ignore the problem for one more day and enjoy the moment—bubbling joy, beautiful nerves, and all.

Al's and my twin berth on the sleeper train was so small, our shoulders bumped when we stood in it at the same time. She showed me how to fold out the sink from the wall and told me I got the top bunk, which had a three-rung ladder. When I stood on the bottom rung, my head brushed the ceiling. No way the bunk would be long enough for Luke's tall frame.

Why was I thinking about Luke in bed?

I sprung toward the door. "I'm heading to the lounge. Want to come?"

"You go ahead." Al held her phone. A smirk emerged. "I'm pretty sure you and my cousin would prefer the time alone."

I refused to let my face turn red. "Gotta check in with Ms. C? Her money came from smuggling, didn't it? What was it? Exotic animals? Stolen artwork? Organs?"

"Still not going to work."

I shrugged and grinned and left her alone.

I needed to text Mom. I still hadn't told her about my injury, and I didn't plan to tell her about the kiss. After a memorable couple of days, leaving out those details felt like lying. But I was so close to the end, I'd rather wait until I had good news. As I navigated the hallway, I settled for a short *Still okay*.

The lounge car had low, uncomfortable couches that I suspected came from 1960s IKEA. Based on the room's smell, the upholstery was permanently saturated with the scent of stale beer and old sandwiches. Several people perched at a bar near the door.

Luke sat on a couch at the far end. When he spotted me, his face lit up.

My smile emerged in response. The setting, the smell, none of it mattered. He stood as I approached, and all I cared about was the electricity dancing between us to unseen music, thrumming through my bones.

We ate a bland meal that was one of the best ever, because our knees brushed under the table, my heart skipped, and my stomach fluttered with every bite. Then we moved to a couch, sitting so we faced each other with my feet in his lap and his hands resting on my legs.

We alternated chatting about nothing, glancing at each other and smiling, and watching the sunset out the window.

Ringing shattered the peace.

We jumped and laughed.

"Your dad again?"

He checked his phone and frowned. "No, I don't know who this is." He hesitated before lifting it. "Hello, this is Luke . . . Yes . . . Yes." His eyes widened. He chewed his lip. The lip I imagined kissing again . . .

"All right," he said. "No, I can't get there until morning. I will. Thank you." He lowered the phone, his face pale.

"What is it? Is something wrong?"

"It was a hospital in London." A small line settled into the space between his eyebrows. "My dad checked in with severe chest pain."

I leaned forward. "Oh no. Is he okay?"

"They said he'll be fine. It wasn't a heart attack. He's been asking for me."

"I'm so sorry."

He sighed, his head hanging. "It's not your fault I ignored his calls."

His discouragement twisted my chest and filled me with the urge to make him feel better, the way he always did for me.

Luke played with his phone, turned the screen on and off, flipped it around.

I put my hand over his. "You couldn't have stopped this by answering your phone."

"I could have been there. Instead, he went into surgery and the last thing I said to him was, 'I need a break from you.'"

"I'm sure he understands."

He gripped my hand and squeezed. "Thank you."

Luke sighed and bent to put the phone in the backpack at his feet. He withdrew the small box he kept hiding, turned it over and over.

I nodded at the box. "Want to talk about that?"

He snapped the lid open, revealing the gold watch. "It was my grandfather's." His thumb traced the face. "He gave it to my dad the day he was accepted at Oxford. My dad passed it to me earlier this year when I received my acceptance letter. But I've not worn it since . . ."

He closed the lid and tucked the box into the backpack.

"Do you know I never asked him why he did it?" Luke's gaze focused on the window, like he was speaking to himself. "I told him he'd been stupid, asked if he thought about how it would affect me. But I never tried to understand. He must have been desperate, you know? Or in trouble. I didn't even ask . . ."

"He'll be fine. You guys will talk and figure things out."

He ripped his eyes from the window and focused their intensity on me. "He tried to apologize, but I wouldn't listen."

"Sometimes when people hurt us, it takes time to forgive. You're ready to listen now."

"Have you forgiven Amberlyn or your dad?" The question was genuine, not accusing.

"I don't know. I moved on. Said I forgot about it. But . . ."

"That's not the same," he said. "That's pretending you don't care. Forgiveness is acknowledging they hurt you but moving forward and letting go of the bitterness."

I picked at a loose thread on the couch. "Acknowledging

I care is the part I'm not so good at. It's easier to ignore the hurt."

"If you keep sweeping things under the rug, eventually the rug doesn't lie flat anymore."

"Then you trip on it and fall on your face?" I asked.

"Exactly."

After my dad left, I threw myself into soccer. A few years later, Amberlyn left because I was a dumb jock, so I decided to prove her right and be the best dumb jock on earth. But the practice, the drills, the running, just buried the real issues in tiredness, pain, and busyness.

Maybe Luke had a point, because this trip was making carefully hidden things leak out from under that crowded rug.

He shifted, pulling me to sit beside him, and slid his arm around me. I leaned my head against his shoulder, he pressed his cheek into my hair, and we listened to the clacking of wheels thundering through the room.

No matter what came next, I would enjoy this moment, Luke's warm body and even breathing and the sense of peace.

A sleeper train, I learned, was not created for actual sleeping.

Between the rocking, the rattling, and the mattress that might have been made of concrete, I had lain awake all night thinking. Recalling the passion on Luke's face when he recounted the things he found great about me. The feel of his lips. The comfort of his arm and the way we fit together.

And I'd spent way too long dwelling on our inevitable good-bye. Where would we part? Ms. C's flat, in front of my class-mates? The street? The airport? Would he try to kiss me again, and would I let him?

This time I'd be the one leaving. What did he expect? I wasn't the summer fling type, and he wasn't, either. He liked me. I cared about him. But nothing could come of it. I was setting myself up for another round of pretending not to miss someone.

I had to finish the contest. He had to see his dad. I'd known our quest wouldn't continue forever, but I wished the ending hadn't announced itself so abruptly.

"Are you all right?" Al asked as we packed up our bags.

"Fine. Why wouldn't I be?"

"Look, I'm not one to discuss . . . feelings . . ."

My hand tightened on my duffel. "I never would have guessed that."

"And you aren't, either."

"So perceptive."

She stared at the wall over my shoulder. "But if you need to talk, I wouldn't be one hundred percent opposed to listening."

"What would I need to talk about?" I'd told her about Luke's dad, her uncle, when I'd finally returned to our cabin, but I had no intention of telling her I'd kissed her cousin. Didn't want to confess the missing journal and let her know she'd spent the last week with a lost cause who had no hope of winning.

"I don't know. Life. Or something."

Wow, we really were terrible at this. "I'm fine. Thank you,

though." I zipped my bag closed with a jerk and moved to the door. "Ready?"

I should have said more. I knew it wasn't easy for Al to offer, but we hadn't achieved the friendship level of me unloading all my issues on her. So many issues.

I stumbled off the train in a haze of tiredness and dread. Luke and I walked slowly, the rest of the passengers shuffling past until we were some of the only people left on the platform. Al waited near the stairs, checking her phone to give us privacy.

"So . . . on to Canterbury?" he asked.

"Yep. Last stop. Hard to believe." I fiddled with the strap of my bag. "I, uh, I hope your dad's okay."

He nodded.

"Can you catch a train from here? To the hospital?"

"Yes."

A great wave built inside me. I should say something meaningful. Something real. I studied the lines of his face, the glasses, the warm brown eyes and the lips I'd kissed. I wasn't ready to give him up. But now would be easier than later.

"I'm glad you came with me."

His blank eyes provided no hint to his thoughts. Like he'd drawn blinds over his face to keep me out. He shoved his hands into his pockets. "Thanks for letting me. I hope you win."

"I guess this is goodbye."

It didn't have to be. I could visit Canterbury and return in a day. I could check on him and his dad tonight. But then what? One way or another, we'd have to say goodbye.

Before I could tell myself this was cold and stupid, I stuck out a hand. "Thanks."

He stared at my hand, face closed except a slight pressing of his lips. Finally, he grasped it, less as a handshake and more as a caress. He held on. His thumb made circles on my palm.

My heart tried to beat its way out of my chest. A fist squeezed my throat. I found myself leaning toward him, lips parting, and made myself stare at the ground. *Don't leave things like this. His dad is sick. He needs you. He* likes *you.* I ignored the insistent voice in my head and released his hand.

"Bye, Luke." I waited half a heartbeat, peeked at his mouth once more, spun, and almost ran toward Al.

Luke didn't speak. In the brief flash of his face I saw before turning, I recognized hurt, disappointment, but also resignation and something darker.

My ears strained for the sound of footsteps following me, but I refused to peek. Nothing. Why didn't he argue? Chase me? Say something? All he had to do was ask, and I'd give in and stay. Maybe he knew it was best this way. Or he thought I wasn't worth it. Or I'd hurt him.

No. *Stop thinking.*

It *was* better this way. He'd been a nice chapter, a fun addition to my quest. But now he had his own problems, and I had to finish the competition. Neither of us needed the complication.

Al didn't say anything when I joined her, but her expression held enough condemnation to fill three books.

"Don't," I said, and walked past her to find the ticket office to go to Canterbury.

That was done. Time to move on.

So why did it feel like part of me was staying behind?

CHAPTER TWENTY-SIX

Canterbury should have been distracting enough to make me stop reliving my farewell to Luke. Majestic cathedral spires jutted above the rooftops. The road took me past half-timbered houses straight from Shakespeare, quaint bookshops and cafés, between two ancient turrets forming a gate. I crossed a bridge over a quiet river that was too narrow for punting.

My pilgrimage was coming to an end. Ms. Carmichael had said that in *The Canterbury Tales*, the journey was a frame, and the tales mattered more than the trip itself. I still had those to worry about—writing them and, apparently, sharing one. Which, hello. Way too personal.

When I reached the destination of Chaucer's pilgrims, Canterbury Cathedral, I hesitated.

Luke would've told me the history. Asked insightful questions. Made me laugh.

I wished he were here. Because I missed him, and because the twisting and squeezing in my chest felt a lot like guilt.

As I entered the church, I used precious data to search like he would have. I learned the cathedral was Gothic style, the site of Thomas Becket's martyrdom, had over a thousand square meters of stained glass and an archive of old writings.

If the facts had come from Luke, I might've cared.

I wandered past columns and carvings, stained-glass windows and choir benches, until I found the tomb of Thomas Becket, the ultimate destination of Chaucer's pilgrims.

Luke's voice calling me "Pilgrim" echoed through my head.

I forced it to be quiet.

The tomb was tucked in a small corner, with a statue of a man in a red robe lying on a slab, hands folded over his chest in prayer. Tombstones lined the floor, and candles flickered on a table below four swords hanging on the wall.

My search revealed Thomas Becket had been the archbishop of Canterbury who'd decided to put the church above the king. The swords represented the four knights who killed Becket, thinking they were doing the king a favor. That idea didn't work out for them when Becket was declared a martyr and made a saint, with millions of people visiting his tomb. Talk about a bad decision.

I really didn't want to think about bad decisions.

Or people like Thomas Becket who made brave ones.

"Britt?"

I whirled at the male voice, heart leaping, but my ears registered the American accent a second before I spotted Spence. I swallowed my disappointment. Luke and I had only parted a few hours ago. He was at the hospital with his dad, not chasing after the girl who'd dumped him in a train station.

"Hey, Spence."

My voice came out dull. Dealing with him and the others was going to take too much energy.

"You made it," he said.

"Don't look so disappointed."

He stepped past me to stand in front of the tomb. "After I win, I'll get myself a fancy statue as a monument to my brilliance."

I rolled my eyes. "I think you have to die first, genius."

He faced me and grinned. "Why wait that long? If I'm dead, I can't enjoy it."

I shook my head. "Have you seen the others? Are we supposed to meet somewhere specific?"

Did Ms. C expect us to hang out until everyone was together? What if Amberlyn or Peter didn't arrive until tomorrow?

"Not sure." A glint entered his eyes. "Maybe they're stuck in Scotland."

We ambled through a huge pillared area lined with wooden benches, then down a staircase.

Normally, a crypt would interest me, but this one seemed too cheery for a place where long-dead bodies rested for eternity, with chandeliers providing sparkling light. I'd hoped for dark and dreary, to suit my mood.

Spence kept joking, but I tuned him out. Part of me was glad he offered a distraction. The stronger part wanted to lock him in one of the stone coffins until I could escape.

But we had to find our classmates, so we moved on.

Upstairs, Spence found another staircase, this one to the bell tower.

No matter how nice the view, I wasn't up for five million steps.

"You go ahead." I waved a hand.

"Knee can't handle it?" His question sounded genuine, not mocking, but it prickled.

Again I dug up the teasing smile. "Maybe I already went up there."

Thankfully, he left me to wallow by myself. Solitude made me antsy and depressed, but I wanted that right now.

I found an open green space in the center of the church, lined with arched windows and a walkway. Luke would've known its proper name. I sat on the ledge overlooking the grass.

So far, this destination was not inspiring me. But that was my fault.

What had Chaucer's pilgrims thought when they arrived here? They'd been competing, too, but Chaucer never told us who won their story contest. I hoped I got more closure.

Of course, Chaucer also failed to mention if the travelers made it to the cathedral. They might have been eaten by bears before they arrived.

"Hey."

The female voice was certainly not Luke. It was Amberlyn.

"Hi." The only person missing was Peter. Who I wanted to hold upside down and shake until my journal fell out.

She scuffed the ground. "How, uh, how's your chin?"

"Fine." Stiff, but the pain was manageable. The physical pain, anyway. The reminder of Luke's kindness that day hurt more.

"Good."

Spence reappeared, not winded from his climb. Good thing I hadn't joined him. He would've teased me about how out of shape I was.

"Aw," he said.

"What?"

"Not gonna lie, I was hoping it might just be you and me, Hanson, and the others got lost." He grinned.

Amberlyn frowned. "Hey."

He shrugged. "That where we're supposed to go?" He nodded over my shoulder.

Several people were filing onto the grass in the courtyard. A knight in armor, a woman in a red gown, two with ornamented priest-like robes, several in tunics or cloaks.

Chaucer's pilgrims.

"I'm guessing they're not here for a church service," I said.

We joined them and found Peter with the group already.

A man in a black cloak and head covering said, "Welcome, pilgrims. Please, take a seat."

My chest tightened at being called "pilgrim" by someone other than Luke.

We sat in a circle with the costumed people. I wished Luke were here to identify them from Chaucer's tales. I didn't want to use Google in front of my classmates. Our chaperones lined up along one edge, reminding me of the first day in Ms. C's flat.

We made an odd group, the old-fashioned outfits mixed with shorts and T-shirts for Spence and Peter and a sundress for Amberlyn. Though the sun shone warmly today, I wasn't ready to reveal my scar, so I was the only one in jeans.

"Where's your friend?" Peter asked.

"Where's my journal?" I shot back.

"You have reached your destination." The man's voice boomed through the courtyard. "Congratulations on completing your journey. Shall we entertain one another with tales from our treks?"

Amberlyn stood. "I'll go first. Let's get this done."

"Isn't the point to share our stories?" I asked. "Not race through to check it off a list?"

Amberlyn ignored me and opened her journal—a new one, not the wrinkled one she'd saved from the train tracks while I bled on the platform.

The beginning of her story described an uneventful time in Bath, visiting the Pump Room and attending a ball.

But she ended with, "Anne Elliot went to Bath, even though she didn't want to, out of duty to her family. Duty is a common theme in Austen's work, one I identify with. I would go anywhere, give up everything, to help my family. And like Catherine Morland, who had wealthy benefactors to take her to Bath and give her the opportunity to make something of herself, I also am grateful for the chance and will leave forever changed."

Despite the sucking up to Ms. C, I hated to admit I was impressed with the easy way she tied her story to the novels. Even if I knew that much about the books, I couldn't have written it so eloquently. Was she referring to a specific situation with her family or speaking generally? Like Luke had said, maybe she had more going on than I knew.

When Amberlyn sat, Spence jumped to his feet. Time to learn if he'd succeeded in copying famous writers' styles.

He cleared his throat. "There once lived, in the land of

California, a worthy young man known as Spence, with lofty ambitions of practicing law, who worked hard at two menial jobs while also diligently pursuing his studies, who never expected to find himself in need of stooping to base criminal behavior such as picking pockets to secure his desired future, but unfortunately for Spence, this tale begins with precisely such a requirement."

He'd certainly nailed Dickens's wordiness. His story continued, making him sound like a sad, sympathetic youth. Suspense built as he made his descent into criminal behavior.

Answered that question—at least with Dickens, he'd succeeded quite well.

I was doomed.

Going last seemed cowardly, but when Spence finished, Peter scrambled up before I could. His head ducked, and his cheeks were red.

After learning I'd inadvertently caused people to mock his story being read aloud, I felt a tiny amount of sympathy for him, before I remembered he was the reason I had nothing to read.

What were the odds of an earthquake swallowing the cathedral before my turn arrived?

"Putting it off?" Spence asked me.

"Saving the best for last," I said.

Amberlyn snorted.

Peter began to read, his voice quiet and lacking Spence's confidence. His story centered on a young man stopping at a tavern to refresh himself during a long trip, where he met likeminded companions who appreciated epic stories. Of course he'd selected his Oxford tale. It sounded like he'd written his whole journal as an overarching hero's journey, about a boy leaving home on a quest, like a classic fantasy novel.

After he stopped, I actually wanted to ask what happened next.

I was super-triple doomed.

When he finished, the others watched me expectantly.

This felt harder than sharing with strangers. These people were my competition. In Bath and Scotland, sharing with Nick or the cab driver, nothing was at stake. Words simply came out. My classmates would be comparing my tale to theirs to see if I measured up. And I couldn't exaggerate their roles with them sitting in front of me.

Entertain the strangers. I could do that. And humor was my best bet. Since I had nothing to read, good thing I excelled at winging it. I stood and focused on the Chaucer characters.

"It was a foggy night in the hills of Dartmoor. Silent, until a howl pierced the darkness, waking me from sleep. A light flickered on the moors."

I made my voice low and melodic as I continued.

"My companions and I set off to find the source of these strange phenomena, through the eerie mist, all alone in the countryside. What would we find? And then, in the dirt, we saw them. Giant paw prints. Sherlock's hound was hunting that night."

The costumed people's eyes were locked onto me. Feeling energized, I went on.

"We searched, worried at every turn that something might jump at us from behind a rock. But, after a fruitless search for

307

the mysterious dog, we gave up. If the hound roamed the moors that night, it didn't want to be found. We returned to the campsite, safe and uneaten, when I noticed. Something was wrong." I shifted my tone, now louder and dramatic. "Our fine tents, shelter and protection from the elements . . . they were gone. A dastardly villain had used the distraction, tricked us into leaving, so he could sabotage our quest."

The pilgrims chuckled. Spence laughed loudly.

Making people laugh was always a win.

"But we prevailed. After a cold, wet night, we continued on, and I stand here today, despite the villain's best efforts, undefeated by ghost dogs, camping, or English weather. At my final destination and ready to win."

I bowed. The pilgrims applauded.

I smirked at Peter. "Not bad for not having my journal, huh? Where is it, Finch?"

"Really? Blaming me again?"

"Yeah, because you keep messing with me."

"You took her journal?" Amberlyn sounded scandalized.

"You're taking her side? Figures. Typical of both of you, arrogant and clueless." He stood and glared at me. "Stop blaming me for your failures."

"It's not a failure when someone steals from you."

"I left your stupid journal in the maze. Not my fault you were too dumb to find it."

I refused to let that jab hit, no matter how similar it sounded to my own silent fears. I crossed my arms. "And everything else?"

"How many times do I have to tell you, it wasn't me? Not

the baths. Not your tents. Besides, how do I know you aren't the one who messed with me? When I finished the King Arthur task, and the grail was missing? After we searched forever, my chaperone had to call Ms. Carmichael for the clue."

Spence snorted.

"I have no idea what you're talking about. I finished that one first and was long gone." My jaw tightened. "Not so dumb after all, am I?"

Amberlyn's gaze had been bouncing back and forth between us, and now she stood and faced Peter. "Was it you who locked up my bags in Plymouth? It took me thirty minutes to convince them to open the locker and let me prove they were mine. I missed my train."

Chuckling came from Spence, reclining in the grass.

Peter's scowl shifted to her. "For the last time. It. Was. Not. Me. I'm perfectly happy to beat you all without cheating."

Spence was fully laughing now, loudly.

"What's so funny?" I asked.

"All of you, yelling at each other. It's fantastic."

"What are you talking about?"

"I just wanted to distract you. Get in your heads. But turning on each other, too? Priceless."

I froze. Wheels churned in my mind, processing his words.

Amberlyn, Peter, and I blinked at each other in silence, then shifted to look at Spence, the only one still sitting.

"It was you? The tent poles, the baths?"

His eyes watered from laughing so hard, and he wiped them. "You should have seen your face before you hit the water."

"Told you it wasn't me," Peter muttered.

"You admitted you hate me, and I saw you there. What was I supposed to think?" I whirled on Spence. Shock hardened to simmering fire in my gut. My fists clenched, and my nostrils flared. "I could have been hurt."

"And what if I hadn't been able to get my bags?" Amberlyn's face was red. "That's theft."

Spence waved a hand. "I wondered which of you would hear the sounds and fall for the dog thing. I didn't expect it to be you, Hanson."

"Whatever. I didn't *fall for it*. I knew there was no dog."

Amberlyn tossed her hair. "You don't honestly think you can win like this, do you?"

Spence shrugged. "You're all here. You have tales, which I made more entertaining."

"What about fair play? Good sportsmanship?" I'd expected better from him.

"I didn't interfere in big ways. Just . . . spiced things up."

"You can bet I'm telling Ms. Carmichael about this." Amberlyn snatched her purse from the ground. "Are we done here?" she asked the lead Chaucer guy.

The robed guy cleared his throat, eyes darting among us. "Er. Right." He climbed to his feet. "Thank you for sharing your tales. We wish you the best of luck on the outcome of your quest."

The other characters shifted, glancing at each other. Some watched us openly, eyes wide, while others glanced away like they were trying not to stare at something indecent.

Amberlyn glared at Spence one last time and marched off.

Peter gave Spence the scowl usually reserved for me, then shifted it to me, and followed her.

Now I felt bad for blaming him. Even if he was a jerk, he hadn't acted on it like Spence.

Only Spence and I remained. I stared down at a guy I thought had been my friend. He remained in the grass, leaning back, smiling slightly.

Apparently, competition brought out the worst in some people.

I leveled a finger at him. "Stay away from me, Lopez."

He blinked, as if he truly didn't understand our rage. "Aw, come on. It was just some fun. I thought you'd appreciate it."

"I appreciate people who don't cheat."

I marched toward Al and straight out of the cathedral. A storm churned inside me. How had he blindsided me so completely? I should have seen it, with his talk of doing anything to win, his jokes that hadn't been jokes.

"I can't believe it. I thought I knew him."

"Don't worry," Al said. "I'll report this to Ms. Carmichael."

"Do you think she'll do anything?"

"She won't be pleased. He might not have caused a huge impact on any of you, but he could have hurt you in Bath." A rare dark expression furrowed her face.

Did he have my journal? I should've asked him. I'd nearly forgotten he'd been in the maze that day. He could have found it and picked it up.

Well, I wasn't going back now. I couldn't stand to look at him. And the journal wouldn't help much anyway.

I needed to focus. Now that I'd gotten a taste of their tales,

I had to write mine. Spence wanted to get in my head, but I refused to let his pranks distract me.

We entered London in early evening, the sky a pale white-blue with streaks of silver clouds. I waited until the train approached a random stop, grasped the pole, and jumped off.

"A little warning next time," Al muttered as she hurried after me. "Where are we going?"

"Exploring."

I needed to ignore my anger at Spence, channel it, focus. I ended up strolling along the river, heading toward a giant Ferris wheel. Signs said LONDON EYE, and it did resemble one. Once I knew its name, I felt it watching me. Judging me.

Al walked closer than usual but still behind me. Not like friends enjoying an evening together. More like she was watching, too.

I missed Luke more than ever. I wanted to talk to him about Spence. Discuss Canterbury. Hear his confidence that I'd figure out my stories. Was it only this morning I told him goodbye?

What had I been thinking?

I bought a new journal and sat in a crowded park. Since I had nothing, I supposed I should start at the beginning. I tried to take Luke's advice, considering what I'd say if I told the story aloud. But it didn't translate. If I talked, would Al transcribe for me? Or was that outside acceptable assistance parameters?

My classmates each had a unique angle to their stories, a good one. I needed that.

After chewing on the pen, I wrote about my first day in London, visiting the orphanage and taking a Dickens tour. When I stopped and reread my words, I wanted to chuck the journal in the Thames. It sounded like a picture book. See Britt walk to the train station. See Britt meet Luke. See Britt play soccer.

This wasn't what Ms. Carmichael wanted to hear. But how did I find words for a trip like this? The health issues I didn't want to talk about, meeting someone as special as Luke, confronting lifelong fears. Everything was too big for a pen, paper, and my feeble writing skills.

I could keep writing out simple stories and hope Ms. C wasn't too disappointed. But I wanted to win, and this wouldn't accomplish that.

Gnawing on the pen while I watched people didn't offer any ideas. Neither did another walk along the river. The ice cream bar was tasty but not exactly brain food.

I gave up and trudged to the tube station, shuffling my feet and banging the useless journal against my thigh.

Maybe sleeping on it would help.

It'd better, because I was running out of time.

CHAPTER TWENTY-SEVEN

Amberlyn didn't bother glancing up at my arrival in the dining room the next morning.

I poured a cup of tea, added four sugar cubes, and downed the drink in three swallows, scalding my throat. I couldn't face her without caffeine. I poured another cup and sat.

"So . . . based on your story yesterday, I guess you were able to save your old journal?" I asked.

"Like you care."

"I don't care. That's why I got this"—I pointed to my chin—"trying to help you." I'd showered this morning and removed the gauze. The black stitches stood out gruesomely. I hadn't expected the bonus of freaking her out. "Because I didn't care."

She stared at her tea, face green. "You're right. Thank you."

"I'm sorry, I didn't catch that."

"I'm not saying it again." She twisted her teacup. "Can you believe Spence?"

"I'm furious, but anger doesn't help. I'm trying to focus on my stories."

"That's mature of you."

"Don't sound so surprised." I shoveled food onto my plate—fried eggs, toast, bacon that was a cross between normal bacon and Canadian bacon. I stared at a pot of baked beans.

"They go on the toast, apparently," Amberlyn said.

"Why wouldn't they? That's a perfectly normal breakfast." I scooped beans onto my toast.

We ate in silence.

I'd shoved the last piece of bacon into my mouth when Amberlyn cleared her throat.

"Why do you need this money anyway?" she asked. "Don't you have a soccer scholarship?"

"Why do you want to know?" I asked. "You haven't cared in years."

"You're one to talk."

I took a final swig of now-lukewarm tea. "What's that supposed to mean?"

"Where's your new boyfriend?"

The tea soured in my throat. "None of your business."

She folded her napkin. "You ditched him, didn't you?"

"Why would you think that?"

"Because you're good at that." She sipped her tea but glared at me over the rim of her cup.

"You're one to talk." I repeated her words, not sure what she was getting at.

"I 'think that' because you're afraid to get attached to people. You assume they'll abandon you."

"That's generally what happens, yeah."

"Guess what?" She set her cup down with an uncharacteristic thump. "You leave, too."

"You're big on the cryptic statements today."

She pushed her plate away and leaned toward me. "Have you spent time with the soccer team since you got hurt? Gone to games? Practices? Team hangouts? You haven't, have you?"

Her words hit like bullets.

I didn't reply. She couldn't know what it was like, seeing them enjoy something I'd never have again.

"And Luke?" she continued. "Let me guess. You decided it was too hard being with someone who lives on another continent, so you left him and moved on."

Bull's-eye. She aimed her words better than her darts.

"Better to move on than dwell on the past and things you can't change." I tapped my fork against the table.

"Even if it hurts people? Like when I needed you?"

"What are you talking about?" I felt like we were having two different conversations, and I didn't want to be part of either.

"In sixth grade."

"Yeah, you went away and when you came back, you were too cool for me. I was the dumb jock who ended up in crazy situations and talked too loud, and you wanted serious, more suitable friends."

"I went away because my grandmother had a stroke. Did you ever think to call me? To check on her?"

Why didn't I remember that? Had she told me about her grandmother, and I forgot? Or had she been waiting for me to initiate? I poked the fork tines into my fingertips.

Was it possible I'd been wrong all these years, and she hadn't left me?

"Besides"—she crossed her arms—"when I returned, you didn't care. You replaced me with soccer and didn't seem to mind if I moved on."

She and I remembered that year very differently. "I thought you didn't want to be friends anymore."

"You could've asked me."

"And risk you shutting me down? No thanks." I made myself put the fork on the table. "Moving on myself was easier than admitting I missed you and risking you not caring."

Her eyes flashed. "That's exactly my point. You get mad at others for leaving, but you do the same thing."

Yesterday played through my head. I knew Luke and I would have to say goodbye eventually, so I'd gotten it over with. I had no defense.

"Do you even have real friends?" Amberlyn asked.

"I have lots of friends."

"Real ones. Close ones. Like we used to be."

Like Luke and Nick, who I'd envied. Once again, Amberlyn saw me too well. I was friends with everyone on the soccer team. Had lots of guy friends from other teams. But no one I could call at night to share secrets. None I relied on, needed, trusted.

Other than Luke, a voice whispered in my head. I told it to shut up.

There was a good reason for the way I acted.

"You want to know why I need the money?" I threw my napkin on the table. "Because the one thing I let myself get attached to is gone. This?" I held out my leg and pointed to my knee. "This is nothing. But the other news I got after surgery? The news about a blood condition? I can't play soccer. Ever. Again."

The shock on her face was what I'd been going for, but it didn't make me feel better.

"That's why I don't get attached. When you want something— when you care—it leads to disappointment."

Her mouth pursed. "What a depressing way to live."

"What about you? Perfect grades, every extracurricular ever invented, plus you probably invented new ones. Why do *you* need this?"

Once the words were out, I found myself truly curious. I'd asked everyone else their stories but not the person I'd been close to, the one I'd assumed I knew.

"Yes, my grades are perfect. For seven of eight semesters. The eighth? I failed everything and had to take summer classes because I was busy caring for my grandmother when she relapsed sophomore year. But that's something else you wouldn't care about since it's too hard." She paused long enough for her nail words to drive through me. "One bad semester wasn't enough for colleges to reject me. I got into UNLV's event management program. But they aren't rushing to offer money. And the medical bills weren't cheap. My family needs the help."

Amberlyn's comments about family made sense now. But why did she have to mess up my worldview even more? We hadn't been friends in years. She didn't have the right to challenge me like that.

I stood and walked out.

"Shocker," she called after me. "Run away like you always do."

I stormed into the entryway. Al, my ever-present shadow, trailed.

"Don't follow me, Alexis. I mean it." I strode out and slammed the door.

I took off jogging down the posh street before realizing that running on uneven cobblestones could make me trip. And fall. And bleed. And die.

Stupid genetics.

I slowed to a fast, angry walk.

I meant to head to the park surrounding the palace that Luke—stop thinking about him!—had mentioned, but I ended up in a different one.

Grass spread under giant trees, and a paved area held fountains and flowerpots. I followed a trail through tall, waving grass, passed a muck-covered pond, and came to another, mowed field.

Where a group of kids in school uniforms were kicking a soccer ball.

I seriously couldn't escape. This country insisted on taunting me with its obsession with the stupid sport.

As the ball bounced and rolled, a wave crashed over me.

I needed that ball. Needed to run and dribble and kick forever, and forget, escape, make it stop. Go where I didn't exist. Where I wasn't Britt Hanson, I was Girl with Ball, and nothing else mattered.

The kids moved on, bouncing the ball between them with knees, feet, heads. My gaze didn't leave the ball until I couldn't see it.

I felt empty. Like my insides had been scooped out. If I stole their ball and ran, then what? A few minutes of forgetting? That wouldn't erase the competition I was going to lose. I still had to figure out what to do with my future. And I had to stop hiding my heart from everything that might hurt it.

I sank into the grass, lay on my back, and stared, unseeing, at the trees and sky.

After at least twenty minutes of numbness, I sat up. Was this who I'd become? A coward who gave up? Who conceded competitions because they were hard? Who rejected the people who cared about me?

Amberlyn had accused me of running away. For the first time, I realized there were lots of ways to run away, and not all of them were physical.

That wasn't who I wanted to be.

It wasn't how the heroes in all those books behaved.

I stood and brushed the grass off my pants.

I was a winner. A fighter.

And I wasn't letting this—any of it—beat me so easily.

While I walked to Ms. C's flat, I squeezed my phone. Luke had programmed his number into it—in case of emergency, he'd said. Apologizing counted as an emergency in my book.

My finger hesitated over the call icon. I bit the inside of my cheek. Held my breath. Pressed it.

Doubt hit immediately. *What was I going to say?*

The phone rang once before clicking to voicemail, and an automated message said the mailbox was full.

Of course. Because this wasn't hard enough. I lowered the phone and scowled at it.

When I entered the flat, Al was waiting in the sitting room.

Without giving her a chance to ask why I'd run off, I asked, "Can you tell me what hospital Luke's dad is at?"

Plan B: show up unannounced.

She narrowed her eyes. "Why do you need it?"

I gave her a blank stare that would've made Luke proud. "Why do you think?"

She didn't answer.

"Come on, Al." I shook the phone. "I *will* call every hospital in London if I have to. How long do you think that will take?" I didn't want to know how many hospitals a city this size had.

"I can't." Al crossed her arms. "Sorry."

"Why not? This type of help doesn't impact the competition."

"Maybe I want you to win," she said, "and if you take half the day to do this, there's a good chance you won't."

"I appreciate the concern. But it's my decision. Help, and you'll save me several hours."

She glared at me.

I glared back. I was an expert at this game.

She grunted. "Fine."

"Weren't you mad at me for the way I left him? You should be happy."

"I want you to make up with my cousin." She frowned. "But I want you to take this contest seriously."

"I am. But I need to fix things with Luke first. You don't have to come. This isn't part of the competition."

She appraised me. "I think it is." She stood. "Let's go."

Al navigated, taking us to an enormous building made entirely of blue windows.

I hesitated outside the front doors and stared at the sign that said THE ROYAL LONDON HOSPITAL. Nausea bubbled in my stomach. I wasn't here for me. Nothing would go wrong. I would support Luke and apologize, that was all.

I marched inside and to the counter, steeling myself against the smell of medicine and stale, sick air. "Hi, I'm here to visit Mr. Jackson."

"First name?" the nurse asked.

"Um."

She squinted at me. "Um Jackson?"

Al sighed. "John. John Jackson."

The lady typed on her keyboard. "Are you family?"

"No, but—"

"I'm his niece," Al cut me off. I felt her mentally rolling her eyes at me.

"Room 212. Take that lift and turn right."

When we were in the elevator, I said, "Good thing you came."

Al shook her head.

We stopped outside room 212. My heart thumped wildly. Was Luke in there? How would he react? Would he be mad? What should I say? I took a deep breath and poked my head in the open door.

The only person in Mr. Jackson's room was Mr. Jackson.

I stepped back and scanned the area. A nurse's station, a vending machine, a guy in a wheelchair. But no sign of Luke. Maybe he'd gone for food. My heart sank but also slowed.

I hovered near the doorway, trying to remain out of sight, while Al spoke to her uncle. Mr. Jackson had messy brown hair the same shade as Luke's except with gray streaks at the temples. Bags under his eyes implied he hadn't slept in ages, and he probably hadn't shaved in three or four days. I easily pictured him as a professor. But no matter how hard I tried, I couldn't see this pale, frail man as someone who had cheated, gotten fired, and ruined his son's future.

After Al and Mr. Jackson chatted, Al asked, "Where's Luke?"

"He left. Said he had something to take care of."

"Where did he go?"

"Didn't say."

Left? Left where? Like, to the store for a meal? To help at the orphanage? I had to see him.

I moved down the hall and tried to call again. Still no answer or room to leave a message. This new plan was not off to a promising start. Good thing I wasn't the superstitious sort.

I tapped the phone against my palm. Then I dialed Amberlyn.

"Am? It's me. Can you give me Nick's number?"

"What?"

323

"Luke's friend Nick. I know he programmed it into your phone. I need to find Luke, and he'll know how."

The line was silent so long I thought she'd hung up on me. Not like I would've blamed her after breakfast. "Okay. I'll text you. Britt?" Her voice was hesitant.

"Yeah?"

"Good luck."

I paused. "Thanks, Am."

I held my breath and dialed the number she sent.

"Hullo?"

"Nick? This is Britt. Luke's friend. From America." Like he needed the reminder.

"Hey. What's up?" He sounded cheerful and genuinely curious.

"Listen, do you know where Luke is? I'm at the hospital with his dad, but Luke's gone and he isn't answering his phone."

"He's here. Why?"

My breath caught. "With you?" So much for surprising him.

"Not at this exact moment. He's in Oxford for the day."

He returned to Oxford voluntarily? "I need to see him."

"He said you were working on your project today."

"He did?" Nick didn't sound mad at me. Had Luke not told him what I'd done? Of course he hadn't. Luke was too nice to blab to his best friend that the girl he'd met had been a total jerk. That made me feel worse. Or did it mean I was wrong about Luke's feelings for me, and he didn't care enough to mention what happened? "I mean, yeah, I am. But I can finish on the train. I need to talk to him."

"Call me when you get here. I'll meet you at the dorm."

"Thanks. Don't tell him I called, okay?"

"Sure, why not."

"Thanks, Nick."

Looked like I was going back to Oxford.

CHAPTER TWENTY-EIGHT

We left the hospital, and I told Al what I'd learned.

"Now you really don't have to come," I said. "I've been to Oxford. I'll be fine."

"I'm sure you will. But . . ."

"But you can't bear to be apart from me? Well, okay then." I started across the parking lot.

She half smiled, but it faded. "Are you sure about this? Two hours to visit the hospital is one thing. Going to Oxford will take nearly a whole day. No offense, but your tales aren't exactly writing themselves."

She had a point.

I stared across the sea of cars. In the back of the parking lot, I spotted an RV and thought of the Humphreys. Specifically, Mrs. Humphrey, the budding film enthusiast.

Other moments from the trip raced through my head, along with Luke's comments on my storytelling skills.

An idea sprouted.

I spun toward Al. "I changed my mind. You have to come with me. I need you."

She raised an eyebrow.

This could work. I'd make it work. "Where can I buy a video camera?"

A week ago, she would've said providing that information fell outside acceptable assistance parameters. Now she searched on her phone and directed me to the nearest store.

I bought the cheapest camera they had, which basically did nothing but film.

"Okay," I said. "Let's go."

Once we settled on the train, I gave the camera to Al. While she read the instructions, I retrieved the guidelines Ms. C had given us the first day.

Nerves churned in my stomach. The rules didn't say what I'd hoped to find. But calculated risks sometimes paid off. Right?

"Care to explain?" Al unfolded the view screen.

I smoothed the sides of my hair and tightened my ponytail. Then took my hair down and shook it out. Then changed my mind and pulled it back again. "One thing that made *The Canterbury Tales* significant was that it was regular stories told by common people." I dug through my brain for the word Luke had used. "Vernacular. The way they would've spoken."

"All right . . . ," she said.

"They used their own voice. And the pilgrims told their

stories aloud." I brushed imaginary lint off my shoulders and straightened my T-shirt. If I'd known I was going to film myself, I would've worn something nicer than a soccer shirt. "That's what I'm good at. Definitely not writing. So, I'm going to tell tales my way and hope Ms. C likes it."

Al cocked her head. "Interesting."

"It's risky. She might automatically disqualify me. The rules say to turn in our journal. I'm taking a chance she won't totally hate a video, since our challenge in Canterbury did involve sharing out loud."

"It is rather clever."

"Don't start being nice to me, Al. I don't know how to handle that." I nodded toward the camera. "Can you operate it?"

She glanced around the fairly full train. "Are you sure you want to do this here?"

"No choice. I have to see Luke, and my tales are due tomorrow morning. I have no idea how long it will take." I grinned. "I like to talk."

"Do you plan on sharing anything personal?"

I shrugged. "I perform better when there's an audience."

Al's wrinkled forehead and tight lips said she'd choose death by a thousand paper cuts over sharing anything remotely personal in front of total strangers. I thought it was partly a British thing, and partly an Al thing, but I had no such hesitation.

Plus, like I told her, if I wanted to see Luke, there was no choice.

"Are you ready?" I asked.

She pressed a few buttons and shifted so she leaned against the window, camera facing me. "Tell me when."

I adjusted my angle to face the camera. Took a deep breath. "Action."

A red light appeared. I looked into the lens but pictured Luke's face. Al's. Nick's. Ms. C's. This felt right. I could do this.

"In Chaucer's time, and even now, pilgrimages are a symbol. A person takes an outward journey, but it's a reflection of the inner one they're truly making. A wise teacher said travel changes you if you let it, so I'm going to describe how an outer journey through England changed me."

I began my tale a few weeks before Ms. C's invitation, with the injury and the story I'd told Luke. That had offered a practice run. The words came easier this time since I'd already said them.

"How do you react when you learn the one thing you wanted in life is gone forever?" I fought the urge to tug my hair, settled for clasping my hands out of sight of the camera. "A week ago, I would've said ignore the problem. Hide under a blanket like a kid who thinks, *If I can't see them, they can't see me.* But a wise friend told me if you keep sweeping things under the rug, eventually the rug doesn't lie flat. And then you start tripping on it. That's where we come to the envelope in my locker."

I sensed the lady in front of us leaning to listen between the seats. The guy across the aisle had removed his headphones. But I was committed. They could eavesdrop all they wanted.

From the envelope, I talked about wondering why Ms. C picked a mediocre student, and fearing I had no chance. My first airplane flight. Visiting the orphanage. I included meeting Luke and how he understood me too well for someone I'd just met.

I tried to be less dramatic and more contemplative than

I usually was when I told stories aloud, while still setting the scene and adding action.

When I finished describing the first day, after possibly exaggerating my pickpocket skills, and adding everything I'd learned about Dickens from the tasks and from Luke, I said, "Cut."

Al turned the camera off.

I let my shoulders slump and chugged water. Even for me, this involved a lot of talking.

"You're a natural in front of the camera," Al said.

"Too bad I won't have time to edit this. Ms. C gets to hear me, unfiltered. I hope I have time for the whole week. I might be up all night."

Her lips twitched. "I should buy you a tripod."

"Nope, you wanted to help, you get to stay until I'm done."

"Fantastic."

In describing Glastonbury, I turned the sword battle into an epic tale worthy of a movie and spared no detail from Al's unfortunate encounter with cow poop. Her glare speared me from behind the camera.

A few passengers chuckled. I sat straighter. Knowing they responded the way I wanted gave me confidence.

I shared how King Arthur made me contemplate what I was meant to do, and how thoughts of the future and my life purpose no longer terrified me. Though, most of the credit for that belonged to Luke. Who I was *not* thinking about now.

"Hey, keep it down over there," a voice called from a few rows up.

"Hush," said another. "I want to hear this."

"Me too," said someone else.

"Keep going, girlie," a fourth voice called.

The camera trembled with Al's silent laughter. Would the recording capture passenger commentary? I smiled and did keep going, describing hitchhiking with the crazy RV family, how it dredged up memories of my family and my hopes for the future.

"I avoided it for years. I've never said this to anyone, but . . . I miss my dad." My discussion with Luke came to me, about forgiveness, and I wished he were here for this admission. "I'm still angry at him for leaving, but I choose to forgive him."

I paused. Talking about my dad filled me with longing for my mom, which was strange. We weren't close. We never spoke on the phone, relied on texting. But I needed to hear her voice.

"Hold on a sec," I told Al as I dug out my phone. It was super early in California, but moms always loved to hear from their kids, right? Our texting app allowed for calls as well.

"Britt?" Mom answered, her voice panicked. "Is everything okay?"

"Yeah, fine. I just wanted to talk." And hadn't considered that a rare phone call would scare her. Whoops.

"Oh." She sounded surprised. "That's nice."

"Sorry if I woke you."

"I would wake up anytime for you. How's the contest going?"

I plucked at a thread on the seat. "I feel okay about it, I think. I'll find out tomorrow. I know I have to win."

"It's fine if you don't. I'm glad you had this experience."

"But college. The money. We need it."

"I won't lie to you and say that everything is fine, but we'll figure something out."

I sighed. "I'm sorry I didn't make it easy, like Maya and Drew."

"Hey." Her voice carried unexpected sharpness. "You're following your own path, not your siblings'. I love you no matter what. And I'm proud of you no matter what."

Tightness seized my throat.

Her tone softened. "You've had a hard year, but you fought through it, and that's what you'll continue to do, whatever happens this week. Because that's who you are. A fighter."

"Thanks, Mom." I forced the words out. "I'll call you tomorrow."

I stared at my phone. I'd been so busy trying to please the dad who left when I should have focused on the parent who stayed. While I blinked hard, Al stared out the window, pretending not to notice me. For once, I appreciated her preference for privacy.

"What are we waiting for?" I cleared my throat. "Let's do this."

When she lifted the camera again, I detailed the Sherlock challenge and recreated the story I'd told in Canterbury about having our tent poles stolen. This time, Spence made an appearance as the unscrupulous competitor sabotaging his classmates. I also detailed his role in my unplanned dunking in Bath.

Then I described the rest of Bath, including my new appreciation for Jane charting her own course in life, ending with, "Personality-wise, I'm closer to Lydia Bennet than her sisters.

But the heroines were the ones who learned from their mistakes, and that's what I'm trying to do, too."

I took another break, and the lady in front of me sneaked a peek at me between the seats.

Al raised an eyebrow at the blatant display of curiosity.

The woman flashed me a thumbs-up and faced forward again.

The train slowed as we drew near to Oxford. Filming had offered a distraction from what awaited me, but my tale wasn't over. If Jane Austen were watching, I hoped she might help arrange a happy ending to this part of the story.

This time, I easily navigated through the city. Al and I walked in silence, side by side, and the quiet was comfortable. I found the door Nick had taken us through and tried to push away memories of Luke and me sharing secrets in the dark, him reading to me, almost kissing me.

Today, a tiny old man sat in the booth. I hoped he wasn't supposed to be a guard, because I could've knocked him over with a feather. "Can I help you?"

"I'm here to see Nick." *Whose last name I don't remember.* Man, I was a mess.

"Who're you?" He pushed himself higher in his seat to squint at me over the edge of the window.

"Britt. He's expecting me."

He frowned but picked up a phone. "Some American girl . . . All right. He says he'll meet you." He nodded inside. "Go on."

I entered the courtyard, my gaze finding the spot where Luke and I had lain in the grass. I needed to stop thinking of

333

everything in comparison to him in case this went badly. And Luke had every right to make this go badly.

We sat on a bench, but Nick arrived less than a minute later.

"Hey again," I said, because what do you say to someone who watched you bleed profusely, taught you to punt, and whose best friend you basically rejected?

"Hullo." He hugged me. "Your chin looks . . ."

"Yeah, hideous. I know."

He laughed. "What're you doing here?"

"I guess Luke didn't tell you I was . . ." I decided not to finish that thought.

"He seemed down, but I assumed it was his dad."

"Maybe, but I also . . ." I paused. "Well. I'm here to apologize."

Nick nodded like that was normal and didn't press for details. I thanked him in my head.

"Do you know where he is?" I asked.

"He said he had something he needed to take care of but didn't tell me what. I'm meeting him for lunch." He jerked a thumb over his shoulder. "Want to come?"

"Thanks."

We walked to the main street, Nick filling the silence by asking about Amberlyn, the rest of my trip, Amberlyn again, and telling me the same story Luke had about when Nick got stitches.

At a restaurant on High Street, Nick stopped. Through the window, I spotted Luke waiting at a table. Same jacket. Same hair falling over his forehead. Same lips that were both soft and insistent . . . Nerves tumbled in my stomach like clothes in a dryer, and I rubbed my shaky, clammy hands against my thighs.

Nick entered first, and Luke stood when he saw his friend. I trailed behind Nick, peeking out from behind him when we reached the table. Luke froze, a flash of something unidentifiable in his eyes before he wiped his face clean of emotion.

"Can I talk?" I stepped around Nick. "Before you say anything? Then if you tell me to go away, I will."

He nodded once.

I gripped the back of a chair, the wood slightly sticky. *Just say it.* "I was an idiot. It took Amberlyn to make me see it. My whole life I've gotten used to people leaving, and it made me afraid of getting attached to anyone or anything. Losing soccer made it worse. Then I met you, and I liked you, but all I could think about was the fact that I'm only here for a week. If I got attached to you, it was going to suck when I left. I haven't let anyone in like I let you in this week."

His face gave away nothing.

Ignoring my heart pounding in my ears, the waiter carrying plates of delicious-smelling burgers, Al and Nick and two dozen customers, I forged on. "Amberlyn said that because I feared people leaving, that's exactly what I did—left before they had the chance. Somehow she knew I'd done it to you. It worked before, because I never had anyone I cared enough about to mind losing. But I don't want to lose you. So if I do, it won't be because I ran away or was afraid to try. I'm sorry. I'm especially sorry for leaving when you needed me. You were there for me, and I should've been there for you. Can you forgive me?"

Once again, perfect strangers were observing the most private thoughts of my heart. Luke and I faced each other in the middle of a busy restaurant. Nearby customers had fallen silent, although they pretended not to watch. The waiter unloaded burgers onto tables, more slowly than necessary.

Normally, I could read Luke's expressions, but now I saw why the ability had surprised him. His face was blanker than my useless journal.

I wanted—so, so badly—to fill the silence. But I'd said what I needed to say. The rest was up to him.

"Can we go outside?" he asked.

"Oh. Right." Way to win points, confess my feelings and put him on the spot in a public place.

I trailed him to the door.

We stepped onto High Street, where students, shoppers, and tourists bustled about their business, oblivious to our drama.

As soon as we were alone on the sidewalk, Luke turned to me.

I held my breath, as if that helped me hold twenty additional apologies that wouldn't have any greater effect than the one I'd given.

We studied each other, and the last few days played through my head. The secrets we'd shared, the fun we'd had. The way I'd left. If I thought about the good things hard enough, maybe I could imprint them onto his brain and give him a reason to forgive me.

His arms circled me before I realized what was happening. I'd already run out of breath, and now my nose pressed into his shoulder. I shifted my face, gasping for air. His arms didn't budge. Mine slid around his waist.

"I was hurt," he said, his breath tickling my hair. "But I wasn't surprised. From the first time you pulled away, I tried to convince myself it was better that way. That people let you down, that it was no big deal. But I couldn't stay away from you."

A hesitant, hopeful sensation swelled inside me.

"I hoped you shared my feelings, but we've only known each other for a week. You have to go home soon. I knew you weren't good at emotions. I think I expected you to do something like that."

"Part of me wished you would come after me." I spoke into his chest, afraid that if I released him, he might vanish. "Stop me from running."

"I should have. I knew what you were doing, but I let you get away with it. Somehow, expecting things won't work out makes it more bearable when bad things happen."

I nodded against his shoulder. People hurried past, and a bicycle bell jingled.

"But I'm tired of living like that," Luke continued. "Expecting people to disappoint me. I'm ready to expect that good things can happen, too."

My heart perked up. "Am I one of the good things?"

"Most certainly." He loosened his hold on me and leaned away to look at me.

I swallowed.

His hand trailed down my arm and settled on my hand. "You appreciate things about me that I didn't think were important.

You make the world brighter. You're beautiful and determined and special, and I don't know how I lasted my whole life without you in it."

Warmth swept like a wave from my head down my spine and into my toes.

"You're not so bad yourself." I twisted his hand to slide my fingers between his. "I can be myself, and you still like me. You challenge me to think and make me smile. You make me want to be a better person." I brought a hand to his face, hesitated, but he leaned his head toward me. I traced his cheek with my fingertips. "I've known you for a week, but I feel like you're the best friend I've had."

His gaze softened.

"Forgive me for running away?" I asked.

"If you forgive me for not chasing after you."

"Deal."

He bent his head toward mine, bringing a hint of pine and the featherlight brush of his breath on my cheek. His soft lips claimed mine as if we'd been kissing forever.

My hand slid into his hair, while the other circled his waist. His found the small of my back, my neck, my cheek, my hair. I ignored the people, the traffic noise, the busy life continuing around us. I could have stood there all day.

Luke pulled away suddenly, leaving my lips lonely and cold. "What are you doing here?" He sounded almost mad. "You have a competition to win."

"I'm working on it. But every tale needs a happy ending, so I had to see you first." My gaze darted to his lips.

He swayed toward me, blinked, dragged his attention from my mouth to my eyes. "Let's go eat so you can . . . what *are* you doing? Did you buy another journal?"

"Not exactly. I'll explain later." I gestured to the busy street. "I'm here because I tried to call, but your voicemail is full."

Luke pulled his phone out of his pocket and ducked his head. "Dead battery. I'm so sorry."

"Well"—I nudged him and grinned—"as long as you weren't ignoring me."

"Absolutely not. I was in a meeting and didn't realize." His eyes widened. "I guess I should tell you—and Nick—why I came. Come on."

With a final, lingering glance at my lips, he took my hand and led me inside.

Customers smiled as we passed. At least we'd brightened their day.

"Oi, mate," Nick said when we sat, shooting me a grin. "Are you going to tell me what you've been up to today? Besides the obvious?" He wagged his eyebrows in my direction.

Luke ducked his head, hair falling across his glasses. It was his shy, nervous look. I liked that I knew him well enough to know what his expressions meant.

"I was talking with the Literature Department at Oxford." If Luke were a fiddler, he would've been playing with something, shaking his foot, tapping his fingers. Instead, he folded his hands tightly on the table. "About whether a first-year can apply for student exchanges before they've started taking classes."

"Student exchange?" Nick repeated.

"Is that like study abroad?" I asked.

"They were understanding of my situation," he continued. "And more than willing to help me find a program at another university that would allow me to study in the fall without having to take additional exams. At least, not yet."

My brain couldn't process what he was saying. "So . . . you'd go to a different school. Study literature. And . . ."

"And get away from here for a bit. Give me time to decide if I can bear returning, after everything that happened with my dad, without having to give up on Oxford forever."

Nick's eyes were wide, and his mouth hung open. "I suppose that's great. I wish . . ."

"Me too, Nick," Luke said, quiet. "But I can't."

Nick ran a hand through his messy hair. "I know, mate. I'm glad it will work out." His smile seemed forced. "Who knows, maybe we can get that flat together one day and have movie marathons and live off biscuits and go punting every day."

Luke's mouth twisted in a sad smile. "Maybe so."

"Where are you going to go?" Nick asked.

"They located three schools with openings. I have a couple of days to review the programs and decide." He glanced down again. Peered up. "I'll tell you when I've settled on one." His eyes warned Nick not to push it, which of course made me insanely curious.

"That sounds fantastic." Al spoke for the first time, and I wondered if it was to keep me from interrogating him. "What does your dad say?"

"He wasn't thrilled, but he was supportive. I'll talk to him

340

today. Speaking of London . . ." He turned to me. "Doesn't someone have an assignment due tomorrow?"

"If we're traveling together," Al said, "you get to take over."

"Take over what?" Luke asked.

"You'll find out." Her lips tilted up at one corner. "Trust me, you'll love it."

CHAPTER TWENTY-NINE

After Luke said goodbye to Nick, and I hugged Nick and thanked him for his help, Luke, Al, and I returned to the train station.

Al sat in front of us, dug through her bag, and handed the camera to Luke. "Have fun."

"Aw, you don't want to finish?" I asked.

She smirked. "I figured you'd prefer his company."

He turned the camera over and raised his eyebrows.

"I'm telling my tales Chaucer-style," I said.

The spark that lit his eyes made my insides dance. "That's brilliant."

"I hope Ms. C agrees. I have you to thank for the idea. You're the one who made me see I was good at storytelling. I'm pretending I have an audience—although, on the trip here, I did. Half the train listened. And had opinions." I nodded to the camera. "Can you work it?"

He readied the camera and leaned against the window.

"Where did I leave off?"

"Bath," Al said.

"What would I do without you, Al?"

"Board a train to France. Drown. End up sleeping on a park bench. Starve."

"Okay, okay, I get it. You single-handedly saved me."

"Just want to make sure my contributions are properly noted."

"So noted." I faced Luke. "Ready? Action."

Knowing that Luke held the camera, I had trouble finding words to describe Oxford. We'd shared personal stuff. But Ms. C didn't need to know everything, so I described our trip to the pub and glossed over the fact that my literary discussion hadn't been the most profound ever. I forced myself to mention my insecurities when it came to Amberlyn.

That led me to recapping when I'd told Luke about my injury, how it had felt to talk about it for the first time.

Luke held the camera in front of the lower half of his face, so when I hit challenging parts, I could focus on his eyes and still be almost looking into the lens. Even though his reactions were more subdued than most people's, I read the laughter, the sympathy, the interest at key parts, and it encouraged me to continue.

I was on a roll. I moved on to the Birmingham station and fingered the stitches in my chin. One end of the string was poking out. Bet they looked great on camera.

"Before the knee injury, I used to think I was invincible. Even after, I had trouble believing things had truly changed.

343

Now I realize life will be different than I'm used to, but that doesn't mean it can't be good. And, cut."

I needed water, and I needed to think.

"You're doing great." Luke lowered the camera. "You make eye contact with the camera, and your vocal inflections are spot-on. You're telling your story in a way that's true to you but also touching on what you learned. This is quite good."

"Aw, stop. You're making me blush." I nudged his leg. "So, Scotland . . ."

"Tell it all," he said.

"You don't know what I was going to ask."

"You're trying to decide if you should include our night out. You should. Didn't that help inspire this?" He held up the camera.

"It did, actually."

"Do it."

I opened a Ribena, drank half in one go, and handed the rest to Luke.

A smile played on his lips.

I waved my hand at the camera. "Okay, go."

I talked about our night, the juggler, the comedian. An idea began to form in my head as I talked, a lumpy one, but one that, with tweaking, might become promising. But now wasn't the time to dwell on it.

Al's face appeared in my peripheral vision, and I realized she never knew about that night. I ignored her, moving on to the castle, the maze. I left out kissing Luke in the rain. Ms. C did *not* need those details. Neither did Al, although she probably suspected. Luke smirked when he realized I'd skipped that part, and I fought to stay on topic.

"I've always been competitive. But I believe victory is sweetest if you earn it. I'm not like Macbeth, or Spence, willing to accept shortcuts or cheats. Yes, I'll fight for what I want and work my hardest, but there are lines I won't cross."

By the time I finished Scotland, it was late afternoon, and we were nearing London. I had to describe Canterbury, but I couldn't return to the flat and risk the others hearing me.

Luke tucked the camera into my bag. "Come to the hospital with me? Then we'll go somewhere until you finish."

"How did it go with your dad yesterday? Did he explain?"

"Not yet. Talking tires him." He took the watch box out of his pocket, opened the lid. "He apologized, though."

I studied the shiny gold band and polished face. "Did you forgive him?"

"I didn't tell him, but . . . I suppose listening to you has made me realize life is too short to hold on to things."

Luke stared at the watch before sliding it out of the box and onto his wrist.

Luke led me to his dad's room. Mr. Jackson's eyes were closed, but when we entered, they blinked open.

I hesitated in the doorway. Luke tugged me farther in.

"Dad, this is Britt. The girl I told you about."

What had he told his father? I started to stick my hand out, but realized he had IVs in his arms, so I waved instead. "Hi."

Mr. Jackson's eyes crinkled at the corners like that was all the smile he could manage. "I'm glad you've made Luke so happy."

I shuffled my feet on the linoleum floor. "I hope you're feeling better."

"I went to Oxford, Dad." Luke perched on the chair in the room but didn't let go of my hand, so even though I didn't think I should be present for this, Luke had other ideas. I stood next to him and squeezed his fingers.

"I'm going to study abroad for a year," he continued. "I'll tell you the details later, but I wanted you to know they approved it. I won't leave until next month, and the doctors say you'll be on your feet by then."

Mr. Jackson shook his head. "Don't worry about me."

"But I do. I'm sorry I left." Luke's hand tightened in mine, though I didn't think he did it on purpose.

His dad nodded, opened his mouth, but instead of saying anything else, sagged against the pillows.

Luke stood and gripped his dad's shoulder. His jacket sleeve shifted, revealing the gold watch. "We'll let you rest, but I wanted you to know . . . I forgive you. I shouldn't have blamed you like I did. I know you didn't mean to hurt me. When you're out of here, we'll talk."

Mr. Jackson eyed the watch, and his eyes crinkled again. "Love you, son." The words came out as a whisper as he drifted to sleep.

We stood in the hospital room, the only sounds his dad's labored breathing and a beeping machine. Luke buried his nose in my hair briefly, and we tiptoed out.

Al accompanied us to Luke's flat. I guessed she planned to stick it out until I finished.

Luke's neighborhood had a row of connected flats like Ms. C's, but these consisted of stained brick and lacked the sculpted shrubbery, suited doormen, and marble lobbies.

"Sorry about the mess," Luke said as he unlocked the door and nudged a pile of newspapers out of the way with his foot.

"You were out of town. I can forgive it for now." I grinned, and he fake-glared at me.

The flat was basic, a downstairs with a small sitting room, dining room, and kitchen, and stairs leading to a second floor. Papers, books, plates, and teacups littered the coffee table and couch. Luke scooped everything from the four-seat dining table, dumped it on the kitchen counter, and pulled out the camera.

I positioned myself against the wall and resumed with our return from Scotland. I didn't gloss over my stupidity in leaving Luke. I confessed the same fears to the camera that I had to him. Giving them words and sending them out for people to hear felt like setting them free. Once I did, they no longer had power over me.

Luke offered an encouraging smile to remind me he forgave me, and I returned it briefly before continuing.

I admitted I hadn't fully appreciated Canterbury because I was thinking about him. His soft smile and gleaming eyes made me want to stop filming so I could kiss him again, but I kept going. Luke's head tilted in interest when I described the cathedral and the pilgrims, since he'd missed that. I described how hearing my classmates' stories fueled my worries.

Although I'd mentioned Spence's pranks, I detailed his full confession here. I didn't want to fully turn him into a villain, but

Ms. C needed to know what he'd done. Luke's frown said he wouldn't mind confronting Spence.

I paused briefly to look at him before concluding.

"Sometimes you need other people to help you see yourself more clearly. I was lucky to share this trip with someone special who did that for me. I wonder what Chaucer's pilgrims thought when they arrived at the end. Was the trip worth it? Did they learn anything? Or did they realize that simply sharing the journey and listening to each other's stories was enough?

"Cut." I sagged in my seat. "That's a wrap."

Luke poked a few buttons on the camera. When he stopped, he fixed me with a deep gaze. "This is good, Britt. Really good. I'm proud of you."

My first instinct was to brush off the compliment, but I resisted. "I couldn't have done it without you."

He grabbed a laptop from the floor. "Are you going to watch it?" He plugged the camera into the computer and then a flash drive.

"Are you kidding?" I shuddered. "Of course not. I'll find things to edit or change, and I don't have time. If I don't watch it, I can let it go."

Luke typed on the computer. "Sometimes that whole don't-look-back thing can be good, I think. I admire that about you. You don't second-guess yourself. What's done is done, and you don't obsess over the past."

"I thought that's what I was trying to overcome."

"Depends on the situation. It's fine to admit you regret things or you need closure. But it can also be helpful. Like with this. You did your best, so you're done. Here." He handed me the flash drive. "Don't lose it."

I twirled it and put it in my pocket. "The last video I made was for colleges."

Luke raised his eyebrows, waiting.

I could talk about this. I could. "Like a recruiting video. Clips of me playing soccer—from games, from practice, showing off ball skills. To send to athletic departments."

Luke chewed his lip. His eyes softened. "That one was obviously successful. Even if the result wasn't what you'd hoped, you earned that football scholarship. I've a good feeling this video will help you win another."

It was exactly the right thing to say. No pity, just faith in me. We smiled at each other, the silence stretching out, warm and gentle.

I stood. "I should go. It's late, and I have to turn this in first thing tomorrow."

He nodded.

"I'm not sure what the plan is. We'll be there in the morning, but Ms. Carmichael has to review our stories, so I don't know what I'm supposed to do all day. I'll call you."

"You'd better." He narrowed his eyes in a teasing glare.

"I will. I promise."

He walked me to the door, with Al trailing behind. We paused, shifting. I glanced at his lips then at Al. Luke swiped hair out of his eyes.

"Oh, go ahead." Al pushed between us and let herself into the hall. "Just wait until I'm outside."

Luke's chuckle sounded nervous, but I laughed loudly.

When she tugged the door closed behind her, Luke gave me a short but deep kiss and brushed hair off my cheek.

"Good night," he said, his gaze on my mouth, his voice low and rough.

A delicious shiver coursed through me, and I forced myself to leave.

"Please don't give me details," Al said.

I patted her shoulder. "Wouldn't dream of it."

Darkness had long since fallen when we reached Ms. Carmichael's flat, which was quiet. I said goodnight to Al and fell into bed.

Despite the late hour, I lay awake, thinking about what Luke had said. I'd learned I could survive thinking about the past, admitting I needed closure or was hurt. But looking forward instead of back would remain my natural tendency. And that was okay.

When I entered the dining room in the morning, Amberlyn, Spence, and Peter were already there. We ate in silence, tossing glares around the room like Frisbees. Or ninja throwing stars. By unspoken agreement, after we finished, we filed into the sitting room to wait.

Either Ms. Carmichael had spy cameras in her flat, or one of our chaperones told her we were ready, because we hadn't been there five minutes when she joined us, again dressed to meet the Queen. She must've had a closet the size of a train car to hold her colorful skirt suits.

She perched on an armchair. "I hope you enjoyed yourselves and learned something this week."

We nodded like obedient bobblehead dolls.

"Today, I will review your tales, and when I've finished, I'll meet with each of you privately after dinner to discuss them. Please leave your submissions on the table."

Amberlyn, Peter, and Spence stacked journals in front of her. I added my flash drive to the top.

Ms. Carmichael tilted her head but didn't comment.

Spence smirked. "Where's your journal, Hanson?"

I leveled him with a cool gaze. "You tell me, Lopez."

Peter and Amberlyn scowled at him, too.

Ms. Carmichael stood, silencing us, and scooped up our items. "I have reading to do." She swept out of the room.

After she left, we shifted, glancing around the room but avoiding each other. I was the first to stand, digging out my phone as I headed for the door.

"Where are you going?" Amberlyn called.

"I'm not sitting here all day. We're in freaking London. She'll need hours to get through our work, unless your journals are blank. Which I wouldn't mind."

"You wish," Spence said. "What's up with the flash drive?"

"You'll see."

"But," Amberlyn said, "what are you going to do?"

"See the Crown Jewels? Museums? Tea with the Queen?"

Anything to keep busy so I didn't imagine Ms. Carmichael watching those personal videos. And anything Luke suggested.

Amberlyn straightened like she wanted to say more.

"Want to come?" I asked before I knew what I was doing. *Idiot.*

She longed to say yes. I saw it in her eager posture and the hunger on her face. But she shook her head. I didn't extend the invitation to the guys. I shrugged and left.

Al caught up with me in the lobby. "Britt, wait."

"Are you still babysitting me?" I smiled so she knew I didn't mind.

"No, you're on your own today." She tugged the bottom of her blazer. "I wanted to talk."

"Oh," I said, curious. "Okay."

"I looked at the receipts, and based on what Ms. Carmichael budgeted for each of you, we should be able to donate a good amount to the orphanage."

"That's great."

If I didn't win, at least I'd done something good.

She nodded. Paused. "It's been an honor helping you this week."

I swallowed a smile. "I thought you weren't helping."

"You know what I mean." She shot me an eye roll and shook her head.

"I'll miss that look of frustration and annoyance. Also, don't you think 'honor' is a bit excessive?"

She pursed her lips and punched me lightly.

A loud laugh erupted from my mouth, bouncing off the marble floors. I swallowed it and made myself get serious. "Thanks, Al. You've been great. You can admit you had fun. I won't tell anyone."

"I didn't have a completely awful time. It may have . . . offered a needed break."

"What now?" I asked. "More nanny jobs or back to accounting and your boring office?"

"How do you know my office is boring?"

"Because you do accounting."

She smiled. "I rather like my job. Most of the time. The office portions, anyway. I remain on the fence about nannying."

"Whatever. You had fun this week."

"I didn't hate every second."

I laughed again.

She studied me. "I think you have a chance at this. Ms. Carmichael likes people who think outside the box, and people who aren't afraid to change. You did both this week. I'm proud of you."

"Thanks. For that, and for keeping me out of jail. If you're ever in California, come find me."

"I will." She hesitated before holding out her hand.

I ignored the hand and hugged her. Briefly. "Bye, Al."

Luke and I took a whirlwind tour of the city. We started at the Tower of London, where crazy torture and mayhem went down in years past. A guy in a fancy uniform told us tales of murder and treason. I selected my future tiara from among the Crown Jewels and my sword from the armory, reliving my knight days.

Next, we roamed the British Museum. He liked the Rosetta Stone. I liked the mummies. We laughed at the creepy bog man he'd told me about, which seemed like ages ago. We ate fish and chips. We talked about everything but nothing. No dad, no college, no contest. We held hands and kissed in public places and laughed and enjoyed the magic of London.

Our final stop was Westminster Abbey, a beautiful old church. Luke led me to Poets' Corner, where marble sculptures, plaques, and grave tiles commemorated famous writers. We found Geoffrey Chaucer's burial site and Charles Dickens's, as well as memorials to Jane Austen, C. S. Lewis, and William Shakespeare.

In a way, I was glad it was too late for this to go in a tale. Just a quiet moment with the people—living and dead—who had shaped my journey, thanking them for inspiring me.

At dinnertime, Luke escorted me to Ms. C's, and I promised to call him that night after I learned my fate.

Inside, Amberlyn sat in the same spot on the couch, but dressed in a skirt and blazer like she was awaiting a job interview.

I paused in the doorway. "Did you sit there all day?"

"Of course not. Priya and I went to Harrods. But I wanted to be nearby in case Ms. Carmichael needed me."

"Have you talked to her yet?"

She sighed. "No. Haven't seen her."

"Where are the guys?"

She angled her head toward the dining room. "Dinner's in there."

"Nice. I'm starving."

After another awkward meal, the four of us once again sat in silence, waiting.

Ms. Carmichael called Spence in first. After thirty minutes that seemed like three thousand, he shuffled out, a scowl on his face that rivaled Peter's usual expression.

"Well?" I asked. "What did she say?"

Hopefully that she'd disqualified him for being a nasty cheater.

A muscle jumped in his jaw. "Thanks for getting me in trouble."

I didn't try to hold back a snort. "You got yourself in trouble. I'm not apologizing for telling the truth."

Amberlyn glared. "I told you Ms. Carmichael wouldn't be okay with it."

"Why can't anyone take a joke anymore?" He stomped out.

Amberlyn and I exchanged an eye roll. Of course someone who played tricks like that would blame anyone but himself.

Ms. Carmichael called Peter next, and when he emerged, he looked lighter than I'd seen him. He didn't even frown at me. His good mood meant he'd probably written an amazing mini-novel that Ms. C had loved.

Then it was Amberlyn's turn. I paced. Rearranged knick-knacks on every surface. Ran a finger over the shelves to make sure Ms. C's maid was doing a good job. Had a second helping of a sticky dessert that tried to glue my teeth together.

Finally, Amberlyn returned, her eyes bright, like she'd nailed that job interview and was well on her way to upper management.

Her and Peter's happiness did not bode well for me.

"Go on back," she said.

It was time.

CHAPTER THIRTY

Ms. Carmichael sat behind the large desk, hands folded, regarding me like a queen would a petitioner. "Please, have a seat."

I did, in a chair in front of the desk.

"Ms. Hanson, do you know why I selected you for this competition?"

"Honestly? I've wondered that for weeks." I sat on my hands to keep myself from fiddling with things on her desk.

She removed her glasses and let them dangle on the chain around her neck. "You're a most frustrating type of student."

"I get that a lot."

"Not because you're unintelligent," she continued as if I hadn't spoken. "Quite the opposite. You're bright. You have a broad vocabulary. Your grammar was always impeccable. But you don't like to think deeply."

"Yeah," I said, "I find it's usually pretty depressing."

She took a long breath and probably counted to ten in her head. "I selected you because you have untapped potential. Because you didn't want to challenge yourself, but you needed it."

"Thanks?"

She shook her head and opened her laptop. My flash drive jutted out from the side.

"Ms. Carmichael?" A voice spoke behind me. I spun to find one of her assistants. "You have a phone call from . . ." He glanced at me. "An important call."

"Very well." She rose. "I shall return momentarily."

I should've been disappointed the decision would take longer, but as soon as she exited, I whirled. Maybe I'd find a clue about her in the office.

Stationery on her desk revealed her full name—Patricia M. Carmichael. Mahogany bookshelves. A houseplant.

My gaze jumped to the shelf on my right. It contained two whole rows of books I recognized, the spines with matching styles. She owned the entire library of C. M. Patricks, the famous author of two dozen Elven Realms novels. I'd read the first couple—drama, forbidden love, Macbeth-style scheming, epic battles. My sister loved them. Even my brother and mom had read some.

I plucked one off the shelf and flipped to the inside back flap. As usual, it lacked a picture of the author. My sister had complained that Patricks never did book signings or public appearances, had no social media, was super secretive. I skimmed the bio.

"C. M. Patricks is the author of the *New York Times* bestselling series Elven Realms. When she isn't writing, she enjoys drinking tea, reading classic literature, and watching movie adaptations of classic literature. She splits her time between London and California."

Why would Ms. Carmichael have these? And no other books? They were insanely popular, with rumors of a movie series, but hardly comparable to Chaucer and Dickens. She didn't seem like the type to read—

Wait. Classic literature. Tea. The movies she made us watch. London and California.

C. M. Patricks. Patricia M. Carmichael.

"Shut the front door," I said just as Ms. C walked back into the room.

"Excuse me?" she said, settling at her desk.

I held up the book. "This is totally you."

Her face was blank. "Ah."

"Ah? That's it? It totally is, isn't it? You retired from writing last year. My sister was so upset when she learned there wouldn't be more books. You decided to teach instead, didn't you? You'd be loaded from all those bestsellers. It makes sense you'd do charity work. And teach English." The thoughts came too fast to keep them in my head. "You're C. M. Patricks."

"I would appreciate"—she folded her hands primly on the desk—"if you would keep your voice down. While my employees know my nom de plume, and are sworn to secrecy, your classmates have not figured it out. I would prefer to keep it that way."

I stared at her, speechless for one of the few times in my life. I was talking to the famous author. The famous author held my future in her hands.

I stuck the book on the shelf. "Your secret's safe with me."

"May we return to the matter at hand?"

"Oh right. Yeah." I made myself stop gaping at the books.

"Your tales were . . . unconventional." Her tone didn't tell me if she found that good or bad. "Would you like to tell me how you decided on a different format?"

"I tried the journal thing, I promise. But it wasn't working. I didn't feel like it captured what really happened. If you watched my video, you know I learned things about myself. Like, I'm an attention hog who likes to talk."

Her lips pressed together. To hide amusement? Or annoyance?

I gulped. "I thought about Chaucer, how most of his pilgrims couldn't write. They were traveling, so they would've told their stories as they walked or around a campfire or over roasted squirrel and hardtack or whatever they ate."

One eyebrow quirked. "Indeed."

"It seemed to fit. It was in the spirit of *The Canterbury Tales*, and it was in the spirit of . . . me."

"Interesting. I can honestly say I was surprised."

I held my breath.

She tapped her fingers on the desk. "It seems you had rather an adventure."

Apparently, I wasn't going to learn whether or not she liked surprises. "You could say that. Is it okay to ask . . . did the others, I mean, were they . . . ?"

The others. Peter wanted to study creative writing, and she was an author. Great.

"I will tell you, as I did the others, that Mr. Lopez has been disqualified. I do not approve of those who interfere with their competitors or disregard the rules."

My stomach churned. I shifted and squeezed fists. Technically, I'd disregarded the rules when I decided to ignore the journal. Did she disapprove of me? Would I join Spence on the disqualified list?

"Other than that," she said, "your classmates' tales were not so . . . colorful."

"I'm the kind of person things happen to." I tried to sound positive, upbeat, and not like I was about to hurl fish and chips on her shiny desk.

"Indeed. Are you the kind of person who learns from these things?"

I needed air. Telling my secrets to a camera was one thing. Telling them to a famous author was another. "I think so. You watched the video."

She nodded, arranged a stack of papers on her desk. "If I give you the money, what will you do with it?"

Moment of truth. "I'm guessing you knew before I came that I can't play soccer." Her nod confirmed it. "My life plan was to play at UCLA and then play pro. Not to sound arrogant, but I was good enough, so I didn't need a backup plan."

"Until the diagnosis."

"Yeah. Until that." Did wealth give a person access to medical records? Or had my mom told her when they talked? "I wasn't ready to admit I was lost. How do you accept that your dream has died? Do people get more than one dream? Or is it like the concept of soul mates? You have one soul dream, and if you fail or you miss out, tough luck? You have to settle for something . . . less."

"And what conclusion did you come to?"

"I don't believe in soul mates. So why did I believe in soul dreams? I realized there are plenty of things I can do and enjoy." I studied her collection of books. How much time and dedication did it take to write that many bestsellers? I took a deep breath. "The biggest thing I learned is that it's okay to want things. I found something—more than one—to *want* again. After my injury, even before that, I didn't like caring about stuff. I assumed I would lose it, so it was easier not to want anything. But I lost the one thing I thought I couldn't. It was awful, but I lived through it. Now I'm ready to start wanting things. And people."

"Luke Jackson?" she asked. Was proper Ms. Carmichael hiding a smirk?

I smiled. "Partly. You'd like him. He wants to teach English. And . . ." It was okay to speak aloud. I'd say what I wanted, and I'd work for it. And if it didn't happen, that would be okay. "If I win the money," I said, "I'll be able to start at UCLA. I'm going to study journalism and become a sports broadcaster. Interview athletes. Tell their stories."

There. I said it. I didn't feel any different, except possibly more confident. Like since I'd said it, now I had to follow through.

"Intriguing." She raised an eyebrow. "You realize journalism often involves finding the story? Determining what's important? Examining themes and deeper meanings?" Her hidden smirk became full-fledged.

"All the things you criticized my essays for lacking? I get it." I pointed at the flash drive. "But that's one of the things I learned through this trip. Exactly like you hoped I would."

"Yes, I believe you did." She pulled out the flash drive and handed it to me. Then closed her laptop. "If you'll wait in the living room with the others, I'll be out momentarily."

I studied her face for a sign, any sign, of whether she was impressed, pleased, annoyed. At least she hadn't told me she was disqualifying me. Yet.

I paused at the door, placed my palm against the carved wood frame. "Ms. Carmichael? Thank you. For this opportunity."

A genuine smile softened her face. "You're most welcome."

The others were waiting in the sitting room, including Spence, who must have returned while I spoke with Ms. C.

Amberlyn sat straighter. "Did she say anything?"

I reclaimed my seat on the sofa. "She's coming."

Peter slouched, but his eyes were trained on the hallway leading to her office. I jiggled my foot.

Spence slumped on a couch in the corner, a baseball hat shading his face, arms crossed. If he was here despite being disqualified, did that mean I might have been, too? But she would have told me, right? My foot moved faster.

Ms. Carmichael took her usual armchair. Was she looking at one of us more than the others? Was she hiding a smile? What thoughts occupied that perfectly groomed head?

"First, thank you for your excellent work. I enjoyed hearing about your journeys and feeling as if I traveled with you. I'm most pleased with how this unconventional endeavor turned out. Although"—her lips tightened and her eyes narrowed— "I am disappointed one of you focused energy on his competitors that would have been better spent on examining himself."

I used every ounce of willpower to keep my attention on Ms.

Carmichael and not gloat to Spence. Especially since I didn't know if I'd be joining him in the doghouse.

"I hope," my teacher continued, "that even those of you who do not win had an enjoyable experience. Learned something, saw a new country, experienced new things."

"Yes, Ms. Carmichael." Amberlyn nodded like a dashboard dog. "Thank you for the opportunity."

Suck-up, I thought, but with less resentment than before. All I managed was a nod.

"Each of you demonstrated good writing as well. I appreciated your unique approaches in telling your tales. Mr. Finch showed exceptional storytelling abilities."

His perpetual frown brightened. He couldn't know what a compliment that was from a bestselling author.

"Ms. Hartsfield demonstrated an excellent grasp of themes and what made each classic writer unique and meaningful."

Amberlyn smiled and glanced at the rest of us as if seeking approval.

"I was impressed with Mr. Lopez's varying styles and understanding of source texts, despite his demonstration of poor sportsmanship."

He didn't shift from his sulking position in the corner.

"And Ms. Hanson took an unconventional angle I had not anticipated."

I waited. My stomach tied itself in knots. But she didn't continue. She'd praised the others, even Spence, and did nothing except point out that I was incapable of following basic directions. Not a good sign.

"I hope this trip has changed you and caused you to see the world or the books or yourself in new ways."

Get on with it.

"As for the winner, it was a difficult decision." She regarded each of us.

I dug my nails into the arm of the sofa, leaving dents in the leather. Would she extinguish our torches one by one? Give us roses? *Say something!*

"But I have decided that the one hundred thousand dollars will be awarded to . . ." She paused like those stupid reality-show hosts.

My heart pounded, and the knots in my stomach tightened. A tiny sliver of hope, desperately clinging for dear life, warred with the logic in my brain, repeating the words from that first day in her classroom—that I had no chance against Peter and Amberlyn and hope was for fools.

"Brittany Hanson."

I couldn't move. She'd said my name. Wait. Had she really said my name? I must have imagined it. I'd heard it in my head, and she hadn't announced anything yet.

"Good job, Britt," Spence said, not completely unenthusiastically.

"Hmm." Amberlyn shifted. "Congratulations."

My heart pounded in my ears. My stomach felt as ill as before.

"Are you sure?" I asked. Surely I'd heard wrong.

"Yes." Ms. Carmichael was smiling now, for real. At me. "Quite sure. I enjoyed your out-of-the-box thinking and was pleasantly surprised at the creativity and insight you showed, both in the approach and the stories. Well done."

"Th-thank you." I peeled my fingers from the arm of the sofa. My limbs trembled, and my breath escaped in a whoosh. "Wow. I feel like I should hug you. Should I shake your hand?"

"The thank-you will suffice. Along with a promise to keep in touch and tell me about university."

University. I was going to college. Shock faded, replaced by excitement thrumming through me. "Yeah—yes. Definitely. I will. Thanks."

"I'll be in touch to work out the details." She faced the others. "Your flight leaves at ten tomorrow morning. Please be here with your luggage, ready for the car at seven-thirty. Until tomorrow." She exited.

I let out a wobbly breath, feeling numb and shaky at the same time.

"What was your surprising approach?" Spence asked.

"Guess you'll never know."

He grunted, heaved himself off the couch, and offered me a fist, no hint of remorse on his face. Would refusing make me a sore winner? I bumped it with mine. He'd gotten what he deserved, which made me feel better.

He marched out, and Peter slunk after him.

"Peter?" I called.

He stopped.

"I'm, uh, sorry for blaming you. For that stuff Spence did."

His eyes darted to mine for less than a second. "Whatever." And he was gone.

Oh well. I'd done my part.

Amberlyn lingered. "I'm happy for you. Really."

"Thanks, Am. And . . . I'm sorry. About what happened

between us." I nudged the edge of the rug with my toe. "It probably was at least half my fault. I shouldn't have blamed you all these years."

"Yeah, well, I was a brat to you, so I'm sorry, too."

I considered hugging her, but she wasn't a toucher, so I stuck my hand out instead. "Good luck."

"You too." We shook like adults, and she left me alone.

We wouldn't keep in touch or be close again, but it was fitting that she'd been the one to help me see I could have friends again. And I was glad to put that part of my life to rest in a satisfactory way.

Now for the fun part. I called Luke. I'd save my mom for later.

"Don't tell me," was how he answered the phone. "I'm outside."

I rushed downstairs and through the lobby and found him sitting on the front steps.

He jumped to his feet. "Al told me when to arrive. So?"

"I won."

"I knew you would."

"That's it?" I nudged him. "No fawning over me? No cheers? No victory dance?"

He adjusted his glasses. "I'm in awe of your brilliance? Humbled by your greatness? Honored to know you?"

"Better . . ."

He swept me into a hug and swung me, laughing.

"That's more like it."

When he released me, I plopped onto the top step, and he joined me.

"What are you going to do with the money?"

"I've decided to study sports journalism. I don't know if UCLA has a program for that. Hopefully they do. I'll take my basic classes this year and research options."

"That's brilliant." His eyes lit up. "It's perfect for you."

"I have you to thank." I leaned my shoulder into his. "For helping me discover who I want to be. Not what, but who."

He twined our fingers together. "I have news for you, too." His thumb played across the back of my hand.

"Oh yeah. Did you decide on a college?"

"I did." A small smirk flitted across his face, but he quickly hid it. "I had a good time helping you explore my country this week."

"Subject change, much?"

He smirked again. "How would you feel about helping me explore your state when I enroll in the Literature Department at UCLA?"

"Shut it. Really?" I threw my arms around him. "That's brilliant."

He laughed and returned the hug, burying his face in my hair. "I hope you don't think I'm a stalker. I know we're not, you know, committed or anything." He pulled back, ducked his head, and stared up at me. "But I would like to spend more time with you."

I brushed his hair out of his eyes, my fingers lingering on his cheekbone. "I'd like that, too."

He smiled. "There were three schools with availability, and I'd much rather spend a year in Southern California than New York or Michigan. Especially since you're in California."

My own smile formed. "Just a year?"

"For now. I'll see how it goes. You were right that I shouldn't give up on what I want because of my dad. But university is a small part of that. I can become a professor no matter where I get my schooling. Maybe I'll return to Oxford, maybe I won't."

"Maybe you'll love California so much you'll stay forever?"

He leaned in slowly, deliberately. Slid a hand to the back of my head. His gaze pinned me. "There's a distinct possibility I will love it."

A shiver ran through me as his lips moved toward mine.

I may have lost one dream, but that wasn't the end of the story—and now I had someone to write the next chapter with me.

ACKNOWLEDGMENTS

It feels unreal to be writing these words after years of dreaming about this moment. I'm grateful to so many people who have helped and encouraged me on this journey.

A huge thank-you to my family for believing in me and fully supporting my dreams, and for endless hours helping me brainstorm, listening to me ramble, and reading messy drafts. I love you all more than words.

I'm so grateful to my agent, Eva Scalzo, for working incredibly hard for me and not giving up. Thank you for helping make this happen, and here's to many more books together.

Thank you to my editor, Wendy Loggia, for believing in this story and making it shine, as well as Hannah Hill, Alison Romig, Jen Strada, and the rest of the team at Delacorte Press. I could not have asked for a better home for this book, and I'm so grateful you welcomed me to the family. Thanks to Ray Shappell for the cover design and to Libby VanderPloeg for the absolutely, adorably perfect illustrations.

I wouldn't be here without the Pitch Wars community: My mentor, Marty Mayberry, who was the first person to take a chance on this story years ago and has been supportive ever since. Brenda Drake, who puts in countless hours to help authors. And the class of 2015, who have provided ongoing community, advice, and support.

My critique partner, Jason Joyner, has read literally everything I write, even when it's rough, and offers invaluable feedback. Thanks for continuing to cheer me on and believing this day would come.

The rest of the Fellowship: Tina Gollings, Josh Hardt, J.J. Johnson, Steve Rzasa, Liberty Speidel, and Josh Smith. Thank you for the advice and encouragement, as well as the endless gifs and sarcasm. Friends like you are what make the journey worth it.

Amanda Stevens, your love for Britt and Luke was such an encouragement. Thanks for your character insights and brainstorming, and for always being there to listen.

Thank you to fellow writers who read early drafts and helped shape this story: Sara Ella, John Otte, and Charity Tinnin.

The England team: Aileen, Deborah, Kim, Kristen, Tracy, and Vikki, thanks for adventuring around England with me and being patient while I stopped to take notes and ask random questions of strangers.

Thanks to my late high school English teacher, Mrs. Brannock, who served as the inspiration for Ms. Carmichael and taught me to love British literature and to obsessively watch every Jane Austen adaptation ever made.

Thank you, the reader, for picking up this book. I hope you loved Britt's journey and it encourages you to live your own stories, keep dreaming new dreams, and find your purpose.

Finally, Jesus, my Savior and King, thank You for loving me, saving me, and calling me to the ultimate adventure of following You.

ABOUT THE AUTHOR

BECKY DEAN is a fan of adventures both real and fictional. When she's not writing or traveling, she can be found drinking tea, watching science fiction shows, or quoting *The Lord of the Rings*. Though she lives in Texas with her husband, she remains a Southern California girl at heart.